Neighbours
Nohbasch

Neighbours

Stories in Mennonite Low German and English

Nohbasch

Jeschichte opp Plautdietsch enn Enjlisch

Jack Thiessen

evertype

2014

Published by Evertype, Cnoc Sceichín, Leac an Anfa, Cathair na Mart, Co. Mhaigh Eo, Éire. www.evertype.com.

First edition 2014.

A catalogue record for this book is available from the British Library.

ISBN-10 1-78201-054-8
ISBN-13 978-1-78201-054-8

Set in Minion Pro and Imprint MT Shadow by Michael Everson.

Cover: Michael Everson.
Cover photograph by Amy J. Graber of a "Farmer's Delight" quilt made by her mother, Julia Graber, juliagraber.blogspot.com.

Printed by: LightningSource.

Neighbours
Nohbasch

Ennhault

Contents

Stories for

Shae, Kiana, Tosca, Ellington, *and* Bruckner

Neighbours
Nohba

Ahre Sproak wea doot

Dee Tjoatjhoff enn Baker Lake enne Nuadwast-Territorie licht eene haulwe Stund toofoot vonne kathoolische Tjoatj. Etj hab den Gang mett aulet Toobehea doa emm Mooss enne Wille Hundat dietlich em Dentj, auls etj mie doa huach em Nuade aune 1968 opphilt. Dee Priesta Choque, eena von dem Oblateorda ut Belgien, wea doa Seelsorja. Hee wea een fromma Mensch, dee siene Messe opp Latiensch hilt, wiels, auls hee doa siena Tiet, seea lang tridj aunkaum, kunn hee tjeen Enjlisch. Enn donn auls hee endlich Enjlisch jeleahd haud, enn Fraunzeesisch enn Flemisch sowesoo, wea ahm daut too loht, enn soo piljad hee enne latiensche Sproak soo wieda, enn dee Eskimos ahm hinjeraun.

Daut jefft tjeen gooden Grund omm den Tjoatjhoff doa too beseatje, oba doa huach emm Nuade ess aules soo wiet enn soo eendrajchich, daut sogoa mette Doodes too spezeare, eene Auflentjung ess. Priesta Choque meend, etj sull een Bassemstäl mettnehme, enn unjawäjess een poad Schneeheehna den Kopp aufschlohne; dee wudd wie dann toom Owendkost brode.

Midje bie de Billjoohne doa huach em Nuade send soo riew, daut eene nich mol doavon räde sull ooda bruckt. Wann eena sich äwa daut Jeweehnliche vetalle mott, sull eena Tus bliewe. Enn TV tjitje.

Etj kaum loht emm August aun mien Ziel aun. Doa lage hejchstens twalw Doodes enn flache Jräwa begrowt; dee Sätja weare ut Spoaholt, enn mett Steehna bedatjt. Enn Israel woare uck Steehna oppe Jräwa jelajcht, enn wann dee Doodja doabenne een beriehmda ess, ooda wea, lage omm soo meea Steehna oppem Grauf. Hiea, enn uck doa, ess dee Grund fe dee Steehna oppem Grauf een eenfacha: dee selle dee Leijch fe Raute, Mies, Stapmies enn frätende, rietende Tiere schitze.

A Language Defunct

The churchyard for non-locals in Baker Lake, NWT lies half an hour's walking distance northwest of the Catholic chapel. It is that walk and attendant milestones in the moss of remoteness I remember most clearly of my brief sojourn to the NWT in 1968. Father Choque, an Oblate priest from Belgium was the local curate; he was a genuinely pious man who conducted his masses in Latin since he had no knowledge of English when he arrived in the High North. Then, finally, after having sufficiently mastered the tongue altogether foreign to his own Flemish and French and the language of God, already mentioned, he was too set or old to switch and so he preferred to keep pilgrimming—the word may be outdated but it fits—on as before.

There is no good reason for wanting to walk to that churchyard except that the NWT is so desolate that even *spezeare* with the dead is a diversion. Father Choque suggested I take along a sturdy broomstick and whack a few ptarmigan over the head underway and bring them home for dinner.

Mosquitoes by the billion are so commonplace in the High North that they warrant no mention. If discussing the obvious is one's intent, it is best to remain home.

I arrived at my destination in the middle of an August afternoon. There were at most two dozen people buried in random three ply boxes and all covered with stones, similar to graves in Israel. Jews of prominence, like venerated rabbis for instance, merit a more copious pile of ersatz petrifaction. The purpose of stones on graves, now before me on caskets, was

3

Enne oole Tiet wea daut schiea onmächlijch em Nuade emm eewjen Frost een deepet Grauf too growe. Groota Frost stalt siene eajne Räjle opp.

Daut gauf doa dree Jräwa enn eene Atj opp dem Tjoatjhoff, dee mie oppfolle. Wiels sogoa Doodes Auras habe, lage disse dree "Ruhe in Frieden" noch eensauma doa, enn disse Eensaumtjeit trock mie doahan.

Nich eena von disse dree Doodes haud sienen dartijchsten Jeburtsdach erläwt; oole Schrefte oppem Spoaholt vetalde mie daut. Daut halpt nuscht nich Auntwuate too seatje, woa tjeene send, enn soo sad etj loos, enn heiwd noch een poah Schneeheehnatjess dee Tjapp auf. Disse witte Heehnatjess, soo's tjliene Raupheehna send iewirjch, enn wizhrijch, enn vetalle väl oba saje nuscht, wiels see aula blooß pludre. Etj nauhm noch mol wiedre vea mett, eea etj tridj noh dee Zivilisatsjoon piljad.

Jiede Jesallschoft haft onjeschräwne Räjle, enn goode Manneare velange, eena saul sich aun dee Räjle hoole. Enn wann nich, kunn eenem daut pesseare, daut mett eenmol een Schild mett "Wie welle Die nich" uthong, enn nich Jewullesenne wea daut aulalatzte waut etj hiea enne Wille Hundat wull.

Nohdem etj dee Schneeheehna utjenohme haud enn een bätje Dreimoazharie aunstald, omm Priesta Choque siene Oppmoatsomtjeit too tjriee, muak etj eene Buddel Schnaups op, dee etj fe soohne Aunlausse mettjebrocht haud. Dee jeheemnisvolle dree Doodje muake mie too dentje, enn etj wull weete, waut doa pesseat wea, enn woarom.

Eene Mohltiet mett, enn, uck ut, einheimische Väjel, soo's dee Schneeheehnatjes, wann dann Heehna uck soo domm send aus Heehna measchtens send, schmatjt väl bäta auls nuscht, enn see druage doatoo bie, daut wie biem Ate schmock enne Vetall kaume.

"Etj haud aul erwähnt," sad Priesta Choque bedajchtich fuat, daut etj nich emma gaunz kluak ute Eskimos word, auls etj häakaum mett ahn, enn ähre Seele too oabeide. Aus äähre Schwiejsaumtjeit beidasieds soo wea, weet etj nich. Enn wiels etj ähre Seelensproak nich diede kunn, enn etj oba sootoosaje

identical to those of the Holy Land: to keep foraging carnivores, later idle rodents, from snacking on the dead. In pre-industrial times it was impossible to dig deeper and safer in Canada's north; permafrost dictates its own regulations.

There were three graves in one corner of this hamlet of the dead that stood out. Since even the inanimate radiate auras, this triple was even more remote than their Rest in Peace dwellers; probably their restless muteness attracted me.

Not one of these three deceased had reached his thirtieth birthday; weathered paint scripts said so. There was little point in pondering something to which there is no answer or reason and so I dispatched another round of scurrying chickens of the wild; eager, gossipy little creatures and full of themselves but too stupid to mistrust, before returning to the trivialities of civilization, where I temporarily belonged.

Every society has unwritten rules and decorum of the spirit dictates compliance. Failure to do so might on occasions like mine lead to a not wanted sign posted and not to be wanted was the last thing I wanted. Amenities in the Baker Lake region were too scarce to risk non-conformity.

After dressing the ptarmigan for dinner and fussing about a bit in order to elicit Father Choque's information, I primed the occasion with a bottle of Scotch, brought for such eventuality. The mysterious death of those younger than I was must have a story and I was interested in whatever common denominator marked the demise of the scant remains of these remote dead.

A dinner of the indigenous birds is better than none at all and it was this peasant wisdom which provided conversational meat to our chicken dinner.

"I have already mentioned," Father Choque, reflectively remarked, "that I was unable to read the eyes and the intent of the Eskimo when I arrived to work with them and their souls. Whether this *Schweigsamkeit* was mutual I do not know.

5

een Framda wea, hilt etj mie aun ähre Räjle, wiels mie nuscht nich aundret äwrijchbleef. Dee Eskimos räde weinijch, too Tiede nuscht nich, oba mien Awaläwe hong je jrodentoo von dee Nichredende auf, enn soo fiejd etj mie. Butadem haud etj mie omm ähre Seele too tjemmre.

Wie drunke oppe Jesundheit, Santé, Prosit, enn begauwe ons opp dem Jesprächswajch, woohnen mien Gaustjäwa utläd.

"Mie tjemmt daut soo väa, auls wann Du doa oppem Tjoatjhoff waut erläft hast, woohnt wieda jintj auls dee dree Doodes, dee ver ähre Tiet doa oppem Tjoatjhoff begrowt lidje, joh?"

"Soo ess'ett," gauf etj Auntwuat.

"Ut goodem Grund," meend Priesta Choque. "Dee dree, enn mank ahn wea uck eena mett een mennischen Nohme, worde omjebrocht auls etj aul hiea wea. Enn wiels dee Morde derjch Vesupe niemols nich jeleest word, enn dee Spekulatsjoon nich vebode ess, vetall etj Die miene Jeschijcht doatoo. Daut eena enn soohne Sache diskreet haundle sull, ess dochwoll bekaunt."

Em Jäjensautz too miene Natua hild etj daut Mul, enn wea stell; oba mien Netjkoppe besäd, daut etj vestund, uck wann miene Jedanke wuatloos bleewe.

"Disse Manna worde von oole Eskimos twintijch Joah tridj ommjebrocht, ooda opp Ordasch von ährem Roht. Enn hiea hast Du miene Jeschijcht: Von Aunfong aun, bleewe de Eskimos hiea huach emm Nuade aum läwe, wiels enn wann see sich aune Natuaräjle hilde.

Gaunz opensejchtlich jletjt ahn daut soo lang auls see enn dee Natua sich jäjensiedich aun dee Räjle hilde. Enn wann daut Awaläwe Erfolj bediet, jletjt ahn daut uck, daut ess dochwoll kloa. Enn daut ess dochwoll kratjt soo kloa, daut hiea, woa dee Wintasch kolt enn strenj enn lang send, enn noch dolla auls wann dee von wieda Siede Räjle bestemme welle, ooda, saj wie mol dee vedreide Räjle von dee Onjekroagde, dee sich jearn enmische, enn väl Roht fe aule habe, enn aules bäta weete enn tjenne, uck wann tjeena ahn jefroagt haft. Mensche send je measchtens soo."

Dee Priesta enn etj leehte dee Buddel Schnaups nochmol too Wuat kohme, enn wiels etj dochwoll ziemlich diskreet jewese

6

Since I was ignorant of the language of their soul and I was the stranger who had to play by their rules, I did. The Eskimo spoke little, often less, but survival depended on the unspoken and I so I complied. Moreover, there were souls to be claimed."

We drank to health, santé, Gesundheit and set out on the informational route my host staked out.

"It seems to me that you have experienced something beyond death on the cemetery and if I am right you are pondering the premature deaths of the three buried on the edge of the Kerkhoff, right?"

"Indeed," I responded.

"With good reason," Father Choque replied. "These three, including one with an Anabaptist name were all murdered while I was already here. And since none of the murders by drowning has ever been resolved and speculation is not forbidden, here is my story. Discretion may be advisable, but I am sure you know that."

Contrary to my nature and custom I held my peace; my nod affirmed agreement with tacit confidentiality.

"These men were murdered by the Eskimo elders, or upon their advice some twenty years ago. And this is the story. From their beginning, the native people in the North obviously survived by living as close to nature as conditions permitted or allowed.

Obviously they made do rather well as long as the terms, mutual of man and nature, were honoured. If survival is the mark allotted to success then they fared well indeed, so much is obvious. It is equally obvious that winters are long and demanding, more so by the paradigms of the south and by the, shall we say, warped standards of the uninvited, intent on improving the lot of others. Mankind has such proclivities."

The Father and I de-regalized a little more of Shiva and since I had exercised sufficient prudence to desist from

wea, enn tjeene Froag mett Zocka bestreit jestalt haud, sad dee Priesta fuat. "Eena kaun dochwoll aunnehme, daut daut dee Eskimos dusend Joah ooda noch meea diead, eea see de Sproak vonne Wilw, aulso dee Wilwsproak jeleaht haude, oba daut jletjt ahn. See tjreaje dee rut. Enn sogoa enn miene Tiet hiea, hab etj jeseehne, daut dee Eskimos loht emm Mai mett eenmol oppheade Wintatiere too jäjre, enn platzlich enn ähre Oabeid stellhilde, sich eenfach hansade, enn opp dee Ranntiere ooda uck Caribou jenannt, wachte, wann see vonne Wilw heade, daut dee veabeensche Tiere unjawäjes nohm Nuade weare. Dee Wilw juhlde enn ähre Sproak, enn vetalde dusend Miel wiet von wieda Siede bett hieahäa, daut freschet Fleesch opp veea Been unjawäjes wea. Dee Wilwsproak wea äah Dialekt, dee Uagrootmutta von aule Sproake, enn Tiere enn Mensche, en dissem Faul dee Eskimos, vestunde disse Sproak too diede, enn wisste jeneiw wann'et freschen Brode fe den Buck enn uck dee Brohdpaun jäwe wudd. Daut wisste see een Dach verhäa. Enn daut Vesprätje derjche Wulfsproak troff emma enn. Biblisch enn emma.

Enn dann pessead daut. Missjoonoare vom Siede kaume aun, enn leahde dee Eskimos enn aule aundre, enn meist uck mie, dee Betjearung noh dee latzte Mood, enn dee Sproak vom Harrn. Etj wisst aundasch, vleijcht uck bäta, enn woarnd ahn, disse Bätaweetasch, daut daut tjeen goodet Enj nehme wudd, oba see wisste je aules bäta, enn wann nich see, dann äah himmlischa Voda. Aules jintj een poah Joah goot; see respekteade sich jäjensiedijch, enn uck woomäjlich, wiels daut Langaunjewande sich nich platzlich wajchbuchle lat; enn soo leete dee Eskimos dee Evangeliste soo meea toch, oba dee Unjascheed bleef bestohne. Oba dann worde dee Evangeliste aggressieva, enn vesochte Schluß mett dee Hatjsarie enn Awagloowe, enn mangelndet Vetrue enn "Dee Harr woat aul fe junt sorje," too moake.

Auls een poah junge Eskimos sich toom willen Gloowe betjeade, kaum daut dann doch boold toom Tjriezwajch. Aune 1948, em lohten Mai, muake sich de ellre Eskimovodasch reed fe de Caribou Jäjarie, wiels de Wilw haude ahn vetald, dee Ranntiere wudde morje loht Nohmeddach aunkohme. Priesta

inquiry, he went on, "Presumably it took the Eskimos a thousand years or more to learn the language of the wolf but they did. And even in my sojourn here I have literally seen the Eskimo in late May suddenly stop hunting winter animals, and in the midst of whatever activity engaged simply sit right down and wait for the reindeer to arrive when the wolf relayed observations of promise to points further north. Wolves along the caribou trek for close to a thousand miles howled their dialect, the mother of all subsequent lingos of the arrival of the caribou, and the Eskimo interpreted this language and knew within half a day when to expect fresh meat on the hoof. It never failed.

And then it happened. Missionaries from the south came to attempt to teach the Eskimo but also all others, including me, salvation and the language of the Lord. I knew enough to warn the come-latelys of the consequences but they persisted in knowing better and if not they, then certainly their Lord did. All went well for the first few years; there was mutual respect and possibly the hesitancy of natural inertia, one might conclude, for them to leave each other alone, to tolerate whatever differences existed, considerable as they proved to be. But then the evangelicals became more aggressive in terminating what they regarded as witchcraft, superstition and lack of trust in "The Lord will provide."

Some of the younger generation of Eskimos joined the fervor of the newly saved and a showdown was not long in coming. In 1948 in late May the elders got ready to hunt caribou which the wolves informed would be here the next afternoon.

We drank to the denouement, the unfolding of a strange tale. "The missionary evangelicals also got ready by encouraging their converted charges to sing and pray and ask God's forgiveness for their heathen superstitions."

Choque enn etj drunke een gooden Schluck, wiels dee
Jeschijcht sich nu total omdreie wull, enn uck deed.

"Dee missjoonistische Evangeliste muake sich uck reed enn
gauwe Ordasch, daut de jungbetjeade Eskimos blooß noch
bäde enn sinje sulle, enn Gott bedde sulle, ahn ähre Dommheite too vezeihe enn uck ähre heidnischen Awagloowe."

"Daut Gaunze kaum dann uck seea schwind toom latzten
Tjriezwajch. Dee ellre Eskimons, dee Eltestasch, sootoosaje,
räde een Machtwort enn doamett wea eene kloare Lienje emm
latzten Schnee getrocke. Aum näjchsten Morje, ooda rejchtja
jesajcht, noch enne selwje Nacht muake dee Oolasch sich fe de
Jäjerie reed, wiels ähre Existenz wea oppem Spell. Enn dee
selwje Nacht kaum daut dochwoll toom Schermetzel, enn aule
dree Missionoare vedrunke opp jeheeme Wies. Aule dree. Dee
Bewies doavon lijcht oppem Tjoatjhoff, den hast Du je selwst
jeseehne."

Mie kaum disse erjriepende Jeschijcht mett ein haulwäjes
goteljet Enj doch eenjamohte väa. Oba daut wea see nich.
Nohdem Priesta Choque enn etj dee Buddel ladijch haude,
vetald hee mie dann noch daut bettere Enj, den Schlußsäjen.
Dee Missjoonoare weare mau soo meea symtomatisch: dee
"Siede" mett de Ideologie, daut jieda Watjzel uck eene
Vebäterung bediet, sad sich derjch, enn doatoo noch, daut een
jiedrem aules nu, fuats, enn oppe Städ noh de amerikaunsche
Oat toosteiht, enn daut jiede Tookunft Opfa vonne Jäjenwoat
senne mott. Dee "daut steiht mie too" Enstallinj, dee
Doodesspruch von jieda Traditsjoon sad sich derjch, enn de
Eskimos, nu Inuit jenannt, een wiedra Watjzel bloo? toom
Gooden, schmeete daut Haundduak vonne Erjäwung, wiels
waut bleef ahn äwrijch? See haude vespält, veloare; noch truja,
see wisste daut, oba haude nuscht too saje. See weare auls Voltj
mett ähre Ajenoate aum Enj, enn aum dietlijchsten word ahn
daut, auls see sich mett dem Wolf, ääh Rada äwa dusend Joah,
nuscht meea too vetalla haude. Ahre Sproak wea doot.

The issue quickly came to a head since the very livelihood of a community, a Gemeinschaft was at stake. The elders spoke a *Machtwort*, meaning that a line was drawn in the late scant snow. Within the day, or rather within the night the elders started the annual hunt of the caribou and in the ensuing melee the missionaries, the emissaries of the south, who chose to get involved, mysteriously drowned. All three. You have seen the evidence for yourself."

I regarded this haunting tale as one with a reasonably happy conclusion, certainly a satisfactory *Schluss*. But it was not. After Father Choque and I had dispatched Shiva's Regality, he informed me of the relatively obvious. The missionaries were merely symptomatic: the south with its ideology that every change represents an improvement prevailed with its non-resistable world of instant gratification, that the undefined future be sacrificed to the past and the present. Entitlement, the death knell of every tradition prevailed and the Eskimo, now called the Inuit, another changing improvement of the word, threw in the towel of futile non-resistance.

Within one generation the Eskimo was no longer capable of interpreting the language of the wolf; then nature turned its back on its children and the demise came full circle. The only smile of victory the Eskimo in time took to their grave was that the murder of the intrusive Jesus emissaries was never solved, with the three meddlers from the south remaining victims of the rodent while waiting for God's final decree.

A final word apropos to progress: another *Ursprache*, a language primeval had obviously been relegated to defunct status and that, as we speak.

Hauns

Aum Sindach zeowents ons soo een bät em Darp too trafe jintj ons Jungess scheen, seea scheen. Tüs wea aulewääje besorjcht enn verejcht, enn de schwoare Oabeit vonn'e näächste Wäatj wea noch wiet auf. Wie kaume üt tjeenen Grund toop, bloos so omm een bät too puche enn äwadriewe, enn Bechteriete enn han enn wada, wann'et senne mußt, een bät too rauze. Ooda uck irjendeen Ooltnäsjen den Kopp too veneede. Oh joh, enn dann mußt wie ons noch zimlich foaken äwa de C.C.F'ers jachte enn woo kommunistisch dee Donnasch weare enn aus de Katholitje von St. Pierre aule onse tjristliche Tjinja fuatnehme wudde ooda mau de measchte. Enn donn mußt wie ons noch jachte aus Fraunz App von Lena enn de Vada aun ons eajnen Doft App wertjlich een tjliena Vada aun Syl Apps vonne Toronto Maple Leafs wea ooda noch dijchta Frindschauft aus daut weare, soo's maunche Lied Tüs säde.

Een Sindach em lohten Juli aus aul daut Jeräd een bät nohjejäwt haud, enn wie tjeenen Grund haude noch lenja too bliewe enn noch weenja Grund haude noh Hüs too gohne, kaum mett eemol een ütjeplajta jreena Voltjswoage aunjeduckat and wää daut uck emma wea, he blost ons eene Woltj Stuff enne Uage enn piept ons de Uahre voll soo's een oola Furd. Donn hild'a stell, muak de Dääh op enn donn kaum langsom een ajchta Schlodonz rütjedreit. He wea goot siene sass Schooh lang, druag een Cowboyhamd enn haud uck ajchte Cowboysteewle aun. Aus'a mett eemol doastund, docht een jieda, daut dis Gaust eajentlich bloß een Revolva bruckt, om em High Noon nenntoopausse. Hee wea een stolta Tjeadel, haud uck eenen Cowboyhoot opp: ahm sach'et seea jlei.

Hauns

Hanging around town on Sunday evenings was the highlight of the week. Chores were done and the hard labor of the coming week seemed far down the road of time. We got together for no real reason—we just wanted to engage in some braggadocio, one-up-man-ships and the occasional fight. Oh yes, and to argue about the CCF'ers and how Communistic they were and whether the Catholics from St. Pierre would kidnap all our Christian children in time or just some of them. As always, we argued about whether Frank Epp from Lena and the cousin to our own David Epp was really a second cousin to Syl Apps of the Toronto Maple Leafs or even more closely related, as some people said.

One Sunday in late July, just when the usual session of jawing was wearing thin and no one had any good reason to stay and even less to go home, a VW beetle, faded green in colour, came our way and whoever it was blew a cloud of dust and a horn of antique vintage while approaching. Then it stopped and lazily but with casual authority, a genuine yokel corkscrewed his way out of the tiny car. He was at least six feet tall and wore a cowboy shirt and real western boots. Once he was all there it seemed that all he needed to complete the picture was a six-shooter since he bore the stance of a fellow out of High Noon, cowboy hat and all. He was proud of himself and he knew he spelled presence.

"Hello, all of you, I'm Hauns!" he said, "and I come all the way from Rosengard to inspect the female population around here." We giggled a bit as boys do wanting to hear more from this newly-arrived authority on women. He slouched back

"Na, Goondach Jie aulatoop, etj sie Hauns!" säd'a, "enn sie den gaunzen Wajch üt Roosegoad jekohme omm mie jüne Mejalleberstaund too betjitje."

Wie lachte een bätje, soo's Jungess daut dann doohne, wann se von eenem rechtjen Expert een bätje meea vonne Früeswelt weete welle. Donn jintj Hauns äwaroasch, betjt sich enn siene Koah nenn, hold eene tjliene Buddel Tjoaschewhiskey äwadäl, enn nauhm een langen Schluck doarüt.

Een poah meea Jungess weare nü noch toojekohme omm sich een bätje opptoohoole, enn uck een poah Tjinja, boaft enn nieschierich.

Hauns frinteld noch emma aus'a tridj noh siene Koah jintj enn mett eene Jitoa enn een Mülschiera tridjkaum. Daut Harmoschtje stald hee opp een tjlienet Jeschnees omm sien Hauls enn tjlamd daut faust. Hauns tjlimpad een bät enn stemmd siene Jitoa enn, enn donn word'et gaunz stell. Mett eemol schreajch hee "YIPPIY AYE JOH" enn fong aun too sinje enn too späle enn wea enn eenem Nü aul medden em Konzert. Hee pompt mett'em rajchten Foot, enn donn jintj hee sien Harmoschtje too doak aus'a den Refrain von Red River Valley späld. Donn leet Hauns mett dem Volumen noh, muak de Uage too, enn kusst mau jrodentoo sien Harmoschtje enn plock de Saide vonn'e Jitoa soo zoat enn so saunft, enn hee wea väle Miele wiet auf enn siene Jedanke. Joh, Hauns head uck opp mett siene Hack Tackt too hoole; hee hoof aunstaut siene rajchte Tee opp enn leet dee han en häa weppe, soo lieseltjes, aus wann'a enn Tjoatj wea. Dee Tjinja kaume emma noda, enn de Mäatjess kaume uck dichtabie, enn haude aula Stearns enne Uage enn muake daut Mültje soo een bätje op. Donn späld Hauns Beautiful Brown Eyes enn aus hee eene Bleewuagje sach, endad hee de eene Zeil. You are my Sunshine wea sien näjchstet Leed enn doabie word Hauns, Jitoa enn Mülschiera aulatoop eent.

Hauns späld enn sung noch een poah Leeda, enn donn mett eemol säda: "Nü späl etj jünt noch 'Muß i' denn' väa enn dann mott etj foahre. Morje mott wiet waste jedrascht woare. Oba etj

into his car and fetched a cherry whiskey mickey, taking a long schluck from it.

A few more fellows decided to come and linger, as well as a few kids, barefoot and curious. Even a few girls had emerged, keeping a safe distance but shyly curious and eager.

Still smiling, Hauns returned to his car, now producing a guitar and a mouth organ which he fastened around his neck on a little stand. Hauns strummed a bit, tuning his guitar. Then he stopped and silence surrounded him. Suddenly he yelled "YIPPEE AYE OH" and started playing and singing arriving in mid concert in an instant. He pumped his right boot and then went for his mouth organ for the refrain of Red River Valley. Next Hauns turned down the volume and slowly closed his eyes, kissing the very keys of his mouth organ while it seemed he was strumming away in thought many miles away; then he stopped stomping but raised his right pointed boot toe instead and moved it in beat from side to side, almost reverently. The kids moved within inches of this troubadour and the girls, much moved, came closer and paid open-mouthed attention. Now Hauns played Beautiful Brown Eyes and when he noticed a blue-eyed girl he altered the line just for her. Then You are my Sunshine was next on the agenda with guitar, Hauns and mouth organ becoming one.

After a generous medley, Hauns informed his audience that he was going to play one more tune before packing up and "heading west". He played and sang some version of "*Muß i' denn*", then he winked, promised to be back before the "summer is out", tipped his brown hat and was gone.

We stood around wondering what had happened. Short minutes ago a stream of wonder had flowed all around and through us buoying everyone up and now we were back again on heavy feet on barren ground, weighing much more with the silence driving me crazy. We boys seemed to agree that nothing much was going to work after Hauns had come,

sie wada tridj eea daut toofrisst." Hauns tjnippst sich aum
Hoot, plintjad een bät, enn wajch wear'a.

Wie stunde enn wundade ons, waut pesseat wea. Een poah
Minüte tridj weare Hauns siene Leeda soo's een Strom omm en
derjch ons jerant, enn nü stund wie doa, enn weare mett eemol
wada väl schwanda jeworde, enn de Welt väl ladja. Wie Jungess
weare ons eenig, daut nü nuscht nich meea schaufe wudd
nohdem Hauns sien Kulla Fiea, sootoosaje, omm ons
jeschmäte haud, enn ons nü enn eene stelle Welt tridjleet. De
Mäatjess trocke sich uck tridj, mett ähre Uage noch emma aum
Horizont. De tjliene Jungess jinje toolatst; see wisste nü,
woaromm se jeläwt enn jewacht haude, oba nü wear'et vebie.

Hauns enn etj troffe ons foakna aus wie aulatoop. Mie jintj
dis Jung scheen: hee wißt väl meea, enn ahm fluag aules too.
Waut'a nich vetalle wull ooda kunn, daut deede siene Leeda,
siene Jitoa enn sien Harmoschtje. Uck wea Hauns too Frülied
väl natta, joh soo natt, soo's etj daut niemols verhäa jeseehne
ooda beläwt haud, büta enne Movies. Mie kaum soo väa,
dissem Tjeadel Hauns sull eena noh-ope, dee kunn vleicht
sogoa mett een reinet Jewesse een bätje sindje, wiels Gott opp
siene Sied wea. Weens so docht etj, wann Hauns uck niemols
säd aus'a irjendwoa eene Mejall "jerollt" haud oba etj wißt von
de Oat, woo hee vonne Leew späld enn sung enn frinteld enn
siene Leppe beletjt, daut Hauns enn siene Lomm opp väle
Läwesrivasch jesunge haud.

Loht em August Aunfong de Feftjajoahre reet daut Läwe ons
ütenaunda, oba nich eea Hauns mie den latzen Farzh von
"From this Valley They say you are Leaving" uzhend fe mie
sung enn späld. Den Owend, aus wie auleen weare, tjeem mie
daut soo väa aus wann Hauns de Täne reete, oba etj vegaut
soone Tjlienijtjeite aus hee too mie opp Plautdietsch säd: "Loht
Die daut gootgohne. Enn etj woa de Mäatjess hinja Portage
jreese, wann etj morje drasche foah, o.k.?" Donn jintj Hauns
langsom auf, späld bieaun lieseltjess Jitoa enn sung stell ver
sich han.

Väle Joahre lohta kaum etj vom Läwe enn Leahre tridj enn
wull doahan, woa mol Tüs jewast wea. Noanijch trock mie daut

16

roped his Ring of Fire around us, and then left, so we went home to a quiet world. The girls, also, retreated into the world of everyday, while scanning an invisible horizon. The last to leave were the little boys who had seen what they had unknowingly lived for, and now it was over.

Hauns and I met more often than all of us together. I sought out the easy grace of a knowing fellow who could tell life's stories in song and let the guitar and his mouth organ fill in the gaps and refrains. Then there was his gentle manner with women which no one, and certainly not I, had ever experienced before unless we went to the movies. Hauns struck me as a guy to emulate; he was even capable of sinning, perhaps, without a guilty conscience; indeed he obviously had God on His side. At least so I concluded, because Hauns never came right out and said whether he had courted one or the other but I knew all this from the way he played and sang about love and winked and smiled and licked his lips as he embarked on his craft of song to dozens of tunes on the rivers of life.

Late in August in the mid-fifties life pulled us apart but not before Hauns played the last verse "From this Valley They say You are Leaving" just for me. That evening, alone with him, I noticed Hauns being mindful of his teeth as though they were hurting him but I forgot about such trivialities when he said, in Low German, "Let yourself enjoy life. I'll say hello to all those girls behind Portage, when I go back for threshing time tomorrow, OK?" Then Hauns walked to his Beetle, strumming his guitar and singing softly.

Many years later when I returned from life and learning to what had once been home, there was no one I wanted more to meet again than Fraunz Nickel's Hauns. It was early afternoon one fall day that year and I drove right over to his place, just to see Rosengard and Hauns again, half expecting to find neither at home. Under the yellowing maple tree stood

dolla han aus noh Fraunz Netjels Hauns. Daut wea aum tiedjen Nohmeddach em Hoafst enn etj fuah jlitj doahan, omm Roosegoad enn Hauns too seehne; emm Stellen räatjend etj daut se beid nich Tüs senne wudde. Unjrem jälen Zockaboom stund Hauns siene tjliene Koah, enn etj odemd opp, enn tjreajch Wind von hinje. Wann bloß de Hauns Tüs senne wudd, dann wudd etj ahm een poah Jeschichte vetalle, daut ahm de Tjwiel toopranne wudd, enn nich bloß von Portage enn Draschabonsche enn jleie enjelsche Mejalles, de aul lange Betjse enn Leppefoaw druage...

Etj puttad aune Dääh enn von benne roopt Hauns stell, etj sull nenn kohme. "Komm noh de Hinjastow. Etj sie hiea, Ivan." Joahrelang nich jeseehne, oba he wisst, daut etj daut wea. Hauns wea auleen.

Hauns lach em Bad mett eene Foarmametz mett een aufjeschiedet Schild oppem Kopp. Hauns frindeld soo's verhäa, uck lachd'a wada soo's frähjoah, oba wanna von Hoate lachd, kaum mie daut een bät je-eewd väa. "Mie jeit'et vondoag eenjamohte. Halp mie een bät aules tooptootjriee enn dann goh wie een bät enne Weid enne Sonn romm, joh?"

Wie jinje langsom oppe Netjels Weid enne woame Sonn medden em Oktoba. Etj wißt daut hiea irjendwaut seea, seea schlemm loswea, wiels tjeen Mennist enn siene baste Joahre lach aum Woatjeldach nohmeddach em Bad. Etj wea stomm von de Äwarauschung: waut etj väa haud, wea Hauns vonne Freileins väl wieda ooste aus Kenora, Ontario toovetalle. Enn dann daut Gaunze een bät met Hauns siene Erläwnisse von hinja Portage enne Draschtiet too vejlitje. Oba Hauns wull doavon nuscht weete kaum mie soo väa, enn etj wea enttwei, daut mie daut aulwada nich jejletjt haud, de Jeschicht vom Läwe opptowoame.

We jinje nohm Siede. Hanenwada mußt wie Spannjewäw vom Hoawst ons vom Jesecht stritje. Uck haud Hauns een Schneppelduak enne Haund, woont hee emma verrem Mül hild wanna räd. We kaume aun eenem Klompe Steena hinje enne Weid aun, dijcht bie eene Schopsfenz. Hauns haud sich aul hanjesat; hee tjitjt em Waste nenn enn trock sich daut

Hauns's green Beetle of former times and I was reassured. If only Hauns would be there, too, did I ever have a story or two to tell him this time and not only about Portage and threshing gangs and fast-talking English girls who wore pants and jeans and lipstick…

I knocked and from inside Hauns quietly called to come in. "Come to the back room. I'm here, Ivan." Somehow he knew it was me after years of absence. He was alone.

Hauns lay in bed with a farmer's cap with a much worn bill on his head. His smile was still there and the easy laugh, but his life-affirming chuckle seemed a bit rehearsed. "I'm having a fairly good day, so please help me a bit to get things together and we can take a walk, okay?" he suggested.

We walked the Nickel pasture, slowly, in the lazy warmth of a mid-October afternoon. I knew something was terribly wrong for no Mennonite lay in bed in the prime of his life during working hours. Finding Hauns in bed had shocked me into silence; what I had had in mind was telling Hauns about the girls much farther east than Kenora, Ontario. And then to compare records with his catch west of Portage during threshing time. But Hauns would have none of that, I sensed, and I was disappointed that resuming the spinning of the yarn of previous times had failed, yet again.

We walked towards the south pausing occasionally to brush cobwebs of the fall from our faces. Also, Hauns had a handkerchief in his hand which he held before his mouth when he spoke. We reached a pile of rocks at the edge of the pasture, enclosed by a sheep wire. Hauns sat down, looking into the west and pulling down the worn bill of a cap that was his personal history over his eyes.

Hauns looked more resigned than troubled, more accepting than agitated and I was puzzled. The silence was of Hauns's making and I held my peace.

Schild wieda äwre Uage; de Metzschild wea Hauns sien persönlijchet Jeschichtsbuak.

Etj wea veblefft: Hauns sach'ett meea erjäwe aus oppjereajcht enn etj wea veblefft. Daut wea stell omm ons, enn wiels Hauns soo stell wea, hild etj mie tridj.

Aus etj aul docht, daut dit woll aules senne wudd, hild Hauns sien Schneppelduak ver sien Mül, enn hee fong aun too räde: "Dee Tjräft fong twee Joah tridj aun enn leet donn een poah Mol noh. Nü haft de Krankheit toom latzten Mol nohjelohte enn fangt aun mie von aule Siede tootoosate. Enn nü sie etj aul soo wiet, daut etj mie mett dem Doot bekauntjemoakt hab. Oba etj docht, eea etj storf, haud etj weens vedeent, daut mie eene Frü goot wea." Etj tjreajch soo'n Schock, daut etj bloß Gaunsehüt haud, von bowe bett unje. Etj haud mie soo jefreit mett eenem jescheiden Mensch, dee waut vom Läwe enn vonne Musitj vestunt, mie mol saut too vetalle enn nü saut etj doa mett ladje Henj enn fung tjeene Wead, Hauns too treeste. Etj docht enn docht, daut mie meest schweet, oba tjeen Jedanke kaum mie, nuscht nich. Mie deed daut nü sogoa leet, daut etj en zimlich breedet Schwaut en Dietschlaund jeschnäde haud, enn etj prachad bie aule Mäatjess auf, dee miene Vesprätjunge von Leew enn Trüheit jejleeft haude, enn etj aum nächsten morje oba wiet äwa aule Hundat jewast wea. Toom Jletj fong Hauns wada aun: "De easchte fiewentwintig Joah von mienem Läwe weare bett'em Raund voll Oabeit. Aules waut etj doavon haud wea een oola Voltjswoage, eene Jitoa, omsonst, enn een Mülschiera, woonen etj biem oolen Trajchtmoaka Beand Ditj oppem Ütroop nohm Bejrafnis fe fiewentwintig Cent kofft. Enn daut wea donn uck aules."

Hauns haud daut wada mett sien Schneppelduak drock. "Doa wea niemols jenuag Jeld ooda Tiet fe een Tähnedockta, enn miene Tähne deede mie aul emma weeh, solang etj mie dentje kaun. Nü ess'et too loht dee fixe too lohte, wann mien Oola uck meent, hee wudd daut 'seea wellijch' doohne, soo's 'a sajcht. Uck wudd etj soo jearn weens eene tjliene Foat wieda aus Jrienthol enn Roosegoad moake. Weetst noch, woo etj emma em Waste drasche deed? Enn daut ha etj uck väl jedohne, oba

Just when I thought that this would probably be all, Hauns placed his handkerchief before his mouth and started talking, "The cancer started two years ago and the remission is over for the last time. And by now I don't really mind dying but I thought I at least deserved the love of just one woman before it's over." I was shocked into goose bumps. I had so much looked forward to exchanging confidentialities and now I was busy rummaging around in the vocabulary of consolation and finding nothing that sounded good or remotely fitting the occasion. I even apologized, very secretly, for the swath I had cut among the German girls who had believed my tales of love and fidelity and were discarded the morning after and whom I had intended to import to local life via stories today. Fortunately Hauns continued, "The first twenty-five years of life were filled to the brim with work. All I got out of it was a car, a guitar, free, and a Hohner mouth scraper for 25 cents at Old Chiropractor Bachelor Bernd Dyck's estate auction. That was all."

Hauns again busied himself with his handkerchief. "There was never enough money or time for a tooth doctor and my teeth have hurt me all my knowing life. Now it's too late to get them fixed even though my old man says he'll pay for them, even 'gladly' he says. Also, I would so much like to take one trip beyond Grünthal and Rosengard. Remember, all the threshing I did out west? Well, I sure did but only in my stories. All I ever did was clear stones on our shitty farm. For hours and days all and every summer I gathered dried bush and logs and piled them on a stone and made a huge fire. This I let burn for as long as it took and then when the stone was piping hot I hitched up old Barnie to a stone boat and we dragged two barrels of water which I dumped on the red hot rock. The shock of the water split the boulders and then the real work started. I used a crowbar to break up the rock and then Barnie pulled out piece after piece by chain. Tomorrow

bloß enn miene Jedanke enn enn miene Jeschichte. Aules waut etj jemols deed, wea Steena opp onse schattaje Foarm opprieme. Stundelang, joh Sommalang, jiedet Joah mußt etj dreajet Bosch enn dreaje Beem tooplese enn daut aulatoop opp eenem Steen noppfeahre enn aunstetje. Enn donn läd etj emma noch meea aun bett de Steen jläjendig heet wea, enn donn spaund etj ons oolen Barnie aun enn hold twee Tonne mett Wota oppe Steenschlap. De stelpd etj opp den Steen nopp. Daut koldet Wota vefead den rootheeten Steen soo seea, daut'a plautst, enn donn fong de Oabeit oba eascht rechtig aun. Etj mußt mett'em Koohfoot den Stein ütenaunda ducke enn Barnie trock dann een Stetj nohm aundren mett'e Tjäd rüt, enn etj flied dee aulewäje bie de Düsende opp. Tjitj!, doa lidje se äwa onse gaunze Foarm aum Raund enn oppe Rains. Daut wea mien Läwe."

Wada mußt daut Schneppelduak Hauns siene Tähne verre fresche Loft schütze.

Hauns lacht enn etj hopt soo seea aus etj kunn, daut aules wada soo senne wudd aus Joahre tridj enn daut miene groote Hop de Wunde vonne Tiet jeschloage, vedonste wudde.

"Etj wad, Dü jinjst enn rollsd Mejalles enne Wad mett mie?" fruag Hauns. Etj säd nuscht, mien Jeschichte weare vewaltjt.

"Weetst noch Obraum Krohne Neeta, dee oole Mejall von hinjrem Graundridje doa emm Nuade hinjre Bescha?" fruag Hauns. "Afens," säd etj, oba etj haud ahr niemols jetroffe. "Na, etj head saje, see wea nich mätjlich wann'et toom Bielohte kaum. Enn dis Farjoah aus de Tjräft nohleet mie too piesacke, fuah etj mol han en nauhm sogoa eene guanze haulwe Buddel Tjoaschewhiskey mett. Etj gauf ahr dee Buddel, enn see tjitjt mie soo aun aus Frülied doohne, wann se eenem waut ütdriewe welle. 'Waut feascht Dü emm Senn?' frajcht se mie. 'Dauts soon scheena Dach, etj docht eefach mol aules stohne enn lidje lohte enn häakohme enn seehne aus wie Äwareenet väahaude.'

"'Na tjitj jünt mol aun,' sajcht se. 'Etj weet waut Dü väahast von de Oat woo Dü de Henj enne Fuppe hast. Oba wann Dü jleewst, daut Dü mien Pie-Anna ennstemme woascht, best Dü oppem Holtwajch. Enn etj woa Die uck saje, woaromm. Etj

it all started again from the start. Look at the jagged pieces, thousands of them piled up all around the farm. That was my life."

Again the handkerchief had to protect Hauns's rotten teeth from the air.

Hauns chuckled and I hoped with utmost desperation that everything would be as years before and that my fervent hope would evaporate the wounds of time.

"So I bet you went and competed with my record with the girls?" asked Hauns. I said nothing, my agenda had wilted.

"You remember Abram Krahn's Nettie, the spinster from behind the gravel ridge north behind the bushes?" asked Hauns. "Barely," I answered, having never met her. "Well, she wasn't exactly choosy when it came to a little bucking around, so I heard say. So I drove over to her place at the height of my remission this spring and even took along a whole little bottle of cherry whiskey. I gave it to her and she looks me over like women do when they want to ruin your carefully laid plans. 'What's on your mind?' she says. 'It's such a beautiful day that I decided to take it off and visit you and see if our plans are the same.'

"'Look here,' she says, 'I know what your plans are from the way you have your hands in your pockets. But if you think you are going to tune my piano, you are mistaken. And I will tell you why. I know what it means when menfolk get such pointed noses like you have because then they are close to piping on the last hole. And if I would let you loose on me, guys like you would either scream yourself hoarse from excitement or simply let one final one fly and croak.'

"I tried to convince her that I was genuine stuff, which I believe I am. She said, 'You are of the Russlander stripe and I can almost remember when your folks came from Russia and treated my family like slaves even though you Nickels and Warkentines had not enough to entice a dog from behind a

weet waut daut bediet, wann Jungess soone spetzte Näse habe soo's Dü, wiels dann piepe se aul oppem latzten Loch. Enn wann etj Die bielohte wudd, dann wurscht Dü soo schratjlich loosjuche enn bloß noch eenen foahre lohte enn dann kolt senne.'

"Etj vesocht ahr bietoobrinje, daut etj een ajchta Tjeadel wea, wiels daut sie etj je uck. Oba see säd bloß: 'Dü best noch emma een haulwa Rußlenda and etj kaun mie noch een bät dentje aus Diene Ellre von Rußlaund kaume enn ons behaundelde aus wann wie Dratj weare, wann uck de Netjels enn de Woatjentiens too dee Tiet nich jenuag haude, omm'en Hund von hinjrem kolden Owe too locke. Jie meende jünt aula noch eene Striep, sogoa, oba nü daut Dü Stangefeeba hast, saul etj Die auftjeele. Hah! Enn sogoa wann etj Die bielohte wudd, weet etj noch aus etj Die mol pische sach aus Dü jrotzt üte korte Betjze rütjewosse weascht, enn aul donn säd etj too mie, nü tjitjt jünt bloß mol den Kolbassa aun wann'a tohm ess. Wann dee Tjneppel eascht mol wild woare sull, wudd Fraunz Netjel's Hauns eene jeweenelje Frü oppriete soo's wann eena een Schlachtmassa enn eene Arbüs nennstuak. Enn doawäjen saj etj Die: Nä. Enn doabie blift daut.'

"Donn hold Neeta de Buddel, woone etj mettjebrocht haud, üt eene Fupp enn ääh Schalduak, enn nauhm eenen seea stiewen Schluck enn dann noch eenen enn donn dreid se de too enn schoof mie de tridj. 'Doa hast diene Buddel, dee bie mie nich aunkaum. Nü kaust foahre enn mett Miss Dainty Füst eenen Date moake. Oba nü mott etj ütmeste.'"

Hauns enn etj stunde opp enn jinje langsom tridj. Bie ahm aunjekohme, streept hee sich siene Schooh auf, hee haud sich dee nich mol toojebunge. Siene Metz hild hee opp aus hee noh hinje jintj enn donn lintjsch enn siene Stow nennwankt. Hauns leet sich enn sien Bad nennfaule, enn dreid sich wajch mett sien Schneppelduak wada verrem Mül. Donn nauhm siene lintje Haund daut Schneppelduak enn läd daut äwa sien Jesejcht, enn mett de Rajchte socht hee miene Haund, omm Audee too saje.

"Etj wull blooss eenmol weete, woo daut jeiht, wann eena eene Fru goot ess. Blooss eenmol. Eea etj stoaw."

cold stove at the time. You all thought a great deal of yourselves, a whole pailful, even, but now that you have rod fever you want me to cool it down. Hah! And so the answer to you is no. And that's that.'

"Then Nettie took the bottle I had brought along from a pocket in her apron and twisted it open and took a very sturdy schluck, then another one and then she put the cap on it and shoved it at me with nothing more than, 'There you have your bottle which didn't work with me. Now you can go and settle for a date with Miss Dainty Fist while I manure out the hen house.'"

Hauns and I got up and walked slowly back to the house. He slid out of his shoes which he hadn't even tied. He kept his cap on as he walked along the corridor and then turned left to his room. Hauns half dropped into bed and turned his head away with his handkerchief back at his mouth. Then he replaced his right hand with his left to hold the hanky over his face so that his right could look for mine to say good-bye.

"I just wanted to know what it was like to make love with a woman. Just once. Before I die."

Budweiser Beea—Dits Diene Moatj!

Auls Arbuse Kloßes Peeta vonne jrientholsche Barjch-tholsche Tjoatj soo ritj word auls hee aul emma rachullijch jewese wea, deed de mennonitsche Jemeenschauft kratjt daut, jäjen daut, see aul emma jewettat haude, oba emma wada deede: Peeta kontrollead von nu aun den Kollatjtetalle enne Tjoatj. Eascht vestalld sich Peeta enn säd: "Oba, nä, oba nä, doatoo sie etj doch väl too wainijch, väl too deemootijch."

Oba boold wea hee de Jeldtalla, nu uck aum Sinndach. Enn wann irjendwäa vleijcht dit enn Jant too beaunstaunde haud, enn een bät pludre wull (enn Peeta tjand sich enn soohne Sache ut, wiels siene Fru Gertie, Prädjaschdochta, dee jratzte Klohtjedroagasche tweschen Jrienthol enn Spencer South wea, enn uck veatijch Joah jewese wea), dann säd Peeta blooß: "Jie wulle mie, nu hab Jie mie, enn nu hab etj daut mett dem Jeld drock!"

Daut schauft, enn von nu aun haud Peeta den Tjoatjejeld-biedel unja siene Kontroll. Wiels Peeta aul lang enn foaken von sien MIissjoohnsiewa enn Radasenn vetallt haud, haud hee nu daut offizielle Vetrue, aulsoo daut "Papiea" bett fe aule Tiede enne Fupp.

Daut gaunze flauscht auls een jeschmäda Fortjs; Peeta schmustad biem Earnstsenne, enn Gertie wea stolt, enn dee Tjinja jehuarsom. Emm sassten Joah von sien Aumt noh dee sinndoagsche Erntedankfiea, kaum nich soo väl Jeld toop auls see bie de Barjchthola jerätjent haude. Dee gaunze, groote Dankboatjeit haud nich dee erwachte Dohlaform emm Talla aunjenohme. Väle Joahrelang wea daut mett dem Tallaen-hault plätrijch jewese, wiels dee Lied bie Jrienthol aulatoop

This Bud's for You

When Peter Klassen Jr. of the Grünthal Bergthaler church became as wealthy as he had always been ambitious, the Mennonite community did exactly what it has always preached against but has always done: It made him the collection plate supervisor. Peter initially feigned resistance and professed modesty Mennonite style, namely humility, but then was formally installed as the keeper of the plate and purse. That worked. Should gossip surface, and the chiefest of such wagging was Peter's Frau Gertie, Peter now had the authority vested in him to prevail.

That worked and from that moment on, Peter had the finances under his control. Since he had long professed loyalty and commitment to mission endeavors, the necessary trust for the office was his of now and likely, by tradition, for evermore.

Everything worked just well; Peter was amusedly serious and his wife proud and their children dutiful. It was the sixth year into Peter's term as the keeper of the purse that the finances after the Thanksgiving Sunday celebration did not meet projected and customary amounts of gratitude converted into cash. For many years, previous donations and offerings had been niggardly of necessity but then the dairy, hog and broiler investments gradually produced profits, big time, and every church-bound alley was macadamized, both literally and figuratively.

However, the collection plate, under Peter's lordship had sustained a few miscarriages and now, suddenly, an abortion. Gossip turned to malice and Peter was summoned to what

oam weare. Oba dann nauhm de Maltjwirtschauft, enn dee Schwiens enn Heehnaproduktsjoon doa emm Struck seea too, enn boold word jieda Wajch von, enn noh jieda Tjoatj, enn Jrienthol mett Zement enn Täah schmock breet enn jlitj enn foahboa jemoakt.

Oba mett eenmol haud dee Kollajtetalla nu unja Peeta siene Obhoot een poah Utstelpsels jeläde, enn nu sogoa eene Meßjeburt. Ute Pludarie worde Väaschmietunge, enn donn word Peeta jebedde mol aum Donnadach (ut gooden Grund soo's bie de Menniste enne Tjoatje aulewäje, enn too aule Tiede jenannt, wiels de Donna eene dietlijche Sproak enn aule Sproake ess), enne Tjoatj too erschiene, enn sich too ertjläre. Peeta wrunscht han enn häa, oba siene Utred weare soo ladijch auls eene holle Postanak.

Jenuag: "Du, Peeta, hast bett Wiehnachte Tiet, Dien Fall enn uck Diene Seel enn Dien Roop too rade, enn wann nijch, woa wie Die daut Wundre leahre, aulso Hott aum Diestel biebrinje.

Peeta saut platzjlijch deep enne Sementocha, enne Bredulj, enn aulahaund, too woohnt de Mensche bett nutoo een Uag toojedretjt haude, kaum äwadäl, enn Peeta fong sich aun too schobbe, too jätje enn too schiere.

Arbuse Kloßes Peeta deed, waut eena dann soo deit, wann eenem daut Wota bett aun Luj steiht, enn de Steewle enn uck de Betjze jestritjt voll send. Hee phooned Peeta Thiesses Peeta, dee uck Erfoahrunge emm Dreie enn Wrunsche haud, wann de Rätjnunge nich stemme wulle. Thiesses Peeta haud meea Bildung, wea jleia, enn vestund hejrche Wotawalle too beschwijchtje.

Daut wea earnst, säda, enn wiels beid wisste, woo eena den Stähl emm Mestfortj nennschuwe musst, wann eena sich tweschne Groow enn dem Mesthupe befung, nauhme see sich den Prädja Moatien Dertjse, enn Tjaisa ohne Reich, enn een Seelsorja ohne Seele aun. See wudde mol wada opp earnst

Old Colony men of serious repute called the Day of Thunder, Donnadach. Nothing jibed except shallow and hollow excuses and Peter was given till Christmas to come up with a redeemable course of action.

Peter was in deep trouble and other matters, to which benefits of the doubt had been previously granted him, were rehashed and Peter now had to resort to many nimble tactics to save his skin and his assholian repute.

He did the obvious thing and contacted his life long buddy, a more educated but equally seasoned in niftinesses, Peter Thiessen and asked for urgent accommodation. Such was granted.

Both had over many years honed the sharp edges of absolutes into manageable roundness of less offensive friction and, knowing their community and the priorities that worked, they mobilized an older, restless man of the spirit, one Martin Doerksen, a bit of a self-styled emperor without much of an empire. The Rev. Doerksen handily agreed to their plan to become a missionary among those less fortunate among us, the Indians, the Natives.

To that end, they had to come up with tangibles, namely where and when they could turn their intentions into practical application. And affordable in any case. They knew full well that when it came to native missions the prevailing mind-set was handily exploitable. Money could be mined out of obdurate and resisting pockets of the majority who were mission-minded enough but just as calculating when it came to investments of the Natives, widely regarded as lazy, no-good and useless. All three were agreed on these attributes but they also knew that those of guilty conscience, the Canadian government in this instance, could always be relied upon to disperse funds without many checks and balances in the direction of the Native Cause and Concern.

Indieauna betjeare, enn wann see een Schwitt von soohne vebiestade Gottestjinja emm Hock haude, wudd äah Roop aulatoop schwind vom Tjalla bett dem dredden Stock kohme. Nu word bosijch enn pienijch een Plohn jeschmäd. Oba too diea sull dee gaunze Betjeararie dann oba uck nijch kohme, daut wea jiedem kloa. Oppe aundre Sied, habe Menniste, enn sozialistische Rejierunge aul emma eene wellje Fupp, wann'et heet, Indieauna, too halpe; doarenn weare see sijch eenijch. Een Moonat lohta wear'et dann uck soowiet. See haude sich fe billjet Jeld een oolet Loftschepp jeleased, woohnt oppem Wota launde kunn; daut haud groote Loftkuffe ut Alumium, staut Schneekuffe ooda Reife, enn doamett wudde see vom Red Riefa enn Winnipetj looslaje, enn dann noh Dryden, enn Ontario fleaje, enn dann wieda noh Sioux Lookout, enn dann noh Pickle Lake, enn dann wada noh Hus kohme. Daut Loftschepp heet Northern Dancer.

Unjawäjess wudde see sijch daut Missioonsfeld vonne vebiestade Roodasch auntjitje, Berejcht enne Tjoatje auflaje, Jeld saumle, enn dann tridjfoahre, dee roothutje Indieauna dee Sinde utdriewe, eene Tjoatj opp jieda Städ bue, enn dee Tabun onbetjeade Willasch oppteeme.

Butadem haude see nohm Paulinsche Waut, "Wann enn Room, dann benemm Die auls een Reema" emm Senn, enn daut heet, wann'et enn Pickel Lake een Sweat Lodge gauf, aulso eene Sauna, nohm Indieaunastil, dann wulle see sich doa aufspeele, enn dee Indieauna wiese, woor'ett betjeade Tjriste ohne Betjze oba mett witte Unjabetjze sitt.

Enn wann daut gaunze Unjanehme flausche wudd, dann haud Kloßes Peeta wada een gooden Nohme dijcht bie de Jeldschiew, enn Thiesses Peeta wudd uck mol wiese tjenne, waut hee enn de leewa Gott aules kunne, wann see sijch enne Grauje speaje, enn sich toop enne Säle laje wudde. Enn Prädja Moatien Dertzje wea aul lang seea iewrijch aum Diestel

30

Within a month, the three had leased a bit of an old fashioned DC-7, a reliable old air-horse and a bush pilot to trace the initial route of their endeavors, namely a pontoon craft to fly Winnipeg, Dryden, Sioux Lookout, Pickle Lake and then home again. Old political contacts were re-heated, at least re-warmed, and they were off in the name of the Lord and with a Sweat Lodge, Native style awaiting them in the Sioux Lookout proximity.

The successful completion of this missionary plan would restore Peter Klassen's good name in the collection plate circles, give sense and direction and respectability to Peter's mentor and life-long buddy, Peter Thiessen, who intended to show his own world and himself what the Lord could and would do if finally given a proper chance; and certainly the endeavour would bestow on the ambitious man of the word, Rev. Doerksen an overdue blessing.

Der Mensch denkt
Und Gott lenkt;
Der Mensch dachte
Und Gott lachte.
Man proposes,
God disposes,
is more than an adequate translation and intent.

The three bowed for a word of prayer, boarded the plane and were off on their new endeavour of saving the lost and needy of word.

Even before the ubiquitous water bottle was custom, the Rev. Doerksen, a huge man, drank copiously from every tank except the beer spigot. Flying is exciting enough but the laws of nature still prevail and while bush planes can execute almost unbelievable feats, they lack plumbing. After much re-arranging of legs and intentions, it was between Kenora and Dryden that gravity and a full bladder prevailed over decorum and Martin Doerksen copiously pissed himself for

jewese, enn nu wudd ahm de leewa Gott endlijch mol eene Extramoht Howa ennschedde.

Aule dree steaje see enn, bäde kort oba earnst, dann ruzhd enn scheddad sich daut Loft- enn Wotaschepp, enn dann fluag uck aul dee Wotaschum, enn see weare enne Loft. Sogoa eea jieda Mensch oppe Ead Dach enn Nacht mett eene Wotabuddel noh de latzte Mood rommrannd, drunk Prädja Dertjze ut jiedem Wotakrohn, buta vom Beeataupe. Hee wea een seea groota, forscha Maun von dreehundat enn zastijch Pund.

Daut Fläje ess oppräjend enn scheen, enn wann uck soohne Loftschäp meist aules blooß Dentjboaret doohne tjenne, bliewe doch jewesse Jesatze uck tweschen Himmel enn Ead bestohne. Northern Dancer haud soo meea aules bie, enn enn sijch, oba een Hiestje nich. Nohdem Ohm Dertjze siene Been enn siene Aufsejchte han enn häa enn sogoa doppelt jelajcht haud, weare'ett mett eenmol soo wiet, enn hee bepischt sich toom easchten Mol enn äwa zastijch Joah. Hee haud soo iewrijch jebät, enn soo seea toojetjnäpe, oba daut holp ahm nuscht, enn sien Borm rannd äwa enn äwa, enn dann kaum uck noch een latztet Schulps hinjeraun. Hee haud eenfach nijch jejleewt, daut de himmlischa Voda daut soo wiet kohme lohe wudd, oba Hee deed, enn nu saut Prädja Moatien Dertjze doa enne onmackelje jäle Bräj, enn schämt sijch de Uage utem Kopp, enn de Betjze, Schooh enn Stremp vom Liew. Dee twee Peetasch vesochte ahm too treeste, oba dee Troost wea soo denn auls de Loft woohne bute dem Northern Dancer omme Uahre blosd.

De Dietsche saje dann: "*Wer einmal liegt, kann nicht mehr fallen*", oba soohne huage Weisheite halpe uck eenem Prädja weinijch, wann hee "*muß ich mit nassen Hosen sitzen*" lieseltjes ver sijch hansommd. Daut died dann uck nijch lang bett daut tweedemol toolohte soo wiet wea, enn Ohmtje Dertjze sijch wada vollstrulld.

the first time since age three. He honestly and really did not believe that the Lord would allow this to happen but He did and now the good reverend sat there in wet discomfort and in terrible embarrassment and shame. The two Peters offered lame excuses but all consolations were as thin as the air whistling past them.

The Germans have a bit of an anecdotal response for such occasions: *"Wer einmal liegt, kann nicht mehr fallen"*—'once you're down you can no longer fall'. Such worldly wisdom is sufficient to piss most people off but not Martin Doerksen in his present state. It was not long before a second voiding of the piss pouch in high altitude dampened shorts, pants and lofty spirits. Before the three were deposited for their nightly sojourn in Sioux Lookout, Peter Thiessen, likewise a stout three hundred pounder and the only one with an extra pair of pantaloons in his sparse luggage, assisted the Rev. Doerksen in re-panting.

The only reason the two Peters escaped the embarrassing fate of their missionary for hire is because the plane had on yesterday's trip transported American fishermen to a remote lake and two empty six packs were located in the luggage compartment by those of urgent bent. An oil funnel also came in handy and both Peters hauled out their peters and each pissed full six This Bud's for You somewhere in the remote loftiness between Dryden and the Sioux.

When this motley trinity later that evening emerged from the Sweat Lodge and took a dip in a cold pool Peter Thiessen's naval cavity, the center of his huge pot belly imploded, and two of the local Natives, noticing his receding bud, there and then bestowed on him the nickname of Pothole Peter.

Since Peter Klassen's reputation has somehow preceded him, his new Indian name was Beer Bottle Pete, while Doerksen's airborne fate, fully revealed, occasioned a re-

Auls dee dree enn Sious Lookout aunkaume, haud Thiesses Peeta, uck een dreehundadpundja Tjnewel, enn dee eensja mett een extra poah kackjäle Betjze, dem Prädja utjeholpe.

Dee eensja Grund, woaromm dee twee Peetasch mett heela Hut enn dreaje Betjze onjeschoare kaume, emm Jäjensautz toom "Dee pachtboara Missionoa Dertjze" wea wiels daut Loftschepp Northern Dancer oppe jistreje Foaht veea amerikaunsche Feschasch noh eenem See noch wieda emm Nuade transportead haud, enn disse haude twalw ladje Budweis Beeabuddle tridj emm Koffaruhm jelohte. Uck haft soohn Northern Dancer fe jieden Faul eenen Schmäahtrejchta mett, enn ladje Buddle enn dee Trejchta kaume ahn, Peeta & Co. nu tweschen Dryden enn Sioux Lookout tweschen Himmel enn Ead seea toopauß, enn soo kaume dee twee Peetasch mett dreaje Betjze oba mett volle Beeabuddle Budweiser Dit's Diene Moatj! enn Sioux Lookout aun.

Auls disse bunte Dree-eenijchtjeit lohta zeowends ute Sauna kaume, enn Peeta Thiesse sien Nowel aun sienem Tweemeetabuck gaunz toopjeschrunke wea, nannde ahm dee Indiauna, dee emma een schoapet Uag fe menschlijchet Bute enn Bennaschtet habe, "Loch aum Buck Peeta. "

Enn wiels see uck aul verhää von Arbuse Kloßes Peeta jeheat haude, nannde see ahm noh de Sauna "Beeabuddel Kloße", enn Prädja Moatien Dertjze nannde see von donn bett vondoag eenfach "Prädja Betjzepischa."

AMEN!

christening as well. He was henceforth known simply as The Pissing Pastor.

Tweeback toom Bejrafnis

Auls Doft Jaunze siene Tiet hiea em Jaumadohl too Enj jintj, wea hee mau twee-efeftijch. Auls hee äwa sien Läwe soo nohdocht, foll ahm bie, daut hee aulnoch väl äwa de misroble Doag enn sien Läwe too koojeneare jehaut haud, enn uck äwa Gott siene Onjerajchtijchtjeite, enn äwre faulsche Donnasch enne Tjoatj, enn uck äwre heiwtänsche Frulied.

Oba nu daut'et soo schwind boajauf jintj, wäahd hee sijch mett Henj enn Feet enn mett sien Bennaschtet. Ahm foll daut stoawe aulnoch schwoa. Oba de Prädjasch haude jesajcht: "Doft, diene Tiet ess jekohme omm dien latztet Schemedauntje too packe. Du best boold unjawäajess!" Daut haud uck de Dokta jesajcht enn schliesslijch uck de Trajchtmoaka, enn de wisst. Enn siene Fru sowesoo.

Doft Jaunze foll daut schwoa. Nu daut aules vebie wea deed ahm daut leed, daut hee hiea enn doa too väl uttoosatte jehaut haud, daut hee städwies too väl gromsaujd haud, enn daut hee measchtens too rachulijch jewast wea, enn daut hee dit enn jant nijch äwareen jebrocht haud.

Oba nu wear'et too loht. Hee lach oppe Schlopbeintj enne groote Stow enn tjitjcht noh dem Fensta enn noh de Dääh… vleijcht wudd sogoa eena opp een schwoatet Pead kohme, ooda vleijcht sogoa irjendwaut mett nuscht buta Knoakess enn een Schädel enn deepe Lajcha em Kopp aunstaut Hut oppem Jesejcht, enn dissa wudd mett eene schoape Sans nennkohme, ohne too puttre. Jiedesmol wann hee jleewd, daut irjendwäa puttad, ooda waut knostad, trock Jaunze sien Kopp unjre Datj, enn vestuak sijch soo goot auls hee noch kunn. Boold wisst hee

And that's that

But now that things were rapidly coming to a close and rather swiftly downhill, he resisted with hands and feet and with inner disposition. He found the business of dying difficult. The ministers had said, "David, it is time for you to pack your last travel bag. You are on your way!" The doctor had also said so and finally even the local bone-setter, and he knew. And his wife in any case.

David Janzen had a hard time of it. Now that everything was past and almost over, he felt a little sorry that he had nattered around here, that he had complained there and that he had been too avaricious most of the time and that he had not brought a few things in his life into order.

Now, however, it was too late. He lay on the sleep bench in the big room and looked at the window and the door… maybe someone on a black horse would ride up after all, or maybe even something with nothing but bones and skull and deep black holes in the head instead of skin on the face would stop in with a sharpened scythe. Every time when he thought he heard a knock or a creak, Janzen pulled in his head a bit and hid under the blanket, as much as he was still able to. Soon he no longer knew what was reality and what was fantasy, what was dreamt and what was imagined.

One thing Janzen knew for sure and that was that he had not seen any angels and also had heard no choirs. He started sweating.

Whether he had called him, or whether the little piker had sensed something? Who knows… whatever, suddenly there sat on the little stool close to the sleep bench his little fall-bred

nijch meea waut Wertjlijchtjeit wea, enn waut hee sijch enbild, waut hee dreemd, enn waut hee sijch utdocht.

Eene Sach wea sijch Jaunze sejcha: hee haud noch tjeene Enjels jeseehne, enn uck tjeen Chooah jeheat. Ahm fong aun too schweete.

Auls eena ahm jeroopt haud, ooda auls dem tjleinen Tjnirps waut jeohnt haud? Wäa weet… waut uck emma, mett eenmol saut bie ahm opp een Beinjstje sien tjlienet Hoawsttjitjel, daut tjliene Doftje. De tjliena Doft wea mau tien Joah oolt, bie wiet de Jinjsta von väle Tjinja.

De oola Jaunze haud oba noch jenuag Ducht enn Daump dem Tjlienen kratjcht too saje, waut hee too doohne haud. "Doft, mien Tjliena, mett mie jeiht'et schwind, väl too schwind too Enj. Enn wann etj nu boold wajch sie, well etj daut du die enne School benemmst, enn daut du die bie Leahra Peetasch de Waute ute Uahre nemmst enn goot oppausst. Uck dooh emma waut Mamma die sajcht, enn loht die nijch egol porre enn stoh zemorjess tiedijch opp. Enn behool daut Goode von mie, enn vejat dee poah schlajchte Doag." Enn donn wea hee stell.

"Oba Pappa, vleijcht woat daut wada mett Junt, enn dann foah wie em Farjoah wada fesche. Etj woa junt uck den jratzten jriepe lohte, joh?"

Doft Jaunze wea aulwada emm Biestalaund jewast, enn ahm haud jedreemt, hee haud aul utjespaunt enn wulll jrods nenngohne, auls de tjliena Doft mett ahm fesche foahre wull.

"Waut?" fruag hee.

"Jie selle dissen Winta noch läwe bliewe, daut wie em Farjoah wada toop fesche gohne tjenne," meend de Tjliena.

"Daut wudd etj seea jearn doohne, oba miene Lomm jeiht unja," säd Jaunze enn wundad sijch, daut hee biem stoawe meist soo auls een Prädja jerät haud.

Doft säd nuscht nijch, oba ahm gruselt bie soohne Räd.

rooster, the late-comer, his youngest, little David. Little David was barely ten years old, by far the youngest of many.

Old Janzen had enough steam left to talk straight to the little fellow and to admonish him as required. "David, my boy, with me things are coming to an end and far too quickly. Once I am gone, I want you to behave yourself in school and in Teacher Peters' class you take the cotton batting out of your ears and listen carefully to him. Also, you do what mother tells you to and don't always wait to be told to work harder and get up in the mornings. Think of the good in me and forget the few off-days." And then he was quiet.

"But papa, maybe things will again turn around with you and then we'll go fishing again in spring. I promise I'll let you catch the biggest one, okay?"

David Janzen had again paid a brief visit to Delirium-Land and he had dreamed he had already unhitched his team and had just wanted to go inside when Little David wanted to go fishing with him.

"What?" he asked.

"You shall stay alive this winter yet so that we can fish again together in spring," suggested the little one.

"That I would like to do, but my boat is sinking," said Janzen and was surprised at himself for having said something almost preacher-like upon dying.

David said nothing but he shuddered at such talk. That's the way it was in that room, if you had allowed your spirit to take a picture of it all: the old fellow lying on the sleep-bench with his hands full with dying and his little one sitting on a stool at his side, living, but having a hard time of it all.

As for the woman and the mother? Well, she was Mennonite and was busy. In the kitchen or wherever: she wielded a sturdy set of brooms and set items and people straight whenever necessary. And sometimes when it wasn't even necessary. But

Soo wea daut enn dee Stow, wann eena sien Jeist een Bild von daut Gaunze aufjenohme haud: dee Oola lach oppe Schlopbeintj enn haud de Henj voll mett stoawe, enn de Tjliena saut oppem Beinjstje aun siene Sied; Doftje wea läwendijch, oba ahm foll daut seea schwoa.

Enn waut de Fru enn Mutta aunjintj? Na, see wea mennisch, enn haud daut drock. Enne Tjäatj ooda woa emma: see feahd eene stiewe Fuchtel enn hild Mensche em Schach enn hild uck Rosmack, wann'et senne musst. Uck maunjchmol wann'et nijch senne musst. Oba see wea de Eensje, dee nu aules unjre Kontroll hilt.

Doft Jaunze wea wada emm Biestalaund; hee haud aulwada utjespaunt enn wea nennjegohne, enn haud sijch hanjelajcht. Enn wea meist enjeschlope. Enn donn mett eenmol ritjcht hee waut... dee Jeruch wea ahm bekaunt, enn seea scheen—soo scheen, daut hee noch nijch enschlope wull. Na joh, enschlope, daut joh, oba eascht wull hee doch noch siene Nieschiea een bätje auffoodre.

"Waut ritjcht hiea soo seea scheen?" fruag hee, enn kroop ut sienem Droohm rut. De tjliena Doft vefeahd sijch soo seea, daut hee vom Beinjstje foll. Oba dee Oola, von siene eajne Stemm oppjewatjcht, fruag wada: "Waut rijcht hiea soo scheen?"

"Daut weet etj nijch, Pappa!" säd Doft.

"Goh enne Tjäatj, enn finj mol ut," säd de oola Jaunze lieseltjess.

Doftje jintj. Oba hee kaum fuats tridj enn berejcht: "Mamma backt Tweeback."

"Enn du hast mie nijch mol een Stetjstje ooda een biet Tjarscht mett jebrocht? Goh hol mie eenen!"

Doft jintj. Hee kaum oba fuats wada tridj enn säd: "Mamma sajcht de Tweeback send nijch goot fe junt, dee send too fresch. Jie tjenne dee nijch vedroage, sajcht see."

40

now she was the only one in that realm who controlled all things in and with her hands.

David Janzen there on the sleep bench was again in Delirium-Land; he had again unhitched his team and had gone in and had laid down. And he had almost fallen asleep. Then suddenly, he smelled something… that scent was familiar and very beautiful—so beautiful that he did not want to fall asleep yet. Na joh, fall asleep he wanted to but first he had to give his curiosity a spoonful of attention.

"What smells so very nice?" he asked, crawling out of his dream.

Little David was so startled that he dropped from his perch. The old one, though, awakened by his own voice, again asked, "What smells so good?"

"That I don't know, Papa!" said David.

"Go to the kitchen and find out," said old Janzen softly.

David went. But he soon returned and reported, "Mother is baking buns."

"And you didn't even bring me along a bit of heel or a piece of crust? Go get me one!"

David went. He came back right away and reported, "Mama says the buns aren't good for you, they are much too fresh. You can't handle them, she says."

Old Janzen said as energetically as he could muster, "Buns, I said. Go!"

David went. After a little while he returned and stated, "Papa, I am sorry but Mama says 'No'!"

"Does one have to anger himself to death while dying? Sonofabitch! You go to the kitchen and fetch a bun or only half of one as far as that goes but you will not return empty-handed. Go right now. I am still boss around here!"

David went. This time it took over a minute before he returned. He remained a little distance from his papa while

De oola Jaunze säd soo energisch auls hee noch kunn:
"Tweeback säd etj. Goh!"

Doft jintj. Noh een tjlienet Stootstje kaum hee wada tridj enn
säd: "Pappa, mie deit daut leed, oba Mamma sajcht 'Nä'!"
"Mott eena sijch biem stoawe noch een bät doot oajre? Toom
Schinda han! Du jeist fuats oppe Städ enne Tjäatj nenn enn
holst eenen Tweeback ooda weens eenen haulwen, oba mett
ladje Henj tjemmst du nijch tridj. Enn nu goh. Etj sie hiea noch
emma Baus!"

Doft jintj. Ditmol diead daut äwa eene Minut eea hee
tridjkaum. Hee bleef een Enjstje von sienem Voda auf stohne
auls hee sienen Berejcht aufläd: "Pappa, Mamma sajcht
doaraun endat sijch nuscht, äwahaupt nuscht. Dee Tweeback
send fe daut Bejrafnis, enn doabie blift'et!"

reporting, "Papa, mamma says nothing will change, not even one bit. The buns are for the funeral, and that's that!"

Nohba Jasch Wiens

Dee Joubert Rie rant dree Kilomeeta derjch onse jewesene Foarm enn wiedre dusende Kilomeeta derjch mien Läwe. Etj kunn nuscht doafäa: ons Fluß rand uck derjch mien Tjarpa, derjch miene Seel, enn wea emma reed sijch miene Jeschijchte auntooheare, enn dee wieda too vetalle, enn dee Steena, emm Wota ooda uck dee deepe Städe enne Rie dee too vetalle enn uck dee Wäsels, dee Nerze, Moschraute, Biebasch enn Ottasch ennem Wota enn uck oppe Eewasch durwe dee aula heare.

Bowe fluage Howtjes, dee uck von enn bie de Rie wohnde, enn sogoa hanenwada een Odla, enn een poah Sorte Uhle, enn uck Ente, Holthackasch, Rootbucks and dee jeheemnisvolla Kossemaltja, dem wie Whippoorwill nannde, enn dee de Nacht em Somma Stundenlang soo scheen oba uck grulijch em Diestren sung. Jeseehne haft dit Voagel bett vondoag tjeena, jleew etj. See weare aula dijcht bie, enn omm mie, enn etj bie, enn omm ahn; wie weare ons dochwoll goot.

Em Winta frooah dee Rie too, enn etj musst jieden Dach tweemol doa hangohne enn daut Ies ophacke, doamett onse Tjeaj enn ons Jungveeh doa supe kunne; dee Stijch doahan jintjch derjchen Bosch, wea eene Veadel Miel auf, dochwoll soo omme veea hundat Meeta, enn kolt wea ons niemols, nijchmol bie dee eewje Tjill. Dee Natua woamt mie enn Die enn Janem enn uck Junt soo's eene leewtolje Mutta aune Brost, ooda soo's eene Groosmau biem Jeschijchtevetalle biem Fieaowent.

Aum Sinnowend leeht wie daut Wota äwaschwamme, enn dann muak wie ons eenen Iesrintj enn spälde Hockey. Onse Pead leewade ons dee Pucks, billijch, enn soo väl auls eena wull.

The Plot of Despair

The Joubert Creek ran a few miles through our former farm and a further thousand miles and more through my life. Our creek ran through my being, through my soul and through whoever was around to listen to my stories: the minks, weasels, muskrats, beavers and otters or the rounded banks of the stream. All listened and understood; a compassionate and understanding wider audience of time.

Hawks flew about, screeching, demanding, assertive, possessive. They, too, lived from and by the creek. Occasionally even an eagle soared, hunting for fish with a knowing eye and practiced intent. There were owls of many varieties, as well, and ducks, woodpeckers, robins and the secretive whippoorwill, who sang nightly, hauntingly beautiful. No one ever saw this bird; it sang backstage with the perfect pitch of the knowing for the knowing. They were all close to me, around me, and I with them; we were part of each other and we knew it. Like love.

In winter the creek froze and I had to chop open a soft spot on the ice for our cows and heifers to drink, twice daily. The path to water led through silent bush, a quarter mile, but the intense cold was never a problem; nature comforts in story telling warmth. Come Saturday, a larger patch of ice was flooded into a hockey rink. Our horses supplied the pucks, free and ample.

Money was scarce, hard to come by, and so I trapped weasels and mink and beavers wherever they crossed my trap line. Since fresh meat was scarce in winter, a .22 calibre Browning rifle was my constant guide and companion.

Omm too een bätje Fupptjejeld too kohme, jreep etj Wäsels enn Nerze enn uck Biebasch enne Faul; den langen Stijch, woa etj dee Faule oppstald, nannde se donn een Trap-Line. Wiels wie emm Winta weinijch freschet Fleesch haude, nauhm etj emma onse Twee-entwintijch mett enn schoot entweda Boatjheehna ooda Raupheehna, dee sijch zeowents enne dijchte Asta bie de Rie Schulinj sochte; dee plock etj oppe Städ, enn dee worde Tus fein toom Owendkost jebrode.

Wann de Winta eenfach nijch oppheare wull, kaum de Aprel, enn meist äwanacht wea de Triebsaul too Enj, enn daut Wota rand enn schäld, enn de Welt word Wotamusitj; daut head sijch goot. Enn dann kaume de Moschraute von aulewäje, enn läwde opp'e Rie opp. Etj nauhm eene lange, ditjche Bohl, spreed doa Eadschocke enn Wrucke nopp, enn sad doatweschen eene Reaj Faule opp. Dee Moschraute fraute daut Jetjätjs soo iewrijch, daut see dee Faule nijch mol too seehne tjreaje, enn mett eenmol haud de Faul ahn uck aul aune groote Tee faust; see sprunge em Wota nenn, enn vedrunke, enn etj haud nohm Aufladre enn Falldreaje wada twee Dohla fe jiede Raut eene Fupp. Daut wea too dee Tiet väl Jeld.

Äwanacht wuake uck dusende Pogge opp en sunge kratjcht soo auls wie emm Tjoatjechooah seea dankboa eascht aula Bauss, dann piepste uck mett eenmol een poah hundat easchte Stemm, enn dann kaum de tweede Stemm enn de Tenors hinjeraun, enn aule freide sijch, daut een nieet Joah aunjefonge haud. Enn dann fonge de Krauje, dee aul wäatjelang wada enn Manitoba weare, sijch heesch too tjreie; see vetalde de Väajel, noch em Siede, daut'et woam jenuag wea tridjtookohme, enn aum näajchsten Morje weare uck aul de Rootbucks oppe Weid, enn fuats kaume uck de Turtelduwe hinjeraun, enn de Holthackasch rätade aune Beem enn sochte Warm. Aum Meddwäatj weare de Tjiewitjs oppe Stap, enn dann kaume de Schwaulmtjess.

Peiheehna enn Kuhne kollbätjre, Hoftjess tjriesche, Duwe kurre, Heehna koakele, Tjitjel piepse, Rootbuks enn Kosemaltjasch aka whippoorwills sinje, Sproakheitasch schindeare,

Prairie chickens and grouse looking for shelter in the trees were handy and easy prey and a frequent welcome for a ready kitchen skillet.

Just when the severity of winter showed no reprieve, April arrived and almost overnight the wait was over and faith restored. Not even Handel's Water-Music sounded as good to ear and soul as did the rushing waters of spring of our Joubert Creek.

It was then time to shove sturdy pieces of rough timber into the creek and to strew left over cellar vegetables on them to hide waiting traps, nailed to the underside of the planks, connected by a length of chain. Muskrats were so eager for veggies that they were oblivious to the traps. Traps jump and hold, the muskrats dove for cover and drowned. Skinning and curing the skins was routine. Two dollars for a muskrat skin came in handy when money was as scarce as a Nazi's good repute.

Overnight a thousand frogs awoke and sang similar to a church choir, full of the gratitude of new life. With one difference: Frogs all sing bass initially, then a few dared a soprano peep, then altos emerge and the tenors fall into the line of song but all chanted the praise of new life, a new beginning, Nature's New Year!

Then came the crows quarreling in raucous chiding while simultaneously announcing to the birds waiting further south that all was safe and good to return. The very next morning the robins cocked along on many lawns with the mourning doves a week behind. Woodpeckers rattled on many trees within a day, while meadow larks and killdeers likewise frolicked wherever the human eye and ear went visiting.

Two weeks later swallows with their slant curves of bewildering joy finalized the return, and outdoor swimming season was open.

Krauje gaulme, Rowes tjrejche, een Tjennitjsvoagel jeft Orda
aun enn koojintjat doabie, Jans rope, Spree sinje em Fahrjoah
soo's een ruscha Chooah em Falsetoo, aulso emm Tjenstlatoon,
oba emma dankboa, Tuntjennitjs vetalle, Kukucks räde
Domms, Uhle trure, Nachtigaule klautsche enn pludre, enn
vetalle aules noh, Krauntjess grunze, Tjiewitjs prophezeie,
Boatjheehna puttre, oba Schwaulmtjess schwietere, enn
doawäjen woat opp Jantsied vetalt, daut'et eea daut Schwaulmtjess gauf, tjeene Nähvereine bestunde. Eascht derjch daut
Schwietere vonne Schwaulmtjess fonge Frulied aun ähre Red
uttooputze, enn straume Dommheite äwa de Nohbaschtjinja
too vetalle, enn Nähvereine too organiseare, mett biblische
Nohmes, doamett see dann uck respatjtobla worde enn
Mensche ähre Utneiarie enn Jehätjeldet earnst nauhme.

Wann een Schwaulmtje mett Famielje eene Doages em
Fahrjoah enn Jrienthol ooda enn Reinlaund opp Jantsied
oppduckt, enn von Panama oode Mexiko vetalt, enn biem
Fleaje ve luta Freid Kullasch dreid enn sich putzt enn prunt,
enn vonne scheene Aupelsiene enn Mangoes wiet, wiet em
Siede vetalt, en dann noch een Farsch von eene riepe Arbus em
Siede bieaun erwähnt, dann kohme Frulied opp Jedanke, enn
dann jeiht een gaunz nieet Läwe aulewäje loos. Dann woat
jeschwietat

Enn too gooda latzt sinjt mett eene Kolaraturastemm dee
Pirol; dit Voagel, to dem de Dietsche dee Voagel saje, ess
strauma auls eene rusche Pastje; haft eene Brost soo root, oba
noch strauma auls een Stop-Schild, enn sinjt, soo's een
säwentienjoaschet Mädtje nohm easchten Kuss biem Monlijcht
em Mai hinja Jrienthol.

Dree Wäatj lohta summde de Kolibries uck aul iewrijch
romm; de measchte Mensche nannde de tjliene Wizhasch
Hummingbirds. Oh joh, etj haud boold de Tuntjennitjs vejäte,
dee aulewäje toojlitj saute enn kollbeatjade ooda uck fuschelde;
dee weare soo besorjt auls ellre Mädtjess, dee sijch dissen
Somma jearn befriee wulle. Mett eenmol wea daut Bosch enn
de Staul enn de Spitjasch voll; wäa de Nacht kaum enn huach

And while the swallows busied themselves building nests in barns and stables, a thousand Canada Geese flew overhead a mile and more to report on a winter well spent in cottage country.

The geese were the largest bird to occupy the sky in uncounted numbers; their littlest counterpart on every yard was the wren who twitters by the name of Fence King in Mennonite Low German, while an even smaller remote cousin is the humming bird, known as the colibri of Latin ken.

Geese attract and pay attention and even when flying a mile high they held a radared eye on the forever-curving Joubert Creek, which directed them on their way north, then north further still.

Every bush and meadow was full of singing, chirping birds, full of happy gibberish as were the girls of school and church. "Maybe," they silently hoped, the dice of union will roll my way before the clover blooms?

Grouse fascinate the living condition: they drum and putter with a volume totally beyond their size and intelligence, much like an eager tractor in the bush, not yet patented. Also, they have a moralizing prance to them, not unlike a minister of raised index finger with many warnings; grouse are preferable; they do not mind being laughed at, humoured.

Our Joubert Creek was a friend to everyone. You could wallow in it, be boisterous and do in it as you pleased; it carried you, pardoned you with wash, and consoled and comforted. This flowing body of sustenance listened patiently, spoke of the many places it had been, never meddled, never intrusive, knew much, always joyful and forgiving. When it embraced you in early summer it was as warm and good as my mother's arms.

As to whether the creek really meant so well, or whether I imagined it, I do not know, and it is of no matter; if you

äwa ons fluage weare de Jans bie de hundad Dusende. See hilde
een Uag opp onse Rie, wiels dee noh Nuade tjrenjeld, enn doa
wulle see han. Woohn Voagel oba besondasch oppfoll wea dee
Boatjhohn, dee soo lud puttad auls een oola Tjätel, dem
maunjche Mensche Trakta nannde.

Dee Schwaulmtjess weare ons besondasch wellkohm, wiels
wann dee tridjkaume, auls aum Nippa enn Russlaund ooda bie
ons aune Rie, meend, daut daut Wota woam jenuag wea omm
too bohde, enn wie rannde mett de wintasche lange Unjabetjse
äwren Schullre jlitjch noh de Rie omm too schwamme.

Wiels de Odla aul aulewäje enne Bibel väatjemmt, enn uck
bie ons han enn wada von Bowe vebiekauhm omm nohm
Fräde enn Aunstaund too tjitje, enn luda mohnd auls een
Evangelist, wann hee, kratjt soo's de Odla, mol eene ooltmood-
sche Sind too seehne trjeajch, mott etj den erwähne. Dann
roopt de Odla, daut eenem de Tjnees too Kolledets worde.

Onse Joubert Rie wea jiedrem Frind. Doabenne kunn eena
toobe, enn sijch freie, dee druag eenem, enn sung doabie een
Trostleed; joh, dee Rie head emma too, vetald, woo see
aulewäaje jewast wea, mischt sijch noanijch enn, wisst soo
meea aules, enn wea emma schaftijch. Wann de Rie eenem
daut easchte Mol emm tiedjen Somma ommfooht, wea daut
meist soo scheen auls wann Mutta eenem em Oarm nauhm.

Auls de Fluß daut wertjlijch soo goot mett ons meend, ooda
auls etj mie daut bloos väastald, weet etj nijch, enn daut ess uck
eendoohnt; wann eena daut jleewd, wea daut soo, enn daut
reatjcht too. Waut etj wisst, ess daut de Rie mootijch wieda
schäld nohm Rat Riewa opptoo, dann em Rooden Fluß nenn,
dann nohm Lake Winnipeg, von doa wieda word daut Wota
von dem jewaultjen Nelson River nohm Hudson's Bay
jedroagt, enn dee sich dann enn doa befriede, enn aul dee
tjliene Mädtjess-Ries ähre Nohmes oppgauwe, omm Mr. enn
Mrs. Nelson too woare, dann kaum dee Schluß, Endstatsjoon.

Jiedet Joah spoad etj jiedre ladje Buddel opp, enn em Farjoah
biem Huagwota schreef etj mienen Nohme opp eenen Zadel,
schoof den enne Buddel nenn, enn dann schmeet etj dee

believed it, it was so and that was all that mattered. What I did know is that Mother Joubert bubbled blithely and courageously to the Rat River, then joined little forces with the bigger Red, on to Lake Winnipeg. From there it gained speed and size with ever more waters; they gave up their previous little identities as they married into the Nelson River Clan which bore them to the common endeavour of Hudson's Bay. Endstation, Arrival. On time, every time!

Every year I saved every empty bottle of my home, and in spring, come high water, I penned my name and station on paper, shoved it into the bottle with a prayer and the hope that someone in the wider world would find that part of me and announce arrival. Then I hurled it into the high water of spring and watched it rock away. Over many years I did just that a hundred times and more.

And sure enough—Father Choque, one day went for a walk towards the end of June along the banks of the mighty Kazan River, where it flows into Hudson's Bay in the Northwest Territories, just by Baker Lake. Where the two great waters confluent, they hold still for a piece of peace; happy to have met.

Father Choque found the bottle with my name in it and he wrote me and I answered him and we back-and-forthed for some twenty years until I finally visited him high in the north, where the radio broadcast Moscow news. Father Choque had attached my name to a piece of caribou skin and framed it with walrus teeth, curved and menacing, even in repose. Father Choque shook my hand by the wall and stated in Flemish, that faith ultimately is rewarded and I believed him.

From that day on, I saw Joubert Creek with and through different eyes. I knew it was on my side, in my corner and that it would never leave me, nor forsake me since it had presented me with the first miracle of my life.

Buddel mett een Jebäd enn mett miene Identität doabenne,
emm huagen Boage enne dunkle Walle nenn, enn hohpt, dee
wudd irjendwoa enne Welt aunkohme, enn daut dee Finja sijch
malde wudd. Daut hab etj äwa väle Joahre hundade Mol
jedohne.

Enn wess woah—dee Priesta Father Choque jintjch aum
Eewa von dem Kazan Fluß eenmol Medde Juni spezeare, enn
doa woa dee groota Riewa bie Baker Lake ennem Hudson's Bay
nennrand, doa fung hee eene Buddel mett mein Nohme
doabenne. Hee schreef mie, enn etj schreef ahm tridj, enn daut
jintjch soo twintijch Joah han enn tridj bett etj ahm endlijch
doa huag emm Nuade besocht. Hee haud mienen Nohme enn
eenen Rohme ut Caribou Lada aunjebrocht, enn mett een poah
Waulross Tähne doaromm utjestraumt aune Waund henje.
Father Choque säd de Gloowe word emma beloohnt, enn etj
jleewd ahm daut.

Von dem Dach aun sach etj onse Rie mett aundre Uage. Etj
wisst daut Wota wea opp miene Sied, enn daut daut mie
niemols emm Stijch lohte wuud, wiels dee Rie mie daut easchte
Wunda em Läwe jebrocht haud.

Auls etj een Farjoha mien Voda fruag, auls daut aum Nippa
bie Gortietz wertjlijch soo schmock sach, auls väle Mensche,
enn aule Menniste emma vetalde, säd hee: "Daut weet etj nijch;
waut etj oba weet, ess daut de leewa Gott emm Farjoah, emm
Somma, enn em Hoawst bett dem Oolenwiewa-Somma, emma
oppe Kaump aum Nippa Meddachschlop hilt." Aha, docht etj
mie, wann mien Voda mie soohne Jeschijchte oppbinje well,
dann kaun etj uck, enn vetald ahm, daut David sien "Der Herr
ist mein Hirte" bie ons biem Biebadaum enne Rie jeschräwe
haud.

Onse Rie wea Troost enn uck Beijchtmutta fe ons, enn uck fe
onse Mutta, enn fe onse Hunj; eascht Karo, dann Mopps, enn
dann mien Buddy äwa väle, väle Joahre. Opp eene Städ haude
de Mensche von eenem Darp, Barjchfeld, mol eene Bridj jebut,
oba daut Darp word oppjeleest, enn dann vefoll dee Bridj. Oba

When, one spring, I asked my father whether the Dnieper around the Choritza Island was as beautiful as always claimed by every Mennonite, living, dead and yet to be born, he answered, "I don't know, but what I do know is that every spring, all through the summer, and up to Indian Summer God chose that very area for his afternoon nap, *Meddach-schlop*." Aha, I thought to myself, if that is what the telling of the tale is all about, then it's my turn, and I told him that the Psalmist David had composed his "The Lord is my Shepherd" right by the beaver dam of our own creek.

Our creek was the water of consolation and mother confessor for my mother, and me, and for our dogs: first Karo, then Mopps and then Buddy for more than half a lifetime.

At one narrow juncture in the creek, inhabitants of the Mennonite village of Bergfeld had once built a bridge. Then the village disbanded and the bridge fell apart. But then again, travel by horse and buggy again resumed; that was in my early days.

It is neither nice nor fair of me and I never complained but I believed in my heart that no one had a right or a claim to my creek, our little river, and I also believed that God knew that all others unfairly meddled when setting foot or wheel in it. And yet it happened. Also, I knew that if the creek would have had a say in the matter, the answer would have verified my sentiment. No. *Nein!*

On a distant hill, on the other side of the creek, which my father always called a crooked piss puddle in comparison to the only river that mattered, the mighty Dnieper, there was an empty, semi-deserted farmstead. On the little hill a mile's distance, stood a two-storied house, a barn, two little granaries and all a bit rundown, as well as a small shed built over an artesian well. The house attracted attention, as if to

53

dann, een Somma jintjch daut mett Pead enn Buggy derjch onse Rie foahre wada loos.

Etj weet: daut wea nijch fein ooda fair von mie, enn etj hab mie uck niemols nijch bekloagt, oba etj jleewd, tjeena haud een Rajcht opp miene Rie, ooda onse Rie, enn etj jleewd uck, daut dem leewen daut Gott goanijch jefoll. Oba daut pessead trotzdem. Etj wisst oba, daut wann dee Rie haud mettrede kunnt, haud dee sijch daut nijch jefaule lohte.

Oppe aundre Sied von dee Rie, woohne mien Voda emma een kruggeljet Pischpuddel nannd, emm Vejlitjch too dem eensjen Fluß, woohna äwahaupt tald, dee Nippa, enn derjch den Bosch, eene Miel auf stund eene ladje Fieastäd. Doa wea ee tweestoockjet Hus opp eenem tjlienen Boajch, een Staul, twee tjliene Spitjasch, aula een bät vekohme, enn velohte sowesoo, enn uck eene tjliene Schenn äwa eenen Äwarannsborm jebut. Oba daut Hus lentjcht opp sijch, auls wull daut saje: "Waut dooh etj hiea, soo auleen, soo onjeforwe, enn dem Wada utjesat?"

Een langbeenja Tjeadel mett een Gangwoatj auls eene Klock, dee tien verr twee weess, enn mett een vedutzten Utdruck oppem Jesejcht, enn mett väl Tähne, dee hee rund omme Klock spield, kofft den Fahrjoah dee Foarm. Hee heet Jasch Wiens, enn mett eenmol wear'a doa, enn etj weet noch emma nijch, woa hee häakaum, enn etj jleew, doa wea uck sesst tjeena, woohna daut wisst. Meist soo auls wann hee vom Himmel jefolle wea, omm ons Noba too woare. Waut etj weet ess, daut hee foaken zeowents oppem Schafott von onse Sommatjäatj saut enn sijch mett miene Mutta vetald. Miene Mutta kunn vetalle enn oabeide toojlitjch, enn etj wisst, daut see mett dem Noba Wiens foadijch word, enn sijch fe ahm Tiet nauhm. Uck jleew etj, daut Wiens mett de Welt kloa kaum bloos soo lang auls hee dijcht bie Mutta saut, wiels wann hee ahm näajchsten Dach nohm korten Besorje tridj kaum sach'et ahm wada vewillat enn vebiestad. Nu wear'a wada doa, runselt de Stearn, reet de Näslajcha op and spield een Sautz Tähne and krautzt

say, "What am I doing here, all alone, unpainted and victimized by the elements?"

A lanky pilgrim with a gait like a clock, reading ten to two, and with a puzzled expression on his many toothed face one spring acquired this very farmstead. His name was Jake Wiens and I still do not know where he came from, and I do not know anyone who did know. It was as if he had fallen from some distant sky to become our neighbour. What I do distinctly remember is that Jake would very often sit on our summer kitchen porch and talk to my mother. My mother could converse and work at the same time and I knew that she could handle Jake Wiens, since she took time for him.

I also believed that Jake managed to make sense of the world only when close to my mother, since, when he returned the next day to sit and talk, he again looked bewildered and lost.

Now he was back again, furling his brow, stretching his nostrils and baring his teeth while scratching himself when mother wasn't looking, while listening to what she had to say. Sometimes Jake would day in Low German, "Woo? Woo?" much like a dog who cocked his ears in puzzlement when the surprises of life proved too much for his measure.

"How, how, just how was that?" and then my mother started to knead the bread dough again, while turning to Jake with strips of dough dangling from her hands, and introducing some example from Russia and how things had been there; Russia was their common denominator and when thusly introduced, Jake claimed to understand. While Jake was catching on, he rolled a piece of straw in his mouth and scratched himself underneath his cap, and looked relieved that there was, after all, some sense to this world.

Then Jake lowered his shoulders an inch or two and I could tell that he decided from now on everything would be different, better. I did the same thing on an almost daily basis, so I knew how it went. When my mother continued to talk, enn schobbd sijch, wann see nijch tjitjcht, enn horjcht beiaun, waut see ahm too saje haud.

Maunjchmol säd Jasch: "Woo, woo?" meist soo auls een Hund, dee uck een Ooah spetzt, wann ahm de Jeheemnisse vom Läwe too groot worde. "Woo, woo, woo wea daut, woo wea daut?" enn dann fung miene Mutta aun wada den Bultjedeajch too tjnäde, enn dann dreid see sijch nohm Jasch enn vetald wieda, während ahr den Deajch vonne Finjasch hong; see säd, woo daut enn Russlaund jewast wea; daut wea ähre Heimat enn uck siene, enn daut Biespell vestund hee, weens soo säd hee. Enn dann wann hee waut vestohne haud, dann rolld hee een Stetjch Strooh em Mul romm, enn krautst sijch unjre Mets, enn tjitjcht erleichtat, daut'et enne Welt doch een bätje Ordnung gauf.

Dann leeht Jasch siene Schullre een poah Zoll raufa faule, enn eena kunn ahm aunseehne, daut hee sijch väajenohme haud, daut von nu aun aules aundasch woare wudd. Etj deed daut uck, enn doawäjen wisst etj, woo daut rannd. Wann miene Mutta emma wada vetald enn sijch doabie wadahohld, musst etj mie äwa ähre Jeduld wundre. Doa weare uck aul aundre bie ons jewast, enn wann de nijch schwind vestunde, kaum daut väa, daut Mutta eenem ooda uck janem een Stejtch Deajch opp een schwoaheajet Ooah launde leeht.

Endlijch jewonne dann doch Jasch siene goode Manneare, enn donn packt hee aul siene goode Aufsejchte enn een bennajet Schemedauntje, enn dann läd hee loos, enn jintjch noh Hus. Wann de Doag emm Somma lang weare, kaum hee noch eenmol tridj omm Troost too tanke. Daut wea aul diesta wann Jasch dann noh Hus jintjch, enn dann red hee emma eene gaunze Striep enne Dunkelheit nenn, enn piept enn sung Stetjatjess von Tjoatjeleeda, enn vejuag doamett de Wilw, enn wille Tiere enn vleijcht uck Diewels, jleew etj, dee ahm oppe Hacke hinjeraun weare. Wann Jasch derjche Jäajend mett siene Oarms roodat, dreid hee sijch maunjchmol biem Gohne een vollet Kulla romm, omm aul dee woohne ahm oppe Hacke weare too vedriewe. Etj wea noch niemols nijch biem Jasch loht

endlessly, and repeated her examples I marveled at her patience. There had been others who, when not choosing to understand her wisdoms, had quickly found themselves with a finger of dough on an ear of hard hearing.

Finally Jake's good manners prevailed and then he packed all his good resolutions into his inner little bag of resolve and took off on his lonely walk home.

In summer when the days were longer, Jake returned in the evenings to replenish his tanks of consolation. It was dark when he finally walked home and he always talked whole reams into the black, and whistled some errant tune while at other times he sang portions of a hymn, thereby dispersing wolves and wild animals, and who knows, maybe even a few devils hard on his heels. While Jake was rowing forth with his lanky arms, he sometimes stopped and spun a whole circle to better chase away whoever was nipping at his cracked leather boots. I had never been at Jake's place late at night but had I walked there, I, too, would have sung some appropriate hymns and I, too, would have recited Bible verses aloud and resolved to be a very nice boy, and I would have walked on silent tiptoes, at the speed of silent stealth. Bears, my mother said, never attack people if they just strictly mind their own business and avoided eye to eye contact.

Mother said Jake was a good *Mensch*, but that he was seriously wrestling with malevolent spirits, since he had been an orphaned child. I believed that since in the Prairie Farmer, a weekly paper, Little Orphan Annie was featured with her *Schutzhund*, her protective dog, and I now knew that she, her dog and Jake Wiens were related.

Jake Wiens spoke Mennonite Low German, but occasionally a High German word slipped into his conversational transmission and our father was quick to catch the glitch. Then he silently started a sneering scoff, observing that Jake had hung around the lesser muddy *Molotschna*

zeowends jewast, oba wann etj doahan jegohne wea, haud etj
uck jesunge enn Bibelfarzh lud oppjesajt enn mie väajenohme
oba seea, enn fe emma schmock too senne, enn haud mie soo
stelltjess auls bloos mäajlijch derjche Jäjend oppe Tees
jeschlitjcht. Boare, haud miene Mutta jesajcht, jriepe tjeenen
Mensch aun, wann dee sijch omm nuscht nijch tjemmat, enn
wann eena dem jriesen Plästa nijch enne Uage tjitjcht.

Mutta säd, Jasch wea een gooda Mensch, oba hee haud seea
mett schlemme Jeista too rinje, wiels hee aul auls Tjind eene
Wais jewast. Daut jleewd etj, wiels daut gauf enne Zeitung,
enne Prairie Farmer, een Waisentjind, Little Orphan Annie,
enn dit Waisenmejaltje haud eenen Hund, daut wea äah
Schutzhund, enn dee twee weare, jleewd etj, omme Atjch mett
Jasch Wiens Frindschauft.

Jasch Wiens red Plautdietsch, oba hanenwada jleppt ahm een
bät Huagdietsch enn sien Sproakjedriew nenn. Enn dann
spetzt ons Voda de Uahre. Enn dann fong hee lieseltjess aun
too jnerre, enn säd, Jasch Wiens haud sijch too lang en dem
moddajen Molotschnapuddel oppjehoole wiels soohn
muckajet Tjeadeltje haud sijch em Nippa de Betjse nijch bloos
von bute nautjemoakt.

Daut wea aulwada loht auls Jasch noh Hus jintjch, enn daut
wea emma een bät Grund sijch too sorje, wiels doa lach je de
Rie tweschen ahm enn ons, enn doa musst hee sijch de Schooh
enn de Socke uttratje. Maunjchmol kaum Jasch boaft aun enn
leeht eenfach daut Graus enn den Wajch ahm de Feet dreaje,
eea hee sijch aulwada oppem Schafott von onse Sommatjäatj
hansad, enn sijch Schooh enn Stremp auntrock.

Eena word Jasch jewant, enn vondoag wear'a wada doa. Oba
mett een Unjascheed. Hee haud siene Schlaubbetjse enn sien
jreenet Hamd aun, uck druag hee siene Mets, enn siene oole
oppjeweppte Schooh, oba Jasch sad sijch nijch han. Hee lehnd
sijch jäjen onse Sommatjäatjedäah, enn haud een Been äwa
daut aundre jewintjelt.

"Na, waut's nu?" fruag Mutta, enn Jasch frinteld sogoa, enn
dann schmustad hee äwrem haulwen Jesejcht.

Puddle in Ukraine too long because such a noodle of a guy would have wet his pants in a proper river and not only from the outside.

It was again late when Jake departed for home and always reason for concern since the creek lay between his place and ours and to ford it, Jake had to take off his shoes and socks. Sometimes Jake arrived barefoot, allowing the grass and the road-path to dry his pedestrian members en route. Then he sat down, as usual, on the little porch of our summer kitchen where he pulled on socks and shoes.

You got used to Jake and today he again arrived. But with a difference. He wore his overalls and a green shirt, with his billed cap pointing skywards and his cracked shoes, bent upwards at the toes, avoiding full contact with the earth. Today Jake did not sit down. He leaned against the summer kitchen door and angled one leg over the other.

"Well, what's up?" mother asked, while Jake even cracked a little smile, and looked happy over half his face.

"Well, what's up?" he repeated and then he inwardly un-raveled himself, produced a hand out of pocket, giggled, adjusted his cap, turned his mouth straw into confusion and started, "I am in love and fully intend to marry in June of this year." My mother was surprised, more than just a bit, and waited for the excitement to subside before wiping the bread dough from her hands. Then she shook Jake's hand most amiably before he could take it back for hiding. I was surprised that my mother was capable of joviality and to talk and even ask about love and home and his plans and the wedding all at the same time, and possibly not even in given order and sequence.

I was of two opinions on the matter. The creek and I wanted Jake to leave us alone, but then again, visitors on the yard were so rare that you actually enjoyed them. Human contact, they called that in time. And so, I felt a bit sad that Jake would

"Na, waut's nu?" wadahold hee, enn dann wrabbeld hee sijch ennalijch auf, hohld eene Haund väa, tjichjad, läd siene Mets trajcht, hilt enn, dreid daut Stetjch Strooh enn sien Mul dreemol drall, enn fong aun: "Etj sie veleewt, enn etj woa mie loht emm Juni befriee." Miene Mutta wundad sijch dolla auls een bätje, enn donn wacht see bett aul de Oppreajnis von disse platzlijche Nieijchtjeit vebie wea, eea see äahre Henj vom Bultjedeajch aufwescht. Dann haundread see mett ahm fetjs, eea siene Haund sijch vesteatje kunn. Etj musst mie wundre, daut miene Mutta fähijch wea een bät Spohs too driewe, enn Jasch äwre Leew, enn Tus, enn sien Plohn, enn dee Tjast utfruag, enn vleijcht nijch eenmol enn de Räajlang.

Etj wea äwa daut gaunze von twee Meenunge. Dee Rie enn etj wulle, daut Jasch ons tochlohte sull, oba Jast kaume soo selden vebei, daut eena sijch dann doch uck wada freid. Daut deed mie een bätje leed, daut Jasch nijch meea soo foaken spezeare kohme wudd. Oba dann wea je uck eene Tjast waut besondret, enn tjeena wisst, wea wem enlohde wudd, enn wea nijch jekroagt word. Daut kunn aulso loosgohne... de enjelohdne Jast stunde opp een Blaut Papiea, schmock jeschräwe, enn wann dee Breef dann endlijch aunkaum stund doa, "Es ist des Herren Wille, daß am... die Braut Anjuscha Töws und der Bräutigam, Jakob Peter Wiens, Sie, samt Familie zu ihrer Hochzeit einladen..." Voda unjaschreef daut, enn wie nauhme daut Konvart dann nohm näajchsten enjelodnen Noba. Uck meend eene Tjast, daut eena sijch aun Worscht, Tjees, Zockastetja enn vleijcht sogoa Cake saut äte tjenne wudd.

Miene Mutta haud fuats emm Senn, sijch een nieet Tjleed mett Help von Ungasch Liesa neie toolohte. Daut wisst etj, wiels see een Mohtbaund too Haund nauhm, dee Sommatjäatjedäah toomuak, enn sijch mäte deed. Mutta haud daut Zeijch doatoo von äahrem Brooda Jeat jetjreaje, enn dissa oabeid fe de Board of Colonization enn vedeend schratjlijch väl Jeld enn Winnipeg, wiels hee seea gegrommt wea, enn uck seea intelligent. De näajchste poah Doag stald see sijch ennalijch väa, woo'ret ahr em nieen Tjleed lohte wudd, enn daut stemmd

no longer come visiting as frequently. But then, a wedding was special and even exciting, with no one knowing for sure as to who would be invited and who not, with such invitations nicely written in highest German on fancy paper, reading, "It is the Lord's Will that the bride Anjuscha Töws and the groom Jacob Peter Wiens, are hereby inviting you and your family to their wedding on..." Our father signed the festive card invitation and we took it to a next invited neighbour. Also, a wedding meant that you could eat your fill of baloney, cheese, sugar cubes and maybe even cake.

My mother immediately planned to have Liesa Unger sew her a new dress for the wedding. I knew that because she took a measuring tape and closed the summer kitchen door, where she obviously let the tape have an evaluative appraisal. Mother had the material for a dress given to her by her brother Gerhard who worked for the Board of Colonization in Winnipeg and earned "terribly" much money because he was so highly educated and intelligent. The next few days my mother imagined what she would look like in her new dress and this put her in a good mood. She also knew that the upcoming wedding was important enough so that her husband and our father would not pose the usual question-commentary "A new dress, again? Is such necessary?" and would not express his predictable moral of the tale as to where this god-forsaken English country with its outlandish modes and customs might yet take us.

Jake's customary ways changed. He now owned a small, lively horse and a buggy, red and black, with upholstered seats for his Sunday-like bride Anjuscha. Once or twice a week and always on Sundays the bridal couple crossed the creek and then drove across our yard via Gnadenfeld, where other Wienses resided, and then, most likely on to Grünthal to church. I had never seen such a dainty and beautiful lady and

ahr vejneajcht. See wisst uck, daut disse Tjast wijchtijch jenuag wea, daut äah Maun enn ons Voda ahr nijch mett siene jeweehnelje Froag "Een nieet Tjleed, aulwada? Ess daut needijch?" kohme wudd, enn sijch uck noch wundre musst, woa daut aulatoop en dissem vefluchten enjelschen Laund mett de Mood hangohne sull.

Jasch siene Jewahnheite veendade sijch. Hee haud nu een tjlienet läwendjet Peadtje, enn een Buggy, root enn schwoat jeforwe, mett plischne Sette fe siene sinndagsche Brut Anuscha. Eenmol, ooda tweemol de Wäatjch, enn emma aum Sinndach fuah hee derjch dee Rie,enn dann bie ons äwrem Hoff noh Jnodefeld, woa uck Wiense wohnde, enn vleijcht fuah hee sogoa noh Jrienthol too Tjoatjch mett siene Brut. Etj haud noch niemols nijch soohne schmocke Lady jeseehne, enn etj schämd mie meist, daut miene Uage sijch nijch aun ahr saut tjitjche kunne.

Miene Mutta säd, daut'et Anjuscha soo auls eene schmocket Duftje sach, soo leeftolijch, soo leijcht oppe Feetjess, soo schmock jebut, enn een bät jeheemnisvoll, wann see äähre Tjenn entrock, omm Mensche nijch emma noh de mennische Oat soo stiew auntootjitjche auls wann see ahn een Tjleed ooda een Aunzug schniedere wulle. Auls see utem Buggy kroop, wiels see noh ons toom Jungetpoatje-Owendkost, soo's daut donn emma jedohne word, kaume, leeht etj miene Fantasie bie ähre Beentjess schwind spezeare gohne, enn mie word schwoat fe Aufgonst äwa Jasch, den Briegaum, dee sijch bloos schobbe kunn, enn tjeene eajne Meenung haud.

Dee Tjast wea enn dree Wäatj enn wea oppreajend. Miene Mutta druag äah nieet Tjleed, dunkel bleiw mett tjliene witte Placktjess, Tippeltjess, enn Voda trock sijch sienen meist nieen Aunzug, noch ut Russlaund aun, enn siene Droagbenj haude een Polizeistampel; dee haud hee sijch vom Eaton's Katalooh fe fiefenndartijch Cent bestallt.

Oppe Tjast rede dree Prädjasch von wiet auf enn see bede uck; etj entnauhm äähre Red, daut uck Anjuscha eene Wais wea, dee em Winta noh Biebelschool jintjch, enn em Somma

I was almost ashamed of myself since my eyes simply could not get enough of her splendor.

My mother said that Anjuscha looked like a most beautiful dove, so loving and so light on her feet, and of such dainty figure and even a bit mysterious when she tucked in her chin to avoid full eye contact, as was the Mennonite peasant custom of control of all the eyes occupied. When she alighted from the buggy for a festive little bridal dinner in our home as was the custom, I let my fancy take a quick stroll up and down her legs and I was black with jealousy of Jake, the groom who, all he could do was scratch himself, and did not have a single independent thought in his silly head.

The wedding was in three week's time and very exciting. My mother wore her new dress, dark blue with little white dots, while our father wore his almost new dark suit, of Russian tailoring, still, and with new suspenders, marked "Police" which he had ordered for the occasion from the Eaton's Catalogue for thirty five cents.

During the ceremony, three ministers from far away spoke and also prayed. I gathered from their talk that Anjuscha was also an orphan who attended Bible School in winter and worked as a maid at the Old Jacob Neufeld's farm, half a mile south of Jake's stead. Then our regular ministers, Johan Enns and Heinrich Warkentin spoke, with a little extra verve. They obviously intended to let everyone know who the cocks of the walks were and that guest ministers were guests and nothing else. I was very young at the time but I got the message so I assume so did all the others.

After the formalities were over, all the visitors and guests were invited for a festive lunch in the church basement which shortly advanced to the "Lower Auditorium" in name, only.

Baloney sandwiches were served, as well as cheese and double-decker buns which the church women had baked and there were sugar cubes by the many dozen for the guests to

bie Oole Jeat Niefelds, siede von Jasch Wiens siene Foarm, Tjäatsche wea. Dann rede onse Prädjasch Enns enn Henritjch Woatjentin, enn see rede forscha auls jeweehnlijch, see wulle dochwoll wiese, wäa hiea enne Tjoatjch Bauss wea, enn daut aundre Prädjasch bie ons Jast weare enn sesst nuscht nijch. Toom Schluß worde aule Jast em Tjoatjetjalla, woohne boold Auditorium heete sull, enjelohde. Daut gauf Balonie-Worscht, enn Tjees, enn dobbelde Tweeback, woohne de Frulied jebackt haude, enn dann gauf'ett uck noch väl Zuckastetja fe de Jast äahren Koffe enn fe ons Jungess äahre Fuppe. Biem Äte saut wie Jungess mett opne Miela, enn kunne daut nijch jleewe, woo schmock eene Brut lohte kunn, enn woo'rett uck Jasch soo opjeriemt auls een Peihohn sach. Hee spield uck nijch eegol siene Tähne, enn hee deed uck aundre nijch auldagsche Dinja, soo's den Koffe em Schattel jeehte, enn dann den kolt puste eea hee den drunk; sien nieen jreenen Aunzug velangde goode Manneare, enn dee haud hee uck vondoag.

Jasch siene Weaj haud mol enne Schlopstow opp eenem Chutor jestohne, enn doa wea siene Seel jebuare, vetald mie miene Mutta, enn etj jleewd ahr daut. Anjuscha äahre Stemm head sijch noh eene Fiddel, woohne Leahra Heidebrajcht maunjchmol enne School späld, wann Schuberts Forelle besondasch scheen heare sull.

Beid weare se stell enn schmocktjess, enn see aute mett lange Finjasch enn uck mett dem tjlienen Finja oppjeweppt. See kusste sijch nijch verr Mensche, enn haude sijch uck tjeen bät noh de latzte Mood domm. Etj docht enn hohpt, daut de aundre Jungess aufjenstijch senne wudde, wiels dee Brutlied onse Nohbasch weare, enn etj vetald dee Jungess, waut fe eene straume Wirtschauft Wiense haude, enn daut opp dem Hoff, daut dusend Jeheemnisse gauf, dee etj aula tjand.

Twee Wäatj verre Tjast hilt miene Mutta mett Voda Unjared wiels Jasch Wiens nijch meea bie ons äwrem Hoff fooah, wiels Voda ahm emma tjräjeld. Eenmol säd Voda: "Wann de Hahn sijch hansatt, dann mott de Hohn sprinje enn tjreie," enn etj schämd mie, wiels etj wisst, waut Voda doamett meend.

dunk in their coffee and for the younger set to stuff in their many pockets. While eating, the boys sat open-mouthed in amazement at the beauty of the bride and how Jake for once looked like a pea-cock. And today he kept his toothy smile to himself and showed off good manners for all to see like not pouring coffee into his saucer and then blowing it cold and slurping it; Jake's new green suit demanded good manners and he had brought them along for the occasion. Jake's cradle had once rocked on a royal estate, on a Chutor, and it was there that his soul was born, my mother told me, and I freely believed her.

Anjuscha's voice sounded like a violin which Teacher Heidebrecht occasionally played in school, particularly when he wanted Schubert's The Trout, *die Forelle* to sound as nice as it should. Both bride and groom ate so quietly and refined with long fingers and with their pinkies in decorous action.

They did not engage in public kissing and roundhouse wedding tactics Hollywood style were simply not in. I thought and hoped that the other boys, my age, would be a bit jealous of me since the newly-weds were our neighbours, and so I told them what a fine farm the couple owned and that it was home to a thousand secrets and I knew them all.

Two weeks after the wedding my mother had a serious word with our father because Jake Wiens no longer drove his buggy across our yard since father had teased him. Once, father said, "If a hen sits down, then it is time for the cock to jump and crow," and I was embarrassed at my understanding.

And then last week Jake appeared alone and then our father stopped all his teasing and my mother was concerned, first a bit and then more troubled as the days progressed.

Was there something in the air in late June when it was already unbearably hot from early morning on, and humid as well? Or had there been some heavenly omen which I should have grasped?

Enn donn tiedijch latze Wäatj kaum Jasch auleen noh ons, enn donn head Voda opp ahm too tjräajle, enn mien Mutta sorjt sijch, eascht een bätje, dann emma meea.

Wea doa aun dem Sinndach waut enne Loft loht emm Juni, auls daut aul tiedijch seea heet enn schwool wea? Ooda haud doa waut senne sullt, woohnt etj haud vestohne kunnt, enn daut auls himmlischet Teatjen haud diede sullt?

Jenuag, wie haude jrods jemoltjche, enn Mutta muak kratjcht Freehstitjch auls daut pessead. Mutta tjitjcht ute Sommatjäatjch nohm Siede, auls see Jasch aunjerannt kohme sach; Jasch huppad soo schwind auls een Peat, enn hee schreajch, enn bload, enn jaummareahd, enn jaumad auls hee aunjedonnat kaum.

Mutta juag ons Tjinja schwind em Hus nenn, woa daut diesta enn tjeel wea, enn Voda rand mett eenem grooten Schlachtmassa noh Jasch Wiense. Jasch rannd Voda hinjeraun, oba Voda rannd väl stoatja, enn Jasch wea ahm hinjeraun, enn etj sach Jasch tweemol unjaweajess omstelpe.

Nu weare se aul eene Veadel Miel auf, oba etj kunn noch emma seehne, woo dee Sonn opp daut Massa blitzt wann Voda doamett biem ranne Kullasch dreid. Jasch fluag aulwada han, stund opp, enn fong aun noh ons Hoff too ranne, oba dann word hee dee Himmelsrejchtunge wada enn, dreid sijch omm. enn rannd Voda hinjeraun. Jasch sach'et aunjeschohte, soo auls een Hos, wann eena dem em Kopp jeschohte haft, enn dee drall ess.

Miene Mutta stund bie de Däah aune Sommatjäatjch, enn bäd soo seea, daut etj een Strieptje Ruak noh Himmel foahre sach. Dann fong see aun opp Rusch too bäde, wiels see haud mie eenmol vetald, daut de Russe relijeesa auls wie en Kanada weare, enn daut ahn meea heilijch wea auls ons.

Dann sad uck ons Hund Karo loos; dee Manna weare aul aune Jlad bie de Rie aunjokohme. Mutta roopt den Hund tridj, oba see kunn bloos noch fuschle, enn doamett wea Karo uck aul veropp. Karo wisst väle Dinja, von dee wie nuscht nich vestunde, enn daut bewees hee uck nu wada.

Whatever, we had just finished milking and mother was fixing breakfast when it happened. Mother was looking south from the summer kitchen when she saw Jake come running. Jake was galloping like a horse while screaming and yelling and lamenting and yammering as he came thundering along.

Mother quickly guided us children into the house where it was dark and cool, while father, equipped with a butcher knife, took off for the Jake Wiens farm. Jake ran behind our father but father was much faster and so Jake loped after him at his full speed but I saw him fall flat on his being twice in the quarter mile interval up to the first line of bush.

They were a quarter of a mile away now but I could still distinctly make out how the sun blitzed on the butcher knife executing bright arcs and circles. Jake fell down again and then got up and came running for our yard; then he realized the error of confusion and took after our father. Jake reminded me of a rabbit, shot in the head, thoroughly confused.

My mother stood by the summer kitchen door and prayed so hard that I saw a wisp of holy smoke arise to heaven. And then she started praying in Russian because she had once told me that they were more religious than people in Canada and that their sense of things holy were more reliable than ours.

Karo, our dog, ever the custodian of the unknown, after having sized up the human condition, had reached his own conclusion and set out as well. The two fore-runners had already reached the dip of Joubert Creek. Mother called the dog home but her voice was gone. By the time she managed a bare whisper, Karo led the pack; he knew, he always knew.

There is nothing that can be reversed or changed by prayer, I concluded and I knew; after all I was five and fully in the know. And yet, surely there must exist a clock somewhere which can be re-set and adjusted anew so that everything can be started afresh, all things to become new again, I thought to

Eena kunn nuscht nijch omdreie ooda derjch Jebäd endre. Daut sull doch irjendwoa eene Klock jäwe, woohne eena nie enstalle kunn, doamett daut Gaunze noch eenmol von veare loostoosatte wea, docht etj mie. Etj vespruak dem leewen Gott, daut wann Hee hiea fuats enjriepe wudd, wudd etj bett aum Enj von mienem Läwe schmock senne wudd, seea schmock, wann Hee blooß noch eenmol, blooß dit eenmol...

Aum Meddwäatjch word Anjuscha, Jasch siene Fru begrowt. De Manna druage eenen langen Kauste mett schwoatem Doot, enn hilde den sijch vom Lief, soo auls eenen Ama mett Maltjch, woohna ahn nijch de Lempre beplenjre enn vestentjre sull.

Aule sass Soatjdroagasch druage den Kauste bett oppe Trapp, enn leehte den doa bute verre Tjoatj stohne. Enn doa bleef daut Soatj. Donn weschte see sijch de Henj, enn jinje jlitjch enne Tjoatjch nenn, stiew auls Kossebatjch, enn total veblefft.

Daut Soatj stund gaunz auleen bute, auls wann daut nijch doahan jehead, einsam und verlassen, enn etj sach väle tjliene schwoate Placktjess verr miene Uage, dee mie wundade; Mutta säd nohäa, see haud dee uck jeseehne.

Dem Jasch leide se toom Deel, toom Deel druage se ahm enne Tjoatj nenn, enn hee hield enn hee kloagd, enn jaumad auls wann een groota Doodeschooah stähnd. Hee jintjch aun auls een wildjewordna Hund, enn juhld mett eene Stemm, dee nijch von ahm kohme kunn. Vleijcht wea daut mau aulatoop een Onjletjch, vleijcht kunn eena den Hund, woohna soo aunjintjch, mett eenem Tjneppel eent ärem Kopp heiwe, enn dann wea aules too Enj, enn wie kunne wada jletjchlijch von Väare aunfange.

Oba daut jintj nijch wajch, enn dee gaunze noaktje Woahrheit bleef bestohne. Wann Jasch doch mol wada bie ons oppem Schafott sette, enn sijch schobbe enn een bät vewillat biem Vetalle tjitjche wudd. Aul daut Jletjch kaum mie wiet, wiet auf väa, wieda auls de Nippa, woa Voda siene Seel jelohte haud.

Aule Traditsjoone habe Jrind, woaromm see too Staund jekohme send, enn soo wea daut uck bie ons, wann'et uck meea 'Du saulst nijch' auls 'Du doafst' gauf. Eene onjesproakne

myself. I promised God right then and there that if He were to get involved right then and there I would be obedient and good till the very end of my life, as long as it might be, if He only just this time, just this one time...

Anjuscha was buried on Wednesday. The men carried the long coffin with Black Death at a distance like a pail with milk so as not to pollute their pant legs. All six pallbearers carried the coffin up the front stairs to the church and then dropped the coffin outside, in front of the church. And that is where the coffin remained. Then the pallbearers wiped their hands and walked straight into the church as stiff as billy-goats, and with much puzzled features. The coffin stood isolated and lonely as if it was misplaced, ill at ease, lonely, deserted. I saw many little black dots before my eyes, which surprised me. My mother later told me she had seen them as well.

Jake was partly led into church, and partly carried while bawling, then howling with a deadly, indeed death-like choir of voices emanating from sources unknown. He reminded of a mad dog whose cry is not of his own making. Maybe, I thought, this is just a mistake, an accident... smack him a good one over the head and let the dog die, and we can start all over again in better faith. But nothing happened. Nothing went away and the stark naked truth of death, pitch black, prevailed. If Jake would only once again sit on the porch of our summer kitchen and scratch himself where he wanted to and look bewildered and confused as formerly... But all that faded happiness was remote, very remote and farther away than the Dnieper where our father had left his soul.

All traditions are based on reasons for their coming to be and this held true for us as well, even if "Thou shalt not" prevailed over "You may!" One such unspoken decree stipulated that the dead shall be buried with their head to the west and their feet facing east. If they lie in such manner, then

Räajel besajt, daut eena de Doodess mett dem Koppenenj nohm Waste, enn daut Feetenenj nohm Ooste begrowe saul. Wann see soo lidje, dann send see emma reed, den Morje, de Hohp enn de Opperstohnung vom Ooste too bejreese.

Oba Jasch siene Fru? See, Anjuscha, word omjedreiht begrowt, wiels soo haud eene earnste Tjoatjestemm noch utem Darp von miene Ellre enn Russlaund daut bestemmt. See begrowde Anjuscha siede vom Tjoatjhoff opp eenem tjlienen Acka, enn dem uck twee aundre daut Schetjsaul enn äahre eajne Henj jenohme haude.

Etj head Jasch Block enn Henritj Unga enn woo see dee twee Poatnasch von Anjuscha berede. "Jana doa," säd Block, "wea een seea rucha Schinda, dee meea Schnaups auls Vetaund emm Kopp haud. Enn dee aundra? Daut wea een Bearnd Faultj, een äwabrestja Turbauss, dee uck mea red auls oabeid. Hee kaum ut'e Tjrimm. Hee wea eena vonne Tabun, woohne eenen ruschen Jung vepriejeld, dee nohäa storf. Von eenem Mord derjchtoogohne ess eene Sach, von sien eajnet Jewesse wajchtooranne ess eene gaunz aundre Sach; hee tjreajch waut ahm toostunt auls de Diewel ahm daut Jenetj mett Bearnd sien Strang tooschnäad," soo säde see.

Mett soohne vebiestade Jeista mott Anjuscha nu lidje enn opp dem Rejchtungsdach wachte; doarenn weare sijch aule Predjasch eenijch, enn scheddade äahre lange Finjasch noh ons soo auls eene Pitsch bett wie ons aula een poah mol bie de Aundacht betjeade. Enn etj vesproak uck fuats sogoa Predja too woare, ooda sogoa een Missionoa, enn uck too bliewe, wann etj blooß noch eenmol onjeschoare doavon kaum, enn wann dit schratjelje Triebsaul noch eenmol vebie seene wudd...

Eene Stacheldrohtfenz trand den Haupttjoatjhoff von dem Vetwiewlungsacka een poah Schooh auf. Een poah Schooh auf, oba doch eene Eewitjeit lach doatweschen, docht Jasch sijch.

Een poah Doag lohta trand sijch Jasch Wiens von aulem, woohnt ahm aun siene kortet Jletjch erinnad. Sien Peadtje wea wajch, enn uck sien Buggy, enn Jasch jintjch wada toofoot, enn siene Feet weare wada Klockewiesasch tien verr twee.

70

they are always ready to greet the morning of hope and resurrection from the east.

But as for Jake's wife? She, Anjuscha, was buried the other way around, as per decree by the voice of the church born in my parent's village in Ukraine. Now these men of the Cloth of the Word stipulated that Anjuscha was to be buried south of the churchyard proper in a little plot of despair, the contaminated 16 by 16 feet of the damned, together with two others who had taken their ultimate fate into their own hands.

Jacob Block and Heinrich Unger discussed the fate of the other two suicide partners of which Anjuscha now formed a trio of the damned. "That one, there," said Block, "was a rough scoundrel who had more homebrew in his head than brains. As to the other one? He was one Ben Falk, a bullying reprobate who was more talk than work. He stemmed from the Crimea. Falk was a member of a gang who beat a Russian labourer to death. To run away from a murder is one thing, to run away from your own conscience is an entirely different matter; he got what he deserved when the devil came calling with a length of rope and pulled it taut around his scrawny neck," the men concluded.

Anjuscha now had to lie with these lost partners of despair and await Judgement Day, that was the consensus of the ministers as they shook their judgemental fingers at the congregation like a bull whip until everyone present decided to get converted a few times running. I promised to become a minister, a preacher and even a missionary right then and there and to remain one if only this ordeal would be reversed.

A barbed wire fence separated the main cemetery from the Plot of Despair; just a few feet away, but an eternity lay between the two, Jake Wiens concluded.

Within a day, Jake Wiens divorced himself from all which reminded him of his brief happiness. His sprightly horse was

Vääje Wäatj, twee Doag nohm Bejrafnis, kaum Jasch Wiens noh ons, enn miene Mutta gauf ahm uck fuats Erlaubnis daut too liehe, waut hee bruckt. Hee nauhm sijch eene Tjnieptang, vestoak dee enn siene Schlaubbetjse, enn jintjch noh dem Tjoatjhoff, eene Stund auf. Daut gauf tjeene Zeij auls Jasch sass Stacheldräd derjchschneet, dree vom vefluchten Acka, enn dree von dem respektablen. Donn flocht Jasch dee Dräd toop. Jasch haud dee Tjoatjhäw toopjelajcht, enn nu lach siene Anjuscha mett de Seelje enn Hohp toop. Eene earnste Stemm red, enn de näajchste Nacht word dee Schohde wada goot jemoakt, enn jiedra lach wada oppoat. Daut jintjch soo dree Nachte hanenhäa; dann gauf Jasch opp, brocht dee Tjnieptang tridj enn schorrd opp onse Sommatjätjeschwal toop.

Jasch Wiens kaum wada jieden Owend noh ons enn saut wada bie ons oppem Schafott verr onse Sommatjäatj. Sien Strooh wea nijch meea em Mul. Oba hee hield de Tiet äwa, enn siene Trohne rannde soo's eene tjliene Rie, stell enn eendrajchtijch.

Etj hild mie tridj enn bäd, daut daut doch aula mol wada aundasch woare wudd, enn wie wada von veare aunfange kunne. Wann Gott de Eewijchtjeit aunlaje kaun, dann sull Hee doch uck disse schratelje Trua ommdreie tjenne, wann uck bloos eenmol, bäd etj. Während miene Mutta mett ahm red enn red, stelltjes mett ahm red. Daut wea nuscht nijch fe Tjinjauahre, daut wisst etj.

Donn jintj loht zeowends etj toop mett Karo noh miene Rie, enn auls etj mie vesejchad haud, daut tjeena nijch doabie wea enn toohead, vetald etj daut Wota aules, enn lohd miene Trua doa auf enn wajch, enn dee Joubert Creek nauhm miene gaunze Laust, enn druag dee wajch, wiet wajch, woa dee emm Wota enn enne Jnohd vedunst enn veschwung.

gone and also his buggy, and Jake again walked with his clock like feet, ten to two.

Last week, two days after the funeral Jake Wiens came to our place late that evening and my mother immediately gave him permission to borrow the item of his request. Jake pocketed fencing pliers in his overalls, and walked to the cemetery an hour's distance. There were no witnesses as Jake cut the six wires of containment: three from the Plot of the Damned and three from the Plot of Hope of Resurrection. Then Jake spliced the wires together.

Jake had incorporated the two cemeteries into one and now his Anjuscha lay together with the saved and those waiting in hope. A serious voice from the pulpit had a say in the matter and the next night the infraction was righted and the dead were again in their rightful places. This went on for three days and nights running and then Jake got the message. He returned the fencing pliers and gave up.

Jake Wiens returned to our place and again sat on the porch of our summer kitchen. The straw in his mouth was gone. His tears were constant but silent. I held back, praying, that everything would be different again, and that we would simply start all over again. If God could get an eternity off and running, just like that, then He surely could reverse this horrible mess of a tragedy, even if only once and for a little while, was my prayer. During which my mother spoke to Jake in a comforting whisper, and then again. This was no matter for the ears of children, and I knew it.

Then I silently took off for our creek with Karo and after having cased the cause and determining that there was no one around to listen in, I unburdened myself and laid off my heavy load into the confidence of the running water of Joubert Creek. The water accepted my load gladly and carried it away, far away where it evaporated in time and grace.

Dee Buran

"Wann daut soo scheen blifft, dann woat de Väasenja morje woll enne Tjoatj 'Hallelujah, schöner Morgen' aunsaje," säd Voda aum Nohmeddach aum 21 Moaz aune 1943 bie ons oppe Foarm.

Voda haud rajcht; daut wea soo scheen, daut onse Tjeaj sijch bute opphilde, enn de Tjalwa Jriepa spälde, enn de Hohn sijch den Mestuhpe utsocht, omm sien Leed auntoosaje.

Wiels daut soo scheen woam wea, enn wie soo väl Schnee haude auls etj domme Jedanke emm Kopp, haud jieda opp onsem Hoff eent ooda twee mett eenem Schneebaul verrem Bless ooda aune Näs aun dem Sinnowend Nohmeddach jetjreaje, auls Mensch ooda Veeh, auls Buschtje ooda Busel. Bieaun haud etj de Väaleew soo auls jieden Sinnowend voll Brennholt jeflieht. Nu wea bloos noch daut Veehdrentje aune Reaj, dann maltje, enn de Fieaowend toom Sinndach kunn loosgohne. Wiels daut soo lind enn woam enn windstell wea, head eena sogoa de easchte Krauj sijch heesch roope. Dee wea den gaunzen Winta enn Mexiko jewast, wiels äahre Stemm wea Sponsch belajcht.

Etj haud jrods daut latzte Pead aum Drentjchtroch verrem Hus toom supe jeholt. Maschka soop twee Schluck, enn donn dreid see sijch platzlijch toop mett mie, auls tjliena Huppupp, wajch enn drebbeld haustijch tridj nohm Staul, enn schlapt mie hinjeraun.

The Buran

(*Buran* is Russian for 'Blizzard', only bigger and better)

"If it remains so nice outside, then the precentor, (also called singing leader in church), will probably have the congregation sing, 'Hallelujah, wondrous morning' in church tomorrow," said father on the afternoon of the 21st of March 1943 at home on our farm.

Our father had it right; it was such a beautiful Saturday that our cows were outside and the calves were playing catch and the rooster looked for the crown of the manure pile on which to sing his cocky song.

Since it was so nice and warm and we had even more snow than silly notions in our head, every living and moving object on our yard had received a snowball or two on the head or on the nose from my major league potential pitching arm that blessed Saturday afternoon, be such targets human or equine, nag or nag, noun or verb.

I had already filled the shed adjacent to the house with firewood like every Saturday and now I had only one chore left, to take the stock to drink by the barnyard trough close to the house and then the milking of many cows by hand was due before the day came to a close by the fire of our cosy home. Because it was so mild and wind still, one could even hear the first crows calling themselves hoarse. They had been in Mexico all winter long and I could still hear the remnants of Spanish inflection in their ravenous demands.

Waut nu? Ess dee netjsch jeworde, ooda ess dee sesst ruhje Kobbel aunjeschote, docht etj mie.

Wie weare noch nijch mol de dartijch Meeta tridj biem Staul aunjekohme, auls de Auntwuat opp daut Vehoole vom Pead vom Himmel aunjedonnat kaum. Soo auls jesajcht, tjeene tien Sekund wea wie nohm Schulinj unjawäajess, oba etj kunn metteenst nijch mol meea den Staul ver mie seehne. Dee Blizzard haud soo loosjelajcht, daut eenem Heare enn Seehne vejintj; dee Wind schluag soo stoatj tridjaun, daut nijch mol een menschlijchet Jebäd doa bowe aunkaum.

Mien Voda wea eajentlijch aul emma eene groota, schratjlijch stoatja Turbauss, oba wann Noot aum Maun wea, word hee gaunz wacka, enn wisst, waut too doohne wea. Hee wea enjeworde, daut de leewa Gott vondoag loht nohmeddach nijch spoße wull, enn soo haud hee soo schwind auls een Blitz eenen Strang tweschen Stauledäahretjlintj enn Husdäa jetrocke, daut eena bie dem korten Wajch enn soohnem Faul nijch vebiestad, doamett eena nijch noch eea auls de Sinndach oppe Ead, doa bowe emm Himmel aunkaum.

Benne word goot aunjelajcht, enn wiels nijch mol daut Radio meea eene Stemm haud, saut wie bie de Kerosienlaumpe, de Kooleeljlaumpe, enn bie de Letoarns, enn heade ons doa bute den Storm aun. Dee rätad enn juld, dee toobt enn dee tocht, dee trock enn dee schindead, dee ständ enn dee pust, denn romood enn dee bullad, dee rocheld enn dee däwad, dee schreajch enn dee fleatjcht, dee prohld enn de pucht, dee piesackt enn dee blosd, dee bload enn de donnad, dee breld enn dee jescht, enn dann noch eenmol von Väare daut selwje Leed enn aule Strophe, enn donn läda noch een poah Farzh too.

Auls wie ennworde, daut sijch de leewa Gott tweschen dem Storm doa bute enn ons hiea benne jestald haud, fong Voda aun too vetalle: "Dit Stormtje ess em Vejlitj too eenem

I had just taken the last horse to the drinking trough before the house. Maschka had barely taken two gulps when she suddenly whipped around, dragging me ass over teakettle on her lead rope in a short gallop straight for the safety of the stable condition.

What gives? Has Maschka gone obstinate or nuts, or why is she so spinsterish, I wondered that Saturday afternoon. We had not yet managed the thirty-metre track to the stable when the answer to the horse's behaviour came thundering from heaven above. As I was on the point of saying, before heaven interrupted my story, we were not ten seconds to refuge when I suddenly could not even see the stable somewhere in front of me. The blizzard was in full swing and I was robbed of all hearing and seeing; the wind blew with such force that even a human prayer failed to make it to the TOP.

My father was always a ruffian and stronger than any Old Testament heavyweight to boot, but when need arose he suddenly became alert and knew what to do for man and beast to survive. And so he had noticed that God in heaven was not in a jovial mood late this Saturday, and as fast as lightning he had fastened a rope between the barn door latch and the house door, so that you would not get lost when navigating the short stretch of path and to prevent you and me from arriving at heaven's door prior to Sunday on earth.

We stoked the stove and the furnace in the house and since even our radio had lost its voice in the fury, we sat by the coal oil lamps and lanterns, listening to nature's symphony of fury raging outside with crescendo. The Buran persisted: it rattled and howled, then thundered and shuddered, it roared and it cursed, it boasted and it threatened, and then repeated the fury of the same song and refrain until the program of duration had run its course.

When we sensed that God had positioned Himself between the storm outside and our huddled presence inside, our father

wertjlijchen Buran enn Rußlaund een lieset Windtje. Hiea
tjenn wie noch emma doohne soo's wie welle, oba wann soohn
Burjan doa enne Ooltkolnie dijcht biem Nippa mol
perseenlijk word, dann musst wie ons doch jehearijch stiepre
enn uck benne fausthoole. Enn noch schlemma: wie musste
ons dann doagelang bloß mett Mannajrett enn Joaschtnejrett
bejneaje, wiels wann Mutta Worscht ooda Schintjefleesch too
Aufwatjzlung brode wull, dann died daut tjeene fief Minute,
enn dann saut ver jiedem Fensta een Wulfpack enn spield de
Tähne enn keiwd aul em Verrut. Wann disse Baund jebrodne
mennische Worscht ritjcht, dann räd sijch daut bie ahn, auls
Dach ooda Nacht, enn eenem Nu romm, enn dann kaume se
bie ons aune Lohde aunputtre.

"Enn doawäjen haud wie je dann uck Staul enn Schien enn
Hus unja eenem Dack. Em Nobadarp gauf daut eenen
drettienjoahschen Radakopps Willie, enn dissa docht, hee wea
aul too groot de Nacht benne oppen Topp too gohne, enn auls
hee dee tien Meeta hinjrem Hus nohm Zetjreet jintj, enn nijch
trdij kaum wisste de Radakopps je uck aul, waut pesseat wea.
Een Schnippsel Footkodda funge se dree Doag loihte, enn een
Bietstje von siene lange Unjabetjse haude de Wilw dochwoll
auls Tjwittung tridjjelohte, doamett daut Rohtsel jeleest woare
kunn.

Nu aut Voda eene jeheaje Portsjoon Schwoatemoag enn
Silltjees, mett Zipple enn Äditj, enn dann haud'a wada Daump
jenuag omm siene Jeschijcht derjch'e Vetal wieda veraun too
schuwe.

"Dee rusche Wilw weare väl jrata enn jefährlijcha auls de
utjewosssne bietsche Boschhose hiea em Bosch, uck wann disse
een bät jule tjenne. Enn hinjeraun enn oppdrenjlijch enn
vehungat weare de Wilw uck aul emma soo auls een Evanjelist
vonne breedajemeendsche Sort" (auls dit stemmd ooda nijch
wisst etj too dee Tiet noch nijch, wiels miene Mutta kaum ut

on earth started his tale. "The storm out there as compared to a real buran in Russia is but a zephyr. Here we can still do as we please but when a buran in the Old Colony by the Dnieper got personal then we had to really stand our ground and even hold on to things in the inner man. And worse, still, we had to make do for days on end with only cream of wheat and pearl barley porridge, because if mother for a change wanted to fry sausage or ham or bacon then, within five minutes, there was assembled before every window a pack of wolves fletching their teeth and chewing human flesh in raw anticipation. Whenever such pack smelled fried Mennonite farmer sausage, then talk of the aroma got around within minutes, be it day or night and they arrived in hordes to knock at the shutters.

And that is why we had stable, barn and house under one roof. In a neighbouring village there was one thirteen year old Redekop's Willie and he thought he was too big to use the night potty inside and when he insisted on visiting the outside biffy, and did not return for a spell, the Redekop family knew what had happened. A segment of foot rag was found three days later, and when a remnant of his long johns was also located within a week we knew that the wolves had left a receipt to resolve the riddle of the missing kacker."

Then our father on earth devoured a goodly chunk of collared pork, head cheese, six centimetres cubed, with onions and vinegar and then he had steam enough to continue the telling of the tale.

"Russian wolves are much bigger and more dangerous than fully grown cannibalistic bush rabbits in our neighbourhood in the Prairies, even if these hairy ones here manage a bit of a howl now and then. Those Russian wolves were as persistent and tenacious as an evangelist of the Mennonite Brethren stripe" (whether this part of the story was really true I don't know because my mother was a member of this fervently elite

79

dem frommen Hock, enn mien Voda jintjch daut scheen, ahr tweemol den Dach een entspreajtended Dentjzaddel too vepausse).

Toom Schluß haud Voda noch dree rusche Wilw dootjeschohte, enn ons jewese woo eena ahm eenmol aum Schänebeen aunjegnoagt haud, eea hee dem mett siene boafte Grauje eenfach aufjewarjcht haud.

Onse Angst haud sijch jelajcht; wie weare dochwoll mett de Tiet too Bad jegohne, enn enjeschlope, enn auls wie korz noh säwen zemorjess wacka worde, wea uck de Burjan too meed toom wieda toobe jeworde, enn wea enjeschlope. Tridjjelohte haud'a städwies huage Diene, koldet Wada enn Stiemväjel bie de Dutz. "Soohn Buran ess soo's een Machnowitz," säd Voda, "eascht raundeleaht dee auls de Beesa, enn dann wann'a aules kort enn tjlien jeschloage haft, dann frat dee Donna sijch opp Koste aundra ditjch enn drall enn voll, enn dann schmustat hee noch biem ennschlope."

Noch eea wie em Staul besorje jinje, meend Mutta, wie sulle doch, wann irjend mäjlijch, veseatje auntoospaune enn mett dem Schläde noh Tjoatj too foahre. "Maunjchmol," soo docht etj mie, "kohme Frulied opp schnorrje Jedanke."

Nohm Freestitj wea wie unjawäjess. De Väasenja wudd dochwoll aundre Leeda auls noch jistre vääjenohme aunsaje, wiels daut Wada soo platzlijch doch seea goastrijch jewast wea.

Wie haude onse oole Kobbel Fannie enn äähre Dochta Gracie aunjespaunt. Fannie wea tjleatja auls daut Wada, enn Gracie spetjcht dee Howa uck aum Sinndach. Auls wie de latze korte haulwe Miel von Tobias Jaunz noh Weltje äähre oole Schmäd vom Siede nohm Nuade fuahre, spetzt Fannie mett eenmol de Uahre, enn pust derjche Näslajcha, enn wundad sijch. Daut foll miene Mutta opp, enn see stund von dee Schlädebeintj opp, enn tjitjcht woahan Fannie ahr mette Jedohnte hanwees.

group and our father liked to give her the works on this account once or twice a day).

To make a longer story short, my father had shot three of these Russian wolves and even showed us how one of them had inflicted a visible bite wound on his right shin (attributable to a sleighing accident at age five but which he carefully guarded for whatever appropriate occasion of a story to be told till age 96); this audacious scoundrel of a wolf had paid for the nip with father strangling him with his bare hands.

Our Angst had abated; we had probably found our way into bed and fallen asleep and when we woke up shortly after seven the next morning, the buran had exhausted itself and had also fallen asleep. It had left behind huge snow banks, chilling temperatures and snowbirds by the dozen. "Such a buran is like a Machnowitz (a roving band leader and murderer during the Russian anarchy)," said our father, "first he rampaged all over hell like the devil and when he had smashed everything into bits, then this hooligan devoured everything in sight at other's expense before crawling off to s drunken stupor with a sneer on his smirk."

Even before we had gone to the stable to do the chores, our mother suggested, that, if at all possible, we should go to church by horse and sleigh this Sunday. "Sometimes," I thought to myself, "womenfolk arrive at strange ideas."

After breakfast we set out. The song leader would probably be choosing different songs than planned after the weather had suddenly behaved so badly.

We hitched our mares Fannie and her daughter to the sleigh. Fannie was more astute than the weather and Gracie felt her oats even on Sundays. When we drove north from the Tobias Janz place to the Woelke residence and past the old Woelke smithy, Fannie suddenly pricked her ears, snorted through her nostrils and acted startled. Our mother was the first to notice

"Bozhe moi, na oba!" säd Mutta, enn wull ons Tjinja noch vom Tootjitje auflentje, oba daut wea too loht. Wie sage uck dee Bescherung lintjsch enne Schneediehn steatje. Ute Schneediehn stuak eene Burrsteewel aunjewintjelt, enn een Stetjstje boafta Foot. Daut Äwaje wea emm Schnee begroft. Onse Mutta enn ons Tjinja worde verre Tjoatj aufjeloht, enn dann fuah Voda mett Onkel Wellm tridj, soo head etj väle Joahre lohta saje.

Auls Hipp Footh dit Fahrjoah storf, word disse Jeschijcht endlijch gaunz vetalt.

Aun dem jenannden Sinnowendnohmeddach storwe meahrere Mensche enn onse Nohbaschauft; soo uck Alexander Faust, Leahra enn Breedajemeendla vefrooah, enn twee Fraunzoose bie St. Pierre Jolys vebiestade auls äahre Kebus em Blizzard ommstelpt, enn äah Kunta derjchjintjch, enn see aum Stacheldrohttun vefroahre... soo word ons aum Mondach enne School vetalt.

Joh, enn Hipp Footh? Dem wea een Foot enn een haulwet Been schwoat jeworde, haud aulso Braund jetjräje, enn daut Been word ahm aufjenohme, oba sesst woamd hee sijch bie Diedrijch Rampels biem Heehnasuppäte eenen Dach enn eene Nacht jrindlijch opp, enn bleef jesund.

Äwa Hipp Footh, dee Sommafelda, word dann zastijch Joah lang nijch jearn jerät, wiels hee bedrunke jewast wea auls hee nohm Schachspäle bie Tobias Jaunz sijch entschlohte haud noch schwind noh Hus too gohne.

Hee haud sijch daut doa enn sienem Igloo unjawäajes schwind macklijch jemurjchelt, enn wiels hee sienen ruschen Pelz druag, haud hee sijch daut "soo goot auls etj kunn doa enne Schneediehn enjerejcht.

Blooss haud etj dochwoll biem enschlope dee eene Burrsteewel, soo auls aul emma verrem Schlopegohne jewant, aufjestreept. Daut woat mie wiedahans nijch soo schwind wada

this as she stood up from her comfortable bench on the sleigh to observe what Fannie might have in mind and gestures.

"*Bozhoi moi*, can you believe it!" said mother while intending to divert us, the children's attentions, from what she had noticed. But she was too late. We also saw the element of surprise sticking out of a snow dune. Out of that snow dune stuck a thick felt winter boot, made in Russia, and a strip of bare leg. The rest of who's there was hidden in the snow.

Our mother and we kids were loaded off at the church while our father returned to Uncle William's farm, I heard say many years later.

When Hip Foth died earlier this spring the whole story came to light and may now be told in its truthful entirety.

On the named Saturday afternoon several people in our neighbourhood froze to death, among them one Alexander Fast, teacher and a Brethren, while in St. Pierre Jolys three Catholic Frenchmen got lost when their caboose capsized and their gelding took off with all three perishing by a barbed wire fence where they came to rest. This news of death was fresh and told in school on Monday, first thing.

And as for Hip Foth? His one foot and half a leg had turned black, also called gangrenous and an amputation was due. Aside from the minor interruption, he stayed at the Dietrich Remple's place for a day and a night with ample chicken soup being served and he went on to live another day and fifty five years.

People were reluctant to talk all that much about Hip Foth because he had been under the influence after a series of chess games with Tobias Janz and had insisted on quickly walking home against better advice and the stern elements.

When the blizzard hit, he had scrambled to dig himself a little igloo in a deep snow bank and since he wore his heavy Russian fur coat he had managed quite well in his den in the dune. However, it had always been his habit to remove his right boot

pesseare, wiels eena saul mett siene Feet doch spoasomma omgohne."

before falling asleep. "That is something I'll not be doing again soon because they can tell me what they want to, you have to act sparingly with your members and extremities; they take an awfully long time to re-grow."

Feftijch Cent, bitte

Disse Jeschijcht fong kratjcht too dee Stund aun auls enn Jrienthol de Bottafebritj toojemoakt word, enn bie de Tjeesfebritj de Räda aunfonge too dreie.

Een jiedra red aul donn von aul den jewaultjen Fortschrett, enn von dem Wohlstaund, enn woo ritjch wie aulatoop woare wudde, wiels de gaunze Welt hungad noh onsem Tjees, enn nu wea Jrienthol daut biblische Laund, woa Maltjch enn Honijch enne Wad ranne wudd. Enn woo jletjlijch wie toop mett onse droagendje Tjnippsbiedels boold senne wudde. Meist soo word'et dann uck.

Oba daut stald sijch dann doch boold rut, daut dee Säjen mol wada een jemischta word. Waut wea?

De Sommasch enn Siedmanitoba woare soo heet, daut omm een Hepptjeshoah aul donn meist eene Bonsch Näajasch noh Jrienthol trocke wulle. Oba donn kaum em Oktoba Schnee enn see dreide omm, enn jinje noh Hus. See bleewe ohne äah Jletjch, enn wie vereascht noch ohne Banane vonne Stud.

Oba nu doch mol tridj noh de Tjeesfebritj... Daut ess soo: Wann Schmaund een bät sua jeworde ess, jefft daut noch emma gotelje Botta, oba wann eena ut sure Maltjch Tjees moakt, dann woat de Menschheit fiestnäsijch, enn at dee Tjees ooda uck den Tjees nijch.

Aulso, waut nu? Wie haude noch nijch Elektrizität omm Wota toom tjeele too pompe, oba wie musste dee Maltjch äwa den Sinndach kolt hoole, wiels too dee Tiet wull Gott daut noch nijch habe, daut eena aum Sinndach oabeid. Joh, dee

Fifty cents, please

This story started at the very moment when the creamery in Grünthal was closed down and the pulleys at the new cheese factory started to hum.

Everyone started talking about the mighty progress of things and how prosperity was on its promising mission and how wealthy we would all shortly be because the whole world had developed an appetite for our cheese and how Grünthal would shortly turn into the Biblical land where milk and honey would competitively race down the tracks of riches. And how pregnant our billfolds would shortly be. And that's just about how it all turned out.

And yet, it shortly turned out that this blessing would be a mixed one. Why that? The summers in southern Manitoba were so hot in the mid-Thirties, that we came within an inch of becoming inhabited by Black folk who liked it hot. But then we had an early snowfall that October, and they turned around and went back home. And so they remained without the promise of fortune, and we had to make do without bananas straight from the palm.

But let's get back to the cheese factory… It's simply fact, that if cream turns slightly sour you can still churn up an acceptable batch of butter, but if you try the same with milk turned to cheese, mankind balks and the product is turned down by men, his relatives and all customers.

So what was to be done? We still had no electricity to pump cold water but we had to keep the milk cool even on Sundays. Those days God still looked unfavourably at people working

leewa Gott enn de measchte Menniste wulle too dee Tie aum Sinndach noch lenja Meddachschlop hoole.

Enn nu, soo auls jesajcht, waut nu? Gaunz eenfach: Wie musste aule Maltjch enn achtgeloonje Maltjchkaune nennjeehte, enn dee—emmahan hundat Pund de Kaun—aun eenem langen Strang aunbinje, enn dann dee em Borm nennhenje, woo see em kolden Wota den gaunzen Sinndach toobrochte. Enn doa wea daut soo tjeel, daut de Maltjch eascht goanijch opp sure Jedanke kohme kunn.

Bie ons Tus wea daut tjeen Probleem, wiels ons Voda "een Thiesse ut Elloag" leet de veea Kaune aum Sinndach em Borm nenn, daut'et bäta nijch bruckt. Bie eenje Nohbasch, woa de Manna mau schmajchtijch weare, enn nijch soo studijch jebut weare, word dee Maltjtjeelarie toom Probleem. Soo auls aunjediet: de Maunsmensche oppem Hoff haude eenfach nijch jenuag Loft enne Meiwe, omm de Kaune aum Mondach tiedijch utem Borm too hohle.

De Maltjkaune rauf too lohte kunn je meist een jiedra, wiels uck enn Jrienthol jintjch aul donn aules schwinda rauf als nopp, enn aun daut Jesatz jleewde soogoa soohne woohne sesst jleewde, daut de Welt veea Atje haud.

Na joh, oba de Maltjkaune henje noch emma em Borm enn selle rut, enn noh de Tjeesfebritjch jebrocht woare. Enn daut aulatoop een bät jicha! Enne Nohbaschauft sach'et soo's dit: Bie Wiense musste Voda enn mien Brooda enn etj han, wiels de Oola too oolt wea, enn siene Jungess eenfach too groote ooda tjliene Huppupps weare. Wie fuahre han, enn hohlde aule twee Kaune rut. Verhäa wull Voda ahn noch biebrinje, daut see sijch enne Grauje spiee sulle, dann jeiht daut leijcht'a, säd'a.

Bie Schusta Boajess wea daut nijch bäta, enn dee Schwitt haud sogoa vesocht too fleatje, oba "daut haud uck een Schiet jeholpe", säd Boaje; "fleatje ooda nijch, de Maltjchkaune wulle leewa emm tjeelen Schaute doa unje em Borm bliewe." Oh joh, wiels Boajess Sommafelda weare, wea daut fleatje doa nijch soo

on Sundays. The bare truth, though, is that in those times God and most Mennonites simply preferred to take longer naps on Sunday afternoons.

And so, as already mentioned, what was to be done? Simple enough. You and we had to pour all the milk into eight gallon cans and then lower the hundred pound containers straight into the cold water of the well where they spent Sundays. In the well it was cool enough so that milk was prevented from whatever sour thoughts in might otherwise entertain.

At our home, none of this was much of a problem, because our father "a Thiessen born and bred in Elloag on the Dnieper" home to the roughnecks widely known, and even more feared for a thousand miles up and downstream, lowered a series of hundredweight cans into a deep and dark well in a smooth jiffy. Such, however, was not the case at some of our neighbours, and cooling milk for the cheese plant presented a problem. As suggested: some of the men folk in the neighbourhood were of lesser mettle and lacked the wind power in their sleeves, as the saying went, to raise the milk cans from the well on Monday mornings.

To lower the cans was a different matter and something which most anybody could do because even around Grünthal things went down more quickly than up, and even those who still insisted that the globe was four-cornered, believed in gravity.

But just a minute, now... the milk cans are still in the well and are to be lifted up and out and taken to the cheese factory. And a little giddy-up and go, was the order of Monday mornings! In the general neighbourhood things looked like this. At neighbour John H. Wiens, our father, and brother Pete, and I had to attend because Old Man Wiens was too old, and his boys were too slouchy when it came to a heavy pull. We travelled over to their place and pulled out the two cans in very short order. Just prior to doing so, our father told the little gang

89

schlemm auls wann een Russlenda daut deed. Bie de Molotschna wea daut fleatje äwahaupt nijch mood; de Lied säde, dee kunne daut nijch mol, wann see daut uck han enn wada proowde.

Aulso fuah wie romm, enn holpe aulewäaje, oba auls wie donn noh dem oolen Grunzkujel Oole Jeat Niefeld kaume, jintjch dee Sposs loos, enn disse Jeschijcht fung aun.

Daut Niefeld een tjniepaja Scherniesel wea wisst etj aul mett fief Joah, enn etj hilt mie nijch enn siene dijchte Nobaschauft toom Äwajen opp. Etj truhd ahm daut too, daut hee junge Benjels em Jeheemen tjniepe wudd, eenfach wiels ahm daut scheen jintjch wann hee Hunj enn Tjinja koojintjre heare kunn. Auls bie disse Niefelds de Heehnastaul aufbrennd tjitjcht dee Oola sijch een haulwet Joah measchtens äwre Schulre, enn auls hee donn noch sienen Vesejchrungsscheck tjreajch, schmustad hee sogoa wann'et reajend.

Butadem wea hee een ditja Scherwaunda, dee sijch mau selden em Staul opphild, wiels, soo's hee säd, "daut Maltje ess Fruesoabeid.."

Na joh, oba disse Niefelds haude uck eene Kaun Maltjch, dee aum Mondach zemorjess utem Borm sull. See weare onse Nohbasch, sesst wea wie doa nijch too Help hanjefoahre.

Soo auls jesajcht, ooda weens aunjediet: Ons Voda, dee ut Eloag, predijcht uck opp siene Oat dolla enn bäta, wann hee een vollet Hus verr sijch haud. Enn doamett meen etj, daut ahm daut scheen jintjch siene Muskle späle too lohte, wann hee een Publikum haud. Enn wann doa dann noch een poah Langhoaje doabie stunde, dann druag ons Voda, dee vom Nippa, uck ruhijch twee Kaune Maltjch, enn weppad doabie noch sogoa mett dem Hinjarenj.

Oba wann tjeena tootjitjcht, dann foll ahm daut sogoa schwoa eenen mässjen Nachtopp zemorjess bettem Mesthupe too droage.

90

of incompetents that if you spat into your hand properly and with fiery gusto, things went easier, so he said.

At Shoemaker Bergens things were not much different and that little gang of nincompoops had even commenced the effort with some choice cussing but that didn't help much a shit either, said Old Man Bergen. "Cuss all you want" he said, "those milk cans simply prefer the shade of cool of the well." Fact is, that cussing among the Bergens was not all that terrible, because they were Sommerfelder Mennonites; among us Russlanders it was a different matter. And among the Molotschna elitists? People said they could not even cuss, even if one or the other had given it a try.

And so we travelled around and helped, but when we arrived at Curmudgeon Old Man George Neufeld's place, the fun of it all started and this story began. The fact that Neufeld was a penny pinching cheapskate was something I already knew at age five, and I kept my distance from him. I would not have been surprised if he would have given me a nasty pinch in the ass just for the fun of it, because he liked to hear dogs and kids howl and wail. When the Neufeld hen house burned down that summer, Old Man Neufeld looked over his shoulder for half a year and more, and then, when he received a cheque from the insurance company in the mail, he smirkingly sneered even when it was raining.

Also, he was a chubby cruiserweight, who was rarely to be found in the stable; "milking is women's work," he claimed.

And yet, these Neufelds also had a can of milk in the well and we had to help lift it out early this Monday morning.

As mentioned, or at least implied: Our father, he, the one from Elloag, enjoyed preaching more to a full house, so to speak. All I am trying to say is that he liked to display a goodly strand of rippling muscles if the audience was abundant. And if a few of the long-haired gender were in attendance, then our father, he from and of the Dnieper, carried two one hundred

Na joh, oba de Kaun mott je noch utem Borm bie Grunzkujels Jeat Niefeld. Kratjcht auls Voda sijch aul den Strang omme Grauje jewetjelt haud, enn dee Kaun ruthewe wull, kaum tiedijch zemorjess dem Jungen Jeat Niefeld siene Brut ute Tjäatj rutjedaunzt, enn looht toom Freestitjch enn. Auls Voda dee too seehne tjreajch, schwoll ahm de Kaum aun, enn hee sad sijch sien Garry Cooper Jesejcht unjrem Hoot opp, enn donn huppst hee soo auls een Hohn oppe Floak, enn stald sijch breetbeensch äwa dem Borm, enn wull de Kaun gaunz schmeissijch Haund äwa Haund nohhejcht tratjche.

Etj freid mie aul emm stellen, daut mien Voda, wann'et senne musst, soohn schratjlijch stoatja Donna wea, dee aul eenmol dree Chochole mett eenem Drusch daut Lijcht utjepust haud.

Oba aul daut Jewesne holp ahm platzlijch nuscht nijch, wiels de Schortinj enn Niefelds äah Borm vefuhlt wea, enn noh gauf, enn Voda, Hoot, willet Jesejcht enn tien Sekunde rusche Fleatjweada aulatoop enn Grunzkujel Jeat Niefels äah Borm hinjenaunda veschwunge.

"Bozhe moi," säd de Niefeldsche, enn Niefeld säd bloos: "Schinda em Schiet!" enn donn speajch hee ut, enn säd noch hinjeraun: "Wann diss Sposs bloos nijch noch too diea tjemmt!"

Wie stunde aula aum Borm enn tjitjchte rauf, enn reatjende mett een Bejrafnis, ooda weens mett een Krankenbad mett Voda doa benne.

Oba waut wea? Doa unje oba nu aul oppe Kaun saut Voda, doll auls een nauta Hohn, enn schreajch: "Na, opp waut wacht Jie, von auleen kohm etj nijch ut disse Bredulj. Niefeld, woa ess Diene Lada?"

Soo auls Jie weete, läwd Voda noch achtefeftijch Joah lenja nohdem Niefelds äah Borm ahm breedajemeendsch jedeept haud, aulso mott hee doa dochwoll irjendwoo rutjekohme senne.

92

pound milk cans with an easy flair, while wiggling his ass cheeks for all to admire as he sauntered along.

However, if there was no one around to applaud, then he found it difficult to transport a chamber pot plus cash and carry goods from the bedroom to the manure pile early mornings.

Whatever, the can of milk is still in Curmudgeon Neufeld's well, waiting for a helping hand. Just as our father had already wrapped the sixteen foot of rope attached to the can around his hands and readying himself for the pull, young George Neufeld's bride danced jauntily from the kitchen to invite us all for breakfast. When our father caught a glimpse of that sprightly feminine morsel, his coxcomb swelled mightily and he put on his Garry Cooper face under his hat, jumping like a rooster to the highest roost, while widely straddling his legs over the top of the well, intending to pull up the can hand over hand like nobody's business.

I was enjoying the prospect of my father, who if need be, was a mighty powerful operator; rumors had it, that he once blew out light and intentions of three roving bandits in the Old Country with one mighty sweep of his right haymaker. And now he would show them all and a bit in my name as well what our Thiessen genes were all about and for all to see.

But all things past availed him little or nothing because the shorting of Neufeld's well was rotten and gave way with father, hat, a wildly furious face followed by ten seconds of Russian cussing vocabulary, dangling participles, and all crashing down, down, down into Curmudgeon Neufeld's well.

"*Bozhe moi*," said Mrs Neufeld, while Chubby Neighbour only said, "Devil in the Shit!" and then he spat, Russian style, and added, "Hope this damn *Scheiße* won't cost too much!"

We stood around the well and looked down and reckoned that we would shortly be attending a funeral or at least a sick bed with our father in it.

Bett de Nobaschauft "doa bowe" von Peeta H. (Heehna) Jaunze de Braundlada jeholt haude, enn Voda daut Lijcht wada erläwd, weare meist dree Stunde vegohne. Waut Voda nijch vetald, de oola tjniepa Niefeld oba fuats enword, ess daut Voda em Borm dochwoll aunjefonge haud too darschte, enn hee doa een Schruwglaus Schmaund fe de erwähnde Brut äahre Tjast enn eenem Amma jefunge, enn daut ladijch jedrunke haud.

Auls wie donn endlijch lieseltjess mett eenem stellen "Gott sei Dank!" utenaunda jinje, jintjch Niefeld noch noh mien Voda opptoo, enn säd too ahm: "Du Thiesse, dee Schmaund woohnen Du doa unje utdrunkst kost feftijch Cent. Aulso bitte… "

But what was? There, a dark half world away and much below sat our father on the milk can, as mad as a wet rooster, yelling, "What the devil are you waiting for? I can't make my way out of this shitty mess on my own. Neufeld, where is your ladder?"

As you may know, our father lived another fifty eight years after Neufeld's well had so unceremoniously baptized him Mennonite Brethren style by full immersion, and so, obviously, he must have escaped that dreary dungeon.

Until the neighbourhood "there above" had managed to fetch a sturdy ladder from Peter C. (Chicken) Janzen's place, and our father again saw the light of day from a reliable perspective, three hours had passed. What our father did not tell, but what tight-fisted Neufeld had immediately noticed, is that father in the well had become very thirsty, and since a handy double quart of cream in a Jewel jar had been hung down for the bride's wedding, our father had drunk it to the lees.

When we finally departed with a quiet "Thank God", old Neufeld sidled up to our father and said, "Thiessen, the cream you devoured while down there costs fifty cents, please!"

Weight-Watchers mol äwaroasch

Em Oktooba aune 1976 kaum Professa Viktor Pijaschew
enn siene Fru Marguscha ut Moscow aune Universität enn
Kiel aun: hee sull doa rusche Jeschijcht enn Literatua
unjarejchte, enn see sull mol em Waste daut Shopping gohne
leahre, enn beid sulle se soo väl Mensche auls mäjlijch toom
Kommunismus betjeare.

Mien Frind Viktor Peetasch enn etj kaume vonne aundre
Sied enn Kiel aun: etj sull doa halpe daut Praische Weadabuak
toopstalle, enn Viktor sull mie doabie too Haund gohne.Wiels
etj eene Koah, een Jetta VW haud, wull Pijaschew schwind
mett mie Frind woare. Ahm sach dee Koah schmock, enn
butadem musst hee sijch jieda Wätjch eenmol biem ruschen
Konsulat enn Hamburg malde, doamett see doa seehne kunne,
daut de Dietsche ahm noch nijch jekidnappt haude.

Daut sijch opp dee Oat malde wea mie een bät bekaunt, wiels
mien ellra Brooda wea too dee Tiet bie de Breeda enn
Nuadkildona biejegohne, enn doa wea daut uck mood sijch
een poah mol de Wätjch enne Tjoatjch, ooda uck noch feina,
emm Bethus too malde, entweda toom Gottesdeenst, ooda too
de Bibelstund, ooda too eenem ooda uck twee Fundraisers de
Wätjch, enn uck woo eena daut äwaje Striepsel Welt noch
verrem Joahresenj betjeare kunn. Enn butadem weare de
Fundraiser-Banketts ahm wijchtijch doamett hee siene
dreehundat Pund Läwendjewijcht oppe Wijchschol uck voll
brinje kunn.

Daut easchte Mol auls Pijaschew noh Hamburg aumtlijch
hanmusst, fruag hee, auls etj ahm doahan feahre wudd. "Auls
Kapitalist woat Ahn daut leijcht faule, joh?" meend hee. Etj

Weight-Watchers in Reverse

In October 1976 Professor Viktor Pijaschew and his wife Margusha arrived from Moscow at the University of Kiel in Germany; he was to instruct Russian History and Literature, while she was meant to learn to go shopping Western style, and both were to convert as many Germans as possible to Communism.

My friend Viktor Peters and I arrived in Kiel from the other direction, so to speak: I was meant to help compile the Prussian Dictionary and Viktor was to keep me company in so doing. Since I owned a VW Jetta in Kiel, Pijaschew quickly decided to become my friend. He said he liked my car, and, moreover, he had to report in person to the Russian Consulate in Hamburg weekly so that they could check on him and make sure the Germans were not about to kidnap him.

This reporting to higher authorities was familiar to me since my older brother at the time had become a member of the North Kildonan Mennonite Brethren, and there the custom held sway that you were meant to be seen in church several times a week, which they called the House of Prayer, a step above the competition, and to worship, or do Bible, attend Bible Study and also to attend, or even organize Fundraisers, so that before year's end the few remaining heathens of this world could be saved and brought into God's favourite fold. Fundraisers were my brother's forte, because most of them were of the All You Can Eat Variety so that he could more readily maintain his three hundred pounds plus frame. Keeping very busy in God's garden and purpose was also part of the agenda and upped the stock of personal repute.

deed daut. Oba kratjcht soo auls daut mang sijchtje Mensche aul emma wea, wull hee dann uck wiedahans een Free Ride doahan habe. Oba etj säd: "Towarisch Vietja, de Dietsche Bundesbohn woat mie dann doll, wiels etj ahr Konkurrenz moak, enn daut well wie dann doch nijch doohne, nä?"

"Nä."

Oba etj nauhm Kollege Pijaschew jieden Dach uck wiedahans noh de Uni. mett, enn jieden Dach wundad hee sijch enn säd biem Kopp schliesre: "Ivan, waut ess hiea bloos los? De dietsche Mädtjess send je soo denn enn muckrijch auls wann see utem Gulag kohme, dee sitt'et aulatoop noh Hunjsfooda. Woo haft sijch daut? Etj docht bett nu, Dietschlaund wea een ritjchet Laund, oba disse Frulied send measchtens utjehungat, nijch?"

"Weit gefehlt, leewa Vietja, Gospodjien Tovarisch," säd etj, "Nohm Tjrijch aute de Dietsche sijch easchtmol aulatoop jehearijch saut enn voll, enn fonge aun soo auls een Schwitt Jans romm too wackle, daut wea de Fresswelle, oba dann kaum de Tiet, auls dee dietsche Mädtjches nijch meea soo auls arabische Haremmejalles rommulwere wulle, enn dann aute see measchtens Seloht, dreemol den Dach, bett see soohne Been auls Krohntjess enn Reiasch tjreaje. Enn doabie ess daut jebläwe; butadem tjenne de dietsche Mädtjess irjendeenen amerikaunschen Soldoht biem Gohne ooda uck biem Ranne utschluwe. Disse Mädtjess habe Konditsjoon jleew mie, oola Molodetjz!"

Oba dem Vietja Pijaschew sach siene Marguscha schmocka wiels, soo säd hee, dee meea Holt verre Däah haud. Waut dee Utdruck Holt verre Däah bediet, daut tjenne sijch de measchte Manna selwst utdentjche. Enn wann nijch, sulle see aun daut Schmettewief enn Barbados (toom Jletjch doot) dentje, dee zwoa eenen ladjen Bähn haud, oba een Buck voll Pelle enn soo auls Marilyn Munroe uck een haulwe Cord Holt verre Däah oppjefliet haud.

The first time Pijaschew had to officially go to Hamburg, he asked me to take him there. "As a capitalist, this little favour is easily enough done for you, *da*?" he suggested. I complied. But as things generally transpire among the wealthy and busy, Colleague Pijaschew suggested that trips to Hamburg by Jetta become routine; he wanted a free ride. So I said, "Tovarish Vietja, the German Federal Railway is going to get good and mad at me for competing with them, and you wouldn't want that, would you?"

"Not really, *nyet*." He was a fast learner; very fast indeed by academic standards.

However, I did take Colleague Pijaschew along from the Professorial Guest House in my Jetta to the University daily during which he routinely shook his head in disbelief, like so, "Ivan, what is so really wrong here? The German girls and womenfolk are so thin as if they have just returned from the Gulag; altogether they look like so many dog bones. What is here the matter? Up to now I thought Germany was a rich country but most of these women look emaciated and starved, right?

"You are sadly mistaken, dear Vietja, Gospodin Tovarish," I replied. After the war, the Germans sat down and ate their fill of pork around the clock and it was not long before they looked like so many fatted geese; that was *die Freßwelle,* the eating wave, but then the girls decided that they no longer wanted to look like candidates for Arabian harems, and they started munching on salads thrice daily until they had the legs of cranes, storks and herons. And their salad days have remained with them to this day. And, don't forget, those ladies are in shape; German ladies can outperform any American soldier day or night, walking or jugging, no kidding, *molodets!*"

But Vietja Pijaschew much preferred his wife Marguscha, because, as he said, "she has more firewood stacked in front of her door"; most men of the earth and woods quickly grasp

Na joh, dee menschlijche Jrimse kohme enn gohne, enn daut diead dann uck nijch lang bett de Amerikauna fatt enn ditjch enn drugglijch worde, wiels see bloos noch mette Koah fuahre, enn eenfach nijch meea gohne kunne, wiels see too fat weare, eenfach väl too fat, enn jeweehnlijch je fatta je domma noch doatoo. Enn boold haude de measchte Amerikauna dann uck meea Holt hinjre Däah auls verre Däah, weens dee Frulied, enn daut word soo groff, daut de measchte Maltjtjeaj sijch grodentoo schämde, wann see de Frulied mett ähre ditjche Bucks enn druggelje Been sage, dee mien Voda enn Arbuse Klosse emma Schietstendasch nannde.

Enn donn jintjch daut groote Jeschaft mett Weight Watchers loos, enn uck aundre Diet Kurse soo auls Shakers enn Quakers, enn aula koste se seea väl Jeld, oba halpe deede se jeweehnlijch een Schiet.

Joh, enn donn läde sijch de steinbachsche Tjoatje uck em Toch, enn derjch daut MCC holpe se fe biljett Jeld Mensche Jewijcht mett een tjristeljet Rezapt "Slim enn Trim" auftoonehme. Oba uck dit holp bloos toom Deel.

Joh, enn dann kaume een poah Frind enn etj opp foljenden Jedanke, enn wiels daut mang ons Menniste jeweehnlijch aulatoop nuscht nijch woat, wann de Tjoatjch nijch de Henj em Spell haft, organisead wie Jungess eene Jemeend, dee mau eene strenje Bedinjung haud: Wea nijch weens tweehundat Pund wuag, word nijch oppjenohme. Waut wie wulle wea eajentlijch gaunz eenfach: wie Jungess wulle derjch den mennischen Gloowe mol too Jeld kohme. Enn stalt junt mol väa: enn eenem haulwen Joah haud wie onse easchte Tjoatjch voll: Luta straume, forsche Manna, enn frindlijch auls eene Tabun freschbetjeade Breeda enn veeahundad Frulied, aula jestuckt, enn frindlijch auls een Darpvoll druggelje Frulied enne Dartjajoahre, enn aula vejneajcht enn utjelohte enn ohne Komplexe, enn ohne Psychologe ooda Social Workers, enn

what he meant by firewood in front of the door. And if not, that Smith Lady from the Bahamas (long dead, prescription overdose) should come to mind; she had an empty loft but a belly full of pills and she, like Marilyn Munroe, had half a cord of firewood neatly stacked in front of her door. Also, both were favourite sugar daddy candidates.

Whatever: human moods and fads come and go and it was not long before the Americans had become very fat and foolish, then obese and bullyish, as it becomes Sumo wrestlers and their apprentices; they travelled everywhere by car or SUV, and shortly they simply could not walk because they were too fat, much too fat, and for once the generalization "The fatter the dumber" roundly applied. In short order, then, fast food prevailed and the American gender of feminine persuasion had more firewood stacked in the rumble seats than in the frontal parts.

It was then that the Big Business of Weight Watchers commenced and even Shakers and Quakers and related diets got into the swing of things with all costing huge amounts of money with most amounting to fat purses and fatter urses.

It was then that the Steinbach churches got into the swing of things, so to speak, and for cheap bucks the MCC helped the needy to lose with a program titled Slim and Trim. This generally amounted to a fat failure as well.

It was then that a few friends and I hit upon the following idea, and since nothing gets airborne unless the church has its hand in the noble endeavour of loftier pull, we boys organized a chain of congregations which had only one strict condition: Only such weighing two hundred pounds or more were accepted. What we, the ever alert, had in mind was really quite simple: we intended to come to big money ("cash grab" for those of lesser faith) via the Mennonite faith. And just imagine! Within half a year we had our first church chock full.

tjeene Neurose, enn aula mett eene Haundtausch voll jespoadet Jeld, wiels Weight Watchers haude se lenjst begrowt.

Eascht wea daut Sposs, oba donn birjad sijch daut enn, enn uck sogoa een ruscha Nohme fe onse Jemeend feahd wie enn: wie nannde dee kort enn eenfach de Marguscha Jemeend, enn dis Nohme bleef stohne enn uck sette!

Enn disse Jemeend (nu jefft'et uck aul eene Filiale enn Wintjla, enn twee enne Kildonajäjend enn uck dree enn Abbotsford, enn Clearbrook doa dijchtbie, enn noch eene haulwe Dutz enn Vancouver, enn twee enne Niagara-Jäjend, woa de Mensche derjch den Prosperity Gospel aule Henj enn Fuppe voll Boajeld habe, enn sijch saut äte tjenne enn uck doohne, enn measchtens een Schemedauntje ver sijch han enn häa schuwe, oba von sijch schäme? Tjeene Spoah, enn tjeene Räd!

Enn aule Jemeende send sijch eenijch, wiels see sijch aum Desch enn uck sesst nijch jäjensiedijch eegol aufbiete. Enn aule Marguscha Tjoatjche habe daut oole Motto: "De Wind blost den Kurrei toop, enn uck soohne Hinjarenjs!"

P. S. Etj sull noch erwähne, daut wie, aulso dee Väastaund vonne Marguscha Jemeend jearn noch Franchises vetjeepe well; noch nijch besat ess haulf Dietschlaund, Curitiba enn Brasilien, Kazakhstan, Mexiko, enn China, enn woa de Menniste sesst noch nijch de Näs nennjestoake habe.

Nothing but handsome, rugged stout rovers and all friendlier than a herd of freshly converted Brethren, and four hundred women, all portly and jovial like a village full of women in the Dirty Thirties, and all forthcoming and without complexes or neurosis and without psychological makeovers or social workers on the prowl. All came with handbags fat with cash from all the money saved from long since failed Weight Watchers. First we did it for all for the good of you fun, but shortly things became established and we even introduced an obviously Russian name for our congregational churches: we called them the Marguscha Gemeinde with good reason and this term was accepted by total majority.

And this church (there now are franchises firmly established in Winkler, two in North Kildonan, three in Abbotsford, one in Clearbrook, and half a dozen in Vancouver, and two in the Niagara Region where people have their hands and pockets full of cash, compliments of Prosperity Gospel) has in its membership those happily rounded, with all allowed to eat their fill and enjoying it; stout and merry and everyone pushing and pulling little shopping carts, bodily attached, full of merry tidings and walking testimonials to our enterprising endeavour. And as for complexes and guilt complexes? You must be kidding. All Marguscha congregations are of common accord and in a forgiving mood because no begrudging of grub competition prevails among those who have it right. Further, all Marguscha churches have a guiding motto, which, roughly translated from Plautdietsch reads: "The wind blows together tumbleweed as well as sturdy posteriors!"

P. S. It should be mentioned that we, meaning the Board of Directors of the Marguscha Congregations Inc., still have available for sale choice franchises in: half of Germany, Curitiba in Brazil, Kazakhstan, Mexico and China and wherever else Mennonitism, Weight Watchers and Competitors have not yet polluted the rounded potential.

De Reemabeintjch

Peeta Niefeld haud enn Rußlaund eene groote Wirtschauft enn fief Jungess. Waut Niefeld besondasch scheen jintjch wea goot buhre, oba waut ahm noch scheena jintjch, wea de Schustarie. "Daut ess siene Flus," säd siene Fru foaken, woon'e Niefeld "Mame" nannd.

Niefeld haud enne Väaleew een Stoftje enjerejcht mett Neimaschien, Leest enn eene Reaj Hohmasch enn Tange enn Pleiasch enn Oate enn Nodle; kromme uck jeboagne enn jlitje. Uck Petjtwearm haud'a enn een ladanett Schaldoak enn siene Reemabeintjch.

Enn doa moak Niefeld Säle trajcht, enn uck Schooh, Pereestje enn Schlorre wann'et senne mußt. Enn doa emm Stoaftje wea Niefeld foaken opp siene Reemabeintjch auntootrafe. Emm Winta ooda noh Fieaowent neid'a daut "de Schnodda Fiea foot,"—enn bät een groffe Utdruck, säd'e de Mensche, wiels Niefeld too de Breedajemeend jehead, oba tjeena säd daut opp Ludes, wiels sonst diead daut Neie ooda daut Fletje bediedent lenja…

Oba schnorrijch wear'ett, wann Niefeld enn siene Schustarie saut, dann wea hee een aundra Mensch; dann wea hee frintlijch enn oppjeriemt, enn utjelohte; joh, dann sung hee rusche Leede enn uck Dietsche. Rusch sung hee, "Ich bete an die Macht der Liebe" enn "De Lorelei" enn "Scheen ist die Jugend" opp Dietsch, oba waut ahm daut scheenste jintj wea "Hab oft im Kreise der Lieben". Joh, donn hold Niefeld foaken siene Junges, siene Bonsch Junges toop en donn word doa enn'e

The Cobbler's Bench

In Ukraine, Peter Neufeld had a large farm and five sons. Neufeld enjoyed the farming well enough, but what he enjoyed even more was making and repairing shoes or leather items of every kind on his cobbler's bench. "Yes, that's his quirk," said his wife Anna, whom Neufeld always called "Mamme."

On the porch connecting the house and the stable, Neufeld had equipped a tackroom with a sturdy sewing machine, a last, a series of hammers and pliers, awls and needles—some crooked, some curved and some straight. There he also kept rolls of pitch-yarn there, and his cobbler's apron.

In this room Neufeld worked on harnesses, shoes, house slippers, whatever was made of leather and needed repair. Whenever he wasn't in the fields or couldn't be found anywhere else, that's where he was bound to be. During the winter or after the day's work was done, he cobbled and sewed "until his snot caught fire" in the irreverent words of a fellow Mennonite Brethren member, who took care to remain anonymous because one's repairs tended to take a little longer if such remarks came full circle.

Yes, this was there Neufeld was truly at home. No matter what anxieties might be bothering him or what troubles loomed, when he sat down at his cobbler's bench he became a new man, a relaxed, cheerful free spirit. In no time at all he would begin to sing, Russian songs and German songs: "I Pray to the Power of Love", "Die Lorelei", "Youth, Beautiful Youth", but best of all he liked to sing "Often in the Circle of My Beloved". He often assembled all five sons in the cobblery, and

Schustarie jesunge waut Zeijch enn Lada helt, säd Niefeld. Enn schmustad.

Aundre Mensche sunge measchtens opp'e Stap wann see mett'e Pead oabeide deede; wann de Sonn unjagohne wull, enn de Pead wellja worde, enn daut Onjezeffa nohleet, enn de Loft frescha word. Joh, donn sung Niefeld uck, enn hee sung daut Orlik enn Maschka de Ohre spetzte enn maunjchmol sogoa Schrett hilde.

Oba aum scheensten jintj Niefeld daut enne Schustarie mett siene Jungess toop sinje. Baus, Tenor, twee ooda dreestemmijch… see sunge. Enn wann de Mensche daut Sinje nijch soo scheen jeheat haud, haud'e se woll jedocht: "Schnorrijch, schnorrijch, woa jeiht daut bloß han mett Niefeld enn siene Jungess?"

De Tiet kaum enn de Tiet jintjch. Enn donn fong de Tiet aun too ranne. Enn donn wear'et mett eenst sowiet: Schwoatja gauf'et aum Himmel, enn de wulle nijch meea vetratje. Joh, enn donn gauf'et Jewitta, enn daut worde diesta.

Joahrelang. Niefeld docht: "Daut woat aulwada, mau aufwachte." Enn hee buad enn neid enn hee sung. Oba mau een bätje, enn mau langsom, enn mau eenstemmijch, wiels Niefeld siene Junges, Obraum enn Johaun enn Peeta enn Jasch enn Isaak lenjst enn Kanada weare. Eascht schreewe se foaken, donn worde see doch woll ritj enn haude daut väl too drock, joh väl too drock, enn donn word daut Schriewe emma wietleftja…

Enn Niefeld buad, enn donn buad hee ut; hee schustad noch, oba boold dreid de Neimaschien langsomma enn Niefeld haud den Schustahohma boold lenja enn lenja opp sien ladanet Schaldoak lidje. Enn siene Brell bleef lenja enn lenja enne Fupp. Enn sinje? Bloß noch aum Sinndach enne Tjoatj. Sesst saut'a doa enn Rußlaund emm Darp Tus enne Schustarie. Enn wea een bät vebiestat. Siene Fru, Mame, uch han enn wada Auna jenannt, nu daut de Tjinja utjefloage weare, wull ahm auf

then they sang fit to raise the roof. And Neufeld smiled. He sang and smiled. Other people usually just sang while working the fields, when day's end was approaching and the insects were diminishing, and the horses had caught their second wind and were more willing again for the final pull of the day. And Neufeld sang then too, sang enthusiastically and melodiously to his two horses Orlik and Maschka, who pricked their ears and kept better time as they did. But most of all, Neufeld like to sing in his cobblery.

Times came and times went, and then time started to gallop. Suddenly there were dark clouds on the horizon, and they wouldn't go away. Then there was thunder and lightning of an evil kind that no wind seemed able to move and no prayer alter. A malignant darkness set in over the Mennonite villages of Ukraine…

For the next few years Neufeld consoled himself constantly with this thought: "Things will be alright, eventually. Just have patience. Patience." And he kept on farming and cobbling and singing as best as circumstances would permit. Often, circumstances didn't. And as one son after another left for Canada, his singing became sadder and quieter and less frequent. The sons wrote back often at first, long accounts of the freedoms and riches in this new land, but then they seemed to have become rich themselves, too rich and too busy, yes, far too busy and their letters arrived less and less often.

Neufeld kept farming, but his farming proceeded as unenthusiastically as his sewing machine. His cobbler's hammer remained untouched on his leather apron for days and weeks, and his spectacles remained in his vest pocket. As for singing? Well, only on Sundays in church. And finally he took to idling away long hours in the cobblery, doing nothing at all. He seemed a little lost. His wife, now called Anna since the children had left, tried now and then to lift his spirits by singing "Often in the Circle of My Beloved" and Neufeld did

enn too een bät Troost tooräde, enn stemmd daut Leed
"Scheen ist die Jugend" aun, enn Niefeld rauspeld sijch uck den
Hauls enn sad uck loos, oba ahm fehld de Freid enn dann
vestommd daut Leed. Maunjchmol wees de Niefeldsche ahm
Bilda vonn'e Groottjinja ut Kanada.

"Sitst, daut ess Kennett, dat ess Heather, doa hinje steiht
Catrien, aules Peeta siene," oba Niefeld sad sijch nijch mol de
Brell opp... "Dee tjenne je nijch mol Dietsch," säd'a, enn
jintjch lidje...

Hunga enn Trua puttade bie Niefelds aune Däah. Jrebble,
dentjche "woo ess'et bloß mäjlich." Enn boold word de Heimat
jäjne Frieheit vetuscht, enn Niefelds foahre loos noh Kanada
opptoo, noh de Tjinja enn Grootttjinja, enn wea weet, waut
noch aules...

See kaume enn Kanada aun. Niefeld tjreajch noch eenmol
Wind von Hinje enn hee läd noch eenmol loos. Oba woahan?
Woa sie etj hiea Tus? Wea finjt sijch hiea bloß trajcht? Joh,
sogoa siene eajne Tjinja weare ahm framd jeworde, Joh, joh,
see nauhme ahn fein opp enn gauwe ahn Kost enn Queteea,
oba Niefeld reatjcht daut nijch too... Enn waut de Niefeldsche
wea, dee säd nijch väl, see säd bloß, see wea fe daut Laund too
oolt, see word hiea nijch soo rajcht tusijch. "Mie bangt," säd
see, enn ahr flautad de Tjenn. Enn donn läd see sijch han enn
foljd de Henj enn hield. See socht äah Schaldoak omm sijch de
Trohne too wesche, fung'ett oba nijch. Enn bruckt daut uck
nijch meea... "Auna ess wajch," säd Niefeld bloß.

Auls enn wanneea enn woaromm dee Mensch too sijch
tjemmt, enn woaromm de Mensch hiea enn Kanada noch
seldna too sijch tjemmt auls sesst woa—wea weet soohnt aules,
docht Niefeld bie sijch. Oba waut halpt daut Räde?... Jenuach,
nohm Bejrafnis kaume Niefeld siene Jungess, Obraum enn
Johaun enn Peeta enn Jasch enn Isaak toop. Enn toom
easchten Mol enn Kanada noh twintijch Joah—noh äwa
twintijch Joah—haude see Tiet, nauhme sijch Tiet; see vetalde,

try to join in but his heart wasn't in it and he usually faded away. Sometimes Anna showed snapshots of their grand-children in Canada: "See? That's Kennett, that's Heater, and there at the back is Cattrien, all Peter's children." But Neufeld didn't even bother to put on his spectacles. "They don't even know German," he shrugged… and went to bed.

Hunger, sorrow and loneliness now knocked regularly on Neufeld's door. Neufeld spent much time brooding, questioning his fate. How was all this possible? How could God forget his children so callously? Eventually patience could no longer sustain even the patient Neufeld. Then Peter Neufeld and Anna packed a few small possessions and joined the throngs of the fleeing. And arrived in Canada, eventually, to join their children, their grandchildren and who knew what else. For a short time after their arrival, Neufeld's sails seemed to catch a breeze. But his new fate was overwhelming. What direction should he take now? Where was he to find a new home in this huge country? His own children had become strange to him. Oh certainly, they offered room and board, but somehow it was not enough. Anna said very little, but you could see she was having the same problem. "I think I'm too old for this country," she said finally, her chin trembling. "I'm homesick." And then she lay down and folded her hands and wept. She looked for her apron, but she couldn't find it. Worse than that, she didn't really need it anymore. "Anna is gone," was all that Neufeld said. And whether people here or there or anywhere else had any more luck in squaring themselves away he didn't know, but somehow this country wasn't an easy fit. But then again, what was the point of such thoughts, Neufeld thought to himself. What was the point of thinking?

After the funeral, Abraham and John and Peter and Jacob and Isaac got together. For the first time since they'd come to Canada, it seemed, they found the time, they made time to reflect on the image of their father, standing alone at the grave

beroatschluage, enn jinje enn sijch, auls see mett eenmol sage, daut äah Voda doa biem Grauf auleen stund enn sienen schwoaten, oolen Hoot aum Raund enne Henj hild enn rund enn rund dreid. Enn donn wada… Voda wea ahn soo goot auls framd jeworde… woo wea daut aules mäajlijch, wea haud daut jedocht… See haude daut väl too drock jehaut, joh, väl too drock jehaut…

De Jungess wudde Voda noh Peeta nehme enn Jnodenfeld. Eascht wudde see ahm halpe siene tjliene Wirtschauft opptoorieme, enn donn, enn twee Wäatj sull hee bie Peetre enn Oat nenntratjche. Em Darp Jnodefeld.

Enn wess woah, enn twee Wäatj wear'ett donn uck sowiet. See weare aule fief Junges noch mol toopjekohme, enn holpe Voda nu biem Ommtratjche.

Joh, enn waut meen jie, waut doa tweschen Hus enn Staul dijchtbie dee Väaleew stund? Eene enjerejchte Schustarie, mett eene Reemabeintjch enn mett aulem Toobehea…

Enn donn sad sijch Oomtje Oola Peeta Niefeld uck aul opp'e Reemabeintjch dol, moak sijch daut doa macklijch, enn fung aun too neie enn Näjeltjess enntooschlohne. Enn donn sad'a de Neimaschien enne goh, daut de Schnodda Fiea foot. Enn donn mett eenmol stemmde aule sass groote Niefelds enn noch enne haulwe Dutz Tjlienatjes enn uck Oat enn noch twee Schwäajasches daut Leed aun, "Hab oft im Kreise der Lieben". Enn donn bleef de Tiet stohne, joh, dee Tiet dreid tridj enn rand äwaroasch. Enn Niefeld tjitjcht äwre Brell, enn derjche Brell enn säd: "Mie ess vondoag tusijch." Enn neid enn sung enn sung enn neid. Enn schloach Näjeltjess enn. Enn schmustad.

turning the brim of his black hat over and over in his hands. He was as much a stranger to them now as they to him; how had all this managed to happen? Who would have thought that if would come too all this? Yes, it was true, they had all been too busy, far too busy…

The time had come, they resolved, to move him to Peter's place in Gnadenfeld. To move in there with Peter and Agatha. Anna's effects remained to be dealt with, of course, and his few possessions too; but in two weeks they would return and accomplish this. They all agreed on it.

Two weeks later they all showed up at the appointed time. And when they arrived at Peter's farm in Gnadenfeld, take a guess at what had been set up between the house and the barn, in a little room on the porch. Yes, a fully equipped cobblery, with a new cobbler's bench and every cobbling tool imaginable.

Then old Peter Neufeld sat himself down on that cobbler's bench and made himself good and comfortable. Then he picked up the hammer, filled his mouth with nails and began to drive them experimentally into the heel of an old boot. And then he set the sewing machine into motion and then he pounded some more nails, and soon he was cobbling and sewing as if his snot had caught fire. And suddenly all five Neufeld sons and half a dozen wee Neufelds and also Agatha and to other daughters-in-law burst open into "Often in the Circle of My Beloved."

Well, you might say time stopped, and then time reversed, and then it started galloping backwards. Old Neufeld looked over his glasses and then he looked through them, and then he had just a thing or two to say. About how he felt pretty comfortable, about how he felt all right in this new home he was in, not too bad, really, not too bad at all. And Neufeld sewed and he sang a little more, and then he sang and he sewed. And now and then he hammered in a few more little nails and smiled.

De Dokta säd...

Auls etj eenjefäah tien Joah jinja wea auls Peeta Pota Wiens nu ess, wea daut doktre enn daut krank senne noch nijch mood. Easchtens haud wie nijch Tiet schaubijch too senne, oba measchtens wiels wie ons daut nijch leiste kunne. Wann eena krank wea—enn daut wea je dann measchtens Kopprietinj enn meist emma bie de Frulied—tjreajch hee, oba measchtens see, een Aspirin, ooda wann dem Betroffenen de Buck weeh deed, tjreaje de Kranke Aulpentjreita. Haud hee sijch jestatt, dann wea eene Buddel Wundaeelj aune Reaj, enn wann eenem de Hauls weeh deed, dann word eene woame, naute Stremp, verhäa jewosche, eenem ommen Gorjel jedronselt enn dem Weehgauljen too Bad jeschetjcht. Wann de Krankheit sijch lenja auls twee Doag opphilt, word jebät.

Joh, daut gauf uck noch een poah aundre Meddel, soo auls bie miene Taunte Marie, dee sijch Blootiele satte leeht, enn wann dee sijch voll Bloot jelutscht haude, weare de Iele vejneajcht enn drall, enn Taunte Marie koasch enn munta. Bie Peeta, aulso Arbuse, Klosses, worde oppem Menscheridje uck Tjapp jesat, oba wiels dee wieda auf wohnde, woa etj mett junt vondoag nijch doahan gohne, omm daut nohda too unjaseatje.

Oh joh, enn dann wea je noch mien breedajemeendscha Grootvoda, dee Predja, dee emma straum aunjetrocke wea, enn niemols nijch oabeide deed. Mien Voda gauf ahm eenmol eenen Spodem enn eene dreetinjsche Fortj, hee sull entweda Heikepitze moake, ooda Eadschocke satte. De oola Heilja säd, hee wudd daut jearn doohne, oba hee kunn sijch nijch betje, wiels hee haud mol aus Tjind eenen Noagel oppjeschluckt, enn de spetjcht ahm seea, wann hee sijch betje deed.

What the doctor said

When I was a kid being sick was not yet much in vogue and mostly so because you couldn't afford it. And if you were sick, generally a headache, and mostly known to womenfolk, then you got an aspirin; if the patient suffered from a stomach ache, it was time for a schluck or two of Alpenkräuter, herbal medicine, alcohol based. If the afflicted had sustained a bruise, a bottle of Wonder Oil came in handy, and if you suffered from a throat ache, a warm, wet sock, previously laundered, was wrapped around the human anatomy between head and body and the "work avoider" was dispatched to bed. If the illness lasted longer than three days, a round of prayer was due.

Come to think of it, there were also other varieties of folk medications practiced. My Aunt Marie had leeches applied and when these were rounded and fat and happily full with her blood they were removed by shaking salt on them, then Auntie was up and around in a jiffy and bossy to boot. At the Peter Klassen family, meaning the Arbuse (Watermelon) Klassens, suction cups were placed on the human back but since they lived a good six miles away, we will not take time to explore the details of the case today.

Speaking of illnesses and sickness and what not all… my grandfather of Mennonite Brethren persuasion comes to mind. He was a preacher of, and to that select fold, and he was always dressed in a suit and tie and never did a lick of work that I can remember. My father once handed him a spade and a three tined fork and he was meant to mound hay for drying or plant potatoes. The holy senior said he would do both gladly but he

113

Na joh, oba soo langsom bestunde de Frulied bie ons noh Wienepetj tweemol daut Joah too foahre enn rejchtijch too doktre. See fuahre dann entweda noh Dokta Kolja Niefeld, ooda noh Dokta Heinrich Ölkers, dee beid Dietsch kunne, enn beid emm Boyd Building äahre Tange enn Spretze reed lidje haude.

Entweda jinje de Frulied noh eenem von disse Beid oba nijch noh aule twee, wiels donn word noch nijch hanennhäa jedoktat. Wäa strenj enn frohm wea, jintj noh Dokta Niefeld, wiels hee een Brooda wea, enn wea daut mett dem Dietsch-senne dolla hild, jintjch noh Dokta Ölkers, dee bloß Huagdietsch räd, oba dem 'ett strauma enn oppjeriemda sach, wann uck jesajcht word, daut hee aul mol eenen Schnaups jedrunke haud.

Na joh, wann daut nohm Dokta foahre soowiet wea, aulso tweemol daut Joah, dann socht de jeweilja Maun fief Dohla, en gauf siene Fru daut Jeld, woabie ahm de Henj enn de Stemm flautade, wiels ahm den Aufscheed von dem grooten Klompe Jeld soo weeh deed, enn donn troffe sijch de Jasch Klosche, dee Kooltje haud, enn de Henritj Peetascha, dee Zucka haud, de Tjnals Niefeldsche, dee meist aules weeh deed, enn de Doft Appsche, dee mett äahre Kraumpodre daut drock haud, enn de Henritj Ungasche, dee sijch äwa pienjet Hoatkloppre bekloagt. Miene Taunte Marie fuah nijch meea nohm Dokta, wiels hee haud jesajcht, see wea väl too drugglijch, enn sull aufnehme. See haud jesajcht, hee sull ahr leewa de Gaulesteena aufnehme, dee weens twalw Pund wuage, enn see wudd dann noh de Operation weinja auls tweehundat Pund oppe Wijchschohl brinje.

Na joh, dee kranke Ladies kaume en Jnodefeld toop enn wachte opp Krohne Bearnd, dee eene stohtsche Koah haud, enn dann kunn de groote Reis noh Wienipetj loos gohne.

Diss Bearnd nauhm een Dohla, de Dokta tjreajcht dree Dohla, enn een Dohla nauhm jiede Fru mett toom veprasse.

114

had accidentally swallowed a nail as a child back in the Old Country and try as he might, stooping or bending was out of the question ever since.

Well, time and progress imposes its own set of rules and so the womenfolk of our neighbourhood insisted that they wanted to do some proper doctoring twice a year in Winnipeg. To that end they visited either Dr Kolja Neufeld or Dr Heinrich Ölkers, who both knew German, and with both having medical utensils, pliers and needles at the ready in their offices in the Boyd Building of Winnipeg.

The women of our immediate area consulted one or the other but not both since doctoring back and forth was not yet a TV hobby. If you were strict of faith and given to piety, you went to Dr Neufeld, because he was one of the Brethren; if you wanted to keep up your German ways and language you consulted Dr Ölkers, who spoke High German, and who came well dressed and dignified in looks and manners even if it was claimed that he had once been seen to have had a strong drink.

When the time came for a doctoral visit twice a year, the respective husband searched around for the necessary five dollars which he handed to his wife during which transaction his voice and his hands trembled since bidding farewell from such a tidy sum of cash hurt his hands, his heart and his billfold. Then the women, consisting of Mrs Jake Klassen, who was colicky, Mrs Henry Peters who had diabetes, Mrs Cornelius Neufeld who had most every illness then known, Mrs David Epp who was busily being ill with varicose veins and Mrs Henry Unger who suffered from a rapid heart beat, assembled. My Aunt Marie no longer doctored because Dr Ölkers had determined that she was too simply too stout and ought to reduce before he would get on with treating her maladies. To which she replied, he should rather get on with removing her gall stones which would reduce her weight by a

Eenfach toom vequose, soo auls ahn daut aul emma soo scheen jintjch, head etj saje.daut jintj Joahrelang soo, eenjefäah noh de Melodie: "De Medizin stintjcht enn schrinjt, oba halpe deit se."

Enn waut besondasch wijchtijch wea, daut de Frulied nohm Doktre enn biem nohhus fuahre sijch dann vetalde, waut de Dokta bie ahn aules jefunge enn jesajcht haud. Enn daut jemeensaume Uadeel wea een seea eenfachet: "Dee Dokta säd, hee haud soo waut Schlemmet auls waut mie schoht, noch niemols nijch verhäa jeseehne."

Krohne Bearnd haud de Jungess eenmol vetald, dee Frulied puchte jrohdentoo, wea aum kranksten wea, enn worde sijch maunjchmol enne Koah bie ahm doll, wem daut measchte schohd. Jeweehnlijch, säd Bearnd, wea daut de Tjnals Niefeldsche, wiels see haud daut dollste unjaweajess biem Nohusfoahre jehielt, enn doabie de aundre Frues ähren Bruch een bestje jewese, enn uck een Strieptje Kraumpoda. Butadem haud see eenmol unjawäajess äahre Haundtausch soo meea volljekotzt. Aulso wea see weens een Joah de Champion emm Kranksenne.

Wäa opp de Idee kaum weet etj nijch, enn woll uck tjeen aundra. Etj wudd daut oba de Jeat Dertjsche von Steinbach tootrue, wiels dee kaum opp schnorrje Idee, enn wea uck heiwtänsch jenuag, äahre Meenung von sijch too jäwe.

Jenuag, eenmol auls Krohne Bearnd de Frulied aula biem Eatons Stooah, soo auls jeweehnlijch aufjelod haud, wea uck de Obraum Krohnsche mett, enn dee wea aul een bät modern, ooda weltlijch soo auls se vondoagdendach doatoo saje. See haud dee aundre Ladies vetalt, daut wann eena sijch een bett tweemol daut Joah mol scheen bie Eatons em Grillroom saut aut, holp daut kratjcht soo väl, auls nohm Dokta too gohne. "Spoat junt daut Jeld," haud see jesajcht, "enn well'we daut mol dropaun kohme lohte. Onse Manna brucke doavon nuscht nijch too weete, enn, butadem wudd mie daut nuscht nijch

116

good twelve pounds after which she would qualify for medical attention, weighing less than two hundred pounds.

All these sick ladies assembled in Gnadenfeld awaiting the arrival of Ben Krahn who owned a stately car and shortly the trip to Winnipeg could start.

Ben charged them a dollar, the doctor got three, and each lady took an extra dollar along just for the joy of squandering it, as has always been their custom, their husbands claimed.

This went on for years on end with the melody in common being, "The medication prescribed may well stink and sting, but shortly all its praises you will sing."

An important part of the routine was that on the way home the women were much engaged in comparing notes as to what the doctor had all found wrong with them. The common denominator of medical findings generally concluded with, "The doctor said that he had yet to see a condition as serious as my affliction; he had never seen the likes of my suffering."

Ben Krahn once told us boys that the lamentations by these doctoring women and the bragging rights as to who was sickest bordered on competition. "Generally," said Ben, "it was Mrs Cornelius Neufeld who had the most numerous of serious ailments to report; she cried loudest on her way home, and had even shown the other woman a little sample of her hernia, and also an inch of her varicosity. And during all the weeping and wailing she had pretty well puked her purse full to the brim; so she was the champion of the sick this time around."

As to who arrived at the idea yet to be presented, I do not know, but I wouldn't put it past Mrs Gerhard Derksen from Steinbach since she was given to unconventional ideas and was also forward enough to express wayward intent.

Whatever, once Ben had unloaded his family of the afflicted at the Eaton's Store in Winnipeg as usual; Mrs Nettie Krahn was also along this time and she liked things modern, or worldly, as they now call it. And it was this Nettie who had told

wundre, wann soo eene scheene Brezhauj eenem nijch sogoa bäta deit auls eegol nohm Dokta too wanke."

See leete sijch äwarede, enn jinje aulatoop doahan.

Na joh, enn wea saut doa bie Eatons emm Grillroom? Tjeen aundra auls de Reisepredja Wellem Faultj, dee de Mensche räjelmässijch de Sind utdreef, enn doafäa kollatjchte deed, auls enn Jrienthol ooda sesst woa enn gaunz Kanada. Faultj haud aum Desch eene Daum mett eenen oppjeweppten Hoot oppem Kopp, enn mett eenem tjlienen Finja, dee kruse Kullasch enne Loft mohld.

"Von Sind woare de twee woll uck nijch väl too vetalle habe," säd de Krohnsche. Auls see aun dem Desch vebiejinje, red Predja Faultj mett eenmol zimlijch lud, enn seea vetieft, von dem Kloageleed Jeremiah, enn hee wea mett siene Jemeinde-schwesta soo em Toch, daut hee de jrientholsche enn jnodefeldsche Frulied nijch mol bejreest, joh nijch eenmol sach. Ooda nijch seehne wull, wäaweet?

De Ladies bestalde sijch jieda fe twee Dohla enn tien Cent een scheenet Schmoasel, enn daut schmatjcht ahn vetrafflijch. Mett eenmol, auls see noch jieda een Schiewtje Läpelkost too sijch nauhme, heade see aum Nohbadesch Dietsch rede. Na, woo ess dann soowaut mäajlijch, dochte see sijch, enn soo wiet von Tus, oba soo scheen tusijch, auls see doa Dokta Kolja Niefeld enn Dokta Heinrich Ölkers sage, dee sogoa een Glaus Wien toom Äte drunke. De Ladies wulle sijch noch ducke, oba daut jletjcht ahn nijch; de Doktasch kaume opp ahn too, enn bejreeste ahn soo frindlijch, auls wann se jrohds aulatoop noh dartijch Joah ut Russlaund utjetjnäpe weare, enn toom easchten Mol äah Frindschauft bejreeste.

Eea Krohne Bearnd ahn Klock fiew bie Eatons em Waiting Room oppicke kaum, haud de Obraum Krohnsche eene Buddel Melissengeist von dem äwajebläwnen Jeld jekofft, enn enn fief tjliene ladje Buddle den Jeist enjedeelt, doamett see Tus doch bewiese kunne, woo seea see aulatoop jedoktat haude.

118

the other ladies that if they were to go for a good meal or two each year at the Grillroom at Eaton's it was just as good for you, if not better, than to visit the doctor. "Save your doctor bill" she had said, "and let's just risk it. Our husbands at home need not get wind of this little adventure, and, I would not be the least bit surprised if a good little banquet on the sly would do us more good than all this doctoring around."

The whole lot was easily persuaded to do just that and they followed the Lady Whether Bell.

They had barely entered the stately Grillroom when they were in for their first surprise. None other than the itinerant minister/cum evangelist William Falk of no fixed address, but who regularly excised sins for hire and cash here, there and everywhere and anywhere in the land was holding forth to a stylish lady who wore a feathered frilled hat at a cocky stance and had her pinkie execute curlicues in the air above a choice table.

"I wonder what manner of sin needs discussing," remarked Nettie Krahn, as the ladies of healing intent passed softly by the pastoral table. When they briefly were in ear shot while en route, Pastor Falk spoke animatedly of the Prophet Jeremiah and he was so much into the lament of things that he paid his last week's church visitors from Grünthal no heed, deliberate or not.

The ladies were assigned a choice table and everyone of them ordered a choice morsel for two dollars and ten cents, and speak of good! Then suddenly, when they were even into a little dish of dessert, they heard German spoken at a neighbouring table. Now how is such a thing possible? So far from home and yet so homey as they heard Dr Kolja Neufeld and Dr Heinrich Ölkers in conversation not five feet away with the two doctors even enjoying a glass of wine with their lunch. The ladies went into the ducking mode but too late: the good doctors came their way and extended the most cordial of greetings, almost

Auls Bearnd daut oppfoll, woo scheen jesund enn utjelohte siene Passazheare vondoag weare, froag hee: "Na, waut säd de Dokta vondoag?"

"Hee säd, hee haud sowaut noch niemols nijch jeseehne!"

as if they had not seen each other for thirty years after all having fled from Russia in a dark and stormy night.

Before Ben Krahn came to fetch the lot from the Eaton's Waiting Room, Nettie Krahn had purchased a small bottle of Spirits of Melissa from the leftover money and distributed it into five vials so that they could show and tell at home how busily they had doctored today.

When Ben Krahn noticed just how well his passengers today looked and felt and talked, he asked his passengers, now, en route, "*Na*, what did they doctor say today?"

"The doctor said, he had never not seen anything like today!"

Gauspelle

Auls etj Oohmtje Wellem Leewe toom easchten mol too seehne tjreajch kunn etj jrods afens de Kaup vom Groffbrot auleen, enn ohne em Koffe em Schatel too ducke, biete. Leaje, aulso flunkre ooda bleiwe kunn etj noch nijch gaunz, wiels etj haud daut aul dreemol jeproowd, word doabie oba jiedesmol root, enn de Lied lachte mie ut. Daut diead oba nijch lang enn dann kunn etj daut uck aul meist soo goot auls een Diakoon, nohdem hee daut Jeld em Kolletjtetalla auleen jetald haud.

Oba tridj noh Oohmtje Wellem Leewe. Wann wie een Mennonietischet Oolet Testament haude, aulso schmock opp Plautdietsch jeschräwe, dann wudd Oohmtje Leewe doa eenjefäah em Dredden Kapitel stohne. Oba wie habe noch emma nijch soohn Testament, oba wann de Tjoatjemanna mol de rejchtje Offenbarung tjriee, dann tjenne see mie saje, etj saul daut schriewe, enn daut wudd dann uck aul dit Joah unjrem Wiehnachtsboom too finje senne. Aulso, bitte!

Oohmtje Wellem Leewe saut enne knaupe Tiet, aum Zoagelenj vonne Groote Depression aulso, foaken, eajentlijch jieden Dach, enn Winnipeg bie Eatons em Waiting Room enn vetald doa Jeschijchte, enn reet Resse, ooda hee dreef doa Jeschafte. Doa weare dann emma soo väl Mensche omm ahm auls bie eene gotelje Schwienstjast, enn horjchte too ooda schnackte opp.

Wann eena Oohmtje Leewe mol gaunz kort beschriewe sull dann wudd eena saje motte, sien Jesejchtsutdruck enn uck sien Tjarpa haude jrods: "Doch nijch! Mensch, waut du nijch sajchst?" jesajcht. Aulso, ahm sach'et emma, soo auls wann hee sijch selwst jrods daut Staune biejebrocht haud.

Butadem wea hee oba uck polietsch. Hee jintjch mett dit enn jant soo omm auls mien Groospau, dee Prädja mett siene Peppermint Candies. Dee vedeeld dee Oola eenmol de Wäatj wann etj seea

Gas Pain Pills

When I first met Mr William Loewen, I was just at that stage of growing up, where I managed to chew the crust of dark bread on my own. Another area of growing up is mastering the lie, the fib, the deception. This came easily enough since role models abound. And yet, I had not mastered a decent fib although I had already tried it three times, but still blushed furiously at the failed effort.

But back to Mr William Loewen. If we had a Mennonite Old Testament, nicely written in Plautdietsch, Mr Loewen would be written up on in the third chapter, and if our churchmen ever receive the proper Revelation, and commission me, I will have the book under the tree come next Christmas.

During the tail end of the Great Depression, Mr William Loewen frequently was to be seen in Winnipeg at Eaton's in the Waiting Room telling tales, or swinging little business deals. People came to listen to him; to be seen in his presence was a social ritual. If I were to briefly describe him, I would conclude that his facial expression, and his portly corpus and quick smile for that matter, revealed, "No kidding, man, is that really true?" or like astonishment. In short, he looked like the element of total, sudden and happy surprise.

Also, he possessed the political touch of contagious, slightly mischievous, stealth. In exercising this attribute, he reminded me of my grandfather, the minister with peppermint candies in his pockets. Both Grandpa, Preacher Krus and Hell-Raiser and all in one person and my personal Holy Trinity, and Mr. Loewen, had in common with our Father in Heaven that they

schmock jewese wea. Oba wanneea hee soohne Candy enn siene
Fupp finje wudd wisst tjeena. Hee säd emma, hee jintjch mett dee
Candy-Vedeelarie omm soo auls de leewa Gott mette
Entretjchung: Tjeena wisst jeneiw, wann de leewa Gott siene Tjinja
hohle kohme wudd, enn wea too de uterlesde Famielje jehead, oba
eent wisst de leewa Gott, Groospau Krus enn uck etj: wie musste
dach enn Nacht schmock senne wann wie em Himmel kohme
wulle, enn wie musste emma reine Unjabetjze enn een reinen
Hauls enn Ohre habe. Sesst wudd wie opplatzt hiea sette bliewe,
enn dann wear'et opp Tiet enn Eewijchtjeit too loht, oba too loht!

Daut aundre, waut Wellem Leewe, Groospau Kus enn de leewa
Gott soo eenjemohte jemeinsaum haude, ess daut blooß de leewa
Gott daut emma drock haud; hee haud emma enn aulewäje de
Henj voll, enn wea de Tiet äwa oppe Stroht.

Wellem Leewe wea mea een blue collar Oabeide, während
Groospau Krus auls Tjind mol eenen Noagel oppjeschluckt haud,
säd hee, enn ahm daut Betje von donn aun schwoa foll. Butadem
säd hee, hee schoond sich fe de Eewijchtjeit, enn daut hab etj
foaken jenuag jeseehne, omm ahm daut too jleewe. Enn doatoo
wea hee emma schmock aunjetrocke, easchtens wiels hee stets enn
stendijch mett'e Entrejung rätjend, enn tweedens wea hee
"Brooda" enn ahm stund soomett emma een extra Strämel too,
"eene extra Wurst" saje de Dietsche doatoo, enn daut wea ahm uck
lenjdhan auntooseehne; Groospau Krus wea jlei enn rund enn
tjeeneswäjess muckrijch.

Enn noch eent: Wellem Leewe haud een schmocken Schneizat
tweschen Tjenn enn Uage, Groospau Krus, druag eenen seea
schmiedjet Boatje, woohne see eene "Goatee" enn opp Plautdietsch
een Puzhel ooda Kozzeboat nanne, während de leewa Gott eenen
straumen, vollen Rabbinaboat druag.

Von dee dree Erwähnde, leet blooß Wellem Leewe sich emma enn
jearn betohle; dee leewa Gott enn Groospau Krus haude measchtens dee Tjnippsbiedels nich mett, oba leete sich jearn feehde.

Joh, oba Oohmtje Leewe well nu opplatzt aul een Jeschaft moake,
enn wann wie nijch doabie sent, dann vesiem wie daut.

Etj haud mie jrods aun ahm raunjeschlitjcht auls een jewessa
Joakob Jeatze ut Manitou Oohm Wellem Leewe een bät de Glauje

held the authority, indeed represented a personal mystery of the seen and the unseen, things hoped for and expecting that you better be better than good.

Joh, but Mr Loewen is about to execute a bit of business and if we don't hurry to his presence right now we might miss out on a grand occasion.

I had just completed my worming way in his direction when a certain Jacob Goertzen from Manitou was already reading a brief chapter of the Riot Act to Mr Loewen in the Eaton's Waiting Room. It was obvious to all that Goertzen had come with a red head, animatedly eager as an evangelist in full swing, while Mr Loewen tried with many gestures to pacify this unruly, slightly wild man and customer.

What caused this minor kerfuffle in a miniature peppermint tea cup, you and all others ask? As already mentioned, those were hard economic times and since we had almost no politicians who daily lied and exaggerated and played loosey-goosey with the truth, we were not accustomed to anything but straight talk and straighter tactics. If anyone missed the mark of truth by even a trifle, people got properly excited.

Back to the action. Mr William Loewen possessed a bit of his very own laboratory in the back part of his residence on William Avenue and it was there, in his secret chambers, biblically speaking, that he had invented a pill which, popped into the gas tank of a car, that car, so equipped, would double or triple its mileage every time. No sweat. And of this kind of pill Mr Loewen had manufactured more than a thousand, and people far and wide swore to its efficacy. A little bag of these wonder pills cost a dollar, one to a customer, and if you strictly followed directions and inserted Mr Loewen's wonder pill into a full tank of gas and according to directions, whether you lived in Steinbach, Grünthal or Manitou, then your car, be it a Chevy, Dodge, Essex or a Ford would double its mileage without fail.

jelest haud. Jeatze haud eenen rooden Kopp, enn wea soo iewrijch auls een Erwatjungspredja, enn Oohmtje Leewe vesocht ahm mett Henj enn Feet enn väl Jedohnte too beschwijchtje. Aulatoop erinnad mie daut aun eenen judschen Besoa enn Elloag, enn wiels etj noch niemols doabie jewast ooda jewese wea, wisst etj je omm soo bäta, woo daut doa toojeiht. Waut wea? Soo langsom word mie de gaunze Loag dietlijch: Wiels, soo's jesajcht, daut too dee Tiet schwoare Tiede weare, enn wie donn noch lang nijch soo väl Polietitja haude, dee ons de Lunze dach enn Nacht volluage, enn aules äwamorje tooschetjch halpe wudde, foll daut noch dolla opp, wann een Mensch mol jeloage haud. Aulso: waut wea? Oohmtje Wellem Leewe haud bie sijch Tus enne stelle Kohma oppe William Avenue, im stillen Kämmerlein, omm biblisch too bliewe, eene Pell utjefunge, dee, wann eena dee enne Gaustank bie de Koah nennläd, de Koah twee bee dreemol soo wiet foahre leet. Enn von disse Sort Pelle haud Oohmtje Leewe nu aul äwa dusend Stetjch vekofft, enn de Mensche weare wiet enn breet seea toofräd. Een Konwart Gauspelle kost een Dohlah, enn wann eena eene Pell schmock de Räjel enn Väaschreft noh, Tus, saj wie mol enn Steinbach, Jrienthol ooda Manitou verrem loosfoahre enne Tank schoof, dann fuah de Koah, auls Essex, Chevy ooda uck Fuurd tweemol see wiet auls ohne. Joh, oba woarom wea dann Joakob Jeatze dem Wellem Leewe soo doll, enn woarom word hee doa ver een vollen Waiting Room bie Eatons soo fuchtijch? Seea eenfach: Wiels Joakob Jeatze een mennischa rachullja Jietsknubbel wea, haud hee Tus enn Manitou fuats dree Pelle enne volle Tank nennjestoppt, wiels dree dochwoll meea veschlohne wudde auls eene. Enn kratjcht soo wear'ett dann uck jekohme, enn nu wea Jeatze seea doll; Hee haud tweschen Manitou enn Winnipeg fief bett sass Mol stellhoohle musst, wiels ahm de Gaustank emma wada äwarand. "Daut tjemmt von diene eajne Dommheit," säd Oohmtje Leewe, "enn doawäjen jelt miene money-back Garantie nijch. Audee! Reis jletjlijch!" Enn wajch wear'a.

126

Jacob Goertzen was one of those ever present Mennonite men of avarice and greed, and tight-fisted to boot, he had, at home in Manitou, stuffed three pills or even more into his gas tank before taking off, expecting, obviously, a triple or more performance run. And the expected had transpired without fail, meaning great failure, or so he claimed. And that's why Goertzen was so damn mad. On his way to the big city of Winnipeg from Manitou, he had had to stop five or six times since his gas tank constantly kept overflowing and now he demanded his money back.

"You have only your own stupidity and greed to blame," said Mr Loewen, "you did not follow my explicit directions and so my money back guarantee does not apply! Goodbye! Have a good trip!"

Daut Bruttjleed

Onkel Tjnals wea Elloaga. Enn soo's de measchte Elloaga nu mol weare enn send, wea hee een läwendja enn lostja Tjeadel, enn nijch oppet Mul jefolle. Aulnoch foaken jintj hee emm Darp han enn häa, enn maunjchmol weppt hee uck een bät mett de Scheestje. Joh, hee wea een oppjeriemda enn een utjelohtna Tjnäwel. "Een strauma Uchazhor," säde de Frulied, "een jleie Tjeadel," säde de Mäadtjess, "een prautsja Deffat," säde de Jungess.

Oba eenes Doages leet uck bie Onkel Tjnals daut Stolzeare noh; hee wea veleeft. Seea veleeft wea hee, enn nu trock hee de Flijchte een bät enn. Enn boold haud hee eene Brut. Enn waut fer'ne Brut!: Eene schmocke, lostje Buschtje met Vestaund enn Hoat. Enn Jemiet? Gaunze Spitjasch voll. Enn Uage? Gaunz Rußlaund speajeld sijch doabenne.

De Tiede weare schwoa enn hoat, enn de Woltje enn Rußlaung wulle nijch meea vetratje. Enn soo kaum'et, daut de Ellre von'ne Brut, Peeta Radakopps, sijch entschloote noh Kanada uttoowaundre. Onkel Tjnals wull noch een haulwet Joah enn Rußlaund bliewe; vleijcht word'et doch noch aulatoop bäta. Wann joh, wudd Jreeta, siene Brut tridjkohme, enn wann nijch, wudd hee noh Kanada kohme. Noh sass Moonat sull'et Tjast jäwe, hiea ooda doa… Woo schwoa soohn Aufscheet ess, kaun tjeena beschriewe. Wäarett erläwt haft, weet soo waut, wäarett nijch erläwt haft, woat daut uck nijch derjch Weada bejriepe.

Aum 23. August, 1928, wea de Dach jekohme, enn diss Dach bestemmd: Aufscheet nehme. Jreeta enn Tjnals weare stomm enn meist jelähmt—soo schwoa word ahn daut. "Audee, mien

The Bridal Gown

Uncle Cornelius was from Elloag (Kitschkass) on the Dnieper. Like most Elloaga were and are, he was a live wire and outgoing, bright and talkative. Young people of the villages walk the streets most summer evenings, others strut, with all showing their stuff, while the remaining swing their coattails with a little extra flair. "Pretty hot stuff, that young fellow," was the going opinion. "A handsome Uchazhor, quite a find, dentist and all," said the ladies. "An ostentatious cock pigeon" is what the masculine competition had to say.

Then one day Uncle Cornelius swaggering and strutting came to an end; he was in love. Indeed, very much in love as he pulled in his jaunty plumage to appear respectable. In short order he had a bride. And what a bride! Greta was a beautiful, lively lady, intelligent and with a heart, rare and giving. As for soul? By the binful. Her eyes? All of Mother Russia sparkled in their brilliance.

However, their happiness, indeed their very future was soon beset by clouds and this darkness persisted over all the land. Greta's father, Peter Redekopp, looked long and hard at the many horizons, both personal and political and decided that a move to Canada was the only solution. Uncle Cornelius decided to remain behind in Russia for another six months, maybe things would improve. If so, Greta, his bride, would return and if not, he would join them in Canada. In six months they were to be married, either here or there. How difficult the impending farewell was cannot be described; words fail. Those who have experienced the agony of separation know; those who have not, cannot be convinced into comprehension by the word.

Tjnals, vejat miene Uage nijch. Etj sie die goot." "Audee Jreeta,
nemm mien Hoat enn dit Packtje mett noh Kanada."

Enn Rußlaund jinje boold aule Lijchta ut, enn daut
Menschehoat leewad boold meea Angst als Leew, enn meea
Meßtrue auls Vetrue. Oba woa bleewe Tjnals enn Jreeta? Tjnals
haud een Plemenitj en Kanada enn dee vetald. Eascht wea hee
eene lange Tiet stell, oba eenes Owends noh Joahre, auls wie
toop enn Dietschlaund weare, vetald hee. "Intressaunt,
schnorrijch, schnoppijch, ooda waut uck emma, etj kaun disse
Jeschijcht nijch enn Kanada vetalle, oba hiea kaun etj nijch
senne, ohne dee too vetalle."

"Ons Onkel Tjnals," soo fong Jeat aun, "wea Tähnedokta.
Dee Doktarie haud hee enn Dietschlaund studeat, enn hee wull
vleijcht uck aul enn Dietschlaund bliewe, oba ahm fehld de
Stap, de Nippa, de Sonn enn siene Mensche, enn siene Sproak,"
säd hee. Enn soo fuah hee tridj noh Rußlaund, enn wea doa
Tähnedokta. Hee wea enn Elloag aulnoch een Dandy, soo's se
enn Kanada saje, oba eenes Doages veschwung hee platzlijch
von'ne Gaus. Jreeta äah Hoat haud ahm een Beentje jestalt, enn
nu wea hee bloß noch fe de Tookunft mett ahr enjestalt. Onkel
Tjnals docht kratjcht soo auls de measchte Menniste: daut de
Kommunismus mau een kortet Onnwada senne wudd. Oba
daut word meea, väl meea; Jreeta, siene Brut äah Voda, säd hee
trud dem polietischen Brode nijch, enn hee veleet mett
Famielje toop noh Kanada. De oole Radakopp haud aul enn
Rußlaund jesajcht: 'Dee woare mett ons opprieme, enn nijch
bloß wäajne Relijoon.' Dis Utsproak wea eene schwoare
Hypothek fe Radakopp, enn disse Belaustung naum hee mett
noh Kanada. De Menniste enn Kanada säde, hee wea
Kommunist, ooda meist eena, oba see säde daut nijch too ahm
sonda unja sijch. Daut uck de Eppaschte disse Aunsejcht
weare, word Radakopp enn, auls hee mett siene Famielje toop
sijch de mennische Jemeend aunschlute wull. 'Eacht betjanne,
eascht aules betjanne', word von ahm velangt. 'Etj hab mie enn

On August 23, 1928 the day had come and this day determined: Farewell. Greta and Cornelius were dumb, paralyzed with the grief of parting. "Goodbye, my dear Cornelius, do not forget my eyes. I love you." "Farewell, Greta, and take this parcel along to Canada."

Shortly the lights in Russia went out and did not come back on again for another 17 years. Everywhere there was more fear than love, more suspicion than trust.

And as for Cornelius and Greta?

Cornelius had a nephew in Canada and he started talking. Initially, he chose to be silent on the matter, but one evening when we were in Germany together he commenced his reverie, "Strange, indeed puzzling, or whatever, I was never able to tell this tale in Canada while here I can do no other but to reveal this enigmatic tale."

"Our Uncle Cornelius," George launched the telling, "was a dentist. He had learned his profession in Germany and had been tempted to stay there but then, he missed the steppes, the Dnieper, the angle of the sun, and his people. And the language of his people, the *Muttersprache*. He had been a bit of a dandy in Elloag, as they call such elegant rovers in Canada, but one day he disappeared from the village street. Greta's heart had tripped him up and as of that hour his every thought and action revolved around Greta and a future with her. His very being had transformed into two souls in one body.

Uncle Cornelius thinking was similar to the thinking of the majority of Mennonites: Communism was but a fleeting dark cloud, shortly to disperse. But things turned out very differently and with much more permanence. The cauldron of radical change had been brought to the boil and life itself was being rendered into a different form and essence. Greta's father stated that he no longer trusted the smell of things and so he decided to gather his round and depart for Canada. "They will clean up with us and our lot," Old Man Redekopp had stated "and not

Rußlaund nijch jebetjt, enn etj woa mie uck hiea nijch betje",
säd Radakopp, enn hee trock mett Famielje toop wajch. wajch.
Enne dietsche Jääjend em Siedwaste Saskatchewan, 'woa de
Preisse wohne,' säd hee, 'enn etj nehm aule Tjinja mett, uck
mien Popptje Jreeta. Enn miene Adrass? Dee weet de leewa
Gott. Aude!' Enn fuah auf.

Tjnals Thiesse, de Briegaum enn Tähnedokta enn Elloag,
word mett eenmol platzlijch enn, de Wääj, de Däare, enn de
Puate weare enn Rußlaund noh bute han too. Too, dijcht enn
vesiejeld. "Enn doamett basta!' säde de Russe. Oba hee saut enn
Elloag enn hohpt enn wacht, enn hee bangd sijch krank. Hee
wull noh Jreeta enn Kanada. Enn sien Läwe beweajd sijch
tweschne twee Polaritäte: Hohp enn Vetwiewlung. Mol haud
eene de Bowahaund, kort nohäa daut aundre. Maunjchmol
wea hee siene Sach sejcha, maunjchmol sach hee schwoat.; enn
soo jintj'et de Tiet äwa. Daut Jreeta ahm tru senne wudd, daut
säd ahm sien Hoat, oba woa see jebläwe wea, daut kunn ahm
tjeena saje… Han enn wada tjreajch hee opp Omwäaj eene
wietleftje Nohrejcht, oba daut wea uck aules. Breew kaume
nijch meea aun. Enn Jreeta? See wohnd doa tweschen
Liebenthal enn Rastatt enn wacht. Enn wacht. De oola
Radakopp word Manager von eenem tjlienen Jeträjd-Elewäta,
ess soo schluage see sijch schlajcht enn rajcht derjch. Jreeta
schreef jiede Wäatj, enn see sad Bloome fe de Tjast enn eene
Myrte fe äähren Brutkraunz. Enn Oppjoah wada, enn donn
noch eenmol… Woo foaken Jreeta ääh Bruttjleed woll aunjetrocke haft—joh, daut's waut doa emm Aufscheetsjeschentj,
emm Packtje wea—weet woll tjeena."

Onkel Tjnals sien Plemenitj head nu opp too vetalle, hee wea
oppjestohne, enn een bät rutjegohne, oba nu kaum hee tridj.
Wie saute noch emma enne Schentj, Niedlingsmühle heet dee,
enn hee vetald wieda. "Dann kaum enn Rußlaund wada eene
Hungaschnoot, enn donn worde aule Famielje enne Ukraine
veräte enn donn gauf'et Tjrijch. Enn nu kaume de Dietsche

only on account of our religion." This statement was shortly to become Redekopp's mortgage, which he took along to Canada. The Mennonites in Canada claimed he was a Communist, or as good as one but, of course, like all things political, this was meant as a handful of grist in an indeterminate mill spoken in a silence of raised eyebrow implications. The fact that such was also the opinion of the Mennonite Establishment became obvious when Redekopp applied for membership in a Mennonite church in his new home in Canada. "First, you fess up, and every detail of it" was the demand. "I never bent to authority in Russia and I am not about to do so now," Redekopp answered, and shortly he moved on and further west, family and all. They located in southwestern Saskatchewan, close to the Great Sandhills, where a sprawling German settlement offered home and new hope, "where the Prussians live," he said, "and I am taking along my kids, including my favourite pretty daughter doll, Greta. And as for my address? It is known to our Father in heaven. Goodbye!" And then he up and left.

Our Uncle Cornelius, the dentist bridegroom in Elloag, was shortly to discover that all roads, all doors, and all exits in Russia were closed to the outside. Closed, shut and sealed. "And that's that!" said the Russians. And he was sitting in Elloag, while he hoped and waited and longed for his bride until sick. His life vacillated between hope and despair. At times hope prevailed, then, again, despair. Sometimes he was sure of his lot, other times he doubted his every decision, and this is how his life went. His was certain of Greta's faithfulness, of that he had no doubt, but as to where she was? No one could provide a reassuring answer... Occasionally, a sparse roundabout rumors came in the air but that was all. However, no letters arrived, no reliable word at to Greta's whereabouts reached him.

Fact is the Redekopps had settled between Liebenthal and Rastatt where Old Man Redekopp managed a grain elevator and they managed after a fashion. Greta wrote her Cornelius every

133

bett enne Ukraine nenn. De dietsche Wehrmacht haud biem Tähnedokta Tjnals Thiesse äah Hauptquateea enjerejcht. De Jrind weare eenfach: Onkel Tjnals haud een grootet Hus, enn hee tjand waut von'ne Medizin, enn hee kunn goot Dietsch, enn butadem wea hee een veninftja Mensch. Dee Tjrijch schluag aune '43 tridjaun, enn eenen Owend säd de dietscha Major too Thiesse emm Vetrue, 'wie woare ons morje tridjtratje enn äwrem Nippa mascheare, enn eene niee Stalung betratje. Saj diene baste Frind, see tjenne mettkohme, Enn du uck. Morje Klock tien ess daut sowiet. Wäa bett dann nijch äwre Bridj ess, dee blifft hia, wiels de Nippabridj woat nohm latzten Soldoht jesprenjt. De Russe send dijchtbie.'

Wada jintj mien Berejchta enn Vada Jeat een bät wajch, wada ohnd etj Onheel. Hee kaum boold tridj, bestald sijch een Glaus Moot enn vetald wieda. Nauhm eenen gooden Schluck—etj nauhm twee—enn vetald wieda.

"Onkel Tjnals wull den gaunzen Owend rut, wiels hee noch waut drinjedet too beschetje haud, oba de dietsche Offiziea haud noch väl too berede, enn too doohne, enn doabie musst Onkel Tjnals ahm too Haund gohne. Enn soo vejintj dee Owend enn een Deel von'ne Nacht. Vleijcht zemorjess… Mett de Dietsche mettgohne? Daut wea beschlohtne Sach. Omm haulf näjen fonge de Dietsche aun äwrew Bridj sijch tridjtootratje; veadel noh näjen weare de latzte Offiziere enn Soldohte wajch. Verhäa porrde see enn foddade Onkel Tjnals opp, hee sull sijch spoode. Auls see aula fuat weare, jintj Onkel Tjnals mett eenem Spodem emm Oaftgoade nenn, besonn sijch eene Stootstje, enn donn jintj hee jlitjch noh eenem Aupelboom opptoo, enn fong aun too growe auls een Willa. Eascht fluage de Soode, dann de Ead, enn dann een bätje Grund. Enn je dolla hee groof, je dolla vejintj de Tiet. Daut Loch word jrata, de Tiet doajäjen tjarta. Klock tien wearet vebie, haude dee Offiziere jesajcht, dann word de Bridj jesprenjt.

week and she planted flowers for the wedding to be, and lovingly tended a myrtle plant for her bridal wreath. She repeated the planting of the flowers of hope with every spring. And again next year, and then again. As to how often she tried on her wedding dress,—that is what the parcel Cornelius had presented her at their farewell contained—is something known to no one.

Uncle Cornelius's nephew halted his tale and had gone out for a spell to stretch his legs but now he returned. We were still in the *Niedlingsmühle*, a cosy den of hospitality, and he resumed the telling of the tale. "Then famine struck all of Russia with every family in Ukraine being torn apart; then came the rumors of war, skirmishes of roving bands ensued and then a full scale war broke out. In 1942 the German Wehrmacht arrived in Ukraine and since Uncle Cornelius, the dentist, had the necessary, adequate house and home, the military headquarters established its command post in his premises. The reasons were simple: Uncle Cornelius knew his way around, he knew German and he was a bright and reasonable presence. In 1943 the war turned, and one late evening the German major informed Uncle Cornelius in confidence that a retreat was imminent and to that end a march across the Dnieper River bridge was necessary to assume a new position, to re-group. "Tell your best friends, that they can come along, and you, obviously, as well. Tomorrow at ten in the morning is the deadline. Anyone who is not across the bridge by then will remain behind because the bridge will be detonated after the crossing of the last man. The Russians are closing in on us."

My reporter again left and again I sensed gloom. He returned, ordered a glass of cheer and resumed his conversational track. He took a good swig and I took two while he reported.

"All evening long Uncle Cornelius wanted to depart the house since he had an urgent matter to attend to but the German officer had many matters yet to be discussed and urgencies to resolve at which our uncle had to assist him. And so, gradually

Tien ver tien haud Onkel Tjnals nu endlijch daut Jesochte jefunge. Waut? Goldresarwe toom Tähne blombeare lage doa emm leiwendjet Biedeltje unjrem Boom vestoake. Emmahan tien Pund Gold sulle nu noch schwind mett. Enn nu packt hee daut Gold schwind enn'en grooten Sack, woa hee uck reesche Tweeback fe unjaweajess benne haud, enn loos jintj'ett mett dem Biedel oppem Ridje noh de Bridj opptoo. Onkel Tjnals, soo säde see, haud jerannt auls de Jud enne lange Nacht, vleijcht noch stoatja. De Dietsche sage ahm kohme enn schreaje, soo's bloß Dietsche schriee tjenne: 'Spood die, Mensch, schwinda!' während de aundre 'Tridj, tridj!' schreaje.

Onkel Tjnals wea jrods oppe Bridj aunjokohme, auls de Sprenjstoff loosjintj. Hee dreid sijch omm, enn rannd tridjaun, soo word mie vetalt, oba auls hee sijch noch radde kunn, ooda auls de Russe ahm mett reesche Tweeback enn Golde fuats jeleewat jenohme habe? Wäa weet? Jenuag, Onkel Tjnals, ons Onkel Tjnals: "Er ward nicht mehr gesehen!"

Enn siene Brut Jreeta? Toop mett Onkel Tjnals sien Plemenitj, mien Vada Jeat aulso, fuah etj noch denselwjen Hoafst noh Siedwast Saskatchewan. Enn doa fruag wie, enn sochte, enn fruage wada. "Vleijcht eent von de dree ladje Hiesa, dijcht biem vefollnen Elewäta aune Bohn, aun de stelljelajde Stratj doa hinje emm Struck." Wie kaume doa aun: Aule Nohmes weare nu opp enjlisch ommjewatjselt worde, oba wie funge den Elewäta. De Fenstre weare twei, Schindle fehlde oppem Dack. De Jeträjdtrubb dreid emm Wind mol hia enn mol doa han, enn muak doabie soohn onheemeljet Jereisch. Dee Trubb knoad enn piepad enn knoad soo jetjwält, enn fong donn uck noch aun too jule, auls de Wind doa derjch blosd, daut ons grusled enn onmacklijch word. Wie haude Angst, oba wie wulle daut Jeheemnis lefte. "Sajcht doch waut jie weete," wull etj too aul daut Velohtnet saje, "vetallt mie doch von aul dee, woohne hiea jeoabeit, jelacht enn jehielt habe. Wiest mie doch dee Städe, woa see wohnde, enn woa see jehopt enn

136

the evening slipped into night. Possibly first thing in the morning…" To accompany the Germans was a foregone conclusion. At eight thirty the next morning, the Germans started their retreat on the bridge; by nine fifteen the last of the German officers and soldiers had departed. Already earlier they had insisted that our uncle get on with it. When the last soldier crossed the bridge of no return, Uncle Cornelius grabbed a spade, ran into his garden, hesitated a fraction, then made straight for an apple tree and set about digging like a dervish. First sods flew, than mounds of earth shot every which way and then a scoop of gravel or more. The more he dug, the less time he still had remaining. The size of the hole increased, with time left decreasing in direct proportion. Ten o'clock was the deadline, the officers had stated, then the bridge was to be blown up.

Ten to ten Uncle Cornelius had finally located what he searched for. Just what was it? Gold reserves for teeth fillings were deposited in a canvas bag hidden under that very tree. The exact amount came to exactly ten pounds and urgency was an ultimate dictate. He grabbed that sack, added it to the other bag of bun rusks on his bag pack for the trail ahead, and then he took off for the bridge on the river Dnieper. Uncle Cornelius, so eye witnesses later reported, had taken off like a sprinter, probably faster since he was widely known for his motoring skills. The Germans saw him thundering along and screamed as only Germans will scream, "Move, Mensch, go for it, on the double now!" while others yelled, "Back, too late! Back with you!"

Uncle Cornelius had just arrived on the bridge when the charge exploded. He whirled around in mid air and raced back, I was told, but whether he managed to escape or whether the Russians seized him with his bag of gold and toasted buns? Who knows? Uncle Cornelius, our Uncle Cornelius was not ever seen again.

jetwiewelt habe." Tjeene Auntwuat, nijch mol eene Echo. Nohm Elewäta-Besuch besocht wie aule dree ladje Hiesa, enn funge uck doa nuscht. Vleijcht enn jant, daut tweestockje Jebied doa hinje? Een Hus mett Leew jebut, enn mett eenem Goade, woa noch Dell enn een poah Bloome wild emm Oktoba wosse. Dee Schornsteen stund noch, oba daut Dack wea een bät toojekuakst. Wie jinje nenn, de Däah wea nijch toojeschlohte. Wie tjitjchte ons omm, funge oba nijch väl. Enne Tjäatj stund noch een oola Heat mett kruggelje Been, enn aune Waund hong noch een oola Kalenda von freajoah, enn emm enjebuhden Atjschaup wea een Eaton's Katalog, enn daut wea aules. Eene doodje Sproak wea hiea läwendijch.

"Wann du de Däa opmoakst, goh etj de Trap 'enopp." Jeat foot aune Däarejräp aun enn trock. Eascht stiepad sijch de Däah, see knoad enn wäahd sijch, oda donn leet see noh. Enn etj läd noh miene Wies loos… Oba mau eene Stoop. Enn donn hild platzlijch onse Welt eenen Uagenbletj den Odem aun: Aune Waund hinjre Däah hong een langet, wittet Tjleed mett Spetze enn Kruzheltjes. Een oolet Tjleed, oba njich aufjedroacht. Enn aum Kroage, unjre Spetze, stunde utjeneiht mett utjeplatjte bleiwe Sied, de Buakstowe "M. R. von C. T."

And Greta? That autumn when we got back from Germany Uncle Cornelius nephew and I went to Liebenthal. There we asked around and looked and then inquired again. "Possibly one of those three empty houses over there close to the dilapidated elevator next to the deserted stretch of spur line," an old-timer suggested. We arrived at the place. All the former names had given in to English translations but we managed to find the elevator. The windows were mainly broken and damaged shingles let in the sun. The grain spout turned and twisted in the wind, eerily moaning with each gust. It was enough to make you shudder, but we persisted. We were afraid, but we wanted to find out what had happened. "Tell us what you know," I appealed to everything gone and forlorn, "tell me of those who lived here, who worked here, who laughed and who wept. Show me the spot where they laboured and loved, there they hoped and despaired." No answer, not as much as an echo. After visiting the elevator, we headed for the three empty houses but found nothing. Possibly in that house further to the back, the two-storied dwelling? A house constructed with love and a garden with some last dill of the season and a few autumn flowers still alive in mid October. The chimney was still upright but the roof had caved in. We looked in, the door was unlocked. There was little of interest. In the kitchen stood an old stove with crooked little legs and on one wall hung an old calendar of yesteryear and an old Eaton's catalogue in a corner cupboard. That was all.

"Might try the upstairs," I suggested. Uncle Cornelius nephew gave a tug at the stairway door.

At first it wouldn't give. But then it did. And that's where we found it, on a hanger, grey with age. A long, white wedding dress, with lace and frills and beautiful puffed sleeves—old but not worn out. On the collar below the lace were some letters embroidered in blue silk thread. They read: "G. R. from C. T."

And that was all.

Eene rusche Stradivarius

Auls wie ons endlijch noh väle Joahre aune Eenenzastijch wada too seehne tjreaje, haud Ohmtje Wellem Boaje sijch erstaunlijch weinijch veendat. Hee wea een bät staumja enne Schimmedaunjäjend jeworde, enn siene Räd een bätje groffa jeworde, oba sesst wea hee gaunz de oola jebläwe. Etj bruckt ahm goanijch dentje halpe, daut hee mie noch eene Jeschijcht schuldijch wea; hee wisst daut. Enn hee fung uck fuats oppe Städ aun: daut wea aum Sinndach Morje oppe Tjoatjetrap em Schaute aun eenem heeten Dach.

"Daut wea noch enn Rußlaund, too dee Tiet aus'se ons aulewäaje bestreepte enn hinjret Lijcht feahde. Wann wie nijch soo dijcht bie de Tjoatj weare, wudd etj noch waut aundret auls 'bestreepe' saje, meend Boaje. Wie Menniste weare meet eenmol äwa Nacht too de Näaja em Laund jeworde, enn ons piesackte se lintjsch enn rajsch, enn dann uck noch een bät von hinje. Na, eenes Doages, auls mien jinjsta Onkel enn etj noh Peetaborjch fuahre, docht etj soo bie mie, eena sull bie aul daut Toakel, enn daut Derjchenaunda, doch een bätje too Jeld kohme.

"Etj haud mie daut kratjcht utjedocht, woo etj daut aunstalle wudd, enn doatoo liehd etj mie von mienem Schwoaga Johaun Konraud eene oole Fiddel, eea wie noh Peetaborjch fuahre.

"Mien Onkel Obraum, soo heet'a, kunn sien Wunda nijch lohte, waut etj mett dee oole Fiddel wull, oba etj säd nuscht, ooda etj buag auf. Oba aus hee unjawäajess wada fruag, waut daut mett dee Fiddel opp sijch haud, säd etj too ahm: 'Etj hab doch mien Deel vonne Foaht hieahan betohlt, saul etj nu noch extra fe de Stradivarius betohle?' Donn meend Onkel Obraum,

A Russian Stradivarius

When finally we were to meet again after many years in the year sixty-one, Uncle William Bergen had changed very little. He had become a bit more stocky in the bin area and his speech had lost whatever refinery it had ever had but other than that he had remained pretty well the same. I did not have to remind him that he still owed me a story; he knew that. And he started on the spot. Right then and there on the church steps on a hot day in the shade.

"It was still in Russia at the time when they started cheating us at every opportunity. If it weren't so close to the church I would tell you what they really did to us," he said. "We Mennonites had almost overnight become pariahs in the country and they let us have it left and right and then also a bit from the rear.

"Well, one day when my youngest uncle and I went to Petersburg I thought to myself, why not try to make a ruble or two from these ruffians.

"I had the plan all ready and to that end I had borrowed from my brother-in-law, Johan Konrad, a fiddle before we set out.

"My uncle Abraham, that was his name; well, this uncle really wanted to know what I was up to with the fiddle I had along. But I said little or nothing or I pretended to be lost in thought. But then when underway he asked again what it was with my fiddle, I said to him, 'I have paid for my part of the trip; shall I now also pay extra for my Stradivarius?' Then Uncle Abraham said, 'Well, maybe one might be allowed to ask a question once in a while, just to keep the conversation going,' but from then on he left me alone and put an end to his questioning.

eena wudd doch hanenwada een bätje froage durwe. Oba von
donn aun leeht hee mie toch, enn stald de Froagarie enn.

"Na, wie weare aul enn Peetaborjch anjekohme, enn nauhme
ons doa eene Stow, dijcht bie de Neimaschiene Sinja siene Städ,
nijch wiet auf vom Nevsky Prospekt, soo väl aus etj mie noch
dentje kaun.

"Toom Jletj räjend daut em Huachsomma korts nohmeddach meist jieda Dach enn dem Deel von Rußlaund, enn
daut kaum mie donn uck seea too Pauss. Den tweeden Dach
auls wie enn Peetaborjch weare, jintj etj mett dee Fiddel soo
gaunz langsom noh eenem Pfaundhus, ooda Paunlauftje, soo's
se hiea doatoo saje. Enn jrods auls etj doa aunkaum, fong'ett
wada kort oba jehearijch aun vom Himmel too poasche. Etj
wetjeld nu schwind Konraud siene Stradivarius enn eene oole
Zeitung enn, enn rannd enn daut Lauftje nenn, woa eene
Ooltestamentla-Bauss stund, enn mie kort bejreesst: kort wiels
doa väl Mensche bie ahm em Lauftje stunde enn haundelde,
enn sijch vetalde, enn sijch een bät jachte, soo aus daut dann
soo mott wann eene Bonsch Molotschna ut Palastina sijch
toom Schisnickäte trafe.

"Etj saj nu opp Rusch too ahm schwind: 'Kaun etj disse
Fiddel hiea een gaunz kortet Stootje lohte, daut de Pracht nijch
naut woat? Etj tohl uck jearn tien Kopietje, bitte.'

'Joh,' sajcht'a, 'woaromm nijch?'

"Etj laj ahm tien Kopietje oppem Desch, enn moak mie rut.

"Fuats etj nu tridj em Hotel nenn, enn tratjch mie
grootsinndagsch omm. Etj sad mie eenen straumen Hoot
opp—etj jleew, daut wea een jreena mett eenem breeden
Raund—tjneep mie soohn Starschie-Schnurrboat aune Näs,
sad mie eene Jeleahde-Brell oppe Näs, soo eene mett
Schlenjedroht omme Uahre, soo auls daut dee Intellijente mett
Jeld deede, trock mie spetze Schooh aun, enn goh tridj noh de
Paunlauftje. Doa wea vleijcht eene tjliene haulwe Stund
vegohne, auls etj doa wada aunkaum. De Rääjen haud

"Well, we arrived in Petersburg and took a room close to the sewing-machine Singer's establishment, not far from the Nevsky Prospect, as far as I can remember.

"As luck would have it, it rained in high summer every day shortly after noon in that part of Russia and such weather was very much part of my plan. On our second day there, I walked very slowly with my fiddle to a pawnshop. Just when I arrived there, it began to rain briefly but torrentially. I quickly wrapped an old newspaper around Konrad's Stradivarius and ran into the shop where the owner gave me a quick hello; quick because all kinds and manner of people stood around in his shop, bargaining all over the place as one would expect.

"Now I said to him in Russian as quickly as I could, 'May I leave this fiddle here for just a little while so that the precious piece doesn't get wet? I'll even pay you ten kopecks, please!'

"'Yes,' he says, 'why not?'

"I placed ten kopecks on the table and left.

"I went to my hotel and there I put on my Sunday finest. I put on my top hat—I think it was a green one with a broad rim—then I clipped a bossy moustache in my nose, and then I fixed an educated pair of glasses on my nose, such with a piece of heavy snare wire around my ears, the way the Intelligentsia with big money did it; then it was the turn of a pair of sharp-toed shoes to be slipped over my feet. Then I headed back to the pawn-shop. It may have been about half an hour before I returned. The rain had let up and was almost over but there were even more people in the store and they were bargaining and smoking and all talking at the same time.

"Well, I looked around at this and that and the other thing when suddenly I pointed at Konrad's fiddle. And then I said, 'Good sir, what kind of a rare fiddle you have got there? I like it; what would you ask for it?'

"'I can't sell it to you. It's not mine; I am just holding it so it doesn't get wet,' he says.

nohjelohte, enn wea meist vebie, oba doa weare noch meea Lied toopjekohme, enn de haundelde, enn daubade, enn vetalde aula toojlitjch, enn dann uck omzajcht, enn aute Schisnick, daut daut mau soo reatjad.

"Etj tjitjj mie nu dit enn jant aun, enn mett eenmol wies etj noh Konraud siene Fiddel. Etj saj, nu oba oba Judsch: 'Groota Meista, waut hab jie doa fe eene seldne Fiddel, de jefellt mie; waut doaf dee jelle?"

"Dee kaun etj nijch vetjeepe. Daut ess nijch miene; dee hab etj hiea mau toom Schulinj unjajebrocht," sajcht'a.

"Doaf etj de weenjstens mol een gaunz tjlienet bätje enne Haund nehme?"froag etj ahm, een bät stelltjes.

"Von mie ut, oba loht dee nijch faule," sajcht'a enn foaht aule miene Jedohnte mett siene Uage hinjeraun.

"Well, etj betjitj mie nu dee Fiddel, enn pletj een bätje oppe Seide, enn saj soo gaunz bieleifijch too dem Lauftje Maun: 'Wudde twee Dusend Rubel tooreatje?'

"Etj jleew joh, oba soo's etj aul säd, daut deit mie leet, oba dauts nijch miene Fiddel, de wacht hie opp äah Bauss," sajcht'a.

"Na, daut dem Lauftjemaun nu langsom den Tjwiel aunfong tooptooranne… soo väl kunn etj dann doch uck aul seehne. Na, etj tjitj mie nu noch een bätje omm, enn kohm wada soo langsom opp dee Fiddel tridj. Etj nauhm dee wada gaunz saunft enne Henj, enn saj: 'Fief Dusend Rubel Boajeld, dauts mien basta Pries! Waut saje See doatoo?'

"Mensch," sajcht'a "fiehre mir niecht enne Versiechung!" ooda soo een bät opp Bibeldietsch, "allain, se jehiert mir niecht!"

"Fief Dusend Rubel ess een Klompe Jeld, uck en Peetaborjch. De Fiddel well jearn mett," saj etj.

Enn goh.

"Bie de Dääh tjemmt hee mie hinjeraun, enn fuschelt mie too: 'Weetst waut, komm wada, soo om Klock sass ut, eea etj too moak; vleijcht tjenn wie dann een Jeschaft moake.'

144

"'But surely I can take it into my hands for just a second?' I asked him as quietly as one does when not exactly whispering.

"'I suppose so, but don't let it fall,' he says while his eyes followed my every move.

"Well, I took a good look at the fiddle and plucked the strings a bit as professionally as I could muster and then I said to him as by-the-way as possible. 'Would two thousand rubles buy this little beauty?'

"'I think so, but as I already said, I'm sorry but it's not my fiddle, it's here waiting for its owner,' he says.

"'Well, I could see that his mind was starting to work overtime, and so I meandered a bit, poking around here and there and slowly I made my way back to the fiddle. And then I took that fiddle very gently into my hands again, while remarking, 'Five thousand rubles in cash and that's my best offer. What do you say?'

"'Mensch,' he says, 'Lead me not into temptation! That violinka, she doesn't belong to me!'

"'Five thousand rubles is a heap of money, even in Petersburg. That fiddle would like to come along,' I said. And left.

"He walked me right to the door and then he whispered to me, 'You know something, come back at six o'clock before I lock up; maybe we can make a little business.'

"Then I walked off in my Sunday best but as sadly as I could manage, right to the first corner, where I quickened my step. At the hotel, I took off my moustache, the high-Sunday clothes, the green hat, my glasses which were already starting to sting my ears a bit, and then I kicked off those sharp-toed shoes. I put on my casual street clothes of the village and again made my way down the street.

"The owner of the pawnshop saw me coming and he was so polite and courteous, almost as subservient as a freshly-caught

"Etj goh nu auf, noch emma grootsindachsch, enn soo trurijch enn soo bedreppt aus etj mau affens kunn. Goh soo langsom bett de easchte Atj, enn dann laj etj loos, aules waut etj kaun, nohm Hotel opptoo.

"Doa aunjekohme, laj etj Schnurrboat, de grootsinndachsche Tjleeda, den jreenen Hoot, miene Brell, die mie aul aunfong aune Uahre too tjniepe, enn miene spetze Schooh auf, enn tratj mie wada soo auldagsch auls verhäa aun, enn goh tridj opp mienen Musikaunte Wajch.

"De Jud sach mie aul kohme, enn wea uck fuats soo heeflijch enn soo deemootijch, meist soo's een fresch jejräpna Baundit, reatjcht mie de Haund enn sajcht, nu wada opp Rusch: 'Goot, daut See wada hiea send, etj haud omm een Hepptjeshoah Äahre Fiddel vekofft... "

"Doch nijch," saj etj,

"Joh," sajcht'a, "mie boot so een Kulack doafäa twee Dusend Rubel. Welle See mie dee nijch fe achtienhundat Rubel vetjeepe?"

"Jearn," saj etj, "oba dauts eajentlijch nijch miene." Enn deed soo trurijch auls etj kunn, oba mau noh bute; ennalijch fong etj aul een bätje too juche, wiels etj langsom een Jeschaft ritjcht.

"Etj woa junt waut saje, etj nehm de Fiddel wada mett, enn wann mien Onkel 'Joh' sajcht, dann brinj etj dee enn twee Wäatjch tridj enn vetjeep Ahn dee!

"Soo's etj soohne Onkels tjann, saje dee emma 'Joh' too een Huptje Boajeld. Hiea habe See tweedusend fiefhundat Rubel', enn dann talld'a mie daut Jeld uck aul enne Haund nenn.

"Mucht dee Onkel mie daut enne Ewijtjeit vezeihe," saj etj. Enn goh langsom auf bett de easchte Atj. Enn dann oba galopp, enn bloos wajch, wajch, en mett eene Japps voll Boajeld enne Fupp.

"Oba nu mott wie nenngohne, dee sinje aul den tweeden Farsch von 'Halleluja, scheener Morjen'."

bandit. He extended his hand to me and said, 'Good that you came back; by the skin of my teeth I had sold your fiddle.'

'Not really!' I said.

"'Yes,' he said, 'some kulak offered me two thousand rubles for it. Won't you sell it to me for eighteen hundred rubles?'

"'Gladly,' I said, 'but it's not really mine!' And I looked as sad as I could on the outside; within myself I started to whoopee a bit because I was smelling good business. 'Let me tell you something; I'll take the fiddle along again and if my uncle says 'yes' to the deal, I'll bring it along in two weeks' time and I'll sell it to you.'

"'The way I know such uncles, they always say 'yes' to a pile of cash money. Here, I'll give you two thousand five hundred rubles!' and having said it, he started counting that cash into my hands.

"'May my uncle forgive me in eternity,' I said. Then I walked slowly to the first corner. And then it was gallop-speed all the way back to the hotel with two fistfuls of cash in my pockets.

"'That's how I became a rich man the first time in my life,' said Uncle William Bergen and then he grinned and placed his head at an angle. And then it was high time to enter the church; the congregation was already into the first hymn by half a verse.

Frindschauft Nohfädme

Nü heat sich dee Dommheet doch langsom opp. Väje Weatj wea etj noch een jestuckta Nobody, soo's de measchte aundre, enn nü kohme se Räajwies aun, enn welle weete, aus Mike Tyson, de niea Champion vonne Schwoare-Scherwaundasch mett mie Frindschauft ess. Jo, de Mensche froage noh mien Autograum enn bliewe lenja bie mie sette aus jeweenlich, enn habe daut nich mol meea "seea drock" uck wann se Menniste send, enn send frindlich aus een Topptje Mies, enn wann etj mie haustig ommdrei, moatj etj emma, daut se noh miene Fuppe ziele, omm üttoofinje, aus de nich een bätje no büte ütjebült send nohm latzten Feit mett Larry Holmes.

Mie ess daut, soo's etj aul säd, aulatoop een bätje too groff jeworde (ooda säd etj 'too domm'?) enn doawäjen, schriew etj daut nü dol, daut jie von nü aun aula weete, woor'ett doamett bestalt ess.

Jo, wie send Frindschauft enn uck goanich soo wietleftig. Taunte Jasch Kloßsche haft goanich soo oracht, wann se meent, daut ditje Bollesjenetj bie aule Thiesses enn Tysons ahr een bätje bekaunt väatjemmt, enn uck daut heete Bloot enne Füste. "De Thiesses kunne aula grülich doll woare, enn wann de mol opp earenst doll worde, dann holde de Lied de Tjinja nenn. Enn wann see aunfonge too schlohne, gauf daut fuats emma Broodaschauft," meend Peetasch, de Chronikler, uck aul emma. De Mensche habe racht.

Dee Jeschicht ess soo's dit: Daut mien Grootonkel no Sumatra jintj enn doa mett de Tiejasch enn de Sind toop oppriemd, daut weet jie.

Tracing Relatives

I've almost had my fill of all this dumbness. Just last week I was a stocky nobody like most of the others and now they come filing up, wanting to know whether Mike Tyson, the new champion of the heavy ones, is related to me. Joh, people ask me for my autograph and stay longer than usual, even if they are Mennonites, "who are always frightfully busy" and they are all together friendlier than a pile of freshly hatched mice and whenever I turn around suddenly, I always notice that they have their eye on my pockets to determine whether they haven't got a bump to the outside after the last fight with Larry Holmes. To me this is one of those 'enough is enough' matters (or did I say dumbness?) and that's why I am now going to write the whole matter down and document it for all to read and see so that you know how things really stand.

Yes, we are relatives and not nearly as distant as you might think. Aunt Jasch Kloßche is not all that wrong when she says that those thick necks on all Thiessens and Tysons look familiar to her and also the hot blood in their fists. "The Thiessens can get awfully mad and when they get seriously angry, people told their children to come into the house."

"And when they started fighting, a brotherhood meeting in the church was not long in coming," the chronicler Peters has said for years. These people are right.

The real story goes like this: my great uncle went to Sumatra and cleaned up on the tigers and sin together and all in one sweep, you all know; however that this very same uncle had an uncle who already in 1802 went to Africa is something you don't know, because all this is written down in a book "Fraunz

Oba daut disselwja Onkel eenen Onkel haud, woon'a aul
aune 1802 noh Afrika jintj, daut weet jie nich, wiels daut ess
bloß en eenem oolen Buak "Fraunz Thiesses Mejchel woat
Missionoa en Afrika: Femielje-Jeheemnis" oppjeschräwe.
Enn dit Buak ess em M. S. C. bie Harry Löwen enne gaunz
unjaschte Schüflod too finje. (Too Nacht nemmt Harry disse
Jeschicht emma no Hüs enn vestatjt se unjre Datj.)
Enn waut steit doabenne? froag jie. Well, nich seea väl, oba
doa steit, -enn dit weet jie woll meist aula- daut Mejchel von
eh enn je, de Nohme vom Darpsboll wea, wiels Michael,
Mechel, Mejchel, Michel ennsowieda emma de jratsta enn de
stoatjsta wea, waut'et gauf. Daut weete se em Himmel enn uck
opp Ead, wiels de Erzenjel Michael drajcht den Nohme nich
omsonst. Enn Gorbatchow enn Jackson uck nich.

Jo, enn diss Fraunz Thiesses Mejchel word soo jenant, wiels
hee aul mett een Joah Kaute aufwarje kunn, enn mett twee Joah
lange Betjse druag enn twintig-pundje Arbüse aufplock, enn
mett de Füst de Nacht oppe Berstaund tweischluag enn
oppfraut. Mett fief Joah haud de Darpsboll fe ahm Schizz, enn
mett twalw haud hee eemol oppem Joahmoatjt enn Ternie
eenen Mongoole em Rastling-Rinj daut Hinjarenj ver aule Lied
volljeheiwt.

Toom Jletj word dis Mejchel tjristlich enn fein mack enn
leahd aus Missionoa. De Lied odemde sogoa een bätje opp,
wiels Thiesses Mejchel wea verhäa doch een "force to be
reckoned with" jewast, soo's Taunte Kloßsche säd, "soo haude
de Lied uck noch äwa hundat Joah jesajcht."

Soo's etj aul säd, siene Mutta freid sich sea, daut hee aunstaut
nohm Circus too gohne omm Mensche de Tjap too febühle,
nü doch noh Afrika jintj enn doa Mensche too schetj holp. Üt
Afrika kaum eascht uck foaken Post enn dann emma weinja,
enn leet donn schließlich gaunz noh.

Jo, enn waut wea, enn woaromm leet de Post noh, enn head
schließlich gaunz opp? Wiels Fraunz Thiesses Mejchel haud

Thiessen's Michael becomes a missionary in Africa: Family-Secret." And this book can only be found in the Mennonite Studies Centre in Harry Loewen's bottom drawer. And what is in this book? you ask. Well, not all that much, but what there is is to be found in that book (and that black on white).

Michael was, since the beginning of time, the name of the village bull, because Mejchel, Mechel, and Michael etc. were always the names of the biggest and the strongest creatures in existence. This they know in heaven and on earth and even, for a while, in the Soviet Union. And the archangel Michael does not bear his name in vain either.

Joh, joh, and Fraunz Thiessen's Mejchel was called so because he was busy choking cats at age one; at two he wore long-legged trousers and picked twenty-pound watermelons and dragged them to the edge of the patch, smashed them open with his fist and ate them up at a single sitting. At age five the village bull was afraid of him and at age twelve he had once entered a wrestling ring at the annual fair in Ternie and administered a lusty beating on the Mongolian champion's bare ass before eight hundred and thirty-three people.

Thanks be to God in heaven that this Mejchel became a Christian and nice and tame and studied to become a missionary. People were relieved far and wide because this Mejchel was a "force to be reckoned with", so said the same Aunt Jasch Kloßche, adding "and that's what people said even a hundred years later."

As I already told you, his mother was happy and relieved that he, instead of going into the circus and knocking peoples' heads together, now went to Africa to work over people in those far-away parts. From out of Africa, mail first came very regularly and then it slowed down a bit and then it became a trickle and finally stopped altogether.

Joh, and what was and why did the mail slow down and then stop altogether? Because Fraunz Thiessen's Mejchel had sich doa mett dem Eppaschta siene Dochta befried, enn daut wea eene grülich jestuckte, schmocke enn frindliche Mamme, "oba schwoat aus Petjdroht", soo steit'et doa em Buak schwoat opp witt, sootoosaje, jeschräwe. Yessiree, daut jefft noch sogoa twee Bilda woa Mejchel mett siene Frü enn drettien Tjinja em huagen Ella steit, enn fief Tjinja sette bie ahm oppem Kopp, oppe Oarms, enn eena oppe Tjnee, dee hee soo een bätje nohhecht helt!

Daut jefft Thiesses, dee sich noch emma schäme, daut wie soon Frindschauft habe, enn se beoabeide de Thiesses Lienje en Afrika enn schreewe enn räde enn deede, se sulle doch weens ähren Nohme een tjlienet bätje endre. Enn daut deede se dann schließlich uck. Mett dem Resultaut, daut een Üa-Üagroottjind von Fraunz Thiesses Mejchel nü dee Champion vonne Schwoare-Scherwaundasch ess! Enn dissa heet Mike Tyson!

married the grand chief's daughter and she was a tremendously stocky, beautiful and friendly mother, "but blacker than pitch"—so it is written. Yessiree, there are even two photos where Mejchel with his wife are to be seen at a great age and with thirteen children, the five younger ones sitting on the missionary's head and arms, with one on his knee which he extends a bit in mid-air!

There are Thiessens who are still ashamed that we have such relatives. And these pleaded with the Thiessen side of the family line in Africa and wrote them and talked and did and prayed to the effect that would they please mind changing their name and even if just a little. And that's exactly what happened. With the result that a great-great grandchild of Fraunz Thiessens Mejchel now is the champion of the heavyweights. And his name is Mike Tyson!

Schmauntfat

Auls de easchte Menniste von Rußlaund noh Dietschlaund fiefentwintijch Joah tridj kaume, weare see rund omm'e Klock fe Seele volla Fräd enn Desche volla Brot dankboa. Daut Jeld, woohnt se vonne dietsche Rejearung tjreaje, wea von ahn een Teatjen doavon, daut Gott ahn besondasch goot wea. Donn hilde se aulwewääje Dankfaste, enn vespruake schmock enn jehuarsom fe de neajchste dusend Joah too senne. Oba soohne Schmockijchtjeite dachennnacht woat dem Mensch auljemeen boold ennoolent, enn de stiewe Sälenstrenj vom Jehuarsom woare measchtens boold schlaup nohdem eena dee enjebroake haft. "Enn dann vezaubeld eena sijch enne schlaupe Strenj, ooda eena klunjt doaräwe," säd Brune Peeta emma. Enn Peeta wisst.

Grootellre enn Ellre, dee sijch enne Effentlijchtjeit niemols omfoohte enn beleib nijch kusste, haude nu enn Dietschlaund Tjinja, dee hundat Joah enn noch meea daut Bedarfnis haude, em schmunje eenjet nohtoohohle. Enn boold nijch blooss de Tjinja. Onse Mensche nanne soohn Benehme weltlijch.

Enn nijch blooss de Tjinja, säd etj? Joh, daut säd etj.

Enn wiels dee Jeschijchte, dee uck wertjlijch soo send, soo ess aus miene fromme Groottaunte Jreeta emma säd: "eene goastaje Jeschijcht ess väl intressaunta aus utjedochte Schmockijchtjeite," well etj junt dee vetalle. Kaun nuscht schohde, Taunte Jreeta word 93 Joah oolt. Enn see wea breedajemeendsch.

Henritj Wiebe wea eena, dee soohne schwoare Lohd von Dankboatjeit druach, daut hee meist nijch steil gohne kunn.

154

Cream Gravy

When the first Mennonites arrived in Germany from Russia some twenty years ago, they were thankful around the clock for having their souls full of peace and their tables full of bread. The cash money that the Germans gave them upon arrival certainly helped to make sleep and dreams more bearable. Moreover such Deutschmarks—*mark* also meaning *marrow* in German—was readily attributable to God's guidance and direction.

So they promised to be nice and well-behaved and obedient maybe even for a thousand years but such good behaviour has a way of becoming unbearable and somehow the traces of the harness of niceness tend to go slack very soon after being broken in. "Then you either get caught in the slack, or you step over it," as Peter Braun used to say. And Peter knew.

Grandparents and parents, who never or rarely displayed any affection in public, now had children in Germany who felt they had a century and more of catching up to do in the smooching department. And soon not only the children. People called such behaviour worldly.

And soon not only the children, did I say? Yes, that's what I said.

Because this is really true I want to tell you about it; after all, "a naughty story which is really true is even more interesting then invented nicenesses," said my grand-aunt Margaret. And she lived to be 93.

Hee haud eenen gaunzen Rucksack voll Dankboatjeit oppem Puckel, kratjcht soo auls daut mott. Oba mett de Tiet, tjreajch dee Rucksack een Lochtje enn doaderjch word Henritj siene Laust leijchta.

Toom Biespell, dree Joah nohdem hee enn Dietschlaund aunjekohme wea, fuah hee aul eene seea groote Koah; fief Joah lohta haud hee sien eajnet Hus, enn meist von Aunfong aun, haud hee dartijch Mensche, aules Menniste, dee fe ahm em Bujeschaft oabeide. Enn zeowents haud hee feftien Frulied enn Mäadtjess, dee fe ahm enn Jeschafte enn Buros rein muake, wosche, enn schieade.

"Daut wausche, schieare woat sijch loohne. Wann jie Wiebe Henritj phoone," stund jeschräwe.

Daut diead dann uck nijch lang bett Henritj Wiebe aunfong auleen Ferien too hoole enn uck nohm Kurort too foahre; hee musst, säd'a: "Mol gaunz auleen entspaune, omm sijch selwst tjanne too leahre." Daut ess soo de dietsche Mood, soo's jie weete.

Enn de Wiebsche? Noh eenem haulwen Joah em Waste, haud see uck een nieet Läwe entdatjcht, enn see jintj boold huachhackijch romm, enn wackeld sogoa een bät mett de Owesied. Boold weare ahr uck aul Kaffeekränzchen nuscht nieet, enn see leeht biem Koffedrintje ut eene Rosenthaltauss sogoa ähren tjlansten Finja enne Loft een bät weppre. Apfeltorte mett Schlagsahne kaume dann boold hinjeraun.

Eenes Doagess haud Trudie, joh soo heet see, "jenuag ess jenuag" enn see säd gaunz eenfach: "Waut Schmauntfat fe den Gaunta ess, ess uck Schmauntfat fe de Gauns," packt ähren nieen Wildlada Schemmedaun enn dann, aun eenem diestren enn schmuddajen dietschen Dach loht em Winta, steajch see enn een Zug enn reist eenfach noh Italien auf. Doa siedlijch vonne Aulpe lachde de junge Mensche, enn sunge 'O solo mio!'enn drunke sogoa Wien, wann'et ahn schlajcht jintj, aunstaut too doohne, waut Menniste enn Dietsche dann doohne: vom Jinjsten Jerejcht ooda vom grooten Triebsaul too

Heinrich Wiebe also belonged to such people, who on account of his heavy load of gratitude, could barely walk erect when he arrived in Germany. He had a whole bag of thankfulness on his back, just like it ought to be. However before long, that bag sustained a hole and lightened Henrich's burden. For instance, three years after his arrival in Germany he drove a really big car; five years later he owned his own house and almost from the beginning he had thirty people, all Mennonites, working for him on a construction gang. And evenings some fifteen women and girls worked for his business, cleaning, washing and scrubbing, mainly offices. "You need cleanin' or some rubbin'? Get Wiebe's staff to do your scrubbin'" it was written.

It was not long before Wiebe started taking solo vacations and going to spas; he had to, "relax completely in order to re-acquaint me with myself," he liked to comment. After all, such is the German mode, as one knows.

As for the Mrs Wiebe? After half a year in the West, she too had acquired a brand new lease on life and soon she knew how to prance about in high-heeled shoes and she even developed a bit of a wiggle on her rumble seat. When having the German equivalent of British high tea, namely coffee, Mrs Wiebe encouraged her pinky finger to dance in the air while she ("call me Trudie") sipped coffee and ate apple torte with fresh whipped cream at wealthy neighbours or in her own home.

Then, one fine day, Trudie she "had had enough" and simply said, "What is Schmauntfat (cream gravy) for the gander is also Schmauntfat for the goose" and packed her newly acquired suede valise and then, in the middle of a dull and dreary German winter day, took off by train for Italy. There south of the Alps the sun shone, young people laughed, people drank a glass of wine and even sang when they suffered trials and tribulations instead of doing what the Germans and Mennonites do, which is to talk about Judgement Day and how terrible,

räde, enn woo schratjlijch doch aules toonijcht enne Welt ess, ooda eene Jebädstund hoole. Ooda vonne Missjoon iewrijch schwietre.

Oba nu ess'ess Tiet, daut jie de tjliena Tjinja too Bad schetje, wiels waut etj junt nu vetalle well, ess bloos fe groote Uahre, joh? "Joh!"

Aum tweeden Owend saut Trudie Wiebe aum Desch oppem Boulevard bute, dijcht biem Forum Romanum enn Rom, enn toom easchten Mol enn äahre sassendartijch Joah aut see auleen Owendkost (fe de Reis haud see selwst jebackte Tweeback, mett jereatjadet Schintjefleesch, een Kulla Formaworscht, een poah Suregurtje, enn een Schruwglaus voll Ditjemaltj mettjenohme). Trudie brocht äahre Henj bie, woohne Gaufel eena too woohnem Ätesgang bruckt, enn woohn Läpel dann aune Reaj wea, enn waut see mett ähre schmocke Beentjess doohne musst, enn wanneea see ähren tjlienen Finja Dirijent späle lohte wudd, aus mett eenmol een jleia Reema sijch aun äahrem Desch hansad. Enn dissa wea soo heeflijch aus een Kavaliea, enn soo grootsindagsch aus een Reiesprädja aunjetrocke, blooss daut dis Giovanni een Paisley Schneppelduak ute Brostfupp rutsteatje leeht.

Senior Roma saut uck mau affens, auls aul eene Buddel mett Rootwien oppem Desch stund, mett twee Jläsa. "Enn Rußlaund em Darp wudd etj dissem Ooltnäs eent mett dem Bassem äwrem Puckel resse, enn en Dietschlaund wudd hee mie vetalle, waut hee aules haud enn kunn, enn enn Kanada wudd hee Jeld fe goode Zwatje saumle, ooda fe de Missjoon, enn hiea?" soo docht Trudie: "Wann hee een Aupel wea, wudd etj ahm een bätje aungnaubre," fuscheld see too sijch selwst, oba donn leeht see Massa enn Gaufel faule, enn heiwd sijch selwst eent verrem Schnoweltje.

See aut gaunz langsom äahren Osso Bucco mett lange Tjieltje noh de italienische Oat enn uck een Tweeback ut Kuckeruzz-mehl jebackt (enn fruach uck fuats noh daut Rezapt), enn

158

how dreadfully terrible things are, or to take off to a prayer meeting. Or to twitter about missions.

But now the time has come to send the children off to bed, because what I am now about to tell you is meant only for adult ears.

The second evening Trudie Wiebe was sitting at a table on a broad sidewalk restaurant, close to the Forum Romanum and having the first dinner in her thirty-six year life by herself (for her train trip she had packed some home-made double-decker buns, smoked ham, a chunk of farmer sausage, a couple of dill pickles and a pickling jar of thickened sour milk). Trudie was teaching her hands which fork to use and which spoon was to do her bidding, and what to do with her shapely legs, and how her new-for-the-trip outfit looked on her, and when she should allow her pinky to play conductor, when suddenly a sprightly Roman seated himself at her table. He was as polite as a cavalier and as high-Sundaily dressed as an itinerant minister, only that this Giovanni had a paisley silk handkerchief doing its own thing from his outer chest pocket.

Senor Roma was barely sitting when a bottle of wine was already standing on the table. "In Russia I would have swatted this cocky slicker one with the broom over his muffler, while in Germany he would tell me all about his ambitions and successes and in Canada he would be raising causes or collecting for charity or the mission, but here?" so thought Trudie. "If he were an apple, I'd take a nibble," she whispered to herself, then dropped knife and fork and slapped her little snoot a reprimand.

She ate her way through the Osso Bucco with long strings of pasta and a salad and white corn meal rolls, (and right away asked for the recipe for these) while just occasionally daring a side glance at this perky dandy. Then she would pull her eyes off him and tell them to stay put.

erlaubd äahre Uage dreemol bie dissem Uchazhor spezeare too gohne. Dann hold see äahre Uagtjess wada tridj enn säd, see haude Tus too bliewe. Fuats oppe Städ!

Oba Trudie gauf äah Glauss Wien Erlaubnis nohda too kohme, wiels Senior Roma biem aunsteete, eene Lienje von dem Drunkleed ut La Traviata doabie sommd. Oba see drunk mau een Neihootvoll, enn nijch eea see sijch omjetjitjt haud, omm too seehne, aus doa uck tjeen Mennist medden en Rom vebiestat wea. Oba doa wea uck nijch een eensja, dem ahr bekaunt väakaum, enn dem'et plautfootijch sach, enn mett eenmol wea daut Glauss wada bie ahr verre Leppedäah. Enn dann noch eenmol, oba mau blooss om uttoofinje, waut see bett nutoo nijch vemisst haud, enn uck nijch wiedahans vemisse wudd.

Dee Reema heet Giacomo Verdimonti enn Trudie späld sijch den Nohme een poah mol väa, dee wea soo jlei... waut dee Nohme woll bediede kunn? Scheen wear'a. Oba doamett nijch jenuag: ahr jefoll diss Tjeadel sogoa een bätje, enn aus Trudie dann noch sach, daut hee Guccis druag enn eene Rolex omhaud, enn daut hee oba uck goanijch, nijch mol een tjlienet Bestje nohm Staul ooda noh Gummschooh ritjcht, enn aus hee dann noch soo lieseltjes een Schnädtje von dee Melodie "La donna e mobile" piepad, word Trudie enn, daut see doch Frindschauft mett Eva wea, enn see muak de Nieschieadäah eene Retz ohp...

Twee Wäatj lohta wea Trudie betjeat. Eascht haud see een grulijch schlajchtet Jewesse enn treest sijch mett de groote Woahrheit utem Oolen Testament, dee see nu gaunz enn goa vestund: Eenmol ess soo goot ess tjeenmol, tweemol ess dautselwje aus eenmol, enn mett de Tiet sogoa noch weinja...

Aus Trudie den Zug noh Hus besteaj, wea Giacomo aune Bohn enn nannd ahr "Schnuckieputzie" enn see nannd ahm "Schmaundbenjel" enn doabie gauf Giacomo ahr een Aufscheedsjeschentj. Een Pelz, Mackenzie River willa Nerz,

But Trudie permitted her glass to submit to the will-o'-the-wisp and she had just a thimble full of the relaxant, but not before looking around to see if any Mennonite was drifting hard by. But there was no one who looked even vaguely familiar and who knew Low German and then she found the wine glass suddenly making its way to her lips again. And then again, but just so she would know in future what she was really not missing.

The Roman's name was Giacomo Verdimonti and Trudie rather liked that name. Not only that, she found him attractive and when Trudie noticed that he wore Guccis and a Rolex and that he bore not even a faint hint of the aroma of stable or gumshoes, and even, occasionally, whistled a lilt of "*La donna e mobile*" to himself, Trudie developed closer connection with our relative Eve: she opened the barn doors of curiosity.

Two weeks later Trudie was converted. First she had a dreadfully guilty conscience and consoled herself with the great Old Testament truth which she now completely and fully and finally understood: Once is as good as nothing at all, twice is the same as once, and as time goes by is even less than once…

When Trudie boarded the train for home, Giacomo was at the station and called her "Schnuckieputzie" while she called him "Honey-Bunny" and Giacomo gave Trudie a gift of farewell. A coat, full length, Mackenzie River wild mink, supple and alive and reminding of the ditty's reversal: "Men of thrifty ilk, give neither fur nor silk."

Heinrich Wiebe was not at the station when his wife arrived in Bielefeld; he was busy smithying money on his pecuniary anvil and doing good works. But what was she to do with this beautiful blanket? Trudie Wiebe headed for a railroad locker, carefully placed her coat in it, stroked it lovingly, then deposited one mark in the slot and deposited the key in her purse.

wallijch enn läwendijch, enn weatjch enn mollijch. Enn gaunz aundasch auls see mol jeheat haud:

"Een Pelz enn feine Sied,
Jeziemt sijch nijch fe mennische Lied."

Henritj Wiebe wea nijch aune Bohn auls siene Fru enn Bielefeld aunkaum; hee haud'et too drock mett Jeld opp sien Aunbolt too schmäde enn uck goode Woatje uttoorejchte. Oba woa nu han mett dem straumen Pelz, oba, oba! Trudie Wiebe jintjch jlitjch opp soohnen Schlutschaup, woavon see hundade enne groote Bohnstatsjoone habe, enn schoof den Pelz doa langsom nenn. Dann stritjcht see den noch eenmol leeftolijch enn gauf dem eenen saunften Kuss, läd eene Moatj enn dee tjliene Retz, enn fuppad sijch den Schlätel enn.

"Henritj, heea! Horch mol häa," säd Trudie too äahrem Maun biem Owendkost: "Etj fung toofallijch eenen Schlätel enne Bohnstatsjoon; wäa weet, vleijcht sullst du mol bie Jeläajenheit doahan gohne, enn tjitje auls dis Schlätel vleijcht fe soohn Schlutschaup pausst, waut meenst?" Henritj Wiebe säd nuscht, oba hee fuppad sijch den Schlätel enn.

Twee Wäatj lohta jinje Wiebe noh de easchte Oper enn Düsseldorf enn ährem Läwe. De Oppfeahrung wea "La Forza del Destino" aulso Dee Macht vom Schetjsaul opp italjeanisch. De Isaak Waulsche, dee uck opp äahre Oat verr kortem dit enn jant vom Schmaundfat Rezapt utjefunge haud, wea een bät eentjannijch auls see Trudie doa troff. Tjeen Wunda, auls see de Oper veleehte, druag de Isaak Waulsche den reemischen Pelz.

"Heinrich, listen," said Trudie to her man while having supper, "I found a key at the train station; who knows, maybe one should have a look and see if there is something in there. It seems like the key might fit a locker there, what do you think?" Heinrich Wiebe said nothing, but he pocketed the key.

Two weeks later Wiebes attended the first opera of their lives in Düsseldorf. The production was "*La Forza del Destino*" (The Force of Destiny) in Italian. Mrs Isaac Wall, who also had recently discovered a thing or two about cream sauce for "ganders and geezers" as she said, made a little strange to Trudie or at least, so Trudie thought. Small wonder, when they left the opera, Mrs Isaac Wall was wearing the Italian mink.

So wie ich bin

"They also serve, who only stand and wait," schreef John
Milton; daut lat sich soo äwasatte:
  Enn dee, dee stohnend wachte bloß,
  See deehne uck.
Lisbeth Peetasch schrift enn eene von ähre vetraflijche Beatja,
daut etj daut Prograum opp meahrere Schäp feahd. Etj jleew
ahr daut. Een Prograum oppem Schepp ess needijch, wiels de
measchte Mensche ohne Oppsejcht enn Unjahoolung nijch
mett dem Läwe foadijch woare. Enn oppem Schepp send see
ohne Oppsejcht. Etj späld aulso 42 Mol den Hoad von 1396
Passazheare oppem Nuadautlauntik, enn leahd too dee Tiet
meist de Halft von aule Mensche oppe Ead tjanne.

Daut wea Friedach zeowents auls ver mien Büro mett eenmol
eene ella-achtje schwoate Frü stund. See wacht, daut kunn etj
seehne, see haud foaken jewacht. See wacht oppe Jerajchtijch-
tjeit, see wacht oppe Eewijchtjeit, enn vondoag wacht see opp
mie. Ähre Uage vetalde mie daut, enn noch väl meea.

"Komm nenn!"

"Wann See aum Sinndach eenen Gottesdeenst organiseare
welle, woa etj jearn een Leed ooda twee sinje." Daut wea aules.
Etj säd: "Mol seehne. De Nohme, bitte?" "Jackson. De Kabiene-
numma es säwen."

Daut wea soo: De Katholitje schetjte emma eenen Priesta
oppe Foaht mett, enn dee hild dann Messen, enn leeht sijch
daut noh de Oat von ähre Sort scheen gohne. Dann reisd hee
drei Wäatj enn Amerikau romm, enn fuah wada bie onsem
näjchsten Tridjkohme noh Europa mett. Entweschen reisd dee

Just as I am

In one of her nostalgic reveries, Elisabeth Peters writes that I was the program director on various ships. I believe her. A program on a ship is necessary since most people do not know what to do if they are unsupervised and without entertainment. And on a ship they are free to do as they please. So I played program director on 42 crossings; I was the shepherd to 1396 passengers on the North Atlantic and got to know more than half of the world's population at that time.

It was a Friday evening when an elderly lady appeared at my office. She was waiting, I could readily determine; she had waited often. She was waiting for justice, she was waiting for eternity and today she waited for me.

"Come in!"

"If you intend to organize a Sunday morning service, I am prepared to sing a song or two for you." That was all.

I said, "Let's see. Your name, please?"

"Jackson. Cabin Number Seven."

This is the way things aboard ship transpired. The Catholics sent a priest along on every voyage and he conducted daily masses and had a good time of it. On reaching port, he travelled through North America, wherever his mission or whims took him, and then in three weeks time at our next call, he boarded the ship and returned to Europe. In-between the next Roman man of the cloth, generally a stiff white collar, paid for by Rome, came onboard.

This became routine, until we took along a huge red-faced priest of God's grace from Ireland, who preferred to conduct

näjchsta reemische Ohmtje mett eenem stiewen witten Kroage, von Rom betohlt, mett.

Daut wea aules scheen enn goot bett wie eenen seea grooten Witjza mett een roodet Jesejcht von Gottes Jnod enn Irrlaund mettnauhme, dee jearn siene Messe büte oppem Achterdeck aufhild. Daut wea Sinnowent-zeowents biem Sonne-unjagang auls hee doa mett siene Schoah jäjen mienen Roht verrem Throon jintj. Hee stund soo bie twee Meeta vonne Räling auf, enn haud daut mett sien Aumt drock. Daut Schepp wea ditmol de Arosa Sun, een Schweizamodell, woohnt de Dietsche kopflastijch, aulso koppschwoa, nannde, wiels daut schwanda bowe auls enne Medd ooda unje wea.

Mott daut maunjchmol soo kohme? Daut deed. Eene sojenannde rogue Wall, aulso Schurkenwall, rolld ons lieseltjess äwa, daut Schepp hoof sijch Väre soo auls een bockschet Pead, donn sad sijch de Arosa Riese oppe Huck, enn tweschenenn pralld de meist säwenschoohja Priesta äwaroasch aune Räling naun, schoot Heistakopp, stankad mett de Been, oakad mett de Oarms, schreajch "Bozhe moi!" opp Enjlisch, enn Plumps, dann wea de Priesta nada. Etj mald daut dem Kapitän, nohdem etj dem Veeahundatpundjen eene Schwamwast hinjeraun jeschmäte haud. Dee nauhm hee mett. Donn dreid wie eene Stundlang den Nelsonkulla, funge nuscht, enn daumpte wieda. Dee Doot brinjt eenem de easchte twee bett dreemol daut Schweete bie.

Etj gauf fuats bekaunt, daut wie aum nächsten Dach, aum Sinndach aulso, eenen protestantischen Gottesdeenst aufhoole wudde. Enn wiels doa tjeen Prädja wea, enn wiels etj bie Prädja Enns enn Jrienthol, bie mienem breedajemeendschen Grootvoda enn Prädja Krüs, Leahre Schäfa, enn Eltesta Bitjat enn Gretna, enn Professasch Bultmann enn Heiler enn Marburg daut Wuat mettjetjräaje haud, läd etj mie enne Säle nenn, enn lauss dreemol Psalm 139 derjch, muak mie reed, säd

his masses outside on the afterdeck. It was Saturday evening when he assembled his flock, contrary to my advice, before God's roving throne under the Divine ceiling. Father O'Brien stood some two metres distance from the railing and got on with his sermon. This time it was the Arosa Sun, a Swiss liner, a top heavy ship, so-called because it was heavier above than mid-ships; heavy and ornate wood furnishings caused this imbalance.

Are some things pre-ordained? They probably are. A so-called rogue wave rolled over us and the ship lifted out of the water in front like a bucking horse, and then the Arosa Sun went down on its haunches, and in-between the priest, just short of seven feet tall, was thrown violently against the railing, turned a frantic summersault, kicked mightily with his legs, waved frantically with his arms, screamed, "Oh my God!" and down he went, meaning overboard. I grabbed the phone on the railing, informed the captain, but not before I threw a life jacket after the four hundred pound father, and which he grabbed, but dragged with him down into the waves all in one desperate effort to cling to life. We executed the mandatory Nelson turns for a full hour, found no trace of him, and steamed on. Death causes witnesses to sweat profusely the first two or three times around.

I immediately announced that next day, Sunday, a Protestant service would be held. And since there was no minister aboard, and I had had ample experience in listening to how it's done, first at the feet of the Reverend Enns in Grünthal back home, then listening to Preacher Kruse, he of Mennonite Brethren persuasion for whom life is a non-stop service to the Lord, and Teacher Paul Schäfer and Bishop Bückert in Gretna, as well as Professors Bultmann and Heiler in Marburg. Then I slipped into the traces of the Word, read Psalm 139 three times, prepared a sermon, informed Ms Jackson that tomorrow at ten

Mis Jackson, daut daut morje Klock Tien soo wiet wea, stald daut enne Scheppszeitung nenn, enn Doloaj!

Doa stund etj nu, goot sass hundat Mensche tjitjchte mie aun, enn etj säd, "Friede sei mit Euch, der Friede, der da größer und mächtiger ist als alle menschliche Vernunft walte über uns!" Daut wadahold etj opp Enjlisch, enn wiels doa een poah Franzoose üt Rimouski weare, dee opp de DeGaulsche Sproak bestunde, wadahold etj daut Gaunze noch opp Plautdietsch.

Dann sung Ms. Jackson "I walk in the garden alone," enn auls see den dredden Farsch sommd, wea doa tjeen dreajet Uag verr mie. Bejleit word see aum Fliegel vetraflijch von eenem irischen Tjenstla enn Schauspäle, dee aulewäje Tüs wea, besondasch enne Nohbaschauft vonne Buddel. Uck ohne Wota wann'et senne musst. Enn daut musst bie ahm senne.

Donn sad etj loos, soo seea auls etj kunn, enn läd ahn den Psalm üt, enn dreef de gaunze Jemeend opp eene Stund jehearijch aule Dommheite ut. Wea den Psalm tjannt, weet, daut sijch David jearn too soohne Zwatje ennlohde lat.

Metteenst kaum de Klavieaspäla, Patrick O'Leary, äwadäl, enn säd, wie wudde noch eene Kollatjt fe aule Schiffsbrüchige enne Welt hoole während Ms. Jackson daut latzte Leed sung.

Etj leet mie nijch ütem Konzept brinje... loht ahm, docht etj bie mie. Etj tjand je siene Schiffsbrüchige, dee nijch em Wota vedrunke weare.

Donn sung Ms. Jackson "Just as I am" enn uck opp Dietsch "So wie ich bin" enn mie saul tjeena vetalle, daut de leewa Gott nijch sogoa oppem Schepp mettfoaht. Hee wea doa meddemang, enn auls Ms. Jackson twee Farzh von dem Leed mett tooje Uage sommd, sad Hee sich lieseltjess bie ahr enne Stemm nenn, enn jintj bie jiedem em Hoat spezeare. Bie mie uck.

Auls wie dree Wäatj lohta enn Montreal emm Howe aunläde, wea doa Post fe mie. Eene Schaulploht wea enn daut Pakeet. Etj muak daut op, enn doa stund jeschräwe: "Abide with me.

it would be her turn as well, announced intentions of a service in the ship's paper, and we were ready for action.

There I stood with an audience exceeding six hundred in number and I pronounced, "Peace be with you, that peace which is greater than human reason and mightier than human endeavour may dwell upon you." Then I repeated the text in English and since there were French people on board from Rimouski who demanded equal treatment and wanted French, I repeated my message in Mennonite Low German.

Then Ms Jackson sang "I walk in the Garden alone," and when she hummed verse number three, no dry eye was to be seen. She was accompanied on the grand piano by an Irish artist and actor who was at home everywhere, but nowhere more at home than close to a bottle even without water, if need be. And with him it needed to be.

And then I took off and sermonized on the Psalm text and dispersed all the nonsense which my congregation might have entertained for a full hour. Anyone who knows the Psalm will agree that it was written explicitly for such purpose.

Suddenly the pianist, Patrick O'Leary surfaced at my side and suggested we should now pass the collection plate around for all the needy shipwrecked of this world, while Ms Jackson sang her final song.

I did not permit him to throw me off balance, but I thought to myself that I knew his shipwrecked needy, who had not drowned in sea water.

Than Ms Jackson sang "Just as I am" in English and in German, and no one can tell me that our Father does not travel aboard ship when it pleases Him. He was right in the middle of things and when Ms Jackson hummed two verses of the song with eyes closed, He softly entered her voice and came to visit every heart. Mine, too.

When three weeks later we laid up in port in Montreal, there was mail. A record was in a package addressed to me. I opened

Love until we meet again in the Garden, from Mahalia Jackson."

Etj hab de Ploht noch.

it, and on an accompanying card was written, "Abide with me, Love until we meet again in the garden, from Mahalia Jackson."

I have that record to this day.

De Doop

Daut Joah 1936 wea een entscheidendet; joh vleijcht soo bediedend enne menschlijche Jeschijcht auls donn auls sijch daut Roode Mäah deeld, enn dee Tjinja Israel doa sondasorj mett dreaje Schlorre derjchwankte. Daut word hiea oppe Prärie soo dreajch enn donn soo heet enn bieaun wada soo dreajch, daut de Mensche dachenacht mett dem Enj reatjende. Enn fe ons Menniste word daut Joah too eene Krise, wiels, soo auls aul irjendwoa verhäa erwähnd word, wea doa fe de Breeda too weinijch Wota toom rejchtijch deepe, enn de Tjoatjelje weare uck aum Enj. Aulso waut too doohne? Daut gauf Konferenze enn väl Jeräd, enn sogoa Jezank, head etj saje. Enn donn? De Breeda funge eenfach aun mett dem Schmaundkauntje too deepe, enn de Tjoatjelje gauwe opp vereascht rain checks, enn doamett soo goot.

Auls etj mie feftien Joah lohta deepe leet, wea daut dreaje Joah noch emma Thema. Woo earnst de leewa Gott doch mett siene Tjinja maunjchmol uck ohne een Wuat too saje räde kunn! Joh, joh...

Bie de Doop wull etj eene oppjestalde Theorie utproowe: Prädja Peeta Toews, de Eltesta vonne Chortitza, enn ons Nohba, sull jesajcht habe, daut see aune '36 mau soo väl Wota bie de Doop bruckte, auls daut jiedrem Doopskaundidoht toostund. Aulso: wea daut een groota Sinda jewast, dann diretjcht een Schulps utem Schmaundkauntje dem oppen Kopp jeete; wea dee Kaundidoht oba mau een tjlena Sinda jewast, dann tjreajch dee mau eene tjliene, haulwe Jappsvoll. Eenem Meddelmässja stund eene volle Japps too, enn een

Baptism

The year of our Lord, 1936, proved to be a decisive one; possibly as significant in the annals of mankind as when the Red Sea parted and the Children of Israel walked right through it, unconcernedly and with dry feet. In the Canadian Prairies it was so dry and so hot and then dry again that people around the clock reckoned that the End had come. And for us Mennonites, that year represented nothing short of a crises, since, as already documented elsewhere, there was too little water around for the Mennonite Brethren to conduct proper baptisms, while the General Conference was likewise at the end of its collective wits. So what was to be done? Conferences were assembled, much talk and more discussions ensued, and even the occasional quarrel broke out, I heard say. And then? The Brethren simply started baptizing with a gravy boat, while the Conference handed out rain checks and that was that.

When I got baptized fifteen years later, that dry year was still a topic widely and hotly discussed. It just went to prove how seriously our loving Father dealt with His children even without having to speak a single word of Yiddish.

During the baptismal occasion I intended to put to test a formulated theory: The Reverend Peter Töws, the bishop of the Chortitza, and our neighbour, had supposedly claimed that in 1936 only as much water as necessary was to be used to baptize a candidate. In practice this meant: if a baptismal candidate had been a serious sinner, then he or she was to get a liberal dash of water straight from the gravy boat and right over the forehead, appropriately bent; however, if the baptismal candidate had been a lesser sinner, then a smaller handful of water generally encased in a cream jug sufficed. A middle of the road sinner was

173

butajeweehnlijch Feina tjreajch mau eenen Neihoot äwrem Czebrientje.

Enn nu wea wie aune Reaj too dee Doop: mien ellra Brooda Peeta, donn etj, enn miene jinjre Sesta Auna, eene Feine. Peeta haud Prädja Enns eemol twee Dohla fe eene Fuah Sweet Clovagoawe aufjenohme, dee, soo haud Voda jesajcht, omsonst wea. Enn wess woah, nu tjreajch hee eene volle Japps Wota äwrem Heeft jegohte, daut'a sijch duckt. Enn etj tjreajch mau weinja auls de Halft, enn Auna mau een Teeläpeltje voll äwa ährem easchten Tonie-Perm, aulso Duawall. Aulso, soo docht etj mie, haud de leewa Gott hiea diretjcht de Finjasch emm Spell.

Oba daut Thema vonne rejchtje mennische Doop wea noch lang nijch too Enj. Toom Biespell, kaum de Eltesta Doft Klosse vonne Barjchtola mett dreehundat Siede Bibelforschung aun, dee etj äwasatte sull, wiels hee nu endlijch wisst, woo daut aulatoop musst. "Kloa enn dietjlijch enn endlijch biblisch," säd'a. Oba Prädja Doft Faust, een kohlkoppja Offenbarungs-expert, säd, daut eena mett dem Heiljen Jeist jedeept woare musst, enn daut jintj bloß emm schälendet Wota, enn nijch enne Gravel-Kuhl ooda em Dooploch medde unjre Tjoatjeflooah.

Daut gauf tjeen Enj vonne Debatte. Enn Steinbach gauf'et eene Jemeend, dee uck unjaduckte, oba noh Hinje; eene aundre Jemeend haud bett nutoo dee Kaundidohte biem noh Väare unjaducke de latzte Sind aufjespeelt.

Wiels mie daut aulatoop too väl word, trock etj mie eenfach tridj, omm mie daut Gaunze mol too äwalaje. Oba nu ess mien Seatje too Enj, enn etj woa mie boold de rejchtje Jemeend aunschlute. Vleijcht well Jie uck? Wann joh, woa etj Junt saje, woo daut nu rajchtschuldijch enn endjiltijch mott.

Eene niee, ajchte Tjoatj woat boold jebut, enn etj sie Shareholder, aulso Aktionär. Disse Tjoatj woat kratjcht soo groot auls de Tempel on the Mount senne, bloß daut se

to receive a cupped handful, while a dainty and hesitant, a strictly amateur sinner got at most a thimbleful poured over his, but mostly her, cowlick.

And now our turn had come to be baptized: my older brother Peter, then I, and then my younger sister Annie, a dainty and semi-saintly candidate. Peter had once charged the Preacher Ennses two dollars for a load of sweet clover sheaves, which our father had said was free. And sure enough: Now he got a goodly and generous measure of virgin well water dashed right over his crown which buckled his very knees. I got less than half that amount, while Annie received about a teaspoonful over her first Toni-Perm of home-made manufacture. Ah ha! I thought to myself. Our Father in heaven obviously has His fingers personally involved in every pie of human wherewithal.

However the topic regarding the proper Mennonite form of baptism was not over by any means. For instance, Bishop David Klassen from the Bergthalers came waddling over with some three hundred pages of biblical research, which I was meant to translate, since he had arrived at the final solution in matters of baptism. "Clear and simple and biblical," he pronounced, since he knew with authoritative finality how it all came together. However, Preacher David Fast, a bald-headed expert on Revelations, said that one was to be baptized by the Holy Spirit and that this was only possible in running water and not in gravel pits or in baptismal pits under church floors.

There was no end to that debate. In Steinbach there was one congregation which baptized by immersion but backwards, while a competing congregation shampooed away all sin by forward inclination of immersion in the water.

Since all this became too much for me, I simply withdrew in order to contemplate and reflect on this matter in its entirety. But now I am finished with my search and my research and I will soon join the right church. Are you interested in joining me? If so, I will tell you the right way and properly explain all the means to that end.

A new, genuine church is soon to be constructed and I am a shareholder in the enterprise. This church will be built exactly

diretjcht äwa eene Rie jebut woare woat. Aulso woat daut Wota derjch den Tjoatjetjalla ranne, dann unjre Kaunzel, enn dann väarewajch nohm Hudson's Bay opptoo, ooda weet etj woahan. Enn aum Enj von dem Meddelgang enn verre Kaunzel woat eene groote Luck jebut, dee soo auls eene Däah ohptooklaupe jeiht, wann sijch eena deepe lohte well. Enn fuats bie de Luck jefft'et een Stäwtje, wiels? Joh, wiels wie haude enn Jrienthol aul feftijch Joahlang gaunz rejchtijch enn biblisch jehaundelt: Fe tjliene Sindasch, soo auls Auna enn etj donn weare, woat uck hiea mett een Schmaundkauntje mau mässijch een Schulpstje äwrem Bless jegohte. Fe derjchschnettelje Sindasch saul dann een Fattkommtje jebruckt woare, aulso een vollet Stelpsel. Fe de Schwoajewijchtla em sindje woat de Luck ohpjemoakt, enn de Sindebock woat doa vom Prädja jrindlijch aufjespeelt, von hinje enn von väare. Enn de Super Schwoajewijchtla em sindje, soo auls ritje steinbachsche Koaredealasch, ooda faulsche Propheete, ooda Investment Dealasch? Dee motte eascht em Stäwtje nenn, enn doa woat ahn de Kopp mett een Lieta Shampoo ennjerubbelt, enn dann de gaunza Tjarpa mett Seep enjeräwe. Dann noch eemol, enn dann woare see aufjespeelt, enn dann woat de Luck ohpjemoakt, enn dann woare see soo lang jedeept auls daut needijch ess. Doabie ess de Prädja aunjebunge, de Kaundidoht nijch, enn daut Wota ess soo rietend, kolt, fresch, enn deep auls Gottes Jnohd. Wiels daut Wota doch bediedend ruzht sinjt bieaun de Jemeend aule Stoophe von dem Leed, opp Dietsch, "Ich weiß einen Strom" von Bordjanksy. Daut pausst toom Thema.

according to the specifications of the Temple on the Mount, with the exception being that this church will be constructed directly over a brook, a creek, a small river, if you will. Meaning, obviously, that the water will run through the church basement, then underneath the pulpit and then ever on to Hudson's Bay or wherever it was meant to go with the flow. At the end of the main church aisle, and just before the pulpit, a sizeable hatch is to be constructed, which can be opened like a door if a person chooses to get on with baptism by immersion. Right beside the hatch a small assembly room will be located, and why that, and to what end? Simply, because we Grünthalers had it right all along; even fifty years ago we had understood with inspired clarity how the Bible had the final and appropriate say in this vital matter.

For lesser sinners as Annie and I were at the time, baptism here is conducted by a cream jug with a small measure of fresh water poured right over the blaze of the forehead. For average sinners of middleweight status a gravy train in miniature is to be used, meaning a goodly measure of Adam's Ale to be dashed straight over the sinner's head. And as for the heavyweight sinners, the latch is then opened wide with the true and literal scapegoat being thoroughly scrubbed fore and aft. As for the super heavyweights in matters of sinning like the wealthy Steinbach car dealers, or false prophets or investment dealers? They are first taken to the small assembly room already mentioned, and a full litre of shampoo is rubbed into their scalp. Then the entire body of the prodigious sinner is thoroughly scrubbed with a premium brand of soap. This ablution is repeated, then the latch is opened wide, and then such previously depraved Men of Mammon are baptized for as long as it takes. While so doing, the baptizing minister is contained by a stout length of rope, while the baptismal candidate is free, not contained, with the water running fast and furious and cold and fresh and as deep as God's grace. Since the rushing water tends to be all too apparent, the congregation sings all the noise subduing verses in German of "*Ich weiß einen Strom*". That does the trick and fits the theme.

De Hiebatsche

"Nu ess'et Tiet," säd de Hiebatsche aum Sinndach, fong aun em earnsten too doktere, läd sijch han, enn wea dree Doag lohta doot. De Hiebatsche word näjentijch Joah oolt, oba ahr sach'et aul feftien Joah soo auls Nooah sien ella-achtje Fru. De latzte veatijch Joah wea see eene Wätfru enn head opp too ellre. Âah Maun wea deelwies een Grunzkujel, Suatopp enn een sturra Priejel. Auls hee noch läwd, haude de Hiebats eene Lauftje, woohnt see oba strenj Stua nannde.

Etj wea mau eenmol, aul lang, lang tridj enn dem Stua, enn daut eenmol reatjcht mie dann uck bett nu too. Etj wull Âditj toom Suregurtje ennlaje tjeepe, oba de oola Hiebat säd, dee wea sua jeworde, enn "de russlendsche Manneare wull uck tjeena tjeepe, enn dee hab etj rutjeschmäte, enn de Darpshunj fraute dee opp, enn tjreaje Liefschniedinj doavon." Dann wisst etj, woo enn woa de Fortj em Stähl stuak, enn etj muak omm den oolen Hiebat eenen grooten Boage.

De Hiebatsche wea vonne Chortitza vom oolen Stil, aulso wea bie ahr, soo auls Peeta Tjäla mie latzt vetald, tjeen Unjascheet tweschen "Läwensgang enn Gloowe, aulso Wuat enn Waundel, enn ons Tjristentum ess nijch bloos aum Sinndach wirtjsom" meend hee, enn wiels hee mett Swaut Al Reima Frindschauft ess, nauhm etj ahm daut auf.

Butadem schreef de oole Hiebatsche aul feftijch Joah fe de *Steinbach Post*, enn soohnt, soo musst etj jistre erfoahre, jefellt dem leewen Gott.

Mrs Hiebert

"My time has come," said Mrs Hiebert on Sunday, and then she started a brief, serious round of doctoring, laid down and three days later she was dead.

Mrs Hiebert was ninety years of age when she packed it in, but she looked like Noah's wife for the last fifteen years of her life. She was a widow for forty years of her life and as of then, she stopped aging. Her husband, in his day, was a curmudgeon, a sourpuss and a killjoy. When he was still alive, the Hieberts owned a store and it is from there that he practiced his nasty nature.

I was in the store only once and that was long, long ago but that one visit was perfectly enough to last me to the end of his days and almost mine. It was my intent to buy some vinegar to pickle dills but Old Hiebert said, "that the vinegar had turned sour, and, also, no one wanted to buy the Russian-Mennonite manners he had for sale, ever since I moved to town and he had had to throw them out. The village dogs had eaten these non-saleable items, and had gotten a bad case of the shits." It was obvious how our two forks fit the handle as we say in the dialect and I made a wide sweep of the man and his store from that day on.

Mrs Hiebert was of the Old Chortitza Style, meaning that there was no difference, as Peter Kehler recently said, between "Walk of Life and Faith, between Word and Deed; our Christianity is not only effective on Sundays," and because he is related to Al Reimer, a friend, I believed him.

Soo auls daut noh de niee Mood Mood jeworde ess, jintjch etj uck nohm "Viewing" aulso noh de Leichenschau em Birchwood en Steinbach.

Wann eena maunjche Mensche, besondasch de rietsche, eentungje Menniste em Soatjch betjitjcht, dann sitte'et de uck noch emm Doot noh "unfinished Bizniss" oba nijch bie de konservatiewe Menniste. Wann see doot send, ess doa em Soatjch tjeena Tus, see send Bowe, gaunz enn goa. Soo uck de Hiebatsche; see wea, soo auls jesajcht, eene chortitzsche Fru vom oolen Stil, vom oolen Kalenda.

Etj bleef weens dree Minute, soo lang auls daut dieat bett aul de hiesje Kroohnsthola eenem jeseehne habe, enn dann jintjch etj mett Bletjch haulf noh Unje jedretjcht aune rajchte Kaunt rut.

Auls etj aum Stäftje vebiejintjch wea de Däah eene tjliene Retz op enn etj, noch emma een Tucks nieschierijch, glupt doa eene haulwe Sekund nenn. Daut sull sijch dann uck meist loohne, wiels doa brennd een tjlienet Tauljlijcht, enn hinjrem Desch en Lehnstoohl saut tjeen aundra auls de leewa Gott.

Mie veschluag mol wada toom tweeden Mol enn mienem Läwe de Sproak, seea soo auls etj Leahra Schäfa toom easchten Mol too seehne tjreajch. Oba dee Oola kaum mie fuats too Help, auls etj ahm dann doch schliesslijch fruag: "Na, Voda, best Du vebiestat?"

Hee sajcht: "Wann soohne mennische Mummtjess, dee noch niemols Betjze ooda Jeans jedroagt habe, wiels see sijch mett ähre aufjeoabeide Been nijch schäme, enn dann uck noch meea auls een haulwet Läwe fe de *Steinbach Post* Goods jeschräwe habe, enn uck sesst eene goode Mutta enn Grootmutta enn uck Nohbasche jewast send, dann kohm etj perseenlijch dee nohm Himmel mett too nehme."

Etj nauhm mie uck fuats väa fe aule mennische Zeitunge too schriewe, waut etj kaun, bloos nijch fe *Den Booten* wiels dissa ess vom rajchtjen Wajch aufjekohme, enn mie nijch well.

Moreover, Mrs Hiebert has been writing for the *Steinbach Post* (then *Mennonitische Post*), for fifty years and this, as I was to experience yesterday, is pleasing unto the Lord.

In accordance with things in vogue, or in style, I also went to her viewing at the Birchwood Funeral Chapel in Steinbach.

When viewing certain people, particularly the eagerly ambitious single-tongued Mennonites in their coffin, they look like so much Unfinished Business; however such is not the case with Conservative Mennonites. When they are dead, then there is no one at home in the coffin; they are gone, have migrated with all they were and had and are. This was also true of Mrs Hiebert; she was, as already mentioned, a Chortitza woman of the old style, from the old Calendar.

I stayed for a good three minutes, long enough for the local Kronsthalers to see me, and then, with my eyes cast down, I exited from the right side.

When I walked past the little assembly room for ministers to the side, the door was slightly ajar and since I was just a tad curious, I threw in a glance, half a second long. That fleeting effort was almost worth the effort as things turned out, because a candle was burning in those little chambers and behind the desk on an easy chair sat none other than God Himself.

For the second time in my life, speech failed me, similar to the time I first met Teacher Schäfer of the MCI, who had more dignity in one finger than does an entire ball team of George Bush lookalikes. However, the Old Fellow immediately came to my assistance, when I asked Him, "How Now, Old Chap, are you lost?"

He responded, "Whenever such Mennonite women, who have never worn pants or jeans because they were not ashamed of their work weary legs and who have, on top of all that written for the *Steinbach Post* for half their lives, and have been good mothers and grandmothers and neighbours as well, then I personally come to take them home when their life is over."

Etj saj: "Voda, waut kaun etj fe Die doohne?"

"Du kaunst mie toom Owendkost ennlohde, etj reisd een bät haustijch von Tus auf," sajcht'a, "enn hab vejäte, mie de needje Dohlasch enntoofuppre, enn hiea enn Steinbach omsonst too äte, wudd mie woll nijch jletjche, meenst nijch uck?"

"Daut kaun goot senne," saj etj, "komm, well'we foahre."

Auls wie toop utem Birchwood enn uck äwrem Hoff doa jinje, tjitjchte de Tjinja mett groote Uage noh mienem Gaust, oba de ellre Mensche worde ahm nijch enn, oba doch: een Prädja mett stiewen Jenetjch, een Tjliewa, vonne Fully Independent Gospellers, meend soo biem Vebiegohne: "Dem Tjeadel sitte't judsch, waut haft dee hiea too seatje?"

Etj haud enn mienem Van soo auls jeweehnlijch onse twee dietsche Schäfahunj mett, enn disse pausse opp mie seea opp, enn brelle jiedem Framden dee Uahre voll, oba jistre zeowentz, auls dee himmlischa Oola ennsteajch, saute see soo aundajchtijch, meist soo auls wann see den leewen Gott toom easchten mol jeseehne haude.

Wie hilde noch schwind enn Bloomenoat aun, wiels de Oola doaropp bestund, een poah Worschtenja fe de Hunj too tjeepe, enn dann fuah wie wieda noh Doehners, woa'rett Giros mett Tsatziki jefft, woohnt dem leewen Gott noch ut siene Jugend auls Hee mett dem Apostel Paulus väl unjawäajess wea, bekaunt wea.

Auls wie mett dem Âte foadijch weare, woohnt je mett Ahm toop emma een bät schwinda jeiht auls jeweehnlijch, wiels eena je nijch danke bruckt, porrd Hee, weils ahm je noch mett dee Hiebatsche toop eene lange Ries, von Kroohnsthol bett Tus väastund.

Enn doa oppem Hof biem Birchwood haundreahd wie, enn dann dacht'et eenmol seea opp, enn wajch wear'a!

I immediately decided to start writing for Mennonite newspapers as well, and whatever I am capable of, except for *Der Bote*, because it has hopelessly lost its way.

I said, "Father, what can I do for you?"

"You can invite me to dinner. I took off from home a bit abruptly," he said, "and forgot to pocket the necessary currency, and to get a free meal here in Steinbach would hardly be possible, right?"

"That's most likely the way it is." I said. "Come, let's go!"

When we left the Birchwood together and walked across the yard, the children looked at Him with very big eyes, but the older people took no note of Him. However, a stiff-necked preacher, a fellow by the name of Kliewer, from the Fully Independent Gospellers mumbled to himself in passing, "That fellow looks Jewish, what might he be up to?"

As usual I had my German Shepherd dogs along with me in the SUV and these guard me with their lives and swear fiercely at any intruder, but last night when the Heavenly Father stepped into my Pilot SUV, they were as reverential as if they had seen God Himself for the first time.

We stopped over in Blumenort briefly because the Old Fellow insisted on buying meat ends for the dogs, before setting out for Döhners Restaurant where giros is served with tzatziki, which The Old Fellow well remembered from His youthful days when he was up and about with Apostle Paul in Turkey and related areas.

When we were through dining with the Old Fellow, which takes less time because saying grace is not called for in His presence, He suggested we get on with it since He had yet to take a long journey, together with Mrs Hiebert, all the way from Kronsthal to Home.

It was on the Birchwood Yard, when we shook hands in farewell, that a brief but intense lightning bolt shot out of nowhere and then He was gone.

Saj "Dankscheen", Peeta

Jeat Thiessen ut Paraguay ess een butajeweenelja Mensch, nijch bloß wiels hee mien Onkel ess, nä, väl meea wiels hee mett eene jeboagne Wead nijch bloß Tjinja eent äwre Huck resse kaun, oba hee kaun mett deeselwje Wead uck Wota unjre Ead finje. Butadem kaun hee billewoohn Poppajei daut sinje enn piepre biebrinje.

Thiessen wull eajentlijch goanijch noh Paraguay, oda daut M.C.C. säd hee sull mau schmock doahan gohne enn Wota seatje enn de Poppajeies doa een bät beleahre. Donn fuah Thiesse mett siene kurrje Fru enn mett siene veea Tjinja noh de Arbuseweaj enn Siedamerikau, noh Paraguay.

"By Gosh, enn by Golly!" säd Thiesse auls'a doa sach, waut'et aules gauf: Ope, Mensche, Indiauna, noaktje Tjinja enn bunte Monkeys. Butadem sach hee doa Väjel, bunte Poppajeies, wille Schwien (oba mau veeabeensche säd Thiesse emma) enn Nordamerikauna mett entjelde Tunge, "de Donnasch räde mau eene Sproak enn dee mau schlajcht," meend Thiesse. Disse Tjräte habe woll auls Tjinja väl too weinijch Priejel jetjreaje. Dee sennt je enjebilda enn noch daumelja auls Tus de Molotschna," vetald Jeat Thiesse emma.

Well Thiessen mußt doa een Loch growe enn doa medde manke Bananestude eene Sirrei bue. Wann Thiesse sijch nijch den Schweet wescht dann schluach hee Näjel enn, enn wann hee nijch de Ope enn de Poppajeies wajchgruld, dann mußt hee siene Tjinja ommhohle, dee nu mett de noaktje Indiaunatjinja späle wulle. Boold haud Thiesse een Hus, een Hiestje, een Staul, veea Foatjel, eene Säj, enn eenen Poppajei,

Say "Thank you", Peter

George A. Thiessen in Paraguay was an unusual person, and not only because he was my uncle. He often cut willow switches with his pocket knife and then converted them into miracles of wonder. Occasionally he used those very switches to administer good works on the naughty behinds of the village urchins, but mainly he employed them to find water. And lastly, Uncle George could teach any pedigree of parrot to whistle and sing in numerous languages.

It was not Thiessen's intention to go to Paraguay, but the Mennonite Central Committee decreed that he go there, because it was God's Will to find water in those parts, and to contain his parrot's salty tongue a trifle. And so Uncle George gathered his wife and his children, four in number, and took off to Paraguay, the watermelon cradle of South America.

Thiessen was used to surprises but this new country contained more Ahas! than he had expected—monkeys, Indians, naked children and hairy apes. "By gosh and by golly," he said even before breakfast on a daily basis. He also saw strange birds, gaudy parrots and wild pigs—but only four-legged ones, he commonly said. "And North Americans with grooved tongues," he observed. "Scoundrels who speak only one language, and even that one poorly." He claimed that the lot had not been properly thrashed as kids. Also, that gang was more conceited and altogether more lacking than the *Molotschnaer* at home.

Finally, when his surprises wore off, he had no choice but to dig a hole in the middle of a banana grove for the base, then foundation of a *serrei* or shack. When Uncle George wasn't

enn dissa wea tweemol soo groot enn dreemol soo straum auls bille een Deffat.

"Een strauma Tjnäwel," säd Thiesse emma, "oba rede kaun hee nijch väl dolla auls een fiewendartijchjoascha doowa Esel. Enn wann daut nijch boold aundasch woat, dann woa etj dem heeschen Schinda den Zoagel bett hinjre Uahre aufhacke."

"Oba nä, oba na!" säde de Tjinja, enn hielde enn prachade: "Pappa, loht dem straumen Peeta doch läwe; hee woat boold sinje auls een Tuntjennitj."

"O.K.", säd Thiesse, "loht ahm noch dree Moonat stohne, oba wann hee dann nijch räde kaun, dann tratj etj ahm de Peesre eenselwies ute Flijchte!:

Nu eewde de Tjinja mett dem Poppajei Dach enn Nacht daut räde; jiedesmol wann hee een Stetjstje Äte tjreajch, säde see aula: "Saj Dankscheen, Peeta, saj Dankscheen!" Oba Peeta scheddad sijch, fraut doppeld soo väl, enn säd nuscht. Ooltnässijch weara ernoa; hee fluach aulewäje romm, lohd sijch selwst bie de Nobasch toom Äte enn, hee gruld de Kaute enn beet de Hunj, hee piesakt de Ope enn vefeahd de Tjinja, oba räde? "Not even boo," säd Thiesse.

Maunjchmol wann Thiesse mett dem Poppajei auleen wea, säd hee toom straumen Peeta: "Du best een schataja Ooltnäs; etj woa die den Schnowel aufhacke, vleijcht bett hinjre Uahre! Du best daumelja auls de Amerikauna, du wesst blooß fräte, enn die auleweaje nennmisiche, oba waut doohne? Nuscht wesst du doohne, nijch mol eene Sproak kaunst du, du krommschnowelja Ami-Schwienäjel. Wach mau, wann etj wada mett die Unjared hool, dann… "

De Tjinja eewde mett dem Poppajei enn säde bie jiedrem Keiwsel: "Peeta, saj doch Dankscheen!" oba Peeta faddad sijch, läd een krommet Ei, enn wea hejchstens netjsch, oba räde? Tjeen Wuat.

Aum Sinnowent haude Thiesses jrots Fieaowend; de Thiessche haud Tweeback jebackt, de Tjinja haude sijch den

wiping the sweat off his brow, he hammered in nails, and when he wasn't dispersing snoopy monkeys, he had to round up his children who were bent on playing with the naked hordes of Indian children. It was not all that long before Thiessen had himself a house, a barn, an outhouse, four piglets, a sow and a parrot twice as big as any pigeon cock. "A magnificent fellow!" Thiessen said. "But talk?" he admitted, "That sanctimonious fatso won't witness any more than a thirty five year old deaf and dumb donkey ass. And if he won't improve on his reputation, then I'll chop his tail off right behind his ears!"

"Oh no, oba nay!" his children cried and lamented. "Let our beautiful Peter live, please do; we'll have him singing and warbling like a wren within a week or so."

"O.K." said Thiessen, "I'll give him another three months. But if he won't talk by then, I'll pluck his feathers out one by one."

So the children worked on moody Peter day and night. Every time they gave him a morsel, they chimed, "Peter, please, say thank you!" But all Peter did was shake his plumage and eat twice as much as he deserved but said nothing. He was a cocky rover, no doubt about it; he roamed and ranged at will, invited himself to the neighbours for free meals, harassed the cats and stabbed the dogs, molested the monkeys and stuka-bombed the children. But talk? "Not even boo!" Thiessen observed disgustedly, and spat in a wide arc. Sometimes when he was alone with the parrot, he whispered threateningly; "You are a smart-ass good for nothing, Peter, and you know that! I'll hack your beak off behind the ears, maybe sooner than you think! You're as stupid as the Americans: you just want to eat and meddle, but when it comes to fulfilling your mission you go AWOL. It is your job to learn to talk, you crooked-beaked Ami-pig-dog! And if you choose to forget that, we'll have to take you to the chopping block and there will be blood and feathers to pay… "

187

Hauls enn de Uahre jewosche. Thiesse haud sijch uck too Aufwatjslung de Feet jeboht, daut Owenkost daumpt oppem Desch! Mett eenmol jrods biem Bäde schreaje de Schwien so jaumalijch, daut Thiesse de Schrootflint too hoole tjreajch enn loos oakad, Thiesses Peeta nauhm de Atjs enn zaubeld hinjreaun, de Thiessche nauhm daut Schlachtmassa enn de Tjinja rannde mett dem Soltstreia hinjeraun!. "Tiejasch, Leiws, dolle Ope enn Diewels manke Schwien," schreajch Thiesse, oba noch väl dolla belltjte de Schwien. Nu stund de gaunze Thiesse Armee verrem Schwienshock, reed toom Aunjriep.

Oba aunstaut Leiws enn Tiejasch, dolle Ope enn Diewels saut de bunta Peeta oppem Schwien, preatjeld dem jraßlijch aune Uahre enn aum Jenetj enn schreajch emma wada: "Saj Dankscheen, Peeta, du fulet Luda, saj Dankscheen Peeta, du domma Molotschna, etj woa die daut Räde biebrinje, saj Dankscheen du M.C.C. Fulpelz. Etj hack die den Zoagel bet hinjre Uahre auf, saj Dankscheen Du fula Kujel, du… "

The Thiessen children redoubled their efforts, withholding food and desserts in a desperate attempt to get Peter to yap. "Why don't you say thank you, Peter; please, please say thank you, just once." But Peter merely preened himself, laid a crooked egg and pouted.

Saturday evening had come and the work of the week had been done. Mrs Thiessen, Aunt Agatha, had baked Mennonite buns, the children had scrubbed their neck and ears, and George Thiessen had even laundered his feet for a change. The evening meal was steaming Mennonite style on the table, aromatic and serene. Suddenly, just as they were saying grace, a horrific donnybrook erupted among the pigs in the barn. "Tigers, devils, mad apes or Americans among the pigs!" Thiessen hollered and went for his shotgun, his double-barreled Nevermiss. His eldest, Peter, grabbed a pickaxe and sprinted after him while Aunt Agatha took the butcher knife to hand and galloped in the parade. The pigs were screaming so loudly, you could hardly hear the yells of the Thiessen family brigade. Within seconds they were lined up and ready at the pigsty gate, their armaments threatening.

But instead of tigers, devils or mad monkeys, it was Peter, big, bright and cocky Peter, who was bronco-riding a terrorized sow, nipping and snapping her horribly about the ears, and squawking at the top of his lungs, "Say thank you, Peter, say thank you, you lazy devil, you crazy *Molotschnaer*! I'll teach you how to talk and yodel and that right now! Say thank you, you pious lazy bastard! I'll chop your tail off right behind your ears, you lazy pig-dog you... "

Tjnippse

Mett de Tiet nehme de measchte Sinde aul noch auf, lohte noh, heare opp, vedonnste eenfach. Maunjche Sind oba bliewe bestohne, jelle aulso uck noch vondoag. Eene von dee Sind, woohne soo oolt auls daut Paradies ess, ess de Unterlassungssünde. Enn doamett wie ons uck rejchtijch vestohne, enn Mensche nijch mett "Etj docht mau" ooda "Meenst wertjlijch?" enn mett opnet Mul kohme, woa etj daut uck fuats opp Enjlisch fausthoole, aulso "sin of omission." Enn nu weet jie.

Enn disse Sind hab etj begohne, oba, oba! Etj wea latzt em Super-Valu Stooa, enn auls etj doa eene jestuckte, oba frindlijche Fru enn eene jewaultje Kordonddoos mett dartijch ooda noch meea Arbuse rundomm sach, foll mie miene Unterlassungssind, soo auls eent mett eenem Bassemstäl äwrem Bless jeresst, bie.

Dee Fru saut doa enne Doos, frindlijch enn besonne, enn fe eenen Dolah tjnippst see Arbuse opp Plautdietsch. Enn säd doabie: "Eene roode, riepe saul daut senne?" Donn tjnippst see dee Arbuse entweda aum Buck ooda aune Uahre, ooda sogoa aum Hinjarenj, enn säd metteenst: "Hiea ess se" hoof dee ute Doos soo eenen gooden Meeta rut, enn dann wea uck aul de neajchste Kundschauft draun. "Nijch aul too riep, soo meea noh de molotschna Oat, toom enlaje saul dee senne, enn wann see een bätje noh Gurtje schmatjcht, dann schod daut uck nuscht, wiels soohne Lied nijch bäta weete, joh?" Enn wada veschwung bie dee Fru een Dohla enne Tausch, enn de Lied

190

Thumping
(Watermelons)

In the course of time most sins tend to slacken, reduce in import, or simply altogether cease to be; just evaporate, as chronology strides on and dictates forgiveness. Some sins, however, remain in effect and are with us, still and always. One such transgression is the sin of omission. To prevent any misunderstanding, with people staring vacuously and talking mindlessly, "But all I did was think that..." or "Are you serious?" or hanging around open-mouthed; I am now going to put the matter in English, which states, and I repeat, is the "sin of omission." And now you know.

And it is this sin I have committed, my, oh my! I recently was in the Super Value Store in Steinbach where I saw a portly, but friendly woman from Kazakhstan via Germany, sitting in a giant sized cardboard box with sixty or even more watermelons keeping her company, and then and there my sin of omission hit me with the full force of a rake handle bashing me a good one on the snoot.

The woman was sitting in the box, friendly but reflective, and for one dollar she thumped watermelons in Low German. While thumping she said, "A red ripe one is what you want?" And then she proceeded to thump the watermelon either on its belly or on the ears, or even on its rear end, before pronouncing, "Here it is" and lifting it a full metre out of the box; then it was the next customer's turn. "Not all that ripe, more in the Molotschna style, for pickling it is meant to be, and if the melon tastes a bit of dill pickled cucumber, then such

191

jinje mett ähre Arbus noh de Kauss. Enn nu de näajchste: "Een bät noh Kaunsus sull de Arbus schmatje, joh?" enn nu word de Tjnippsasche soo iewrijch auls een Trajchtmoaka, enn boold hohld see eene dunkeljreene, strieptje Arbus mett een druggeljet Bucktje utem Klompe. "Een Dohla, oba mett Garantie, bitte." "Enn jie welle de jratzte woohnt'et jeft fe daut Jeld, aulso acht Dohla enn näjentachentijch Zent? Oba groot enn seet mett weinja Tjäna, doamett ditmol dee Tjinja nijch eene Arbusestud em Buck wausse woat, joh? Hiea ess se!" "Enn jie welle de baste Arbus woohne mett de ditjbuckje Scherwaundasch vonne elloagsche Berstaund Frindschauft ess, joh?" Enn soo jintjch daut wieda. Enn emma wieda, enn dann too Enj! De Arbuseklompe wea meist wajch, bloos soo eenjefäah feftien Stetj, woohne de Tjnippspriefung nijch bestohne haude, enn nu eensaum enn velohte doa lage, soo's äwajelohtne oole Mäadtjess, enn em Tjoatjetjalla auleen oolt woare motte.

Joh, oba nu well jie weete, woarenn de Unterlassungssind besteiht, joh? Gaunz eenfach, dee besteiht doarenn, daut de groote, oole Konst—enn bloos fe Menniste toojelohte—joh de seldne Gow Arbuse aum Buck too tjnippse meist veloahre jegohne ess. Enn daut toom Deel derjch miene Schuld, wiels etj hab de Gow enn mienem Hoat enn enn miene Finjasch enschlope lohte.

Etj säd Gow, enn meend uck Gow. Wiels mien Voda, dee jratsta Elloaga enn hundat Joah, kunn buta Tenor biem "Ich weiß einen Strom" dreemol daut Joah enne Tjoatj sinje, enn sijch äwa Stalin oajre, nijch väl waut meea, oba Arbusetjnippse kunn hee bäta auls een Psychiauta, aulso Dokta Phil., daut Jeld talle kaun.

Wann daut Aunfong August soo wiet wea, dann jintjch dee Oola oppe Berstaund, tjneed sijch bie de Arbuse han, muak de Uage too, enn daut Mul op, enn tjnippst, enn horjcht doabie mett scheewet Ooah soo auls ons Hund Bobbat bie een Piepamusloch, enn dann tjnippst hee noch eene, enn dann

is alright, too, because such folk don't know any better, joh?"
And again the thumping woman pocketed a dollar, with the
customer off, dragging the juicy fruit to the cashier. And now
the next customer, just step up, "A bit of Kansas you'd like in
the taste, joh?" and then the thumper became as eager as a
chiropractor and made for a dark green, striped melon with a
chubby paunch, "One dollar, but it comes with a warranty."
"And you are on the search for the biggest one for the money,
like eight dollars and ninety eight cents? But it has to be big
and sweet with few seeds in it so it won't start sprouting in your
children's gut?, joh? Here it is!" "And you are on the lookout
for a fat-bellied one related to the heavyweights from Elloag
on the Dnieper, joh?" And that is the way things went. And
then again, starting from the beginning until finally, the
excitement was over. The pile of watermelons was almost
depleted with only about fifteen remaining, which had not
passed the muster, and were left behind forlorn like so many
overlooked girls of elderly vintage, sitting around in church
basements, left to age in lonely neglect.

Joh, but you are eager to know wherein the sin of omission
lies, right? It lies, pure and simply in the fact that the great, old
gift—and reserved exclusively for Mennonites—namely, the
art of thumping watermelons in the solar plexus to determine
the state of supreme choiceness has almost been lost. And this
has happened in part, through a fault of mine, because I have
allowed this precious talent to wither on the vine of my heart
and in my fingers.

I stated "gift" and that's exactly what I meant. Because my
father, the most prodigious fellow from Elloag on the Dnieper
for a hundred years and counting, could, aside from singing
mightily in a tenor voice "Oh have you not heard of that
beautiful stream?" three times yearly in church, and getting
steaming mad at Stalin twice daily, do little else of any use but

193

noch een poah, enn dann plock hee twee auf, enn dee musst etj noh Hus droage.

Babe Ruth haud een batting average von eenjefäah .350, oba Voda haud een Tjnippsderjchschnett von weens .950.

Joh, enn donn kaume mett eenmol de Arbuse bie de Dusende von Reimasch ut Steinbach mett ähre groote Trocks ut Texas jefeat, enn de groote, wann uck seldne Tjnippskonst, vedräajd soo auls daut Krolltje aune Arbuseranke.

Oba doamett noch lang nijch too Enj, nä, nä, wiels daut gauf en Russlaund uck noch mennische Tjnippsasch, head etj saje, dee Mensche, oba uck Tjinja, entweda aum Kopp, ooda aune Brost, ooda oppem Ridje tjnippse kunne, enn dann fuats oppe Städ wisste, woo daut mett de Tookunft vom Jetjnippsten bestalt wea.

Etj wudd dit nijch jejleewt, enn daut beleib nijch wieda vetalt habe, wann nijch mien gooda Frind, een Ooltkoloniea vonne baste Sort, mie sienatiet nijch vetalt haud, daut een jiedet Mädtje, woohnt de Hejchre-Mädtjesschool enn Chortitza beseatje wull, verhäa jetjnippst word. Wann de Tjnippsa dann mett dem Kopp netjcht, dann word see oppjenohme, wann de Tjnippsa oba Bedentjche haud, dann word dee Kaundidoht entweda noh de Tjrim noh de breedajemeendsche Biebel-school jeschetjt, ooda see leahd neie, ooda see word too de Mulbäarupe fe den Siedberoop utjeleahd. Ooda eenfach noh de Stäts jeschetjcht, wiels doa nijch välwaut velangt word. Daut weet jie, enn wann nijch, dann froagt bloos Bosche Jeat.

Jie tjenne jleewe waut jie welle, oba eent ess bie aul dem eenfach soo: Dem Tjnippsa sien Erfoljsderjchschnett lach wiet äwa .900, aulso mielewiet bäta auls aule Schoolpsychologen enn sesstje Experte toop! Oba tridj noh miene Unjalohtungs-sind: etj woa näajchste Wäatj en Steinbach enn eene jewaultje Kordondoos voll mett Arbuse nennkrupe enn doa tjnippse, enn miene groote, wann uck seldne Gow waulte lohte. Eene Wäatj hab etj vesproake omsonst too tjnippse om miene groote

194

thump watermelons. And this he could do better than a psychiatrist, like Dr Phil, manages to count money.

When the middle of August arrived, our father walked with an authoritative, knowing gait to the watermelon patch, where he knelt down by the fruit of Mennonite choice and then he would reverently close his eyes, open his mouth, cock his ear and listen like our dog Bobbat does at a gopher hole, before gently thumping first one melon, another few in turn, then picking two which I had to carry home.

Babe Ruth had a lifetime batting average of .350 but our father had a thumping average of success of at least .950.

At then, suddenly, as if overnight, watermelons started arriving at Reimer's Store in Steinbach by the truckload from Texas, and the great gift of thumping watermelons withered like the tell-tale curling leaflet on the fruit of that vine.

But there is much more to the story than this. In Russia, there were Mennonite thumpers, I heard say, who were able to thump not only people, but also children, either on the head or on their chests, or even on their backside and were immediately able to determine the future fate of the so thumped.

I would never have thought that this was possible if my good friend, an Old Colonier of the finest tradition, had not told me in his own good time that every girl who had aspirations of attending the Higher Girls School in Chortitza was subject to a thumping prior to admittance. If the thumper nodded, she was admitted; if not, the candidate was dispatched to the Brethren Bible School in Crimea, or she was sent to be trained in the mulberry caterpillar trade to produce silk. Or, as a last resort, she was simply sent off the USA where standards were less stringent. This is common knowledge, and if you doubt my word, then you better consult George W. Bush.

You can believe what you want to, but the fact remains: The thumper's rate of success lay much higher than .900%,

Sind too tilje, dann eene wiedre Wäatj fe de Missjoon aum Arbusebucktje lieseltjess mett mienen Pausoppfinja auntooputtre, enn dann, wiedahans, berooplijch mett miene Konst daut Selwajeld enn miene Betjzefupp too locke.

Vleijcht seeh wie ons em Steinbach enne Super-Valu-Berstaund, joh?

obviously much beyond that of all the school psychologists and associated experts together. But back to my own sin of omission: next week I intend to crawl into one of those huge cardboard crates in Steinbach full of watermelons, and thump for all I'm worth and reactivate my great, albeit rare and almost defunct gift. I have pledged to thump free of charge for a whole week to mitigate my great sin of omission, and then to thump with my knowledgeable index finger for a solid week in the cause of mission concerns, and then finally, after I have done penance, I will be allowed to exercise my gift, allowing coinage to slip into the malnourished pockets of my threadbare pants.

It would be a treat of a pleasure to meet and greet you and yours in the melon patch at Super Value all next week, joh?

Zuka Bumie
(Ich liebe die Erde,
Ja ljublju tebja, Semlja!)

Daut ritjche Mensch emm auljemeenen nijch goode Mensche send, weet sogoa de leewa Gott. Enn wann oba mol een Ritjcha jescheit ess, joh sogoa spendoabel woat, fellt daut soo seea opp, daut eena doavon eene Jeschijcht schriewe saul enn mott. Soo auls ditt:

Eene ella-achtje Fru leet ähren Jeldbiedel dem 14 Aprel, aune 1983 bie mie toom Jeburtsdach een Ei laje, enn enn dem Ei wea eene Reis noh Alaska von Vancouver ut, enn aules betohlt. Daut sull soo om disse Tiet en dem Joah loosgohne.

Wiels etj von dee Sort Mensche sie, dee nijch jearn eena von Väle ess, sonda leewa Väle enn eenem sie, enn etj mie oppe groote Wotasch vonne Welt uttjann, leeht etj mie waut ennfaule. De Leida vonne Lufthansa enn Vancouver wea mien Frind, enn soo bedd etj ahm, morje jäjen disse Klockentiet den Kapitän vonne Staatendam, oppe Holland-Amerika-Linje, mie soo auntooroope: "Etj wudd jearn mett dem wijchtjen enn beriehmden Professa Dokta Johannes van Matheywsen perseenlijch rede. Etj wudd ahm daut tootrue, daut hee unja dem Datjnohme, aulso Incognito Jack Thiessen reist. Oba dit Jespräch ess seea wijchtijch."

Auls etj mie enn miene Scheppskohma oppem Schepp irjendwoa deep enne Tweede Klauss schobbd enn hoojend, enn dee Staatendam aul jehearijch Walle nohm Nuade schluag, puttad daut mett eenmol aun miene Dääh, enn doa stund je

Tsuka Bumie
(I love the Earth,
Ya lyublyu tebya, Zemlya!)

Even God knows that most wealthy people are not all that much good. If, however a wealthy person chances to be good and even generous, this represents such a rarity that a telling of the tale is due. Like this: An elderly lady of the arts encouraged her bank account to lay an egg in my nest on the 14th of April 1983, the day of my birthday, and this egg consisted of a cruise from Vancouver to Alaska, fully paid for.

Since I belong to that set of people which does not intend to be one of many but prefers to be many in one, and because I know my way around the great waters of this globe, I accepted this gift with appropriate humility. The head of Lufthansa in Vancouver happened to be my friend and so I requested him to phone the captain of the ship "Staatendam" of the Holland-America Line "at this time next day" and instruct him as follows: "I would like to speak personally with the important and famous Professor Dr Johannes van Mathewsen, should he be on board. I would not be at all surprised if he will be travelling incognito under the name of Jack Thiessen. Whatever, this call is of considerable import."

When I had managed to locate my cabin aboard, somewhere deep in the bowels of second class, with the Staatendam already making waves in a northerly direction, there was a knock at my cabin door. I answered to a sheepish steward who asked: "The captain of the ship would like to know if you would kindly honor him by accepting his invitation of transfer to first

dann uck soohn schopsnäsja Steward, enn leeht froage: "Dee Kapitän well weete, auls See ahm de Eah aundoohne wudde, enne Easchta Klauss äwatoowatjzle? See send doch Professa Dokta..." Etj leeht ahm eascht goanijch utrede, sonda schoof ahm aul een Schemedaun enn siene Grauje.

Fe mie fong de Reis eascht nu rejchtijch aun. Enn joh, daut Äte, enn dee Wien, enn de Jesallschauft ess enne Easchte Klauss uck bediedend bäta too vedroage.

Noch dolla fong de Reis oba aun, auls wie tiedijch aum Sinndach ver Alaska Anka aunläde, enn een Tender kaum, omm de interesseade Passazheare oppet Laund too brinje. Weda fuhl noch domm, wisst etj daut enn disse Jäajend noch Russe läwde, enn daut'et doa sogoa eene rusche Tjoatj gauf.

Daut jefft Mensche, woohne jleewe, daut etj jeweehnlijch lange Been enne aundre Rejchtung moak von woa eene Tjoatj steeht, oba dee, woohne mie tjanne, weete daut enn soohne Tjoatje, woa dee leewa Gott oppe veaschte Beintj sett, etj Tus sie.

Enn soo uck hiea.

Alaska ess amerikaunsch, daut weete sogoa de Amerikauna; daut'et oba enn Alaska Tjriste jefft, daut weete see measchtens nijch.

Oba daut word etj enn. De Mensche enne Tjoatj weare noch measchtens soo aunjetrocke auls mie daut en Jrienthol ut meine Jugend, soo omme tien Joah tridj, bekaunt wea. De Frulied druage bunte Deatja oppem Kopp, rede Rusch, enn de Manna weare schwoat aunjetrocke, enn staupte lang ut, enn auls eena sijch oppe Tjoatjebeintj de Steewle uttrock wiels ahm siene Heehnauage jeatjte, sach etj wada toom easchten Mol noh väle Joahre, daut'et noch Footkoddre gauf. Enn nu wea etj gaunz Tus.

De Predja red väl enn earnst, enn meend de latzte Tiede stunde, wann nijch verre Däah, dann hinjre Däah, enn luta soohn mie lenjst Bekaundet. Von Missjoondriewe word oba

class accommodation. You are, are you not, Professor, Dr…"
His invitation was still in mid-air when my suitcase had already
been deposited into his second class dukes.

As of that transfer, my voyage had properly started. And,
granted, the food, the wine and the company in First Class
were considerably more enjoyable, on a higher deck.

The voyage became even more pleasant the next morning,
on a Sunday, when the liner dropped anchor in the Alaskan
waters and a tender arrived to take passengers, so inclined, to
land. Since I was neither lazy nor ignorant, I knew that in this
very area some Russians still resided and that their church was
likewise extant.

There are people who believe I generally stretch my legs in
the opposite direction wherever a Church is known to be, but
such who know me well, know that in churches where God
occupies the front pew, I am at home.

This applied to the present circumstances.

Alaska is American, even Americans know so, but the fact
that Christians of my persuasion live there, is generally not
known to them. I was shortly to discover this to be very real.
The worshippers were mainly dressed like I was used to from
my early days in Grünthal, many long years ago. The womenfolk mostly wore brightly-coloured head scarves and spoke
Russian, while the men wore black and took long steps when
walking. When one of the worshippers slowly pulled off a
seasoned boot right there on the church pew the better to
scratch an itching corn, I saw for the first time in some fifty
years that foot rags instead of socks still existed and I was fully
at home, even in Alaska.

The minister spoke long and earnestly, proclaiming that the
End Times, if not standing in front of the door, were at least
lurking behind the door, and he issued all manner of dire
predictions; I was thoroughly used to such sober wagging of
the voice finger from my days at home with Slavic theological

nijch jeret, enn uck nijch eegol vom Jeld, oba waut mie seea scheen jintjch wea äah Jesang. See sunge soo meea ut'e Seel enn vom Hoat; dee Mannastemme weare weens dree Schooh deep, enn de Tenore soo ruhm achtien; dee stuake bowrem Tjoatjedack rut. De Frulied haude biem sinje de Uage too, enn de elre Frulied hielde biem sinje, soo auls daut aul emma mott.

Auls etj docht, daut wudd soo eenjemohte jlei too Enj gohne, dreid sijch soohn earnsta Gospodjien mett eenmol omm, enn säd: "Wie habe Besuch. Wellkohm hiea. Dee Nohme bitte?"

"Gospodjien Ivan Petrowitsch" säd etj.

Donn beschwiemde veea ooda fief haulf, vleijcht wiels etj soo Auntwuat gauf auls wann Ivan Groznie enn etj Frindschauft weare, enn nijch bloß omm'e Atj.

Donn sajcht de Predja: "Habe See een Leed, woohnt ahn scheen jeiht, enn woohnt wie fe Ahn sinje tjenne?"

Etj saj: "Joh, '*Ich bete an die Macht der Liebe*' von Bordjansky."

Waut see je nijch weete kunne wea, daut mien Voda bloß een Leed utwandijch kunn, enn daut weare aule Varzh von dit Leed. Opp Rusch natiedlijch. Etj uck.

Enn donn läd wie aulatoop loos. Oba seea. Veea Balalaikas worde läwendijch, bie dree Jitoare zettade de Saide, enn twee Fiddle kaume äwadäl. Etj sung uck, waut Zeijch enn Lada häagauf, enn auls etj dann vom Baus noh de Tenorpartie bie "Ins Meer der Liebe mich versenken" noh bowe omwonk, enn Vollgas gauf, dann haud wie aulatoop jewonne. Wiels de leewa Gott läd sijch dann uck mett siene gaunze Stemm enne Säle, enn tjeena wisst woll, daut dee Oola soo goot Rusch kunn, enn hiea em wieden Alaska vondoag aum Sinndach loht zemorjess oppjeduckt wea.

Auls wie ons dann nohm Schluß verre Tjoatj troffe, kaum daut meist toom tug-of-war, ooda Strangtratje, soo auls de Dietsche daut saje, oba measchten noh dem Gottesdeenst daut nijch doohne.

flavouring delivered in German. There was little talk about conducting mission work or about all the money needed to make the world as miserable as Americans tend to be, but it was their singing which greatly appealed to me. Their song was of the heart and soul variety; the bass voices ranging about three feet deep, while the tenors ascended some eighteen feet, poking right through the ceiling, then roof. Younger women sang with closed eyes, while the older women wept silently while singing, as it should be.

When I already thought that things would draw to a predictable close, one serious Gospodin suddenly turned to me and said, "We have company today. Welcome! Your name, please?"

"Gospodin Ivan Petrovich," I replied.

Then the minister said, "Do you have a favourite song we can sing for you?"

I replied, "Yes, '*Ich bete an die Macht der Liebe*' by Bordyansky."

What they obviously could not know is that my father knew only one hymn by heart and that one was this very song, all four verses of it. In Russian, of course. I, too.

And then we started singing in mighty accord of voice. Four balalaikas came alive, three guitars let their melodic strings vibrate, and two violins came out of nowhere to offer their manned input. I sang with every chord and cord coming alive, and when I switched from my natural bass to the full throated tenor range and then turned around my voice at full volume in mid air at "*Ins Meer der Liebe mich versenken*", and injecting an extra push into my vocal traces, we attained common ground of grand song of the Russian cathedral tradition. Then, as rarely happens, and only if everything is just right, God himself threw Himself into the hymn as well, with few realizing that God knew Russian so well; He had obviously chosen to descend or surface all on a Sunday morning in Alaska.

Waut wea? De Froag wea, wäa mie toom Meddachäte ennlohde wudd. Aule wulle, aule deede.

Etj meend soo bieaun em Stellen, de Predja wudd bestemmt de Henj mett aundre Sache vollhabe, enn etj wudd kratjcht soo jearn biem Diakoon een Kommtje Supp äte, wiels, soo auls etj daut aul lang tjand, talld de Diakoon aul emma de Kollatjt, enn doa foll dann uck dit enn jant biesied, enn doawäjen kunn eena bie ahm aum basten saut woare.

Wie saute aul biem Desch. Daut gauf suren enn seeten Kapusta, uck Komst jenannt, Bortsch ut Beete, enn uck meea noh de mennische Oat, Chjlebb enn Bultje, dann Fesch, weens fief Sorte, jereatjat enn uck freschen, Eadschocke mett Schal, enn uck jebrodne, Iekra biem Ätläpelvoll, dann "Fleesch utem Woold" dochwoll Elch, ooda uck Moosefleesch, soo auls wie daut nanne, dann Läpelkost.

Medden biem Äte fruag de Diakoon, auls etj waut doajäjen haud, wann hee too de Vedeiwung eenen Sturack aunbeede wudd? Etj säd, etj wudd mie nijch doaraun steete, soolang auls mien Glaus nijch ladijch bleef.

"Butadem" säd etj, "mott etj mie noh dem latzten Leed enne Tjoatj een bät stoatje." Enn daut deed wie je dann uck.

"Noch een bät nohschentje?" wea dee Froag.

"Jun Semmehonn ess soo goot, etj wudd sogoa noch een Varzh vom Leed aunstemme, wann Jie noch een bätje oppjeete wudde."

Daut pessead.

Wie kaume enne Vetall. "Woa kohme See häa? Sejchalijch tjen Amerikauna vonne stätsche Sort, nä?"

Wie drunke noch eenen dobbelden Sturack, enn soo langsom word wie too eene Broodaschauft, enn de Nohbasch kunne äahre Nieschiea nijch lenja emm Hock lohte, enn kaume uck vebie.

When, after the conclusion of that monumental Sunday service, we gathered in front of the church and a bit of a tug-of-war ensued.

Why so? The question arose as to who would invite me to whose place for lunch, which the Russians called dinner. Everyone wanted to, everyone did.

I quietly deliberated as to whether the minister would have his hands full with other matters, and that I just as soon should accept an invitation to the deacon's home for a bowl of soup; I know my way around in church hierarchies and had reason to assume that the deacon counted the money from the collection plate, with larger paper bills dropping beside at the counting, and so chances were that I would get more adequate fill at his domicile.

We were at table. Sour as well as sweet kapusta aka as cabbage was served, borscht, red beet based, chjleb and bulka, bread of various sorts, then fish, five varieties, smoked, graved and fresh, potatoes in their jackets and fried, wild rice, then caviar by the spoonful, with "meat from the forest, moose, elk and venison" and dessert.

In the middle of the meal the deacon asked if I were to take offence if he offered a digestive, a *sturak* known to me. I said, I would take no such offence as long as my glass would not remain wanting.

"Furthermore," I added, "after that last song in church we do need a bit of sustenance," and that is exactly what happened.

"Top off your crystal?" was the question.

"Your home brew is so good that I would be prepared to sing another verse of the song, if you were to add a bit of fuel to that end."

That came to pass.

We launched into conversational mode. "Where do you call home? Certainly not an American of the States variety?"

Enn dann kaume noch meea, enn wie rede, enn vetalde, enn spezeade auls wann wie aulatoop aum Don, aune Volga, ooda aum Nippa aum Eewa em Somma saute.

Enn donn kaum uck de Predja nohm Meddachschlop aun, enn wull weete, woohne Tjoatjejemeend etj aunjehead. "Mott woll eene ajchte tjristlijche senne?"

"Joh, seea, etj jehea too de Zuka Bumie Jemeend," säd etj.

Daut musst etj ertjläre.

"Etj wea eenmol enn Indonesien, enn doa nannde se de Laundschauft fuats hinjrem Talaga-Warna-See 'Zuka Bumie' enn Zuka haft mett jun Wuat Zucka nuscht nijch toodoohne, sonda meend 'Ja ljublju Semlju', Ich liebe die Erde, Etj sie de Ead goot, I love the earth." Enn wiels de Welt doa soo schmock wea, wea daut uck nijch schwoa Gott, enn Mensche, enn daut Fletjch Ead doa aulatoop enn opp eenmol goot too senne.

"Enn too dee Jemeend jehea etj. Dee Himmel oppe Ead."

Enn boold noh aul dee goode Sturacks, kaum je dann uck Zuka Bumie, aulsoo dee Himmel, emma nohda.

Another double shot of moonshine brightened the path of interchange and gradually we became as Brethren; before long neighbours could not contain their curiosity and came around to socialize as well.

Shortly, even more came to visit and we talked with so much community of *Gemeinschaft,* as if we were altogether assembled at the banks of the Don, the Volga or the Dnieper in mid-summer. The Slavic soul is like none other, I knew that, but had rarely experienced in such copious persuasion.

Then the minister arrived, after having taken a post dinner nap, and he wanted to know to which church I belonged. "Probably a good Christian fellowship?"

"Yes, indeed, I belong to the Tsuka Bumie Church," I replied. I had to explain that one.

"I once was in Indonesia, and there the landscape beyond Lake Talaga Warna Lake was called Tsuka Bumie, Ya lyublyu Zemlyu, I love the earth. And since that area of the world is so spiritually bountiful, it was easy to fall in love with God, the people and the very terrain, with each one, then everyone, then altogether simultaneously.

"And it is to that church that I belong: Heaven on Earth."

Soon after all those good digestives, Tsuka Bumie, then heaven itself, came convincingly closer.

Auna, lidj stell!

"Sat junt mol aula han," säd de Jasch Kloße latzt. "Joh, enn du Pa, holst mol schwind noch Knacksoht, enn dann woa etj junt mol de Jeschijcht vom Oolen Peeta Hiebat, woohnen wie emma Betschla, ooda Pieptje Hiebat nande, vetalle."

"Hiebat wea noch enn Rußlaund jebuare, oba auls achtjoahscha Tjnirps kaum hee mett de gaunze Famielje noh Kanada. Enn fuats jintjch daut mett dissem goaschtajen Onnoosel loos, wiels? Joh, wiels auls see bie Moorhead oppem Schepp emm Red Riefa aune 1875 fuahre, feld hee mett eenmol enn aulemaun socht Hiebats Peetatje. Taunte Hiebatsche hield aul, Oole Hiebat speajch ut, tjwelstad em Riefa nenn enn säd: "Sukensien!"

"Well, nu stund daut Schepp emm Red stell, dee Schabräda oakade langsom enn latjte enn stunde dann gaunz stell. Taunte Plume Sewautsche vetald aul, woo Happnasch Obraumtje uck mol emm Nippa vedrunke wea, enn säd, dem Peetatje haude se aul lang goot 'siene druggelje Bultjes' vollheiwe sullt. So säd de Sewautsche. Oba Peeta wea nijch too finje, enn nu jintjch Oohmtje Hieba selwst opp earnst seatje. Enn mett eenmol head daut gaunze Schepp dem Oolen Hiebat loosrescheare. 'Enn sure enuff.enn toom aulen Donna, enn toom Kuckuck manke Klucke, enn Schietreiasch emm Suaromp, doa ess Peetatje!' Em Red schwomp'a doa emm Wota romma. 'Toom aulen Donna!' schreajch Oole Hiebat, 'fuats tjemmst du rut, enn dissem schatajen Puddel lohnt sijch daut goanijch too bode. Enn butadem mott wie noh Kanada, foa fehle opplatzt aul een poah Indiauna auftooladre, enn du murchelst hiea em Blott romma,

Annie, lie still!

"If you will please sit down," said Mrs Jake Klassen recently, "while my Ohmtje Jake will get us some sunflower seeds, I will tell you the story about Old Man Peter Hiebert, whom we called Bachelor Hiebert or Pipe Smoking Hiebert, and whom they kicked out of the Elim Church in Grünthal."

"Hiebert was one of those Mennonite boys born in Russia, but who came to Canada as an eight year old. And trouble followed this mischief maker boy all the way, anyway. When that group of Mennos travelled down the Red River at Moorhead, North Dakota on a side-wheeler in 1875, Peter one late afternoon on July 18, was suddenly missing, and all hands on deck went looking for Hiebert's Peterkin. Mrs Hiebert, the mother, started crying, while her husband spat into the river and yelled, "son of a bitch!"

"Well, and now the ship stood still in the Red, the paddle wheel squeaked to a halt and then came to a complete stop. Mrs Prune Sawatzky started telling how Heppner's Abie had also once drowned in the Dnieper and added, 'that's what happens when you don't tan the hides of youngsters in time on a regular basis.' So said Mrs Sawatzky. But Peterkin was still nowhere to be found, and now Old Man Peter Hiebert started a serious search for his boy. Then, suddenly, the entire ship heard Pa Hiebert's authoritative bellow, 'And sure enough, and Blackie among the carrots, and storks in the millet patch and frogs and tribulations, there is that little rat. And now you get out of that murky puddle, you little devil, this dugout is not meant for swimming. And, also, it is time we made for Canada,

emm deist hiea de Beffeldrentjch ennschwiene. Enn tratj die uck fuats de Betjze aun, enn een bät jicha sonst woa etj die noch de Stars enn Srtipes emm Hinjarenj nenn stample! Enn du, Panna, goh saj dem Capten, hee saul aul Stiem jäwe, wie well fuats noh Kanada foahre!'

"Joh, joh dis Peetatje kaum noh Kanada, oba hiea leete siene Schoose nijch noh, hee wea een hasselja Bädel, enn 'goaschtaje auls Adam, dee sijch uck emma enne Aupelberstaund rommadreef" säd Oole Hiebat. Peetatje säd bloß, hee deed mau prektesse Indiauna too späle, wiels dee sent willa auls de Wille Wiens ut Niegortitz, soo haude de Lied vetalt.

Well, Hiebats Peetaje, boold Hiebats Peeta, dann Peeta Hiebat enn schließlijch Oomtje Betschla Hiebat bleef een Spuchterieta. De Lied säde emma, hee wea goastrijch,oba dauts goanijch soo, hee wea maua utjelohte, enn hee säd 'Joh'too jiedrem Wintjel emm Läwe, "Na, etj weet uck nijch", säd Taunte Kloße wieda, "enn nu kohmt mol aula een bät noda, wiels waut etj nu vetale woa, vetalt nijch wieda, nä, daut vetal etj mau auleen wann'et needijch ess, vestohne? Joh? Na, dann mol wieda; weet jie äwahaupt woarom see Betschla Hiebat ute Jemeed rutschmeete? Nä? Na kohmt noch een bätje nohda, enn du Pannasche, vetal ditmol uck nijch wieda, enn du Krohnsche, vetal uck nijch, wiels diene Jeschijchte vom jnodenfeldschen Peeta Thiesses Haunsa send morschijch äwadräwe. Oba mei, mei, tridj nohm Onkel Hiebat. Oh yes, daut wea soo: Stald junt väa, de Betschla Hiebat wea je goanijch befriet, enn wie wißte uck goanijch, waut hee nohm Fieaowent deed. Oba waut jedohne woat hee woll habe, enn 'Det's fe schur' säd de Boatelsche. Well, eenes Doages saut hee aum Sinndach enne Tjoatj, enn boold schorrd hee een bätje toop, enn mett eenmol schnoatjcht hee uck aul. De Predja vetald nu noch luda, woo Kain dem Abel eent mettem Koohfoot äwrem Tjriez jeresst haud, enn dann noch eent, oba Onkel Hiebat saut tweschen Peeta Leewe enn Tobias Jaunz enn schnoatjt. Joh,

because there may be Indians waiting to be skinned up there while you waddle around in the mud and dirty the buffalo drink. Out with you and now you get into your pants for otherwise I am going to imprint the Stars and Stripes into your shanks in a hurry! And you Penner, you head for the captain and tell him to ply full steam ahead, it's time we went to Canada!'

"Yes, yes, this Peterkin came to Canada but his mischief persisted and his pranks did not abate; he was up to around the clock no good, and 'more disobedient than Adam, who meandered non-stop in the apple orchard in his day,' said Old Man Hiebert. Peterkin merely said, he had only intended practicing playing Indian, because they are wilder than Wild Wiens from Niechortitza, so people in the Old Country had said.

Well, Hiebert's Peterkin, soon Hiebert's Peter, then Peter Hiebert and finally Mr Bachelor Hiebert remained a prankster. People said he was mischief maker but he was more than that; he lived life to the full. "Well, I don't really know," said Mrs Klassen, "but there is still something about him yet to be told. But before I do so, I want you all to promise that this really true story as to why he was kicked out of the Grünthal Elim Church never leaves this room. And this applies to you as well, Nettie Krahn, because you have a tendency to exaggerate stories like about Peter Thiessen's Johnny.

"But back to Bachelor Hiebert. We know he was never married but we don't know what he was up to after working hours, as few as they probably were." "But up to something, he was, for sure," added Mrs Barthel, who generally knew.

"So one day, Bachelor Hiebert was sitting in church on Sunday and it wasn't long before he fell into his relaxed self and then he started breathing deeply before slipping into slumber which wasn't all that surprising since Preacher Froese long-windedly held forth with his favourite sermon of how schnoatjt soo's ne jestritje Bausfiddel ohne Seide, schmustad emm Schnurrboat neen'a, enn hohld noch eenmo derjche Näs enn opnet Mul Loft, enn schmustad, enn hohld wada ut opp siene Bausfiddel, enn frinteld enn pust 'PIRRRHHH!' Enn donn bucheld Jaunz dem Hiebat doch eent mett'em Alboage enne Rebbe, enn waut säd Hiebat? Joh, waut säd'a donn bloß? Well, yes, Betschla Hiebat säd bloß: 'Auna, lidj stell!'"

Cain had worked over his brother Abel with a crowbar and then given him another one for good measure, while Mr Bachelor was sitting between Peter Loewen and Tobias Janz changing gears from sleeping to snoring, like a bass fiddle. Obviously his sleep was pleasant and deep as he smiled and hummed in tune to his vibrato snore and for all to hear five rows fore and aft: "PIRRRHHH!" Then Janz, thinking a sermon in church has more of a green light than a snoring bachelor does, gave him a stiff one, even if quietly, right in the ribs. To which Bachelor Hiebert gently but emphatically responded, "Annie, lie still!"

Adam, woo bist Du?

Daut wea Sinndach-Nohmeddach em Mai, daut fong aun scheen too ritje, enn de Sonn schiend soo frintlijch enn Niegortietz aum Nippa; joh daut niee Läwe jintj aulewäaje loos! Oohmtje Hiebat wea aul dree Doag wajch, enn Arkadak wear'a; hee deed friee, säde de Lied em Darp.

Siene Fru wea aul meist twee Joah doot enn ohne soohne "Langhoaje mettem Rock" wea daut mau plätrijch enne Tjäatj, enn een "bätje wietleftijch enne Schlopstow". Hiebat wea aulsoo enn Arkadak, de Mädtjes enn de Mejalles weare Tus enn Peetate, joh Peetatje, de Twalf-Joascha, de jrala Peeta, de Onoosel tjitjt sijch doa emm Darp aum Nippa omm enn socht waut too doohne; uck Schowanack wann'et senne musst. Mett Mädtjes wull hee nijch späle; dann wull hee doch leewa de Klucke zoaje ooda Kraujeeia utnehme, ooda sest waut. Joh, hee wudd vondoag sest waut doohne. Oba waut? Well, satt junt mol macklijch han enn dann woa etj junt vetale, waut Hiebats Peetatje deed.

Peeta jintj eascht noh Peetasch, oba de Victor, de Vietja wull vondoag leewa lese auls mett Peetatje Domms driewe. Aulso jintj Peetatje noh Dertjzes schrots äwre Gaus. Doa sull hee nijch hangohne, haud Voda jesajcht, oba dem Peeta jäatjcht, joh, ahm spetjcht de wille Howa; ahm jankad een bät Heideldei too moake. Joh, enn Dertjzes Willie kaum uck jrots ruta.

Dee Willie wea feftien enn "hunjsch auls Rasputin" haud Onkel Hiebat jesajcht, enn "pauss opp fe dem, Peetatje!" Oba Peetatje jintj noda, enn roopt: "Goondach, Willie, waut dooh

214

Adam, where are you?

It was a Sunday afternoon in May; full spring was in the air and everywhere, with the sun on high beam in Niechortitza by the Dnieper. New life in full sprout burst from every bloom and blossom. Mr Horse Hiebert had been gone for three days now, in Arkadak; people in the village said he was on a courting mission.

His wife had been dead for almost two years and without a "long-haired presence in a skirt" things tended to be "sparse pickings in the bedroom". The stage of the story was set: Hiebert was in Arkadak, his girls were at home and Little Peter, named Peterkin by the family, that elusive rascal looked around for a little action in the village by the Dnieper; even executing a few pranks would not beyond his realm of possibilities to be entertained. Playing with his sisters was not his idea of fun; he would rather tease the clucking hens or climb a tree in search of crow's eggs, or whatever came in handy by way of a leisurely distraction. Or, possibly, be up to something else. Yes, to do something else was the agenda for this afternoon. But what? If you will sit down and give me five minutes attention I will do as promised and tell you what Hiebert's Peterkin did today.

First Peter walked over to the Peter's place but Victor, his friend Victor, today preferred to read a book instead of inventing foolishnesses with Peter. And so Peter sauntered over to the Derksen's yard, kitty corner from their farm in the village. He had instructions from his father not to go there but today Peter felt his oats, indeed those very oats needled him for action and so he up and went. Things came in handy for

jie vondoag, schlope ooda sohtknacke?" Enn fuats oppe Städ
betjcht Willie sijch enn hoof eenen Steen opp, oba Peetatje wea
fetjsa enn hoof uck schwind eenen Steen opp enn hohld ut,
troff kratjcht derjche Stakeete enn brennd dem Willie eent
aune Moagekuhl- kratjcht aum Solar Plexus troff hee dem
Willie. "Buff" säd'et, de Stoff fluach ut'em Hamd enn Willie
stähnd, schorrd toop enn reahd sijch nijch! "Eijejajejaj" docht
Peetatje, "soo jung enn etj kunn aul Kain heete!" "Fe soohne
Junges habe se emm Himmel tjeen Hock frie!" haud Predja
App jesajcht. Peetatje stund doa verrem Tun, enn wea soo's
aunjenoagelt, hee kunn sijch nijch reahre. Willie lach gaunz
stell, de Welt wea platzlijch seea, seea trurijch jeworde.

Enn de truje Welt word noch diestra auls Onkel Sohtknacka
Dertjze Senior nu rut kaum. You bet, doa wear'a! de groota,
steila, forscha Joakob Dertjze tjlintjt de Däah op, hoojend,
ratjcht sijch enn säd: "Ahem!" schobbd sijch aum Bossem, enn
murcheld enn siene Schlorre loos. Enn fuats fung hee sienen
Willie aum Tun lidje, enn säd: "Waut's mie dit? Feitstanz ooda
Dommheit?" enn schlappd Willie nenn. Oba Willie kaum nu
too sijch enn kloagd: "Nä, nijch Feitstanz, daut haft Hiescha
Hiebats Peetatje jedohne, de flaumd mie eent enne Moagekuhl
mett een Steen. Doa steit'a."

"Na, oba, uck noch sowaut, dann well wie fuats mol seehne,"
säd de Oola Sohtknacka, enn hohld daut Tjnippsmassa rut enn
schneet eene schmocke, ditje Wead ute Akotstje-Hatj. Nu
haud'a se reed, enn Peetatje stund noch emma enn kunn sijch
nijch reahre. Sien Schlucka weppt han enn häa, hee beletjcht
sijch de Leppe, sien Ritja flautad, enn sien Hoat bullad auls
eene Tonn oppem Stuckawoage. Enn hee kunn eenfach nijch
loosrescheare. Oohmtje Dertjze kaum nu langsom noda,
schoof Schlorr noh Schlorr, piepad aul sogoa eenen tjlienen
Siegesdaunz enn säd: "Wann de Oole Hiebat sienen Jung nijch
enne Stoak hoole kaun, dann woa etj ahm utauste halpe"—Säd

his plans of idle pranks because Derksen's Willie just came out of the house as Peter chanced by.

Willie was fifteen and as "rough as Rasputin" his father had said, and added, "you better be on your guard when that kid's around." But Peter kept on walking in that very direction, and, seeing the neighbour's kid, called, "Willie, what are you up to in your parts today, are you all sleeping as usual or are you cracking sunflower seeds?" In a split second, Willie bent down to grab a stone, but Peter beat him to it, made for his own stone and all in one motion threw it as hard as he could between two slats of the garden rail fence hitting Willie right in the stomach area, dead on in the solar plexus. "Buff" was the report of stone arrival, a bit of dust issued from a well worn shirt, then Willie groaned, collapsed and stopped moving. "Ay-yi-yi" thought Peter, "so young and yet my name could well be Cain of Bible fame!" "No room for such kind of kids in heaven," is what Preacher Epp had said. Peter stood stock still in front of the garden fence, as if impaled by a nail of justice; he simply could not stir. Short yards away lay Willie, completely still… all the world had suddenly become very quiet and just as sad.

And that sad world turned considerably darker when Ohmtje Sunflower Cracker Derksen Senior came out of his house. You bet, there he was! That big, stout, erect Jacob Derksen unlatched the door of his home, stretched himself like a tomcat in a foul mood and pronounced: "Ahem!" scratched his chest and moved his angry by nature freight on two wooden clogs to the outside world. Within a second, his eyes caught sight of Willie lying by the fence, and he said: "Now what the deuces is this all about? Convulsions or home-made stupidity?" and dragged Willie inside. In the slight interim, Willie had come around and complained, "No, not epilepsy; this was done by Horse Hiebert's Peterkin, he whupped me one in the gut with a rock. There, he still stands!"

daut enn kaum noda enn emma sacheltjess noda. Enn nu, nu wear'a meist doa, stratjt aul siene Haund ut, hohld mett de Wead ut enn donn pessead doch noch een Wundatje—Peetatje wea mett eenmol loos, donn wear'a fuats emm hejchsten Jedriew enn schisd auf, kratjcht auls de Wead derjche Loft juld.

Peetatje weess nu dem vebleffden Sohtknacka siene jriese, boafte Hacke, enn hee huppad enn stusd loos auls wann ahm twintijch Bramse toojlitj aune Duppsjäjend jeprätjelt haude. Enn Joakob Dertjze drebbled hinjeraun enn vepriejeld de Loft! Enn doll wear'a schudahauftijch, enn speajch dreemol ut enn säd seea schlajchte Weada—waut säd hee? Hee säd: "Hiebat foat friee enn Tus lat hee siene Wirtschauft vekohme, enn hee lat siene Tjinja rommbiestre auls Hocklinja, oba wann etj dem Peeta toohoole tjrie, dann woat hee koojintjre auls Henritjs siene Brood junge Hunj. Dem Peetatje woa etj daut Sette fe twee Wäatj aufwahne, enn daut's soo sejcha auls daut Sonntje aum Himmel," speajch nochmol ut, enn red dann noch een Strieptje Rusch.

"Hallo," säd Dertjze too de Mädtjes enne Tjeatj, "woa ess jun Goaschthaumel?" "Nijch hiea," säd Hiebats Jreeta. "Oho, uck noch leaje doohne se hiea! Dann woa etj mol selwst tjitje motte," enn jintj oppem Bähn nopp. Enn joh, Peeta wea oppem Bähn; äwrem Schienebähn wear'a nohm Heibähn hinje enne Atj jegohne, enn doa saut'a nu.

De Heibähn wea eenfach ut loose Bräda jemoakt, eenfach Bräda soo twee bett dree Zoll utenaunda lage see doa enn eena musst schratjlijch oppausse enn kratjcht velenjd de Baultjes gohne, sonst kunn eena doa noch seea too Splät kohme. Enn nu kaum Oohmtje Sohtknacka oppem Bän noppa—Peetatje sach eascht den buzhajen Kopp, dann siene Komstbläda Ohre, enn donn eene Schoof dolle Tähne. Oohmtje Dertjze word emma jrata enn kaum emma noda enn roopt: "Adam, wo bist Du?" enn sach nu uck aul Peetatje enne Atj hucke. Nu kaum

"Well, well, my goodness me, let us set about as fast as we can and settle this matter up before the next minute has expired," said Sunflower Cracker, and had already opened his pocket knife to relieve an acacia bush of a suitable switch. Now he had it good and ready with Peterkin standing there frozen in time and space right before him. Peter's Adam's apple whipped to and fro, he licked his lips, while his nostrils quivered, and his heart was thundering like a barrel on a schooner wagon. Peterkin simply could not move a muscle. Mr Derksen came slowly closer, shoved clog after clog, already whistled a victory dance and said, "If Old Man Hiebert can't keep a bridle on his son, I might just have to rope him in myself," and while saying so he advanced ever closer. And now, now, he was almost there, had stretched out his hand for the culprit and his switch was already in take-off mode, when a miracle happened.

Peterkin suddenly became unstuck, was in high gear within an instant as if an entire beehive and its angry cousins had stung him you know where, and disappeared just as the switch whistled through the air missing him by a Gillette blade. While Jacob Derksen was after him full speed ahead and laying a dreadful beating on thin air and uttering curses not known to any hymnal. Then he spat three times while reloading foul vocabulary. These consisted of "Hiebert drives off courting while his farmstead goes to the devil and lets his children roam around like so many useless heifers, but when I get hold of his son Peter then the kid will whimper like Heinrich's brood of puppies."

And worse still, if you know anything about Mennonite traditions. You can covet and meddle all for the love and interest of a better walk of life, but when it comes to offering advice about rearing children or managing a farmyard you are taking life itself into your own hands. "When I am through with this kid he will sit lopsided wherever he goes and he will

hee nodatjess, balancead sijch doa oppe Baultjes, fiddeld mett de Wead han enn häa, enn säd doabie: "Kratjcht soo's em Paradies. Eascht hasslijch senne, enn dann sijch noch vesteatje. Adam, dee nauhm weens bloos een Aupeltje, oba dis Misa enne Atj, dem nu de Lempe soo seea flautre, dee nauhm fuats eenen Steen! Joh, joh, oba de leewa Gott tjreajch de Tjräte mack, enn etj woa dissem Scherniesel uck mack tjriee. Joh, joh. Na, Peetatje, dit Mol woa etj die doch wiese motte, woo eena Steenschmietasch daut Lada vollheiwt. Etj woa diene Betjze mol soo vollheiwe, daut daut fe twee Joah veschlohne woat, wacht mau een bätje",—säd daut enn kaum noda enn noda. Enn nu schoot uck aul platzlijch siene Haund nohm Peetatje opptoo, oba Mister Sohtknacka tjreajch mau Loft toohoole, wiels Peeta leet nu een bät haustijch de Kupplung rut enn schoot auf auls een Flitzboage—aun Oohmtje Dertjze vebie enn wajch. Doaropp haud de Paradies-Wajchta nijch jereatjent enn hee veloa sien Jlitjjewijcht enn foll derjch'e Bräda enn kaum oppe Baultjes too riede. De Bräda schnallde enne Hejcht enn Oohm Dertjze saut enne Bredulj, faustjetjlamt! Peetatje wea nu aul unje enn roopd de Mädtjes: "Kohmt schwind enn tjitjt! Oohmtje Sohtknacka Dertjze spält bie ons oppem Jäwel Cowboy! Enn sien Kunta haft ahm raufjeschmäte, enn nu ritt hee oppem Baultje!"

Auls Oohmtje Dertjze daut head, wea hee soo doll, daut hee meist ute Näs reatjad. Hee jescht enn säd: "Dree Wäatj woat Peetaje daut Sette vegohne!" Enn donn haud'et Peeta oba seea ielijch. Bloos wajch, wajch von dissem dollen Cowboy, docht hee. Enn nu schurjeld hee loos enn läd sijch aune Ritsch manke Diedatjiele dohl, lach doa manke Holstjebatj enn Mest-tjniepasch enn vestuak sijch enn odemd mau veea bett fiefmol de Minut. Enn doa bleef hee bett daut schemma word, bett de Lied jemoltje haude enn bett daut gaunze Läwenstempo enn bät nohjelohte haud, enn bett Oohmtje Dertjze wada de Fuppe

list like the Titanic soon afloat, and that's as sure as the sun in the sky," he said, spat again, and concluded his reveries with a verse of Russian curse.

"Hello," said Derksen to the girls in the kitchen, "where is your little shit?" "Not here," answered Hiebert's Greta. "Oho, they are not even beyond lying around here! Well then, I will go and have a look-see myself." While already on his way to the attic, where as bad luck would have it, is exactly where Peter was hiding. Peter had removed himself all the way across the attic, beyond the barn loft, then crossed the hay loft and then to the far corner where he now sat, making himself small.

This hay loft was made of loose planks placed haphazardly over widely spaced joists. Crossing these was only possible by taking risk to soul and body for if you missed a solid joist underfoot, you were in for a rough ride. And now Mr Sunflower Cracker advanced into that realm. Peter spied first a mop of hair. Then he saw a set of cabbage-sized ears. Lastly a whole set of angry teeth came into view. Ohmtje Derksen became constantly bigger and came ever closer while calling, "Adam, where are you?" as he saw Peter hiding in the corner. Now he inched closer, balanced himself on the joists, fiddled around with his switch and commenced a little sermonizing himself. "Just like in Paradise. First they misbehaved and then they hid. Adam, yes Adam, he took only a little apple, but this miserable runt whose pant legs are now trembling like a scared dog's, he took a stone! Well, our father in heaven got Adam and his kinfolk good and meek and I intend to do no less. Joh, joh, Little Peter, the time has come to show you how stone throwers are treated in my neighbourhood; I wouldn't like to be your ass when I'm through with you. My lesson will remain with you and in your pants for two years or more and such comes with a warranty."

Suddenly his hand shot out towards Peter but Mister Sunflower Cracker came up with no more than thin air because

voll Soht, enn bett Willie vleijcht uck aul wada Domms em Kopp haud. Auls'et emma ruja word, head Peeta mett eenmol Jreeta roope: "Oba Peetatje, oba Petruschka, woa best du? Komm doch noh Hus. Oohmtje Dertjze ess aul noh Hus jeschibbelt, enn etj hab mie aul noh die jebangt. Nu komm doch, etj woa die uck Tjieltjemoos koake!" Enn donn ratjcht sijch Peeta, stuak väasejchtijch den Kopp derjch daut Jreens, vesproak noch eenmol von nu aun schmocka too senne, enn jintjch mett Jreeta toop nenn.

Oola Hiescha Hiebat kaum aum Mondach noh Hus. Enn de gaunze Wäatj wundad hee sijch Dach enn Nacht woo pienijch enn woo jehorsom enn ontlijch Peetatje wea. Enn aum Donnadach, auls hee sien Wunda nijch meea lohte kunn äwa sien Mostajung, säd hee: "Peeta, komm mol emm Staul nenn, wie motte ons vondoag zeowents mol vetale." Enn daut deede se dann uck; see satte sijch emm Staul oppe Maltjbeinstjes dohl enn hilde een bät Broodaschauft. Enn donn docht Peeta woll, daut Wada ess opp Jewitta, wiels sien Voda trock sijch langsom den Pojas ute Letse. Den läd hee sijch nu doppelt äwre Tjnees enn säd doabie: "Peeta, waut wesst du mie nu vetale?" Well, Peeta wisst je nijch waut Voda wisst, oba irjendwaut wudd de Oola woll weete, enn so vetald hee nu siene Versjoon von de Jriepa-Jeschijcht.

"Sitt soo waut schmock?" fruach Onkel Hiebat nu, enn läd aul siene Piep wajch. "Nä," säd Peetaje, "oba doa ess noch waut, waut etj junt eajentlijch goanijch vetale wull." "Na waut?" meend Oohmtje Hiebat, "enn nu een bät jicha, sonst woa etj die fuats de Schwoate utwoatje!"

Peeta hold nu doch latzte vestoakne Koat ute Fupp enn läd de sootoosaje oppem Maltjbeinstje. "Voda," säd hee, "etj wull Junt daut nijch vetale. Oba weet Jie, waut Oohmtje Dertjze säd? Hee säd: 'Wann de Oola Hiescha Hiebat sienen Jung nijch enne Stoak hoole kaun, dann woa etj ahm utauste motte'!"

222

Peter released his brakes all in one move on his home turf, and shot off like an arrow, just past Mr Derksen and away. The Guardian of Paradise had not reckoned with such swift action; he lost his balance and crash landed on a joist with the loose spring boards edging up and wedging him in.

Peterkin was already downstairs and called his sisters, "Come quickly and look! Ohmtje Sunflower Cracker Derksen is playing cowboy in our attic! And his gelding has just thrown him and now he rides a joist instead."

When Ohmtje Derksen heard this he was so angry that smoke curled up out of his nose. He panted and pronounced, "Peterkin won't be sitting for three weeks and more!" When Peter heard this he sprinted off for safer regions. Just away, away from this mad cowboy, he advised himself. He headed straight for the dugout and nestled himself among the cattails in the reeds, made himself a cover among the wood ticks and dung beetles and laid low, breathing at most four or five times a minute. And there he stayed until evening fell, until village folk had done the milking, and the tempo of life had somewhat abated. And Ohmtje Derksen again had his pockets full of sunflower seeds and Willie had replenished his head with naughty ideas. When everything became peaceful again, Peter heard Greta calling, "Peterkin, my little Petruschka, where are you? Come home, please, won't you? Mr Derksen has long since shuffled home and I miss you so much. Now come home, please and I'll cook a favourite supper just for you!" Then Peter stretched himself, looked cautiously all around the greenery and promised to be a good boy and went home with Greta.

Ohmtje Horse Hiebert came home on Monday. All of that week he was surprised at just how diligent and obedient and well behaved his Peterkin was. On Thursday when he could no longer contain his wonder at how well his boy was behaving for once he said, "Peter, come with me to the stable tonight; there is something we ought to discuss."

"Daut säd de Sohtknacka?" schreajch Hiebat, "daut säd de Deffat?" enn fädemd nu schwind den Pojas enne Betjzeletse, enn oakad loos noh Dertjzes."Ja tjebbe dam! Dann woa wie fuats mol seehne," säd hee, enn wajch wear'a noh Dertjzes opptoo!

And that is what they did; they sat down on the milking stools and conducted a bit of internal fellowship. Peter thought the weather forecast read thunder, because his father slowly pulled his belt out of the loops and laid it double across his knees while saying, "Peter, what is it that you want to tell me?" Well, Peter did not know what his father knew, but he knew that father knew something; that much was clear. And so he spilled his version of the story of how he had gone over to the Sunflower Cracker neighbour and how Willie had picked up a stone and how he had beat Willie to it, and had landed him a good one with his stone in the pit of the stomach and that Old Man Derksen had then threatened to whip him.

"Is that proper conduct on your part?" asked Mr Hiebert, and already put his pipe on the stool. "No," said Peterkin, "but there is something else which I did not really want to tell you." "What's that? And you better make it snappy, or I'll end the session with a double portion on the seat of your pants."

Peter now produced his trump card and placed it carefully on the milk stool. "Father," he said, "I did not want to tell you this, but do you know what Ohmtje Derksen said?" He said, 'If Old Man Horse Hiebert cannot manage his kid, I'll have to do it myself!'"

"The old Sunflower Cracker said *that*?" screamed Hiebert, sending the milk stool flying. "That's what the Old Rooster Tail said?" and already he had re-adjusted his belt, and galloped full speed ahead to the Derksen place. "I'll show that seed-cracker whose business it is to raise my children! I'll show that overweening presumptuous interfering cockerel!" And the last little Peter Peterkin Petruschka saw of his father, he was barging in through the gate of Derksen's front yard.

"Nä, Hillary, Du bliffst Tus"

"Na joh," säd etj, "dann kohm etj junt aulatoop mol wada enn Washington beseatje." See haude mie too vestohne jejäwt, daut see sijch doa nijch meea von mie aufschnutze lohte wudde, wiels see loohde mie egol enn, enn etj leet nuscht nijch von mie heare. Auls see mie dann noch oppem Phoon klipp enn kloa too vestohne gauwe: "Joh, wie weete, daut du daut auls Mennist seea drock hast, oba wie welle uck mol wada waut von die habe," dann packt etj mien Schemedauntje, talld miene Dolasch, enn waut dann wieda pessead, woat disse Jeschijcht junt vetalle, nijch etj.

Enn soo begauf sijch daut dann, daut etj mol wada enne Medd wea, kratjcht soo auls sijch daut fe de Thiessess von onse Oat jeheat. Wie habe ons aul emma een bät tusijch enn Washington jefeehlt, wann etj mol bie de Woahrheit bliewe doaf. Daut easchte waut etj deed, wea mienen tjlienen Vada, den Gordon Thiesse, dee easchta Jeldtalla enn Ottawa, weete lohte, daut hee derjch mie goot veträde wea. Hee bedankt sijch, enn meend soo bieaun, bäta auls etj kunn hee daut uck nijch doohne. Etj säd doatoo schlijcht 'Aumen!'

Enn nu jintjch daut enn Washington bosijch väarewajch. Wiels dee Staut eene seea jefährlijche ess, woa see eenem em Derjchschnett twee bett dreemol den Dach mett dem Scheetiesa enne Rebbe poakere, enn uck bereibere, kratjcht eendoohnt auls eenem sowaut scheen jeit ooda nijch, enn etj mien Rewolwa Tus jelohte haud, soo auls sijch daut fe eenen Wäahloosen jeziemt, musst etj mie nu mol wada opp mien fetjset Pedaumtje velohte. Eene Bonsch Schwoatasch kaume je dann uck aul vonne Sied enn von hinje opp mie too, soo auls

226

Why I left Hillary behind

I finally consented to go to Washington because Hillary and some other old friends over there let me know, in unmistakable language, that "this is the absolutely last time we are inviting you. Of course we know full well that you are a very busy Mennonite but even here in the capital we are not to be snubbed by you yet again."

So I examined the corners of my pockets in every pair of my pants to determine whether my meager Canadian dollars would suffice, and then I took off. As to what else I packed into my luggage, the story will reveal in time, not I.

And so it came to pass that I shortly found myself in the centre of things, just like it befits all the Thiessens of my acquaintance and stature. We have always felt a bit at home in Washington, if the truth be known. The first thing I did was to inform my little cousin, Gordon Thiessen, in Ottawa (treasurer of the Bank of Canada) what I was up to so that he would have peace of mind; I informed him that, in my humble opinion, Canada was well represented by his relative. Gordon e. mailed me promptly to thank me and let me know that he could now attend to lesser items of business with due serenity, a load now being lifted off his back.

Now matters were allowed to take their due course. Since Washington is a very dangerous city where you get mugged or robbed twice a day on average, whether you like it or not, or become the victim of pickpockets, and I had left my barreled branding irons behind as it befits a non-resisting Mennonite, I had to rely, as always, on my nimble mind to execute an impromptu jig of survival when I spied a gang of Afrose daut doohne, wann se eenem wijchtjen enn ritjen Onkel den Jeldbiedel aufladre welle. Aulso schoof etj daut Tjriedtje aum Oppschlag von mienem Aunzug mie nohda nohm Mul enn räd iewrijch enn een Transmitter nenn, dem'et oba nijch gauf.

Enn mien bastet Rusch säd etj: "Rachulle enn Reibasch send mie hiea em Stijch; saul etj wachte bett jie aula too Help kohme, ooda saul etj miene Sabackasch aulatoop looslohte enn uck dartijch Soldohte hinjeraun, ooda saul etj eenfach uttniepe?" Dann muak etj daut Mul wiet ohp soo aus eena daut deit, wann eena seea horjcht enn gauf lud too Auntwuat: "Karoscho, duzhe dobre!" Enn dann vetrock sijch daut gaunze Pack, heeflijch, enn aufpracherisch enn äahre Jedohnte. Joh, see kaume mie sogoa een bät veleaje väa, enn vleijcht sogoa friewellijch, enn wann etj nijch enn Jrienthol, aulso Tus, soohne goode Maneare jeleaht haud, wea etj de Veseatjung unjaläje, dit Pack selwst omm eene milde Gow too bedde.

Aulso jintjch etj tridj emm Hotel nenn, enn trock mie grootsindagsch aun enn bestald eene Taxi, dee miene deemootje Wijchtijchtjeit noh de National Foundation of Women in the Arts feahre mucht. Auls Bill Clinton, donn noch President, enn etj hauntreade, wisst etj fuats, waut fe eena hee wea. Doatoo haud etj aul jenuag Mol em Speajel jetjitjcht. Fe soohne Sache bruckt Onsaeena tjeene Oprahs ooda niemoodsche Experts.

Daut Bankett wea sogoa bäta aus een Schwiensbrode em chortietschen Tjoatjetjalla Tus em Darp. Enn uck bilja. Disse Mensche wisste waut see deede, enn soo haude se General Colin Powell enn mie aum selwjen Desch jesat. Auls etj mie väastald, enn hee den Nohme Thiesse head, fruag hee auls etj a) Mennist wea enn b) auls etj Dietsch kunn enn c) auls etj een Wäaloosa wea. Etj säd: "Jawohl, Herr Generol, etj sie Mennist, etj kaun Dietsch, enn joh, etj sie meist gaunz wäaloos, bett opp miene rajchte Fust," dee etj ahm weess. Wie haude ons jefunge, enn wann jie vestendlijchawies weete welle, woaräwe wie ons

Americans sauntering my way casually from the front and both sides; this is the way they do things when they want to relieve important and wealthy gentlemen of my ilk of their greenbacks. I casually pushed the boutonniere on my coat lapel up to my mouth, slowed down my brisk pace, and spoke into a non-existent transmitter as follows in my best Russian, "There are ruffians and rascals in my way; shall I wait for reinforcements, or release a few canines and a legion or two of crack storm troopers or shall I turn on my after burner and take off?" Then I listened intently, open-mouthed, into my lapel, nodded and answered, "*Dobre, duzhe dobre!*' (Well, very well). That pack of ruffians quietly dispersed, almost politely and certainly apologetically. They almost appeared in a gratuitous mood themselves and had it not been for my excellent manners, Made in Grünthal, I would have been tempted to ask them for a bit of spare change myself.

I repaired to the hotel and donned my Sunday best, ordered a taxi and had him deliver important goods in modest human form to the National Foundation of Women in the Arts. When Bill Clinton, the president, and I shook hands, I winked at him with a knowing, half-brother in the human arts and crafts eye, and when he responded, I immediately knew what manner of Willie he was. I needed no Kenneth Starr or a Linda Tripper or a million or more of pocket disposables to investigate anything. My only thought was, "There but for the grace of—"

The banquet, shortly in progress, was, a step on a stair, higher, because General Colin Powell had been assigned to my table by fate or competent hands, and when he heard my name Thiessen, he asked if I were a Mennonite and if I spoke German. I answered both questions in the affirmative and seconded the emotion with an audible "Yes, sir!" Then the good general smiled and asked if I were a conscientious objector, still in German. I replied, "*Jawohl*, Herr General, with the exception of my right fist," which I promptly proceeded to

229

de haulwe Nacht vetalde, dann mott jie aul bie mie too Tjoatj
kohme, wiels daut ess de rajchtschuldje Städ groote
Jeheemnisse enn aundre wijchtje Dinja vonne latzte Tiede too
openboare.

Oba nu well wie vonne Kaunzel raufkrupe enn tridj ennem
Auldach gohne. Nohdem Powell enn etj ons seea läwendijch
bett haulf veea vetald haude, enn doabie sogoa een Glauss ooda
Twee Schnaups drunke, doamett wie nijch ennschleepe, gauf
etj ahm lieseltjess too vestohne, daut wann wie aum näjchsten
Dach den aulabasten Endruck opp Hillary moake wulle, dann
sull wie vleijcht doch langsom schlope gohne. Enn kratjcht soo
auls etj daut aul lang jewant sie, wann eena bediedende
Mensche een bät tratjcht halpt, nehme see den Roht stell oba
dankboa aun.

Oba well'we nu mol den näajchsten Dach aunschniede, joh?

Dee groota Golfspäla, enn uck Professa, enn een Maun von
eenem grooten Weete, enn bieaun uck noch Steinbacha, Al
Reima, fruag mie eenmol, woo mie daut soo leijcht foll mett
Mensche von Welt too vetjeare, während ahm daut schwoa
foll. Etj säd, etj wudd ahm daut bie Jeläajenheit vetalle, enn
daut woa etj nu doohne, wiels etj miene groote Gow nijch lenja
fe mie auleen behoole well enn uck nijch kaun. "Een groote
enn seldne Gow, hast Du," säd Reima, enn doa haft'a rajcht.

Daut ess aulatoop sea eenfach, enn etj kaun nuscht doafäa:
Aule Babies tweschen tien Minute bett fief Minute ver Klock
tien zemorjess aum 14 Auprel jebuare send de Uasprung vom
väl jebruckten enn noch meea messbruckten Terminus
CHARISMA... joh soo send wie, enn wie tjenne nuscht dofäa.

Na joh, oba nu sad etj loos, Charisma enn aules. Enn wann
eena von dem Charisma een bät toolat, woare Mensch enn
Hunj enn sesstje Tiere daut oppe Städ enn, enn dee Wirtjung
ess platzlijch enn jewaultijch. Eena haft daut dann nijch leijcht,
oba soo ess'ett. Aulso bleef de Äwarauschung dann uck nijch
ut, auls etj dem stohtschen Sohl betraut, enn een Polizist enn

show him. We talked half the night away in German, and if you are—understandably—dying to know form and content of our conversations then you had better attend my church and give me your ear during the preliminaries and introduction which is the proper setting for such revelations and other important issues relating to the End Times.

But now let's dismount from the pulpit and head back to the everydayness of life. After much animated discussion, lasting till the wee hours and primed by some Scottish Highland libation, I discreetly informed the General that if we intended to make our very best impression on Hillary, we might do well to practice a bit of restraint. And as can be easily imagined, he was much obliged for my gentle counsel. As always, when dealing with functionaries of a higher order, they will invariably listen to well intentioned, prudent advice. (The good general failed to inform me that Hillary had not invited him; even worse, I do not believe it much troubled him).

But lets get on with the reception of the next day.

The great golf player, and writer, and a professor during his idle hours, Al Reimer, once asked me why and how I had such an easy time in associating with venerables and why he found it so excruciatingly difficult, try as he might, which he did. I promised that I would let him know, all in my own good time, but I never really got around to it but now I can no longer contain the pressure of superiority. "A great and rare gift, you have," said Reimer, and he's got that one right. Because:

All babies of the masculine gender born on April 14 between 09:50 and 09:55 are prone to a swelling of the gills every leap year at exactly 12:00 midnight for two minutes. It is then that they release two to three droplets which can be stroked, gently, into a minuscule receptacle. This essence is the original CHARISMA. I had packed this little vial, the size of a hummingbird's head, for the occasion and now I applied a touch of it on the rim of my beard.

siene dree Hunj mie utsochte enn väanauhme. "Waut ess aun die soo aundasch?"fruag hee, auls hee siene Scheetiesasch mie omme Tjnäp schliesre leeht, enn de Hunj sijch fe miene Socke enn Lempe besondasch intresseade. "Waut ess aun mie aundasch? Easchtens see etj een plautdietscha Mennist, tweedens sie etj mau een bescheidna Kenädja, dreddens hab etj toom Freestitj sass Zoll wille Schwiensworscht oppjejäte, enn dee schmatjcht soo goot, daut etj een gaunzet Kulla fe jun President mettjebrocht hab. Jana, doa mett de kugelsejchre Wast, vestatjcht dee hinja sienem Ridje. Na joh, enn daut aundre, waut aun mie aundasch ess: etj droag vondoag mol wada gaunz reine Socke." Enn dann leete se mie endlijch toch, enn daut word uck Tiet, wiels een jiedra en dem Sohl jaumad daut äwa mie, enn tjitjchte mie soo mettliedijch aun, kratjcht soo auls Tus, wann etj enne Tjoatj biem schlope mol too lud schnoatje dooh.

Na, enn nu wea etj aune Reaj, Hillary Clinton de Haund too reatje. Etj veneajd mie, enn läd mie doabie meist doppelt, enn bedankt mie, enn dann deed etj daut, waut mienem Swaut Al Reima emma soo enn siene Jedanke vemuzha. Etj stund soo een bestje mett Wind, doamett Hillary uck een bätje von mienem Duchie mettjriee wudd. Auls daut soo lieseltjess bie ahr aunkaum, enn see sijch fein heeflijch bedankt, daut etj endlijch mol wada oppjeduckt wea, säd etj: "Ess daut wertjlijch soo, Easchte Lady, daut See sijch eascht entschloohte hiea opptooträde, auls Ahn jesajcht word, daut etj vondoag hiea senne wudd?"

Vestendeljawies veschluckt see sijch een bestje, kratjcht soo aus aule Mensche daut doohne, wann eena ahn oppe Schlitjche tjemmt, enn dann säd see soo frindlijch auls eene freschjebackte Brut: "Mien leewa Tjeadel, well'we hiea mol den Teajel een bät lockra lohte, enn enn Glauss Champagner opp miene Räatjnung drintje, joh?" "Joh." Auls wie mett de Jläsa aunstade, fuscheld etj ahr too: "Dee lange Reis haft sijch mol wada

Then I set off. Just a hint of a whiff of this charisma perfume is perceived by men and beast alike and the effect is immediate and obvious. And so it comes as no surprise that the police who had occupied the stately hall first thing that forenoon, singled me out. "What is different about you?" asked one of the FBI policeman, he the one with four barreled branding irons and three canines, which gave my pant legs more than due attention. "Firstly," I said, "I am a Low German speaking Mennonite, secondly I am but a modest Canadian, thirdly I had a goodly chunk of wild-boar salami for breakfast (and this sausage is so good that I brought a whole ring of it along for your president, upon order, and your colleague over there has it hidden in his bullet proof vest because also your canines are interested in wild boar, even in casings), and fourthly I am wearing brand new socks for the occasion." Then they laid off and just as well because everyone in that hall gave me a pitying look just as they do at home when I snore a little too loudly while sleeping in church.

Well, then it was my turn to step up and shake Hillary Clinton, the First Lady's, hand. I bowed deeply, well practiced, and expressed my gratitude and then I did that what so much mystified Al Reimer for the greater part of his, Made in Steinbach, life. I stood gently up wind so that Hillary would catch a whiff of charisma perfume in her delicate little nostrils and when she thanked me for coming, I said, "Is it really true, Madame First Lady, that you decided to appear only after you were informed that I would be in attendance?"

She, meaning the First Lady, swallowed a little harder than intended, like all people do when found out, as she suggested with slightly more than appropriate delight, "My dear gentleman, I believe it is time to dispense with formalities for a bit and make for the bar and have a glass of champagne at my invitation." "It was worth the long trip," I whispered when we clinked glasses. Everyone present was speechless with

jeloohnt, nijch?" See plintjad aus 'ne Popp, enn säd blooss: "Oba joh!". Een jiedra em Sohl wea soo mustjess stell enn seea äwarauscht, buta Hillary enn etj. Daut musst soo kohme, oba blooss wie twee wisste enn vestunde daut.

Mensche woohne nijch blooss weete oba uck vestohne, woare mie daut mett Leijchtijchtjeit jleewe, daut Hillary daut Läwe doa platzlijch ennoolent wea, daut äahre Tjnees nu Kolledetz weare, enn etj blooss haud froage brucke, enn see wea mettjekohme. Oba etj docht mie, na, na Jung, mau een bät langsomma, wiels de Willie, de lestja Scherniesel, dem wudd etj daut tootrue, daut hee een Unjaseeboot enne Hudson's Bay nennschetje, enn mie sondasorj de Wintametz vom Kopp scheete wudd, wann etj onschuldijch oppem Mesthupe hinjrem Staul stohne wudd. Butadem well etj mie uck wiedahans mette Nohbasch goot stohne, enn daut nijch too Scheetariee kohme lohte.

Enn tweedens, soo docht etj mie, haft mien oola Massey Combein mau een seea tjlienen Cockpit, enn Hillary steiht doch wertjlijch eene mackelje Sett biem drasche too, nijch?

surprise except the two of us. It was bound to happen and we two knew it.

Those in the know will believe me when I say with effortless modesty that Hillary was more than slightly amenable to accompanying me back home. However, I decided to give the matter a reflective interlude because, the way I sized Willie up, I would not put it past him to order a submarine into the Hudson's Bay and shoot off my winter cap while I was minding my business on the manure pile behind the barn. Secondly, I delayed any eventual happiness and eagerness on her part since I allowed fore-thought and prudence to prevail, knowing full well that my combine back home is of the kind that has only one seat in the cockpit. And a lady of Hillary's stature deserves more commodious accommodation than that, surely.

Stearntjes aum Himmel

"Komm doch mol een bätje noda, Haunsa," säd Tiena emm wann see mie dretjche wull. Enn etj kaum dann uck een bätje noda, enn Tiena dretjcht enn kußt mie. Schnorijch wea daut, wann mie sesst wea kusse ooda dretje wull, dann wull etj daut goanijch, oba von Tiena leet etj mie daut emma jefaule. Na joh, waut heet daut nu uck aulwada emma, soo foaken pessead je daut nijch, vleijcht dree ooda veeamol daut Joah too Wiehnachte enn biem Jeburtsdach, oba sesst eajentlijch nijch.

Na joh, oba woo foaken daut wea tallt goanijch; etj jleew eena kaun sijch opp sien tjindlijchet Uagemoht doch aul noch velohte, sonst wudd etj nijch nu noch emma Tiena äahre Stemm, "Komm doch mol een bätje noda, Haunsa!" noh äwa zastijch Joah heare. Oba daut pesseat mie foaken, daut etj daut hea: "Komm doch mol een bätje noda, Haunsa," enn daut säd Tiena emma soo leeftolijh mett so väl Hoat enn Seel. Enn doabie lacht see emma, enn wann see lacht, haud see tjliene Kuhltjes enne Backe enn eene tjliene kruse Plack oppe Stearn. Enn Tiena lacht foaken.

Maunjchmol lachte uck de aundre Mensche, de groote, wann Tiena mie kußt enn dretjcht, enn dann schämd etj mie, enn wißt nijch, waut nu enn woahan. Oba miene Mame säd, daut schod doch nuscht, Tiena wea een goodet Mäadtje, etj tjann je ahr noch von Rußlaund...

Etj weet uck noch vondoag, daut de lostje Tiet bie Kloßes mett Tiena enn äahre Ellre enn de Jeschwista emma weens soo scheen jintj auls Wiehnachte. Enn bsondasch em Winta, wann eena eascht de Pead aunspaune mußt, enn dann säwen Miel foahre, enn dann utspaune enn donn sijch oppwoame, wiels

236

Stars in the Sky

"Come a little closer, will you, Hans," said Tina whenever she wanted to hug me. Then I came a little closer and Tina hugged and kissed me. Strange it was, when anyone else wanted to kiss or hug me I resisted but when Tina did it I was always silly with joy. Always? It didn't really happen all that often, maybe three or four times a year, at Christmas or at birthdays but that was about all.

Actually, it doesn't really matter how often it happened; one's childhood impressions should be allowed to stand. Fact is, I can still hear her voice "Come a little closer, will you, Hans," even fifty years later, and Tina said it so lovingly with so much heart and soul. And while saying it, she laughed, and when she laughed she had dimples on her cheeks and on her forehead. And Tina laughed often.

Sometimes the other grown-ups laughed when Tina hugged and kissed me and then I was embarrassed, and I did not know what to do with myself. But my mother said it was all alright, Tina was a good girl, whom I still remember well from Russia.

I know even today that the happy times at Klassen's with Tina and her parents and her siblings were always as delightful as at Christmastime. This was particularly true in wintertime when we first had to hitch the horses to the sleigh, and then travel seven miles, and then unhitch the team and warm up because it was so fiercely cold. Then we ate and enjoyed ourselves and laughed. And then come closer because Tina wanted to hug me.

When Tina was as old as I am now she had been dead for twenty-five years. But Tina still often comes to visit me. And

wie aula soo vetjlämt weare, enn donn äte enn sijch freie enn lache. Enn donn noda kohme, wiels Tiena mie han enn wada dretjche wull...

Auls Tiena soo oolt wea auls etj nu sie, dann wea see aul twintijch Joah doot. Joh, Tiena ess aul lang wajch, oba see tjemmt noch foaken bie mie spezeare. Enn dann sie etj emma tjlien, enn nieschierijch, enn jletjlijch enn frooh... Joh, oam weea wie too dee Tiet aulatoop bettalijch; oame Schluckasch mett oole Poltoos, enn aufjedroagde Tjleeda noch ut Rußlaund enn mett prachaje Burrsteewle aune Feet. "Oba wie send ennalijch ritjch," sät Tiena emma, "wiels wann Mensche eascht noh bute han ritjch weare, dann vedreaje see von benne. "Woo weetst du daut, Tiena?" fruag etj.

"Daut steiht aulewäje jeschräwe. Oame Mensche send ritjch, wiels see emma väl Tiet habe! Ritjche Mensch send oam, wiels see weinijch Tiet habe!" säd Tiena. Oba etj vestunt von sowaut meist nuscht nijch. "Oba daut steiht aulewäje jeschräwe," säd Tiena...

De Tiet kaum, enn de Tiet jintjch. Enn donn fong de Tiet aun de ranne. Oba wann Tiena säd: "Komm doch mol een bätje noda, Haunsa," dann head de Tiet opp too ranne. Enn wann see sajcht: "Komm mol een bätje noda!" dann blift de Tiet stohne. Enn daut pesseat aul noch eahremol... uck noch vondoag.

Aune näjentienhundat enn näjendartijch—etj wea jrohts auls tjliena Tjnirps vonn'e School noh Hus jekohme—(daut wea Hoafst, oba seea woam, enn etj schneet jrods Tjarps fer're Tjeaj twei) vetald mien ellre Brooda mie, daut Tjrijch utjebroake wea...

Auls etj Tiena wada sach, säd see: "Joh, nu feite se enn Europa. De Mensche schlohne sijch eenfach doot. Enn sogoa scheete doohne see, enn see welle sijch uck trafe." Etj wea acht Joah oolt, enn word mett daut Gaunze nijch soorajcht foadijch, enn uck nijch redda; mie wea daut aulatoop too groff. Oba

then I am again little and curious and happy and carefree. To be sure we were all terribly poor those days, poor devils with hand-me-downs and old worn clothes still from Russia, and with lumpy felt boots on our feet. "But we are wealthy within ourselves," Tina always said, "when people become wealthy on the outside they wither within." "How do you know that, Tina" I asked.

"That is written everywhere. Poor people are rich because the always have time! Rich people are poor because they have no time," said Tina. I understood nothing about all that at the time. "But it is written everywhere," said Tina.

Time came and time went. And then time started galloping. But when Tina said, "Come a little closer, Hans," then time stopped running. And when she says, "Come a little closer!" then time still stops. And that happens to me rather often, even today...

In 1939 I was a little shaver; I had just come home from school and it was autumn and I was just cutting up some pumpkins as cattle feed, when my older brother informed me that the Second World War had started.

When I saw Tina again, she said, "Yes, now they are fighting in Europe. And they are shooting and they even intend to harm each other. People just don't seem to be able to stop hurting each other." I was only eight years old and all this was deeply puzzling to me and I could not make any sense of all this fighting at all. I certainly knew that people around me did not behave like that at all. But then Tina took me and kissed me and then all my hurt and uneasiness just melted away.

Then Tina and her sister Lena and her brother Peter and her father started chopping and sawing firewood by the hundreds of cords and sold every piece of it. Everything suddenly could be sold and people came to money. Within months, Tina's father purchased a short wave radio and he always listened to

Tiena nauhm mie enn kußt mie enn dann veschwung daut Weescha von benne…

Tiena enn äahre Sesta Leena enn äah Brooda Peeta enn äah Voda muake nu Holt, Kordholt bie de hundade Kord, enn vekoffte daut. Aules jintjch mett eenmol too vetjeepe, enn de Mensche kaume too Jeld. Tiena äah Voda kofft sijch een Shortwave, enn hee head emma Nieijchtjeite enn hee wißt jieden Dach waut Hitla, enn Churchill enn Stalin säde. Hee wißt aules; daut wea toom staune.

Joh, enn boold doaropp fuahre Tiena enn äahre Sesta enn äahre Elre noh Winnipeg, noh Eatons. Enn doa leete see Tiena äahre Uage teste. Enn donn tjreajch see too Wiehnachte eene Brell. Auls wie ons wada sage, daut wea aum tweeden Heljedach, sach'et Tiena mie soo framd, oba soo framd mett äahre niee Brell. Enn donn fruag etj ahr, auls see dee Brell uck wertjlijch brucke mußt. "Komm mol een bätje häa, Haunsa." säd see, enn dann nauhm see mie noh bute, ver're Däah.

Enn donn wees Tiena mie de groote Schap aum Himmel enn daut tjliene Schaptje, enn donn uck den Nuadstearn, enn woo de groote Schap emma noh dem Nuadstearn zield. "Etj wißt, daut'et dee aula gauf," säd Tiena lieseltjes, "oba eea etj de Brell tjreajch, haud etj dee noch niemols verhäa jeseehne." En donn dreid Tiena sijch wajch, enn wescht sijch eene Trohn von'ne Backe.

Enn von donn aun dretjcht Tiena mie uck nijch meea, enn etj tjreajch von ahr uck tjeen Kuß meea…

the news and he knew everyday what Hitler and Churchill and Stalin said. He seemed to know everything; it was surprising.

A little while later Tina and her sister and her parents went to Winnipeg, to the Eaton's department store where they had Tina's eyes tested. And for Christmas of that year she got a set of spectacles. When we met again on Boxing Day, Tina looked so strange, so very strange to me with her new glasses. And then I asked her if she really, really needed these new glasses. "Come a little closer, Hans" Tina said and then she took me to the porch.

And there Tina showed me the wonders of the sky and the Little Dipper and the North Star and the Big Dipper. And then she pointed out how the Big Dipper revolved but always pointed towards the North Star directly overhead and a bit north. "I knew they all existed," Tina softly said, "but before I got these spectacles I had never seen them." Then Tina turned away and she wiped a tear from her eyes which I had never seen before.

But you know, from that evening on, Tina never hugged me, and I never received another kiss from her…

Lottie

Leahra Fraunz Niefeld wea ruhm een Joah mett Jaunzes Lottie befriet. Niefeld jefoll de Lied doa tweschen Roosegoad enn Burwool, wiels hee kunn buta Leahra senn, uck gaunz fein mett de Tjinja sinje, enn daut wea too Wiehnachte wichtijch. Enn butadem vepriejeld hee de Schooltjinja mau selden, obzwoa hee Rußlenda wea.

Enn siene Fru? De Lied säde, äah Nohme wea een bätje utjeputzt: "Woaromm kaun see nijch eenfach Auna, ooda Merie ooda Neeta heete? Enn woarom soohnen utjestraumden Nohme auls Lottie?" "Daut's meist soo onneedijch auls Spretze aum Unjarock", säd de Wellm Teewsche.

Na joh!

Aum feftienden Aprel aune Veareveatijch schetjt de Peeta Rampelsche äahren elsten Sähn Hauns mett een grootet Schruwglaus voll Heehnasupp noh Niefelds. Ahr ohnd waut, haud see jesajcht, enn donn sprung Hauns opp'et Pead nopp, enn reet noh Niefelds opptoo.

Daut Farjoah wea daut Joah soo grulijch naut enn blottijch, daut de School eene Wäatj äwa Oostre too wea. De Tjinja bleewe Tus, enn wachte bett daut Sonntje enn de Ead den Morast een bätje jedreajcht haude, enn de Wäaj mol wada foahboa worde. Niefelds haud tjeena nijch jeseehne, uck nijch enne Tjoatj aum Sinndach, enn doawäjen säd Taunte Rampelsche doch woll, ahr ohnd waut, enn schetjt Haus mett Heehnasupp noh Leahra Niefelds.

Dee twee-eenhaulf Miel too riede dieade dem Hauns äwa eene Stund—soo naut enn blottijch wea daut. Too Tiede fung

Lottie

Teacher Frank Neufeld had been married for about a year to Lottie Janzen. People between Rosengard and Burwalde liked Neufeld. In addition to being a good teacher, he sang well with the children and he managed to make the school Christmas program special. And, also, he rarely strapped the pupils although he was a Russlander.

And as for his wife, Lottie? Her name was a little too fancy for the average Mennonite ear. What was wrong with Annie, Mary or Nettie? "And why such an embroidered name like Lottie, which is as unnecessary and frivolous as lace on a petticoat," was Mrs Nettie Krahn's opinion.

Well, maybe.

That spring was so frightfully wet and so muddy and the roads so inaccessible that the school was closed for a whole week during Easter time. The children remained at home with all waiting until the sun had dried up their whole little world and the roads became passable again. Nobody had seen the Neufelds, not even in church on Sunday and that is possibly why, on April fifteenth, 1944, Mrs Peter Rempel, after having said, she sensed something, sent her oldest son Hans with a large jar of chicken soup to the Neufelds.

Riding the two and one half miles took Hans more than one hour on horseback—it was that wet and muddy. At times his horse Barnie barely found footing under his hooves and he panted and strained through slush, mud and water. But suddenly, when Barnie, already lathered and puffing like a steam engine, and had sweated himself foamy and trembled from exertion, the last corner before the driveway became

Rampels äah Barnie schiea nijch Boddem unjre Heefta, enn hee ständ enn jescht enn murcheld enn moarachd veropp derjch Modd enn Wota. Oba mett eenmol auls Barnie aul auls een Daumptjeatel stiemd enn sijch schiemijch jeschweet haud, en fe luta Aunstrenjung flautad, kaum de latzte Atj verre Oppfoaht, enn Hauns kaum mett siene derjchjescholtjade Heehnasupp enne Tausch oppem Ridje bie Niefelds aun.

Daut wea haulf veea Nohmeddach, enn Niefelds mußte Tus senne, oba äah Hus dijcht bie de School stund stell en een bätje velohte doa emm Bosch. Hauns puttad aune Däah nohdem hee Barnie aun eenem tjoanjen Boom aunjebunge haud. Hee puttad, head nuscht, hilt sienen Odem aun, wacht, head bloß sien Hoat bullre, enn daut Bloot fientjes emm Kopp ruzhe, puttad wada aun… nuscht! Tjeene Stemm, dee ahm "Komm nenn!" tooroopt. Hauns wull aul daut Glaus Heehnasupp tweschne Däahre hanstalle enn noh Hus riede, auls hee waut head, hinja ahm waut head. Joh, doa wea waut too heare, doa hinjrem Staul emm Bosch haud'et jeknostat. Hee jintj tjitje, enn sach nu uck, woo Leahra Fraunz Niefeld mett eenem ditjchen Boomstaum hinjrem Staul derjch'et Bosch aunjetoßd kaum.

Oba, Lied etj saj, woo sach'et bloß Leahra Fraunz Niefeld? Buzhajett Hoah, auldagsche Tjleeda, daut Jesejcht volla Schweet, enn blottijch wear'a von bowe bett unje. Fuats jintjch Hauns Leahra Niefeld too Halp. "Goondach, doaf etj halpe aunfohte?" "Goondach", säd Leahra Niefeld, enn stratjcht siene Haund rut. Hauns sach, daut dee Haund flautad, enn de Schweet oppem Jesejcht? Doa weare meea Trohne auls Schweet oppem Jesejcht, enn Hauns bleef Odem enn Sproak stohne. "Een Leahra hielt?" fruach hee opp stelles.

Joh, dee Leahra hield, haud jehielt, enn hield noch. "Na oba, wauts hiea bloß los?" fruag Hauns lieseltjes.

"Väaje Nacht Klock tien kaum onse tjliene Lottie aun, enn daut diead, enn diead de haulwe Nacht. Enn endlijch omm

visible and Hans arrived with his thoroughly churned jar of chicken soup in a duffle bag on his back at the Neufeld teacherage.

The time was three thirty in the afternoon and the Neufelds were certainly at home but their house stood a bit lonely and forlorn there in the bush. Hans knocked at the door, but not before he had tied Barnie to a sturdy tree. He knocked, heard nothing, held his breath, waited, heard only his heart pounding, and the faint trickling of his head's blood; he knocked again… nothing! No voice calling a "Come in!" Hans already wanted to deposit the jar with chicken soup between the doors and ride back home again, when there was a noise behind him; there was something he had heard; between stable and the bush there had been a crackling something. Hans went for a look and now saw Teacher Franz Neufeld dragging a thick oak trunk through the bush behind the barn.

But it was the teacher's appearance that startled Hans the most. Disheveled hair, bedraggled weekday clothes, his face was covered with sweat and he was muddy from top to bottom. Hans rushed over to help. "Good day, can I give you a hand?"

"Good day," Teacher Neufeld said dully, and extended a shaking hand. That's when Hans realized that the sweat on the teacher's face was mainly tears. A teacher, a respected teacher crying his eyes out.

"What in the world has happened?" Hans asked fearfully.

Teacher Neufeld spoke to Hans as to an adult, "Last night at ten Lottie began to deliver, and it took so long, so very long, it took half of the night. Finally, around four in the morning little Lottie was born, she was finally born, and she even smiled a bit, the little mite did, and then she seemed to lose all interest; then she moved a bit almost as if looking for a more comfortable place, she moved her head just a trifle, then she closed her eyes, and then she was gone. Simply gone. I tried

245

Klock veea ut wea see doa, wea see endlijch doa, hohld eenmol Odem, frinteld sogoa een bät, oba dann word see soo meed, enn muak de Uagtjes too. Enn schleep enn. Enn donn wea see wajch. Eenfach wajch. Doa holp nuscht nijch meea."

Fraunz Niefeld enn Rampels Hauns schlapte den ditjchen Staum nu enn'em Staul nenn. Donn hohlde see sijch twee Batj, läde den Staum doa noppa, enn fonge aun too oabeide. Mett Atjs enn Soag enn Häwel oabeide see bett Meddanacht. Tweschenenn jintj Leahra Niefeld jieda Stund nenn enn vesorjd siene kranke, schlaupe, schwacke Fru emm Bad, oba sonst oabeide see beid biem Letoarnelijcht bett Klock twalw. Donn jinje see nenn. Jeschlope woare see wull nijch väl habe.

Klock saß zemorjess fonge see wada aun too oabeide, enn Klock twee Nohmeddach wea daut tjliene Soatj foadijch. Enn daut Soatj läde see aula Speena von'ne Holtoabeit nenn, enn donn jintj Leahra Niefeld nenn enn hohld waut; hee hohld siene Fru Lottie äah Bruttjleed enn läd daut schmock äwre Speena, enn muak een tjlient Badtje. Dann jintj hee wada nenn, enn noh eene Veadel Stund kaum hee sinndoagsch aunjetrocke rut. Bleef verre Däah stohne, docht, besennd sijch, enn jintj emm Tjalla nenn, enn hohld een Korftje mett dee tjliene Lottie doabenne. Daut schmocke Popptje schleep noch emma soo ruhijch, enn nu hoof hee Lottie leeftolijch rut, enn kußt ahr oppe Stearn, enn donn läd hee ahr emm Soatj nenn, läd ahr schmock trajcht, enn noagelt daut Sautj lieseltjes too. Donn druage see daut tjliene Backstje noh dem Staum von dem aufjehackten Eatjeboom. Groowe een Grauftje, enn sunge toop daut Leed, "Und die Kindlein, und die Kindlein zieht er an die Brust... O dann werden sie glänzen wie die Sternlein so rein... " Donn leete see daut Soatj langsom enn stell rauf enn scheffelde daut Grauf too... Dee Sonn schiend enn schiend.

Enn donn, eascht väl lohta, donn jinje see, Hauns enn Fraunz, eascht äwaridjes, enn donn väarewajch enne stelle Welt nenn.

everything but nothing helped." And then tears trailed down his muddy face again.

After a while the two of them dragged the tree trunk, some four feet long, into the barn. They hauled in two sawbucks and wrestled the trunk across them, and then they attacked it with saw and plane. They laboured until sundown, then lit the lamps and continued on until midnight. Every hour or so Teacher Neufeld went inside to look after his wife, slowly recovering, and to stoke up the wood stove. When they were finally exhausted they had a bite to eat and slept a few hours. At six the next morning they were back at work and at two that afternoon the little casket was ready. They lined it with wood shavings, and then Teacher Neufeld went inside and returned with Lottie's bridal dress. He draped this slowly and lovingly over the shavings, making a little bed.

When he went into the house the next time, he returned wearing his Sunday suit and carrying a basket with tiny Lottie inside. She looked like she was asleep, so relaxed and so peaceful. He lifted her out gently and kissed her on the forehead, placed her in the coffin and made her comfortable. Then he nailed the coffin shut. He and Hans carried it to the stump of the oak from which it had been made, and dug a small grave. Teacher Neufeld began to sing: "Little children, little children, He holds at his breast... Like the stars, the heavens, with bright lights adorning... They shall shine, like the jewels bright stars in His crown..." and Hans joined in. Then they lowered the coffin into the grave and Teacher Neufeld covered it...

The sun had broken again, finally, after all the mud and slush and rain. It shone brilliantly, almost hurting the eyes. And after a long time the two men turned around and walked silently and sadly into an emptier world.

But from that day on the name Lottie stopped bothering people the way it had done before. Some people, in fact,

Von dem Dach aun, stead de Nohme Lottie tjeenen Mensch meea; joh, de Mensche säde, ahn head de Nohme eajentlijch scheen.

decided that it was rather a good name to have. Others agreed and even said that they'd gotten rather fund of it and might suggest Lottie to their children as a name for a granddaughter some day.

www.ingramcontent.com/pod-product-compliance
Lightning Source LLC
Chambersburg PA
CBHW031121030726
47496CB00002BA/625